One day she would have to return to
her true form . . .

Frothy waves rolled  larger than the last. All mer and in the water form existence, the dead a sinuous dragon clutching a pearl under its bearded chin.

The waves rose and enfolded me, and suddenly I was crying against the mother I had never known. She knelt in the water, her arms around me. Seaweed twined in her black hair.

"I don't want to be alone anymore," I sobbed.

"Hush," she said. Her voice was a whispered roar, as if it were coming out of a seashell. "All you had to do was ask."

She touched her clammy lips to my forehead. Something tumbled from her mouth. I caught it in my hand. It was a jade fish. I placed it under my tongue and tasted salt.

—From "Threes" by E.L. Chen

Also Available from DAW Books:

A Girl's Guide to Guns and Monsters, **edited by Martin H. Greenberg and Kerrie Hughes**
Here are thirteen tales of strong women, armed with weapons they are not afraid to use, as well as fists and feet of fury, from authors such as Tanya Huff, Mickey Zucker Reichert, Jane Lindskold, Kristine Kathryn Rusch, Nina Kiriki Hoffman, Irene Radford, and others. These are urban and paranormal stories certain to appeal to all readers of this most popular genre. So sit back and enjoy as these empowered women take on all challenges with weapons, wit, and skill—and pity the poor monsters and bad guys who'll need rescuing from them!

Timeshares, **edited by Jean Rabe and Martin H. Greenberg**
Welcome to timesharing like you've never experienced before. This is not your chance to acquire some rental property in the Bahamas. The stories you'll find within these pages are your tickets to *real* timesharing—taking a vacation through time. Afraid of flying? The high cost of gas got you down? Want to *really* get away? Step into your local Timeshares agency office, venture through their time travel device, and you can find yourself in exotic, adventurous locations. Of course, you and your fellow vacationers may also find yourselves caught up in all manner of trouble and mysteries—and definitely in danger. With stories by Kevin J. Anderson, Michael A. Stackpole, Greg Cox, Donald J. Bingle, Chris Pierson and Linda Baker, and others.

Cthulhu's Reign, **edited by Darrell Schweitzer**
Some of the darkest hints in all of H.P. Lovecraft's Cthulhu Mythos relate to what will happen *after* the Old Ones return and take over the Earth. What happens when the Stars Are Right, the sunken city of R'lyeh rises from beneath the waves, and Cthulhu is unleashed upon the world for the last time? What happens when the other Old Ones, long since banished from our universe, break through and descend from the stars? What would the reign of Cthulhu be like, on a totally transformed planet where mankind is no longer the master? It won't be simply the end of everything. It will be a time of new horrors and of utter strangeness. It will be a time when humans with a "taint" of unearthly blood in their ancestry may come into their own. It will be a time foreseen only by authors with the kind of finely honed imaginative visions as Ian Watson, Brian Stableford, Will Murray, Gregory Frost, Richard Lupoff, and the others of *Cthulhu's Reign.*

THE DRAGON AND THE STARS

edited by Derwin Mak
and Eric Choi

DAW BOOKS, INC.
DONALD A. WOLLHEIM, FOUNDER
375 Hudson Street, New York, NY 10014

Loretto School

16893

First Printing, May 2010

1 2 3 4 5 6 7 8 9

DAW TRADEMARK REGISTERED
U.S. PAT. AND TM. OFF. AND FOREIGN COUNTRIES
—MARCA REGISTRADA
HECHO EN U.S.A.

PRINTED IN THE U.S.A.

ACKNOWLEDGMENTS

Introduction copyright © 2010 by Tess Gerritsen

"The Character of the Hound," copyright © 2010 by Tony Pi

"The Fortunes of Mrs. Yu," copyright © 2010 by Charles Tan

"Goin' Down to Anglotown," copyright © 2010 by William F. Wu

"The Polar Bear Carries the Mail," copyright © 2010 by Derwin Mak

"Lips of Ash," copyright © 2010 by Emery Huang

"The Man on the Moon," copyright © 2010 by Crystal Gail Shangkuan Koo

"Across the Sea," copyright © 2010 by Emily Mah

"Mortal Clay, Stone Heart," copyright © 2010 by Eugie Foster

"Dancers with Red Shoes," copyright © 2010 by Melissa Yuan-Innes

"Intelligent Truth," copyright © 2010 by Shelly Li

"Bargains," copyright © 2010 by Gabriela Lee

"Threes," copyright © 2010 by E.L. Chen

CONTENTS

Introduction

Tess Gerritsen

I grew up in a household where ghosts and demons were real and ancestors' spirits hovered over our family, where incense was burned every morning and mysterious brews of whiskey and medicinal herbs often simmered on the stove. My mother, an immigrant from Kunming, China, never stopped reminding me that our family came from a land far older than America. She filled our heads with tales from her own childhood, of fighting monks and ghostly lovers and wise men who could magically walk on water.

"It's true, these stories are all true," she insisted. "In China, these things really happen."

And I believed her.

But I grew up. I went to college and medical school and built a career as a doctor, and later as a writer. China may be stamped on my face and in my DNA, but in every other way, I thought of myself as an American. I believed in science, not superstition. As my memories of childhood receded, so too did my mother's tales of ghosts and demons, of a far-off country so ancient that magic is part and parcel of its history. I forgot just how Chinese I really am.

When I read this marvelous collection of stories, my Chinese childhood came rushing back to me. Here, in *The Dragon and the Stars,* are tales of wonder and magic, of immigrant families, and ancient history re-imagined. Each of these writers knows what it means to be part of a Chinese family, to grow up with parents who no doubt spun mystical stories for them, just as my own mother did.

In this treasure chest of stories, you'll discover a point of view that western literature too often ignores. Some of these tales are set in the ancient past, some in the near future. Some deal in magic, some in realism. In "Bargains" by Gabriela Lee, a young woman has a fateful encounter with a Chinatown shopkeeper who has dreams to sell—dreams with consequences. In "Papa and Mama" by Wen Y. Phua, a Chinese daughter struggles to remain dutiful to her parents, despite the fact they are both dead and inconveniently reincarnated as a fish and a bird. In "The Fortunes of Mrs. Yu" by Charles Tan, a blank strip of paper inside a fortune cookie spells an uncertain future to a diner. These three are just a sampling of the wildly imaginative tales you are about to enjoy.

In Chinese numerology, eighteen is a lucky number. The eighteen writers who contributed to *The Dragon and the Stars* hail from around the world, and their stories are each delightfully unique. But all of them have something in common: they reflect the experience of what it is to be Chinese, an identity that none of us ever truly escapes, though we may grow up far from the shores of China.

The Character of the Hound

Tony Pi

*A*UTUMN, *in the Thirty-First Year of the Shao-Xing reign period of the Southern Song Dynasty, on the southern shore of the Yellow River, Henan Province*

Not long past sunset, halfway through my inspection of another paddle-wheel warship, an anxious messenger arrived delivering a strange summons.

"All soldiers who bear the character of the hound, come with me!" he cried.

Our generation all bore a *chengyu*—a proverb—tattooed down our backs. What the herald sought was the ideogram for *hound*, which had two forms:

犬 and 犭

I stepped over the foot-treadle and greeted the herald, fist-in-hand. "I am Wu Fan, and my *chengyu* is *qiū hǎo wú fàn*."

秋毫無犯

I had chosen the *chengyu* when I turned twenty as a vow to my deceased father, and I also took my courtesy name from it. Literally *new feather not harm*, the

3

proverb meant *one who would not commit the slightest offense against the people*; it was my eldest brother who had tattooed those words into permanence at my capping ceremony.

No others aboard bore a tattoo that fit the summons, but my guide seemed satisfied with me and shoved me toward the exit. I had barely enough time to call out instructions to my ragged crew: "Load the thunderclap bombs without me!"

Off-ship, the sandy shore was crowded with makeshift camps and grim soldiers preparing for battle. Snatches of lewd songs and laughter rose amid the sounds of toil, but the overall mood remained bleak. The Jin army had massed four hundred thousand strong on the northern bank of the Yellow River, whereas our river fleet had only twenty thousand men. If we could not stop them from crossing at sunrise, they would lay waste to the lands we had reclaimed from them ten years ago, and the sacrifices of a hundred thousand lives would be for naught.

A flurry of messengers boarded and left other creaking boats, some alone, a few accompanied by men in their twenties like me, called to the same duty. The lack of seasoned warriors with the *hound* mark did not surprise me. Soldiers of the generation before us who had fought under Yue Fei, the Spirit General, all bore the same tattooed motto as he did, *utmost loyalty serve country*:

盡忠報國

It was only after the recapture of the capital Kaifeng, during the years of fragile peace, that men and women began wearing proverbs of their own choosing.

All of us seemed to be converging on the grand vessel holding court among smaller ships—eleven paddle wheels a side and one of the finest trebuchets in the fleet. We called her the *Longma*, after the legendary dragon-horse guardian of the Yellow River. I had admired the flagship from afar but had never set foot upon her.

But I could not dispel my unease about this strange summons. My superiors had not asked after knowledge or skills but required a man merely for the shape of a word on his skin. A blood sacrifice to ensure victory on the morrow?

To my surprise, we approached a stark vessel in the shadow of the flagship, where a handful of scowling men already gathered. A *Qitou*-rank officer guarded the gangplank, wielding a snake halberd as he would a flag-spear, only a red paper lantern hung from the base of the halberd blade. A slip of paper with calligraphic characters swayed beneath the light, the black ink still wet, proclaiming a riddle: *one dog, four mouths*.

"Only a man who knows the answer may board," the officer said.

Three of the men shook their heads and stepped back. Illiterate, perhaps? The rest of us considered the puzzle in earnest.

Lantern riddles intrigued me. As youths in my native Sichuan, my brothers and I had matched wits against many riddle-hands during the Lantern Festivals. Sometimes, a riddle depended on words with double meanings, and other times several ideograms had to be combined to yield the final word. By the puzzle's form, I suspected the latter.

Dog suggested the character for *hound*, which can be combined with four instances of the character for *mouth*. Only one word fit the riddle: *qi*, the character for *tool* or *receptacle*.

器

I was first to give the answer. Satisfied, the officer dismissed the others and stepped aside to let me board.

Unlike the other wheel-ships in the fleet, which had been rigged with trebuchets, this squat vessel held on deck only a windowless cabin with a door slightly ajar. I gathered my courage and entered.

Two men stood in heated argument in the lantern-lit chamber. I recognized the wispy-bearded man in his early fifties as Admiral Zhang, bedecked in his imposing lamellar armor. A veteran of the war against the Jin, Zhang had been given the command of our river fleet by the Spirit General himself.

The other, a balding man in his thirties, bore a deep diagonal scar crossing both lips. His uniform marked him as a *Yongdui*, a platoon commander.

"Our ships and weapons are superior. Even without its magic, we can win tomorrow!" Admiral Zhang insisted. "I, who am beneath your flag, beg you to reconsider."

Beneath your flag? The Admiral's use of the honorific for the *Yongdui* ill-fit the proper chain of command.

The scar-lip man shook his head and answered Zhang in a calm and sonorous voice. "No. It remains the key to holding the Yellow River and must not fall into Jin hands at any cost."

I knelt in obeisance. "I, your servant Wu Fan, am at your disposal." This posture brought my eyes to fixate on a pool of drying blood before a closed interior door. A sudden chill overtook me.

"How will this man help?" Admiral Zhang asked.

Scar-Lips drew his sword from its leather scabbard and stepped so close that his trouser leg brushed against my tied hair. "He has a mind for riddles, it seems." He touched the flat of his sword on the nape of my neck and slid its entire length down my back, between cotton and skin. I dared not move, and held myself as still as I could against the gentle rocking of the boat. A sudden breeze tickled my back, and my cotton tunic fell in two parts, sliding down my arms. "And he has the *hound* upon his back."

Admiral Zhang snarled. "But is he loyal?"

"I, your servant, have known scoundrels who rip their shirts to show honor written down their backs, even as they lie and steal," I said, unable to hold my tongue. "My tattoo may not shout the same allegiance, but I take my *chengyu*'s moral to heart. I am true to the Emperor and would never turn traitor. Let my deeds prove it."

"Would you lay down your life here and now to save the kingdom?" Scar-Lips asked.

"I give it without hesitation," I blurted.

"Then it seems you have the heart as well." Scar-Lips sheathed his sword. "Wu Fan, you will hear many strange and secret things tonight, not to be repeated upon pain of death. If you understand, rise."

I let my arms slip from the sundered tunic as I stood. "I do."

"Call me Kou Shen." *Kou shen* meant *mouth god* or *mouth spirit*, leaving me to wonder about the nature of this man. "There is an urgent matter of the state, the theft of a relic from this ship. Do you know the legend of the *Hetu*?"

"Yes, the sacred River Chart," I answered. "In ancient times, as a gift to the king, the Yellow River sent a dragon-horse from its depths with a magical map of the river's secrets upon its back."

Kou Shen nodded. "The *Hetu* is real, and in the hands of a sorcerer, the hide can raise floods or calm waters on the Yellow River. The currents flow in our favor, and enemies who slip underwater never surface alive. Thanks to the *Hetu*'s magic, the Jin armies have feared the river. But that advantage may be lost." He pushed the door to the adjacent room open. Two robed men and a guardsman lay dead at the foot of a silk-draped table, their throats cleanly cut.

I turned away. I had seen more gruesome deaths in

my three years of military service, but the cold precision of these murders disgusted me. "Who did this?"

"A traitor among us, one of high rank who knows about the *Hetu*," Kou Shen said.

Admiral Zhang's face twisted with anguish when Kou Shen said *traitor*. "The sorcerers may be dead, but our fleet will rise to the challenge."

"I do not doubt it, Admiral," Kou Shen said. "But while there remains a chance to recover the *Hetu*, we must seek it."

"I am honored that you have chosen me for this task, but I am a mere engineer," I said. "I can fix trebuchets and paddle wheels or calculate the trajectory of a bomb, but catching a murderer . . ."

"I see in you a clever man, Wu Fan," Kou Shen said. "You will—you must—use those wits for the sake of the country."

"My apologies, but I, the lowest general, must see to the remaining battle preparations for morning," Admiral Zhang said, bowing. "I leave this matter in your capable hands." He departed, leaving me alone with Kou Shen.

Kou Shen gestured at a stubby stool. After I politely declined, he took the seat himself. "I am one of many *shen* in the service of the Spirit General," he said. "For the sake of our people, Wu Fan, you must allow one such spirit to enter you."

There were rumors of such spirits said to serve the Spirit General Yue Fei, returning with him from beyond the grave to protect the Song Dynasty.

Yue Fei's legend told of his mother, who had tattooed the words *utmost loyalty serve country* on her son's back to remind him of his patriotic duty. That gift of needled words did not save the general nineteen years ago, when he had been falsely accused by the Prime Minister of treason and executed. But it was said that one of Yue

Fei's disciples had taken the same mark of loyalty to honor him and had willingly given possession of his body to his master's ghost, whose work in this world remained unfinished. To this day, the Spirit General kept command of the armies of the Southern Song.

"When Yue Fei died, he discovered that his spirit could leap from body to body, if they bore the same tattooed *chengyu* as his," Kou Shen continued. "But the Spirit General is not the only spirit bound to words on skin, though he is the greatest among us. We call him *Xin Shen*, spirit of the word *heart*."

I understood. *Heart* appears in the word for *loyalty*.

"Then you are the spirit of the word *mouth*?" The man before me was merely a vessel for *Kou Shen*. Judging by Scar-Lips' age, he would have borne the same *chengyu* as Yue Fei. "*Mouth* is part of the character for *country*!"

Kou Shen nodded.

My eyes widened. "Then the character of the *hound* ... I am to host its spirit?"

"Aye. We need the nose of Quan Shen, spirit of the hound, to identify and capture the thief," Kou Shen said.

I was at a loss for words. It would be a legendary sacrifice to serve a spirit. After all, when Yue Fei had taken his disciple's body, he had been able to expose the Prime Minister as a Jin spy and rally the Song army. Under his banner, our brethren won back the lands south of the Yellow River. But what had happened to the disciple who had given his body to Yue Fei?

Sweat beaded on my brow. Could I endure that loss of freedom? "What happens to *me*? Do I die?"

"No," Kou Shen assured me. "While Quan Shen controls your body, you still sense and observe, and your thoughts remain your own. We spirits must obey certain laws.

"One, a spirit only senses the strength, direction, and distance of the summons, but does not hear the *chengyu* used to conjure him. That secret is your hold over him.

"Two, a spirit is a guest. Only you may invite him in, but once he accepts, only you may release him—so long as your *chengyu* remains secret from him.

"Three, if the spirit discovers your *chengyu* and speaks it aloud, the body that hears it must acknowledge the spirit as its master. Thereafter, he may come and leave of his own accord."

Then the sooner we found the thief, the sooner I could send this Quan Shen away. "But for all we know, the thief has already thrown *Hetu* back into the Yellow River!"

Kou Shen disagreed. "Whoever stole it must know its true worth. Whether he craves wealth or power, he is a fool if he does not approach the Jin."

"I do not have the courage for this," I admitted.

"You have. Look where you are: serving in a fleet fighting for your country, ready to die! Why fear a few hours' loan of your body? Study your doubts and cast them aside, soldier."

I gazed into the lantern flame and meditated on my fear. To let an unknown spirit ride my skin and do things with my body without my permission—that scared me witless. But my father and uncles had given their lives fighting the Jurchen barbarians from the north, who stole our lands and dared call themselves a golden dynasty. How could I be afraid to surrender my body for one night, when I had already pledged it to my people?

"Please accept this apology from your humble servant. You are right—it is my duty and honor to serve."

Kou Shen clasped my shoulder. "Good."

But I had to ask one thing that still disturbed me. "You set that riddle to find an intelligent man. Why? Is there something I should know about this spirit of the hound?"

"Ah, you *are* astute, Wu Fan. Quan Shen is the only spirit who can track the *Hetu*, but he has drunk too deep from the well of power. There is a risk in that, for us spirits. We may invoke the magic rooted in the nature of our word at the cost of losing a part of our humanity. For example, the spirit of wine is an inveterate drunk; the spirit of the wind the embodiment of wanderlust; and even I talk too much. As for Quan Shen, he thinks and reacts like a hound and forgets that sometimes he must think before he acts. *You* must be his better judgment. Keep him focused on his mission."

"But what do I do once I find the thief?"

"Leave him to me," Kou Shen said, his hand falling to the hilt of his sword.

"How do I summon him?"

"Prayer. Need. Both. Speak your *chengyu* and wish for a spirit's aid," he explained.

I frowned. "But will Quan Shen come?"

"He dwells for now in a soldier of Kaifeng. I have a host there chanting *chengyu*, awaiting my return. I will convince Quan Shen to come to you. Are you ready?"

"I am," I replied.

"Good. I will return to this body soon," Kou Shen said.

He yawned, letting his head and shoulders slump. When he raised his eyes to meet mine again, he laughed softly and flexed his fingers.

"Kou Shen?" I asked.

"He's gone, for the moment. My name's Ren Chun," he said.

"It is an honor, Ren Chun," I replied. "If I might ask, what is it like to serve Kou Shen?"

Ren Chun stroked his scar idly as he searched for the right words. "Imagine a dragon dance where you're the dragon, rippling and twisting in glory. Only you're at the mercy of the troupe who carries you, dancing to their whim. You watch yourself 'chasing the pearl' or 'circling the pillar', but the beauty-in-motion isn't yours."

"I see. Who is this Kou Shen, in truth?" I asked.

"Kou Shen's the voice of the Spirit General. Every squadron has a mouthpiece like me, waiting and praying at the appointed hours for Spirit General to possess him. He bears messages from far and wide, giving our army a formidable advantage over the Jin. When he possesses me, I wait and listen while he observes the fleet or dines with officers. Whoever you serve, friend, you'll need patience."

"What I have serves me well enough," I answered.

Ren Chun smiled. "If you say so. Come, let's begin." He kicked away the stool, settled into a lotus position and closed his eyes.

I imitated him and intoned my *chengyu*, over and over in a quaking voice. I formed the character of *hound* in my mind's eye. *Come, Quan Shen. Your country has need of you, and I open my heart to you. Come.*

On the twelfth iteration, the spirit entered me.

My voice—no, *our* voice—ceased chanting, and our eyes opened of their own accord. Thousands of new scents overwhelmed our sense of smell, each with a different shade and strength.

When I had been the sole occupant of my body, my thoughts centered behind my eyes, but that place was no longer the throne of my reason. A phantom hound with boundless energy took that seat from me, and my sense of self scattered to the edges like fleas on his hide.

Against my will, we sprang to our feet. Our head strained to see our back, but the *chengyu* tattoo remained out of sight. Growling, we spun in place, a dog chasing his own tail.

I tried to communicate with Quan Shen, but my mouth did not even try to shape my intended words. I tried manifesting my thoughts instead.

Honorable Quan Shen, please cease! You will only make us ill!

Quan Shen ignored me and laughed, spinning us faster and faster. "This could amuse me all night," he said in my voice.

A firm hand gripped our shoulder, stopping Quan Shen's mad twirling. "Quan Shen! Don't bring disgrace to us *shen* with these antics. Behave."

Quan Shen sneered. "I was enjoying that, Big Mouth."

"Show proper respect and call me Kou Shen. You waste time we don't have. Work with Wu Fan to find the *Hetu.*"

"Work with this pup?" Quan Shen said. We sniffed our armpit. The stink was our own, but laced with old tea and sour plum. "He reeks of fear and doubt."

Pup? I considered my words to Quan Shen, and I knew where I had gone wrong. I had deferred to him when I should have acted like pack leader.

Know your place, Quan Shen. I am no pup, I said. *I conjured you to serve the good of the country. There is no place for your selfish behavior among us.*

"So? What if I refuse?" he said, testing me.

I will cast you out of this body, and Kou Shen and I will spread word of your shame throughout the land. Thereafter, only vagabonds would dare take the mark of the hound, much less pray to you. It is your choice: become an outcast, or join us and fight for a victory feast. Which will it be?

Our stomach grumbled, and our lips parted to bare our teeth. "I'm starving now!" Quan Shen complained.

Soon.

"Very well. What do you need?"

The scent of a killer, and the whereabouts of the Hetu. I directed him toward the chart room. Kou Shen observed us from the doorway.

Our nose, enchanted by hound magic, identified an abundance of smells. Quan Shen isolated them one by one.

"Learn these scents, pup. Three deaths, one after the other." We crouched next to the closest body, the guardsman. "This one died first. Never had time to sweat surprise."

We switched to a crisp, spicy odor.

"Skinny one was second. A quick death—a scent of surprise without the bouquet of fear." We tilted our head towards the third and last body. "Smell it on him?"

The scent of old tea.

"Sure, call it that."

But which is the killer's scent? I asked.

We tested a succession of smells, but Quan Shen discarded them quickly. "Bland fish from supper. Month-old ink. Balm for a skin disease on that one." We sniffed again. "Ah. An odd smell."

It was a smoky, earthy, scent of grass.

I knew it. *Mugwort?*

"Close. Smoke from its burning," Quan Shen said.

Moxibustion? I suggested. Some healers burned mugwort on patients' skins to improve blood flow. *Tell Kou Shen.*

We turned toward Kou Shen. "Whoever killed them likely had a moxibustion treatment within the day," Quan Shen reported.

Kou Shen brushed his thumb lightly against his scar as he considered the clue. "I know two healers in the fleet who do moxibustion. They might remember who they treated. I'll ask Admiral Zhang to find them. Is the scent strong enough to track?"

"No, but the *Hetu*'s fragrance is enough," Quan Shen replied. "Let me memorize it."

We bit and tore the silk off the table, gathered it in our hands and inhaled deeply. The blend of smells—

horsehide, watered wine, and salted carp—defied my expectations. So delicate was the balance of the three, their sum became fragrant despite their constituent parts.

Quan Shen laughed. "The bouquet of the river's magic, rarest of the rare. Breathe deep and grow drunk, pup!"

I left him to indulge while I considered another part of the puzzle. How heavy was the *Hetu*, and could a lone assassin carry it and escape notice?

The elm table that held the *Hetu* had been exquisitely carved. Its spindly legs resembled dragon-horses, while the tabletop had been inlaid with a gold-and-bone magic-square pattern. It was not the sturdiest of tables, but it had likely been designed to hold only one thing: the *Hetu*.

The scaly hide of a dragon-horse likely weighed more than horsehide. Assuming the unfolded hide covered the entire table, I calculated the approximate weight of the relic from those dimensions.

The Hetu *would be easiest to carry if the assassin had an accomplice,* I told Quan Shen. *Or, if he acted alone, he would need to be a strong man to manage such a cumbersome relic. Even so, he could not have gone far without a horse. Tell Kou Shen.*

Quan Shen did not obey. Instead, he sniffed the air and growled. "I smell rain on its way. Hurry, or the scents will wash away!" We dropped to all fours, kicked off our shoes and dashed out of the cabin.

Quan Shen! This is undignified! I shouted.

"Think about the mission," he said. We leaped from the deck of the ship onto the rocky shore, tumbling into a predatory crouch. Soldiers around us stared in disbelief. Ren Chun had likened spirit-possession to a dragon dance, but I felt like a lion dance costume worn by Quan Shen the acrobat.

"Wait," Kou Shen shouted behind us. "Take a horse—"

"Faster on foot. Try to catch up," Quan Shen said. We locked onto the scent trail and bolted.

The sight of a shirtless and shoeless man tearing through a camp on the eve of war set off cries of alarm by nervous soldiers. *Everyone thinks I've gone mad,* I said, and prayed no one would attack us.

Behind us, I heard hoofbeats and Kou Shen's voice. "Hold your swords!" he commanded, much to my relief.

Clouds above threatened to blot out the full moon. We cleared the camp, bounded up a slope to the edge of a forest of oaks, and sniffed. "Smell that horse? This way!" Quan Shen said, and raced into the dark woodlands.

The fragrant trail of the *Hetu* lured us southwest through the forest. A few jagged stones underfoot cut shallow wounds on our callused hands and feet as we ran, but we gritted our teeth and pushed on. Occasionally we would stop to sniff and confirm the direction before setting off again.

The moonlight filtered down through the canopy of leaves, barely enough to see by. However, the gloom worked to our advantage; a careful assassin would have had to lead his horse down the path slowly, as a misstep could break the animal's leg.

"Are you loving this!" Quan Shen said, more of a statement than a question.

Surprisingly, I was. Quan Shen's magic granted my body strength and speed it never had, and I never felt more alive. The darkness proved little hindrance with the hound's mystical senses guiding us.

Kou Shen was taking the bigger risk, pressing his mount through the same terrain after us. At first, he held his own on the trail, but Quan Shen had been taking incredible leaps to take short cuts that a rider and horse could never follow. I lost track of where they were behind us.

Turn back and find Kou Shen. We cannot fight the killer alone, I said. *We have no sword, and even if we had one, I had only basic training!*

"You call yourself a soldier?" Quan Shen growled.

I am an expert shot with the trebuchet, I said in defense.

"Easy, I'll rip his throat out with my teeth!" Quan Shen was drunk on the magic of the wild, thirsting for a fight. Even I became tipsy, but I fought to hold on to rational thought.

A few drops of rain splashed upon our back.

Our nose twitched. "Smell that? Mugwort. We're close!" he said.

Take him by surprise, I advised.

But Quan Shen would not listen. We barked a war cry and hurtled forward.

There, the silhouette of a man leading a horse!

The assassin had heard the noise and reached for his sword, but Quan Shen growled and pounced, forcing him to the ground. We sunk our teeth into the man's forearm, but he punched us in the head with his other hand, disorienting us. He rolled away from his frightened mare, drawing his sword in a fluid motion.

We shook off our daze, turned and crouched.

Our enemy rose to his feet, and I recognized his face. *He's one of the healers!*

Quan Shen charged the assassin, but he was quicker, sidestepping our attack. A sword cut connected with our left shoulder, opening a painful gash. We growled and backed out of his reach.

Rain began to fall.

Listen, Quan Shen, his sword gives him an advantage, but we need not fight. I drew his attention to the mare, which had a bulky bundle strapped to her back. *Spook the horse and deny him the* Hetu *until reinforcements arrive.*

We started circling the assassin. "I can take him," Quan Shen said, baring our teeth.

With sword at the ready, the assassin slowly approached his horse.

Obey, or we both die, I said. *If you are the spirit of the hound, draw on your other qualities besides the wild. Loyalty. Dedication. Duty!*

I felt Quan Shen calm. "As you command."

We barked and leaped through the air with supernatural strength toward the mare, grabbed a branch overhead, and kicked her rump, panicking the horse. She reared and bolted.

The assassin surged forward and cut at us, but we swung ourselves up onto the branch. The tree's limb bowed and creaked under our weight. It would not hold for long. Undaunted, the assassin unleashed a barrage of strikes at our feet, but we grabbed the higher branch and pulled our feet out of his reach.

"What now?" Quan Shen muttered.

Our ears picked up the sound of approaching hooves hitting damp earth. Out of the shadows came Kou Shen astride his steed, his blade wet with rain. The assassin turned, but not in time: a swing of Kou Shen's sword as he rode past separated the villain's head from his body.

We breathed easier. "Kou Shen! What kept you?" Quan Shen asked.

"You should've waited," Kou Shen said. "Come down, my friend."

I caught a whiff of old tea in an updraft. *Wait, Quan Shen, isn't that the scent of fear?*

Yes, Quan Shen sub-vocalized. *Strange. Why would Kou Shen still be afraid? The enemy is dead.*

How would Kou Shen know how many healers in the fleet practiced moxibustion? And why did he come alone, when he could easily have brought reinforcements? I asked. *It must be Ren Chun, pretending to be*

Kou Shen. Look at the way he stroked his scar, like an old comfort.

Quan Shen cursed. *I knew Big Mouth was far too quiet.*

"Well?" Ren Chun asked. "Let's find the *Hetu.*"

Ren Chun silenced his accomplice before he could betray him, I conjectured. *He expects us to trust him, so he can kill us as soon as we turn our back.*

"A moment. I can hear the runaway horse better from this height," Quan Shen replied. To me: *Do we fight, then?*

Even with your powers, we would surely lose against a mounted swordsman. I have an idea, I said. *Give the branch below us a strong kick, and it will fall.*

It's hardly enough to hurt him, if it even connects, Quan Shen said, doubtful.

No, but it will be a distraction. Can you get us to the dead man's sword? I asked. The weapon lay in the assassin's lifeless hand, beside Ren Chun and his horse.

I thought you were pathetic with a blade?

I am, but Kou Shen is not. He knows Ren Chun's body well, and likely his weaknesses. One of the words in my chengyu *has the character for mouth, so I will try summoning Kou Shen myself.* I was deliberately vague about which word, in case Quan Shen could figure out my *chengyu.*

You are doomed if I leave! Quan Shen said. *What if he fails to come?*

He will. He must.

Then dismiss me when you are ready. Good luck, my friend.

And you, Quan Shen.

We slammed down with our feet and broke off the branch, catching Ren Chen by surprise. The limb fell, missing him and his horse, but it was enough to startle the mare, which whinnied and skittered a few paces to safety.

We took advantage of the diversion, swung away from Ren Chun, and dropped to the ground, landing soft.

With a cry, Ren Chun spurred his mount back toward us, brandishing his sword, but his blade caught only air as we rolled under the mare and dove for the dead man's weapon. When we had it in our hand, I dismissed Quan Shen. *Go!*

The spirit of the hound fled my body, returning control to me but leaving me exhausted. I staggered to my feet and held the sword up with a trembling hand. I shouted my *chengyu*, my need for Kou Shen never greater.

"Die," Ren Chun cried, leaning from horseback to cut me down.

The spirit of Kou Shen poured into me.

Our grip strengthened on the sword's hilt, and Kou Shen anticipated Ren Chun's feint, parrying the blow that would have killed us.

Ren Chun pressed his attack, but Kou Shen anticipated his strikes, dodging and blocking with our sword. "You cannot defeat me, Ren Chun." Our voice carried a force like thunder.

"Kou Shen," Ren Chun guessed. "Let's put that to the test, shall we? The Jin will pay me well to know if a spirit can die!"

"I think not. Why did you turn, Ren Chun?" Kou Shen asked amid the ringing of blade against blade.

Ren Chun sneered. "This world belongs to the living! I'd rather see the Song Dynasty fall to the Jin than let ghosts like you use and corrupt our people."

"No, Ren Chun, we serve the country even in death. It is you who has betrayed the words on your back—"

With those words, Kou Shen left my body as swiftly as he had taken it.

"—and they will be your downfall," Kou Shen said in Ren Chun's voice, in control of the traitor's body. He sheathed his sword.

Fatigue overtook me again as I kept the sword's point toward him in a shaking hand, not sure what had happened.

"Remember what I told you about a spirit who has learned someone's *chengyu?*" Kou Shen said.

I understood. If the body heard the spirit speak the *chengyu*, it would acknowledge him as the master. "It works even when you speak it in a different body!"

He nodded. "His body is mine."

It was an ability with frightening potential. Legions of Song soldiers bore Yue Fei's tattoo. A spirit that shouted the *chengyu* could leap to any man who heard it, carrying its skills where it was needed on the battlefield. I was beginning to understand the true power of the Spirit General and his ghosts and why Ren Chun feared them. A loyal spirit would serve the good, but if they were all human once, then some might be tempted to do evil.

"I should have known it was him earlier," I said. "I should not have been so trusting."

"The brunt of the blame is mine," Kou Shen said, binding the wound on my shoulder. "It was I who made Ren Chun privy to the secret of the *Hetu*. I will release this body once Admiral Zhang has him safely bound." He opened a hand to gauge the rain, a drizzle still. "The morning creeps closer, and a battle remains to be won. Let us recover the *Hetu* quickly."

"It's strapped to the assassin's horse. I know a spirit who could track it." I smiled.

Kou Shen nodded. "If you will consent to it."

"It would be an honor," I replied. However, it was also my duty to learn more about these spirits, not for profit as Ren Chun did, but to understand what they were and where their loyalties lay.

I spoke my *chengyu* and held Quan Shen's name firm in my heart. *Come, my friend. We have need of you.*

This time, I welcomed the spirit of the hound.

The Fortunes of Mrs. Yu

Charles Tan

MRS. Yu and her lady friends had just finished eating the eight-course lauriat at the Golden Dragon. The headwaiter combined the remnants of noodles, pork, pigeon, abalone, lobster, and fish all into one plate and signaled the rest of his staff to start packing the dishes.

"What's for dessert?" Mrs. Ang asked as she brought out her compact mirror and stared at the reflection of her teeth.

"I'm dreadfully tired of mango pudding and sesame seed balls. I hope we can try something different," Ms. Tan said.

"Not to worry, Ellen," said Mrs. Yu. "I talked to the manager, and he had something special prepared for tonight." Not even Mrs. Yu knew what the restaurant had in store for them as she signaled the waiters to bring in dessert.

Small plates were distributed around the table, and the headwaiter carried with him a modest tray filled with what looked like crusty conch shells.

"Fortune cookies! How *faux* Chinese. I thought they stopped serving these here," Ms. Tan said.

"They kind of you remind you of PacMan," said Mrs. Lu, who admired the curves of the cookie. "Does anyone still play PacMan these days?"

There was a sharp crackle, and everyone turned to Mrs. Ang. She snapped her cookie in half and drew out a thin strip of paper. "I'm not too fond of sweets, but I could always use the advice. Harsh economic climate and all."

Dessert had officially begun, and everyone started eating their fortune cookies, some taking out the paper beforehand, others drawing it out of their mouths like snake charmers.

"Something you lost will soon turn up."

"Do not mistake temptation for opportunity."

"Ideas are like children; there are none so wonderful as your own."

Everyone read their fortunes out loud save for Mrs. Yu, who continued to stare at her strip of paper. Ms. Tan turned to her and asked, "What does your say?"

Mrs. Yu smiled and recalled a quote from Confucius. "Forget injuries, never forget kindness."

Everyone said their farewells except Mrs. Yu, who opted to stay. "Don't worry about me. I just need to thank the manager personally," she said.

Once they left, she approached the headwaiter and asked if he had any fortune cookies left. Hers had been devoid of any sayings, and she felt a certain embarrassment if she were to admit this to her friends. While she had successfully bluffed her way out of that predicament, the night did not feel complete without finishing this particular ritual. The headwaiter motioned for one of his companions, who then brought out another tray filled with fortune cookies.

Mrs. Yu flashed her smile, snatched two of the cookies, and stored them in her purse. She felt fortunate that she was a regular patron and wielded a certain influence with the staff. It was rumored that The Golden Dragon was barely breaking even and would be cutting down on its staff soon. It wouldn't do to disappoint one of their best customers.

After exiting the restaurant, she looked around and made sure no one was about. When Mrs. Yu was convinced that she was alone, she drew out a fortune cookie from her bag, cracked it in half, and pulled out the strip of paper.

It was a blank.

Mrs. Yu, as a reflex, smiled.

"Calm yourself," she said out loud, as merely thinking about it was not enough to assuage her doubts. At least she had the foresight to grab a spare.

She took out the last fortune cookie, and her hands trembled. She wondered what would happen if this fortune cookie was another blank. Shouldn't it be called fortuneless cookies then? How preposterous. Or maybe there were defective cookies in the batch, and she was simply unlucky. But even that fact conveyed a certain fate, a sign of disharmony in her life.

Mrs. Yu cracked open the fortune cookie and hoped to see some etchings in the strip of paper. It didn't matter if the advice was written in Hanzi, a language she never mastered with its endless combination of radicals and reliance on rote memorization, as long as there was some sort of advice.

Like the previous ones, it was a blank. Mrs. Yu stared at the white piece of paper.

At first she felt rage. She will sue the fortune cookie makers! It didn't matter if the cookies contained good fortune or bad fortune, as long as they actually contained something. Why, what would have happened to the Ming revolution if the bakers failed in their simple duty to smuggle messages into their moon cakes? The citizens would never have successfully rebelled against the Mongol invaders.

Once Mrs. Yu's fantasy had run its course, her

thoughts turned in another direction. Maybe the blank strip of paper was the message, a symbol of sorts. White was the color of death, and it was possible the fortune cookie was predicting her demise.

She pondered the implications. Her first thoughts were of Mr. Yu, a stout man who went to work every day without fail. As industrious as Mr. Yu was, he was ignorant of life's basic necessities such as cleaning, cooking, and accounting. She imagined the police breaking into their home, finding Mr. Yu's room cluttered with magazines and clothes, and somewhere in the mess was Mr. Yu himself, who had become as thin as a Chinese brush because he had failed to shop for groceries at the market and had mismanaged his funds with all the take-out he ordered.

And then there was her Sunday group, whom she met on a night such as this. There would be no one to arrange the dinners, schedule the meetings, settle the bills, and rein in the various members of the group. Mrs. Ang would be spending her time watching young men, even if she was the oldest in the clique and married to a faithful gentleman. Ms. Tan was too daring and would get everyone lost, jailed, or bankrupt, depending on the particular thrill she might suggest for the night. And poor Mrs. Lu always reminisced about the past. If she had her way, they would be spending their evenings in her apartment, talking about the days gone by and admiring dusty photo albums.

No, it could not yet be her time to die. The fortune cookies at the Golden Dragon were simply a fluke.

She went to an obscure Chinese take-out in the dark corners of Chinatown. It had the stereotypical phrase Ni Hao, the logo was missing a few characters, and the chef wasn't even Chinese; but it was one of the few restaurants in Manila that still served fortune cookies.

Mrs. Yu didn't even bother scrutinizing the menu. She

ordered the cheapest pack meal and tapped her foot as the staff scrambled to grab her order. When it arrived, she dumped the contents into a fly-infested trash bin, but not before taking out the fortune cookie.

The cookie itself wasn't spectacular. It was brown rather than golden, and the edges were bent rather than curved. At least she didn't have to eat it, Mrs. Yu thought, before she broke it in half and drew out her fortune.

It was another blank. Now, she had four such strips of paper. Four was an unlucky number—it had the same phonetics as the Chinese word for death.

Perhaps it was foolish of her to challenge the will of the gods. Mrs. Yu resigned herself to her fate. Well, if she were to die today, at the very least it might as well be at a venue of her choosing. The apartment she shared with Mr. Yu felt too confining. Besides, she didn't want to leave him in shock should he discover her corpse in their bedroom. The local church seemed a poor fit. True, it was where she met her Sunday group, but she was never as pious as she appeared to be, and the only reason she was so faithful in her attendance was because it was where she chatted with her friends. Maybe she should return to the Golden Dragon, her previously favorite restaurant. They deserved the impending confusion for serving her the fortune cookies in the first place. Hopefully it would become a scandal on local TV; the media would dig up the identity of its owners, one of the waiters would be revealed to have had a secret affair with a celebrity customer, and the kitchen would be investigated for violating health codes. She was even willing to settle for an urban legend, the type that was propagated through email and text messages.

Somehow, the thought comforted her, and she felt a sense of liberation. It was only the foolish, after all, who fought fate until the very end.

The trip back was arduous. She was accosted by thieves who demanded that she surrender her money and cell phone. Mrs. Yu simply had a glazed look as she handed over her purse. Would she die now, the victim of a street stabbing? While crossing the street, she stumbled on the gravel that was eroded by tires and the weather. Her right high heel broke, and Mrs. Yu wondered whether a speeding car would hit her then and there. When all she got was blaring traffic horns, she got up quickly and walked away with a limp. A few blocks from the Golden Dragon, there was a sudden downpour, but Mrs. Yu couldn't be bothered to look for shelter. Perhaps Lei Gong would finally strike her down with one of his thunderbolts. Instead, all she got was disheveled hair, smudged make-up, and soaked clothes.

By the time she reached the Golden Dragon, the parking lot was empty, and the headwaiter was about to put the chains and lock around the door.

"Wait," Mrs. Yu shouted. She had lost all her composure by then and had only a yearning to collapse inside the restaurant and condemn its owners to the eighteen levels of hell. Why did they ever serve her fortune cookies? It wasn't even real Chinese food.

At first, it appeared to Mrs. Yu that the headwaiter did not recognize her. He took a step back and held tightly the chains of the lock. Perhaps it was her limp, which made her movements devoid of grace. Or maybe the rain had ruined her make-up, and she resembled a *jiang shi* more than someone regal. She would have called out his name to catch his attention, but Mrs. Yu realized that despite knowing him for the past eight years, she couldn't recall his name, even when the official uniform required them to wear a shiny nametag.

Mrs. Yu could not tell whether it was recognition or pity that made the waiter relax his grip on the lock and approach her. She could sense some hesitation as he came closer, so she decided to reach out to him, when her strength finally gave out and she fainted.

When Mrs. Yu regained consciousness, she found herself inside one of the carpeted dining rooms. At first, her vision was a bit blurry, and she mistook the headwaiter for her grandfather, a bald and gaunt man who often flashed her a toothless smile.

"Why did you come to the Philippines?" she once asked her grandfather. With all their stories about China, its language, people, and culture, Mrs. Yu wondered what would have made her grandparents leave the mainland.

"I wanted to start over with a blank slate," he replied. He didn't elaborate further, as if his statement was self explanatory. Mrs. Yu didn't comprehend its implications at the time, but right now, it sounded like an adage for a fortune cookie.

Mrs. Yu's vision cleared up when she heard the sounds of a familiar voice.

"What did you say?" the headwaiter asked.

"A blank slate," Mrs. Yu replied. "A blank slate!"

The headwaiter gave her a look of incomprehension, his typical reaction when he encountered customers speaking in Fookien, Mandarin, or Cantonese.

Mrs. Yu was about to rebuke him when she remembered where she was. It was way past business hours, and the waiter didn't have to take her inside to attend to her as if she were his responsibility. There was no profit to be made.

Mrs. Yu fumbled through her pockets and found that she still had the four white strips of paper.

"Pen. Can I borrow your pen?" Mrs. Yu demanded.

The headwaiter took out the pen clipped to his right breast pocket and gave it to her.

Perhaps being fortuneless wasn't necessarily a bad thing. Even though Mrs. Yu wasn't particularly good with Chinese characters, she managed to write on one of the strips of paper the Hanzi for prosperity, a word with which she was quite familiar due to the numerous money-filled red envelopes she received on her birthday.

"Here, this is for you," said Mrs. Yu. She smiled as she handed the improvised fortune, the ink still fresh, to the headwaiter. "May you have good luck."

Goin' Down to Anglotown

William F. Wu

"**WE'RE** goin' down to Anglotown!" Ken Wong yelled happily over the sound of the wind rushing into the car windows as he drove up the freeway.

He was racing east on the 10 Freeway toward downtown Los Angeles from Westwood with his two best friends. They had just graduated last week from UCLA. The big graduation parties were over, but now, on a perfect June evening, the trio wanted one more night on the town together before going their separate ways.

Tonight, Ken was treating his friends. A freshly minted college grad, with a major in business and a minor in history, he was the only one with a well-paying job lined up. Ken had even received a startling amount of congratulatory money in *lai see* from his relatives. So with a big wad of cash to say farewell in style, he was taking his friends out to dinner.

Filling the shotgun seat with his bulk, Garth Endo folded his arms across his broad chest. "I still say Little Eire's better. It's next to Anglotown. We can get drunk and sing *Danny Boy* for the Micks."

Hooting with laughter, Andy Fan leaned between them from the back. "Yeah, I'd like to hear you sing that, you sentimental jackass. Where the hell are pipes callin' *you*, anyhow? Japan?"

Garth gave him a light-hearted swat with the back of his hand. "I'm *gosei, baka*-boy! You oughta remember that by now. Fifth generation! Even my grandparents don't know anybody in Japan. And you got the green hair, dude. Is that Kelly green?"

Ken laughed. Andy's degree was in film, television, and digital media, with a focus on screenwriting. He had a modest new job reading scripts for a small production company, and for a year he had dyed his black hair day-glow green.

"It's an artistic statement!" Andy yelled, laughing.

"It's a lotta snot!" Garth growled back. "Get a snot rag!"

All three roared with laughter.

"Remember that seventies movie *Anglotown?*" Andy grinned impishly. "The one starring Jack Nguyen? The last line is a classic."

Garth turned to Ken. "Damn it, he's going to start in with movie quotes again."

"He's unstoppable." Ken shook his head.

"'Forget it, Jake. It's Anglotown,'" Andy intoned.

Garth gave him another back-handed slap.

Ken sped on, the skyscrapers of downtown in view ahead. He would start work in one soon, with his new business degree and his new job at a financial firm. To-night he was taking his pals to a particular restaurant. A waitress there had caught his eye a month ago. He hadn't told Andy and Garth about her.

Beyond the skyscrapers beckoned Anglotown, a strange and mysterious island of Anglo culture in the fused Asian America of greater Southern California.

Out of sight over the coast, the sun remained high, but downtown and in Anglotown, tall buildings threw shadows that gave the streets an air of mystery. Storefronts were darkened and the streets seemed empty. Most of the people visible from the street were white, many wearing work uniforms or dirty aprons. When they spoke to each other, they sprinkled in their own slang, using words that rarely entered mainstream English.

"I've heard Anglotown has all kinds of underground tunnels, secret rooms and passageways," said Ken. "Maybe it's just urban myth, but the rumors go way back."

"Urban myth," said Garth. "Let's look for the Loch Anglotown Monster, too."

Andy laughed and gave Garth a whack on the arm.

Ken parked and led his friends up the sidewalk, looking around. He didn't remember the name of the restaurant. It was a weeknight, with few tourists out.

Some of the tourist-based businesses in Anglotown had the pointed windows, steep gables, and gingerbread of Victorian homes. The shapes created other-worldly shadows, hinting at ghosts from when California was mostly Anglo and Hispanic. Other buildings reflected Colonial Revival, meaning a rectangular shape, two or three stories, symmetrical façades, brick or wood siding, pillars, and windows with shutters. Yet none of it seemed quite right; the shutters were just for show, nailed against the front walls, and many structures had been added awkwardly. Signs, written in archaic lettering, swung in the breeze from horizontal posts out front that evoked New England or Britain itself. None of it seemed to belong in Los Angeles, yet it all belonged in Anglotown.

"Smells good," said Andy. "Is that meatloaf cooking?"

"I smell pot roast." Garth, who knew about all kinds of food, raised his head and breathed in. "Hey, does this *hakujin* restaurant you like have cheap prime rib?"

Ken ignored him, eyeing a narrow storefront jammed between a big seafood restaurant with a Cape Cod front and a bank with a Victorian-era façade. "Chillicothe Katfish Kitchen" was painted on the door above "Genuine Missouri Style Cuisine."

An Asian couple in their twenties stepped out.

Ken caught the guy's eye. "You know an Anglo named Smith?"

"Ha! You know one who's not?" The guy laughed way too loud.

With a sigh, Ken held the door for Andy and Garth so he could see for himself.

The restaurant was dark inside.

"Hi, welcome to the Chillicothe Katfish Kitchen." Cindy Smith, according to her name tag, gave them a glittering smile and picked up some laminated menus.

"Hi." Ken grinned, glad to see her again. "Three of us."

"This way, please." She didn't seem to recognize him.

Andy stifled a laugh and nudged Ken in the ribs.

Cindy, who was about their age, was a pretty blonde with hair that might have been bleached or, considering her pale skin, might have been natural. She wore a retro 1950s outfit. It included a light blue stretch-fabric halter top without a bra, cut low to show off lots of cleavage and cropped to reveal her toned stomach; very tight, high-waisted white short-shorts; and white socks with red sneakers. Her hair was tied up in a swaying pony tail with a large red bow.

Single candles burned in glass bulbs on each pink Formica table. The flickering candlelight threw myriad shadows. Ken wondered again if the building had secret rooms or hidden tunnels.

She turned at a red vinyl booth. "Will this be okay?"

"Sure," said Ken, sitting down.

"Everything you got's okay with me," said Andy, grinning stupidly.

"Shut up and sit down," Garth muttered.

Cindy laughed, her smile a little too bright. "What would you like to drink?"

"Grain Belt Golden draft, all around," said Ken.

"You know your Anglo beer." She gave him an even brighter smile and walked away, her ponytail and rear end swaying.

Garth pushed against Andy. "Shove over, damn it. I need more space. What the hell's Grain Belt Golden?"

"A Midwestern lager," said Ken. "You can only get it in Anglotown. But Anglotown's turning into Euro Fusion, anyway. Little Eire's got Scottish bars. Frogtown keeps fighting to keep out the Little Deutschland shops. All the *bok gwai los* are adjacent now. In fact, Grain Belt Golden's more German than Anglo, but what the hell."

"Yeah, what the hell, Anglo-Saxons started out in Germany." Garth glared at him. "But if it's lousy, I'm blaming you."

Andy was still admiring Cindy, now from a distance. "If it's lousy, I'll forgive her. I'll forgive her anything."

Garth swatted Andy's arm with the back of his hand.

"She looks great," said Ken. "Thing is, even in Anglotown, no *lo fan* dresses like that except to show off for the tourists."

"Who cares?" Andy shrugged. "We're tourists and we're here."

"The *bok gwai lo* women can be so hot," said Ken. "They have that reserve, you know? An air of mystery to go with the beauty."

"And the different natural hair colors," said Garth. "No green, but they sure do make the world a little prettier."

Andy picked up his menu. "So, what's good in this place?"

"Just remember, in a place like this, everybody orders separately," said Garth. "We each get our own dinner. Nobody shares off a serving plate."

"You think I never ate in an Anglo restaurant before?" Andy demanded.

"Those suburban places don't count," said Garth.

"You think *hakujins* really serve soy sauce with pancakes? Tuna casserole with water chestnuts and bean sprouts? Anglos don't eat it that way at home. You order that, I'll slap you from here to Little Eire."

"You want the real thing, you come to Anglotown," said Ken.

"Meatloaf dinner," Andy read from the menu. "With brown sugar glaze or ketchup. Or maybe the deep-fried catfish fillet. I'm not sure."

"Chicken-fried steak for me," said Garth. "Green beans with bacon. Hush puppies? Whatever."

Cindy came out of the shadows with cold mugs of Grain Belt Golden, leaning low to set them down. Smiling, she waited for their orders.

Ken decided on the meatloaf with the brown sugar glaze, and corn, while Andy chose pork chops with peas and carrots. All the dinners came with a tossed salad and, after a protracted debate, they ordered all the salad dressings on the side so they could try them. Cindy plucked at her halter, thanked them, and swayed away.

Ken sipped his beer and looked around. A white family with two young children was barely visible in a shadowed booth in the far corner. In the front, a middle-aged Asian tourist couple sat at a small table. Otherwise, the restaurant was empty. He supposed it survived mostly on the business lunch trade and weekend patrons.

The front windows had blue and white checked curtains. A big wall clock had been made with a shellacked horizontal slice of a red cedar tree trunk. Eight-by-ten pinup photos, showing blondes, redheads, and brunettes, adorned the walls. Many were posed in Midwestern fields of grain or in cities such as St. Paul or Cincinnati. In the life Ken had always known, this kind of decor could only be found in Anglotown.

"You're the only one leaving the area," Ken said to Garth. He studied his friend. Garth was a published poet already, in several prestigious publications, with a bachelor's degree in fine arts. He was about to start grad school at the University of Iowa writing program. All three had grown up in the Los Angeles sprawl, and none of them had been to the Midwest, where whites and their culture were dominant. "Any idea what it's like there?"

Garth looked away. "Damn. I guess it'll be one gigantic Anglotown. I don't know what they'll think of me."

"No telling," said Ken. "But Toronto and Chicago have Anglotowns. New Orleans, too, 'cause the big cities have dominant Asian populations. I bet from Ontario down to Texas, it's mostly one big Anglotown. Those are the states that supported the Asian Exclusion bills in Congress back in the 1800s and after." He paused. "Think about it. If those bills had passed, everything could've been different."

"You're right," said Andy. "Those states aren't like the rest of the country. They didn't even make the Mid-Autumn Moon Festival a state holiday."

Ken nodded. "But I think it's better now since the race riots. They even elected a Chinese mayor in Pekin, Illinois."

"Oh, good," Garth muttered. "How fitting."

"At least you have an English given name," said Ken. "They can all pronounce it in the Midwest. You have a Japanese name, too?"

"Yoshio," said Garth. "After all these years, you never asked before. But, yeah, my family still gives Japanese names." He shrugged. "It means 'Righteous,' or something like that. I don't really use it."

"Yeah, definitely go with 'Garth' in Iowa," said Ken.

"My Chinese name's An-Ning," said Andy. "It means Peace and Serenity in Mandarin. My grandparents were kids when they came from northern China in 1940-something. They'd lived through a couple of wars, so peace was a big deal to them."

"Why don't you use it?" Ken asked.

"We're all speaking English, aren't we?" Andy grinned. "An Ning sounded too much like 'Annie' to me. So I when I was a kid I started using Andy instead."

Garth gave Ken a playful look. "'Ken' is a Japanese name as well as English. Are you just passing, Mr. Wong?"

"Yeah! I don't want to be associated with you!" Ken laughed, and clinked mugs with them as they joined in. "On my dad's side, we go back to the Gold Rush era. I guess back then, going with English names seemed like a good idea. Asian given names have only been cool for a generation or two. But my folks named me Kendall. My middle name's 'Quong Ta.' It's Toisanese for 'Big Brightness.' I hope it doesn't sound that clumsy in Toisanese. Maybe if I want the extra prestige someday, I'll use it."

Andy nodded thoughtfully. "Maybe once I start writing and directing, I oughta use my Chinese name. I'm gonna think about that."

Cindy brought their salads and six small dishes of salad dressings. She smiled at them brightly before leaving.

"Hey, speaking of detective movies set in L.A.," said Andy, as he studied the bright red Russian dressing. "One of the all-time best is *L.A. Confidential* with the Hong Kong star, Russell Koh. But he turned down the upcoming remake of the *The Big Sleep*. You hear about that?"

"No, and I like it that way." Garth sniffed suspiciously at the blue cheese dressing. "But you're gonna tell me, anyway, aren't ya?"

"George Kulani agreed to star in it. He's *yonsei*, since you're so big on counting generations. But some activist group sent a petition to the studio. They say a white guy should play Philip Marlowe, not some yellow guy in whiteface."

"They got a point," said Garth. "Marlowe's white."

"What about just getting the most talented actor?" Andy stood his ground now that the talk was on his turf. "Kulani's a damn good actor with a huge fan base. He's bankable. The makeup's no problem. He's got the acting chops for it."

"Speaking of chops, shut up and eat," said Garth.

Cindy soon returned, carefully balancing three full plates. With a self-conscious smile, she suggestively leaned down low once again, setting the correct plates in front of each diner. She slowly straightened, looking at them as she played idly with the front of her halter top. "More beer, guys?"

"Make it a pitcher," said Ken, and his companions nodded.

She smiled just at him this time. "Of course!"

Ken watched over his shoulder as she walked away and saw her look back at him. She smiled again. Encouraged, he returned the smile.

Andy looked up at Ken with a mouthful of pork chop. "How'd you find this place?"

"I came down for some new suits and got them tailored here out of English wool. It's cheap in Anglotown. Then I looked for a place to have lunch."

Cindy returned with a pitcher of Grain Belt Golden and topped off all three mugs. "Will there be anything else?"

"Can I ask you something?" Ken asked.

Her smile faltered for the first time. "What do you want to know?"

"Have you heard about George Kulani playing Philip Marlowe in a new movie? I wondered what you thought about that."

Cindy's smile snapped right back. "George Kulani's hot. I love everything he does."

"But should he play a *bok gwai*—uh, a white guy?" Andy asked.

"Oh, I don't care," Cindy shrugged. "I'll go see it."

"Cool," said Andy, his eyes on her cleavage.

Cindy walked away, but this time she glanced behind her. When she saw Ken watching her, she smiled again.

"She's just angling for a big tip," Garth said sourly.

"Works for me," said Andy. "Since Ken's treating us with his pile of cash!"

Ken caught Cindy studying them from across the room. When she realized he was watching her, she turned away abruptly. He was surprised that she didn't smile this time.

"Look, guys." Garth stared into his beer. "I'm not good at this, okay? But I just want to say, thanks for all the good times. It's been really cool. I won't have friends where I'm going next. So, uh, to the three of us, okay?"

Ken and Andy clinked mugs with him. "*Kampai!*" Ken called out, using the Japanese term for bottoms up.

They all repeated it and drained their mugs.

Garth nodded to himself, satisfied.

Andy picked up the pitcher and poured for everyone.

"So Cindy likes Kulani," said Andy. "So what? Women everywhere love Kulani. Lots of white women like Asian guys."

"They want to trade up," said Ken. "Who wants some Anglotown dude who's going sweep floors all his life or get shot up in a gangland turf war?"

"I got that," said Garth. "You get a job outside Anglotown, who owns the company? Who's your supervisor? All Asians. Awkward for a lot of white dudes. But it might be different in Iowa. Backwards, maybe. I dunno."

"Don't forget the mass media," said Andy. "Like Koh and Kulani playing heroes on the big screen. They're like Clark Gable, Keye Luke, and Lane Nakano for earlier generations. But so what? I don't care why white girls like us. And some Asian guys got a thing for them, too." He looked pointedly at Ken. "Personally, I'm not so particular. I still got my Latina girlfriend. "

"Stick to movies," Garth muttered. "Otherwise, I'm gonna puke."

"Ah, yes! 'Forget it, Jake. It's Anglotown.' "

"Sorry I reminded you," said Garth. "I shoulda just puked."

Ken and Andy laughed.

Garth eyed Ken. "And my last girlfriend was Nikkei. But you're hot for Cindy."

"Hey, in Iowa, white women are all you're going to see!" Ken laughed.

Andy joined the laughter, but Garth glowered and looked away.

Ken sipped his beer and looked for Cindy. She was wiping down the empty table where the middle-aged Asian couple had been sitting. Now the only other patrons were the Anglo family in the corner.

Andy leaned down close. "Okay, Ken. Are you going to talk to Cindy or what?"

"What the hell." Ken got up, feeling a light buzz from the beer. He walked through the shadows to the back of the restaurant, where she had gone after cleaning the table. On the wall above her, a black and white clock was shaped like a cat. With every tick-tock, its eyes and tail switched back and forth.

Weird, he thought.

"Is everything okay?" Cindy gave him with a look that was wary, yet still flirtatious.

"Sure, it's great. I was just wondering, you know, what it's like here." He knew he sounded lame. "I mean in Anglotown. Are you from here?"

"Oh. Yeah, I was born and raised here."

Ken's beer buzz was amping up. "Does Anglotown have secret tunnels?"

Instead of answering, she leaned toward him, her manner suddenly intimate. "You okay? Your face is all flushed."

"I'm fine. So, uh, about the secret tunnels?"

"Oh, I know. You've heard about the secret rooms and passageways, underground tunnels, and all that?"

"I suppose it's just urban myth, but I've wondered—"

She placed one finger against his lips. Her voice dropped to a whisper. "It's quiet tonight. I only have two tables left. And it's just my dad, who cooks, plus the dishwasher and me. Would you like to see some secret sights?" She took her finger away.

"Sure," Ken whispered back. "If it's okay—"

"But just you. I'm not telling anyone else 'cause my dad would freak. All three of you would make too much noise. Deal?"

"Yeah."

Cindy made another quick survey of the dining room, then hooked one arm through Ken's. He smelled light, sweet perfume for the first time. She walked him to a swinging door and slipped through. They entered a small foyer with a windowed door on the left that led to the kitchen and a staircase leading down on the right.

In the little foyer, Cindy leaned into Ken as she looked into the kitchen through the little window. "Okay, downstairs, quick."

Ken followed her. The steps were made of old wood that gave slightly beneath him. Few buildings in California had basements, and he had never entered one. He felt a tingle of excitement as he descended into the shadows.

The basement was chilly. In the indirect light from upstairs, Ken saw white freezers humming quietly. Shelves held stacks of canned goods. A big pegboard lined the wall. Cast iron pots and pans of all sizes hung from it, fading into shadow far ahead.

"The freezers are full of frozen catfish and chicken," Cindy whispered, as though this was important. "Come on." She walked away from the stairs, with her big bow and ponytail throwing exaggerated shadows that swayed against the peg board and its pots and pans. "Some of them have frozen rats."

"Rats?" Startled, Ken glanced at her before following her deeper into the darkness. A rat skittered away into the shadowed area ahead, and he flinched.

"You see?" Cindy leaned against him, wafting sweet perfume, and she whispered into his ear. "Sometimes we eat them ourselves."

"What? How do you catch them?"

"We catch 'em with our forks!"

Fighting the beer buzz, Ken tried to picture how that would work but failed.

"And we know you yellows really hate them, so if we don't like somebody, we serve 'em rats instead of chicken!" She giggled.

"I hope you liked us okay," Ken muttered.

"Sure!" She pressed her bust against him. "You guys know Grain Belt Golden."

Still uncertain, Ken allowed her to steer him ahead of her with a dainty hand.

"Look," she whispered from behind. "I know it's dark, but there's a secret passageway." She drew him toward the wall with the big peg board. "The floor gets uneven. Watch your step, okay?"

He looked down, but in the dim light he could barely see the floor beneath his feet. Then he heard a metallic clank behind him and turned.

Cindy came up close, her mouth approaching his.

Buzzed but happy, he leaned toward her in the shadows. Just before their lips met, something hard slammed against the top of his head, with a low-pitched metallic thud. He staggered, not sure what had happened.

When he looked up, Cindy was drawing an enormous cast iron skillet back over her shoulder with a two-handed grip, like a batter at home plate getting ready for a pitch.

He ducked under a home-run swing that could have sent his brain matter over a centerfield fence. Confused, with his head pounding in pain and his vision blurry, he was in no condition to fight. He ran for the stairs, aware of a giant shadow with a bouncing ponytail along the row of white freezers closing in.

Just as he stretched for the second step, the big pan clanged against the back of his head, sounding oddly like a small Chinese gong. He forced his way up the stairs. Her quick, dainty footsteps hurried right behind him.

As Ken reached the top step and entered the little foyer, he saw the swinging door that led to the dining room. Before he could reach it, the heavy skillet slammed against the top of his head again and he fell to the floor.

Dazed, he was aware of Cindy shouting. Hands tugged at his back pants pockets. He heard male voices, muffled by closed doors, from somewhere behind him and somewhere in front of him.

Groggy from the blows, he tried to stand and then staggered forward, banging the swinging door with his forehead and falling out onto the floor of the dining room.

Ken tried to clear his thoughts as he heard several sets of footsteps to his rear. In front of him, he recognized startled shouts from Andy and Garth and their footsteps coming up fast. He drew a deep breath.

"Chill!" Andy shouted to someone. "Stay back."

"She got my wallet," Ken wheezed. He touched the top of his head and felt blood on his fingers.

"Easy, dude," Garth said quietly in his ear.

Andy and Garth took his arms and lifted him to his

feet, at the same time backing away from the swinging door.

Ken got his footing and turned as his vision cleared. His head pounded in pain. Andy and Garth held him up, and all three watched Cindy as they edged backward.

Cindy stood just this side of the swinging door. Two white men had crowded behind her. One was a balding, heavyset guy wearing a stained apron and holding a long carving knife. The other was a lean, bearded twenty-something with muscular forearms. From the wet apron he wore, Ken guessed he was the dishwasher.

For a long moment, no one moved.

Ken realized Cindy held his bulging wallet in one hand and the cast iron skillet in the other. She smiled at him sweetly and handed the skillet to the dishwasher. Then she pulled the big wad of cash out of his wallet and stuck it into her cleavage with the folded centers down and the open edges of the greenbacks still in view like a flat-edged flower.

"Hey!" Ken started forward, but Andy and Garth held him fast.

Cindy tossed the wallet underhand to them.

Garth caught it.

"Thanks for the big tip!" Cindy laughed, with a sneer in her smile this time. "I just love waiting on you rich yellow bastards! Now get out!"

The two guys behind her laughed.

"Just stay right there, *bok gwai lo*," Garth growled, using the Cantonese term, to show solidarity with Ken and Andy.

Andy and Garth began walking Ken backward to the front door.

"Come back any time, guys," Cindy sneered. She put her hands on her hips and rocked her shoulders, making the greenback-blossom quiver. "The money waves bye-bye!"

Furious, Ken jerked forward. "That's my graduation money!"

"Ooh, college boys!" Cindy giggled. "No wonder I hit the jackpot!"

Ken yanked against Andy and Garth's hold. "Come on, we can take 'em! There's just two guys and her."

On the wall in the rear, the black and white clock tick-tocked, its cat's eyes switching and its tail swinging. In the far corner, the Anglo family's table was empty now, except for the dirty dishes. Little candle flames danced on the individual tables in the dim restaurant. Streetlight glowed through the blue and white checked curtains at the front window.

Andy and Garth, still holding him, said nothing.

"Or we can call the cops," Ken added, his intensity fading.

"It's cash," Andy said quietly. "Their word against ours—and we're on their turf."

Ken looked around in the shadows amid the flickering candle flames. The place was exotic, alien. It smelled of pan-fried catfish and chicken-fried steak. A Katfish Kitchen. He would never understand these people.

Glaring at Cindy's smirk and at the thick wad of cash still protruding from her cleavage, he let out a long breath. He forced himself to relax and stand straight, without pulling against Andy and Garth. They released him.

Ken whirled and strode out of the restaurant. Out in the cool night air, the streetlights threw slanted shadows across the buildings and down the block. He looked in all directions. No one else was out here at this hour. The empty streets of Anglotown seemed dark with menace.

Behind him, Andy and Garth warily backed out the door, making sure no one followed them. When they were safely away from the Chillicothe Katfish Kitchen, the three of them fell into step together, striding briskly down the sidewalk with nervous backward glances.

"I would have treated her right," Ken said quietly, his head still pounding in pain. "I would have asked her out, spent money on her. Over time, a lot more money than what she took. Who knows, we could have hit it off."

"Just chill," said Andy. "That's not what she wanted."

Ken stopped and looked back up the street at the restaurant door. Even with the deep, throbbing headache and blood dripping down the back of his neck, he had an urge to go back. He didn't want it to end this way.

Andy seemed to read his thoughts. "No way, dude."

"But it doesn't make any sense," said Ken. "I just want to know . . . *why*?"

"Forget it, Ken," said Garth. "It's Anglotown."

The Polar Bear Carries the Mail

Derwin Mak

PAUL Chu and Jonathan Soong stopped their car and watched the funeral procession pass them. A small crowd of mourners followed the black hearse. To most southerners, these people were simply "Aboriginals," but after six months in town, Paul knew the names of their nations: Cree, Chipeweyan, Métis, Dene, and Inuit.

A few Chinese walked with the Aboriginals. "We should be with them," said Paul. "If only Kate's flight weren't arriving now. At least we got to the church service."

"The only whites in the funeral procession are our employees and the locals," Jonathan observed. "The protesters did not show up like they said they would."

"It's good that they didn't," said Paul. "They say they mourn for Danny too, but the locals blame them for his death."

A white environmentalist from Ontario had killed Danny Eastman, a Cree worker at the methane processing plant. Since the death had occurred at a protest where tempers had flared quickly, everyone expected the accused killer to plea bargain for the lesser charge of manslaughter.

"There's Ray Cassidy," said Paul, noticing one of the non-Aboriginals, a man in his fifties. "Did you get a chance to talk to him?"

"Briefly. He still will not come back," Jonathan said.

After the procession had passed, Paul and Jonathan continued driving past the small, short buildings of Churchill, Manitoba. When they reached the outskirts of town, the scenery changed to crooked, weather-beaten trees, a sparse forest at the southern edge of the Arctic.

Near the airport, Paul saw a sign reading:

WELCOME TO CHURCHILL, MANITOBA
POLAR BEAR CAPITAL OF THE WORLD

However, Paul had still not seen a polar bear. Like the fish and beluga whales, the polar bears disappeared when the methane acidified the Arctic Ocean.

Massive amounts of methane were frozen in the permafrost twelve thousand years ago. For centuries, the methane had been turning into gas and leaking to the surface. Early in the twenty-first century, the seepage intensified, especially from the ocean floor. Nobody knew why the methane was outgassing. Some scientists suspected human-induced climate change, while others said the planet naturally goes through cycles of heat and cold.

The methane killed most of the marine life and polar bears along the southwestern shore of Hudson Bay. The locals used to fish and show polar bears and beluga whales to tourists. Without fishing and ecotourism, Churchill needed another industry.

Ann Alaralok, Mayor of Churchill, told the town council, "Methane ruined one industry, but it can support another one ..."

The town invited Stanley Aerospace, a Hong Kong company, to build a spaceport at the abandoned research rocket launch facility at Fort Churchill. Stanley Aerospace formed a consortium with several Canadian companies to build Churchill Spaceport.

Jonathan Soong, the spaceport's first general manager, came with rocket scientists from China, as well as from Stanley's Canadian partners in Montreal and Toronto. The Chinese brought a Long March CH4-1 rocket, a new model fueled by liquid methane. The Canadians hired the people of Churchill to build the spaceport and a processing plant to harvest methane as rocket fuel. With the new Shanghai process, they could compress methane from gas to liquid cheaply and efficiently with fewer staff than older methods. The locals talked eagerly of starting hotels, restaurants, shops, and other businesses to serve the spaceport's staff, clients, and tourists.

But environmentalists came from the south to try to stop the spaceport and its methane plant. Last week, when they blockaded the methane plant, a riot broke out, and Danny Eastman was killed.

"Sometimes I think the spaceport is cursed," Jonathan said as he parked the car. "The protests interrupted construction work. There are no clients waiting to launch anything. The protesters scared ten people into returning to Hong Kong. Then Eastman died. And now Cassidy has quit working at the methane plant."

"Our luck's going to change," Paul predicted. "After *Polar Bear*'s flight, the space tourism program will take off, clients will line up to launch their satellites, and I'll be the first Canadian to go into orbit on a rocket launched from Canada."

"I wish that day would come soon. Then I will finally be able to return to Hong Kong," Jonathan said.

He pointed at an old Bombardier Q400 turboprop airplane sitting on the runway. "Look, the plane has arrived. Your girlfriend must be waiting for us."

They walked to the terminal and found Kate waiting for them. She wore a black miniskirt and green jacket with the logo of the St. Patrick's Society of Montreal, an image of the patron saint of Ireland.

Paul kissed Kate and stroked her brown hair. "Have you been waiting long?" he asked.

Kate shook her head. "No, not long. Just fifteen minutes."

"I'm sorry about that," said Jonathan. "We had a short delay along the way."

"What's with the black suits?" Kate asked. "You two look like you just came from a funeral."

"Actually, we did," Paul said.

Kate gasped. "Oh, my God, now I remember. Danny Eastman."

"Mr. Soong," a voice called from a distance. It came from a man whose blond hair was styled in a bowl cut. He wore a green army surplus jacket over a T-shirt showing Hugo Chavez, the notorious Venezuelan dictator of decades ago.

As the man approached them, Paul whispered to Kate, "Here comes trouble."

Jonathan flinched as the man stared at them with his piercing, brown eyes.

The man said, "Mr. Soong, on behalf of the Churchill Environmental Alliance, I wish to express our regret that Mr. Eastman has died. We offered our condolences to his family."

Jonathan nodded and muttered, "Thank you. Mr. Eastman was an excellent employee. He was a good person."

After an awkward pause, the man continued. "Are you uncomfortable around me? That's so rude of you. You should be happy to see me. *That's* the Canadian way."

The man turned to Kate. "I don't believe we've met before. I'm Dr. Edward Hackbart. Pleased to meet you. And who are you?"

Kate glared at Hackbart. She must have recognized him from the news. Hackbart was a professor of political science at York University in Toronto. Last year, he spent six months in jail for breaking the windows of the Japanese Embassy to protest against whale hunting. The university stripped him of his tenure, and he drifted to Churchill to fight against the spaceport.

"My name's Kate," she finally replied.

"And what are you doing here?"

"Just visiting."

"Really?" said Hackbart. "In a town this small, it's hard to keep secrets. Aren't you Mr. Soong's new assistant, replacing the one who went back to China?"

"So what if I am?" she replied.

Hackbart grunted. "In the early twentieth century, Manitoba had a law prohibiting Chinese men from hiring white women. It might not have been a fair law, but at least it stopped outsiders from messing with the province."

Kate scowled.

"Outsiders? You're from Toronto, just like me," said Paul. "You didn't live here until you came up as a protester! You live in a tent near the methane plant."

"My tent doesn't spoil the natural beauty of the area, unlike your eyesore methane plant and spaceport," Hackbart retorted.

"Okay, we need to go to the office," Jonathan ordered. "Paul, Kate, come with me."

Without saying any more to Hackbart, they fled from the terminal.

"Did you hear what he said?" Kate complained. "Was he being racist?"

"He became that way when he noticed that his opponents are mostly Aboriginals and Chinese," said Jonathan.

He shook his head. "We could have gone to Florida or New Mexico, but we came here."

They passed the methane plant. "Mr. Ming wanted the tax credits and cheap methane," Paul said.

When they arrived at Churchill Spaceport, Kate got

out of the car and looked at the buildings, roads, and runways around her.

"Wow, this is amazing," she said. She pulled a small sketchpad and pencil out of her handbag and began drawing a spaceport scene. "I would love to paint this landscape."

"She has a fine arts degree from McGill," Paul explained to Jonathan. "She wanted to be a painter."

"But being executive assistant to the president of the Montreal Museum of Fine Arts paid better," Kate admitted.

"I see," said Jonathan.

"Oh, there's your spaceship," Kate said, staring at the launch pad. A Long March rocket stood beside a supply tower. Atop the rocket was the *Polar Bear*, the reusable space plane. Despite the red maple leaf painted on her white body, the *Polar Bear* was made in China.

"Uh oh, no wonder the spaceport has been so unlucky," she said.

"What's wrong?" Paul asked.

"The supply tower has X's and jagged patterns on it. There's also a pyramid on the top. All those intersecting straight lines are bad *feng shui*," Kate said, citing the ancient theory of how the built environment affects fortune.

"How interesting," said Jonathan. "In a spaceport full of Chinese workers, the Irish girl is the first person to notice the *feng shui*."

It was late August, a time when the aurora borealis is visible. Paul showed Kate the northern lights. The aurora formed a moving green, red, and white backdrop to the Long March rocket.

"The northern lights are formed by charged particles from the magnetosphere colliding with gases in the upper atmosphere. I'll be flying into them," said Paul.

"Are they dangerous?" Kate asked.

"No. I'll pass through the aurora in a few seconds, so the electronic systems and I will not get a dangerous dose of radiation. In addition, the spaceship has radiation-hardened components."

Paul heard someone walking. He turned to see Ann Alaralok, Inuit historian, Mayor of Churchill, and a frequent visitor to the spaceport.

After Paul introduced Kate to Alaralok, the mayor asked Kate, "Is this the first time you've seen the northern lights?"

Kate smiled. "Yes. They're so beautiful."

"I bet Paul told you their scientific explanation, but do you know the legends?" said Alaralok. "The Inuit say the lights are sky people playing ball."

The mayor continued. "And then there are the Cree. The Cree call the aurora 'the dance of the spirits.' The lights are the spirits of the dead."

At a videoconference with the consortium partners, Jonathan updated them on the status.

"After the death of Danny Eastman, the police say they will no longer tolerate blockades and protests at the methane plant or the spaceport," said Jonathan. "The environmentalists have ended their blockades, but they remain camped in tents in front of the methane plant."

Donald Ming, President of Stanley Aerospace, gave a bittersweet smile from Hong Kong. "That is good news, although I wish the police had intervened earlier. We could have avoided the death and the delays in construction."

"This is Canada," Jonathan reminded him. "The police let protesters do whatever they want until someone dies."

From Montreal, Jane Holt, Vice-President of Space Tourism at Alouette Aviation, said, "*Polar Bear*'s flight will prove that we can provide a safe and effective space tourism product. But I'm having trouble selling tour packages before Paul goes into orbit."

"I'm ready for that anytime," Paul said. "I flew *Polar Bear*'s sister plane in a suborbital flight from Mojave. No problems. I know how to handle that plane."

From the corner of the boardroom table, Kate smiled at Paul as she typed notes on her laptop.

"The problem is acquiring the liquid methane fuel," Jonathan reported. "The original staff returned to China after the third riot. They trained some local people to take over, but some of them quit after bullying from the protesters. I have convinced most of them to return, but I do not have the compressor supervisor."

"Oh?" said Holt. "Hasn't Ray Cassidy returned to work?"

Jonathan shook his head. "No. Cassidy still thinks the whole enterprise is not worth the trouble if it cost his friend's life."

"Can you promote another person to take over Cassidy's job?"

"Maybe later, but not now. Cassidy has the most experience. I want someone like him on the job when we restart production."

"Please resolve the problem of the methane plant," Ming urged. "The company has spent billions of dollars on the spaceport, and the board of directors is worried that we have launched only a few unmanned suborbital test flights. The spaceport has not earned a cent. If you do not launch within a month, the board will cut its losses and sell its shares of the consortium, if anyone is willing to buy them."

In Montreal, Jane Holt looked startled. "Without Stanley Aerospace, the spaceport won't have enough capital. The rest of us can't operate it without a large partner."

"The board does not want to keep throwing good money after bad," said Ming. "I am sorry."

The conference ended. As the video screens turned blank, Paul saw Jonathan shrug his shoulders.

"I may go home sooner than expected," Jonathan said.

Barred from the methane plant and the spaceport, Dr. Hackbart led his followers to the post office, where the Chinese spaceport workers received parcels of food and gifts from home. The protesters chanted demands for the Chinese to return to China. The protesters lunged at the workers, and fighting broke out.

This time, the protesters fled when they heard the police car siren. Nobody got killed, but one of the Chinese vowed to quit and return to the Wenchang Spaceport in China.

After the fight, Paul and Kate went to the post office to send a toy polar bear to Kate's niece. The broken windows startled them.

The postmaster, Justin Gallant, straightened a poster of the Louis Riel postage stamp. Riel was the Métis leader who founded Manitoba and led two failed rebellions against the Canadian government in the nineteenth century.

The frame around the poster was broken. "At least they didn't damage the poster," he said. "I would be very annoyed if they had. I'm descended from one of Riel's brothers."

The post office lobby had a soapstone sculpture of Sedna, the Inuit goddess of marine animals. Hackbart had pulled the sculpture off its pedestal and hurled it to the floor several times. A small piece had broken off, and the larger piece was covered with dents and scratches.

Ann Alaralok picked up the sculpture. "How could they do this?" she cried. "Those hooligans have no respect for native culture! We should tear down their tents and send them back home!"

"The mayor's very angry," Kate whispered. "Aside from being an image of an Inuit goddess, is that carving important for another reason?"

Paul replied, "Ten years ago, the town council commissioned the statue to honor Aboriginal fishermen. That's when they had a fishing industry."

"It's as if the goddess had abandoned them," Kate commented softly.

She went to the mayor and took the sculpture. Sedna looked like a mermaid, but the tail had broken off.

"It's the bad *feng shui* at the spaceport. This town could use some positive *qi*," Kate said, referring to the energy flow of living beings.

Two Chinese lions arrived at the spaceport. Made of fiberglass, they were the type that guarded palace gates, though these were only a meter tall.

"What are they doing here?" Paul asked.

Jonathan replied, "Ming sent them from Hong Kong. When you fly, he wants the two lions in the passenger seats. After you come back, we will send them back to Ming."

"This is his encouragement for us to launch soon."

"The Minister of National Heritage will be visiting Hong Kong. Ming wants to give the lions to him as souvenirs of the first manned flight of a new Chinese spaceship."

The Minister was obviously the Minister of National Heritage of China, not of Canada.

Paul grinned. "There's a whole collectors' trade in things that flew aboard spaceships: flags, badges, medals, uniforms, mail, and even baseballs. Now the Communist Party wants space-flown fiberglass lions."

"Ming wants our first space tourists to be Chinese, so

that is why the lions are joining you," Jonathan joked. "Everything about this flight will be Chinese. The Minister of National Heritage wants it that way."

"Except that I and half the mission crew are Canadian citizens, and the vehicle will have a Transport Canada registration."

"And how do I explain that the spaceship *Polar Bear* is named after a Chinese animal?" Jonathan mused.

The mood in town was shifting. With Danny Eastman's death and the recent fight at the post office, people wondered whether the spaceport was worth the trouble. Would they always suffer scorn and violence if the spaceport opened for business?

"There are only forty people, all from out of town, who are protesting and causing trouble," Mayor Alaralok argued at a town council meeting. "The spaceport has all the required environmental programs for recycling, waste management, and carbon emission control."

Dr. Edward Hackbart stood up in the visitor gallery. "That's what they say now, but you can't trust these foreign businessmen. In any case, they're already spoiling the natural beauty you have here."

"The fish, beluga whales, and polar bears are gone," Alaralok said. "No fishing, no ecotourism. What will you have us do?"

"You can get government assistance," Hackbart suggested.

Alaralok scowled. "Can't you southern white people ever think of anything else than giving us welfare?"

"Clean the dirt out of your ears!" Hackbart yelled. "I never used the word 'welfare'! I said, 'government assistance' . . ."

As the council meeting degenerated into shouting, Paul wondered if he would ever fly. The spaceport had used up its supply of methane on the test launches. The plant was ready to compress more methane gas into liquid, but the inexperienced staff needed a skilled supervisor to guide them. One supervisor had fled back to China, and the other had retired to his home.

It wasn't only his hopes that were dying. The hopes of many townspeople were dying too. They had worked hard to build the spaceport only to see it turn idle, like past promises from outsiders.

Paul left the town council meeting and walked to Ray Cassidy's house.

"Hey, Paul, come in." Ray Cassidy said as he opened the door. Despite quitting the spaceport, Ray was still friendly with its staff.

"Thanks for letting me in," said Paul. "I've seen you many times, but this is my first time in your house."

Ray asked, "Can I get you anything? A beer? A coffee?"

"Thanks for offering. I'll have a beer," Paul replied.

"Coming up," said Ray as he went to the kitchen.

Paul looked at the living room. On the wall was a family tree showing Ray's descent from an English fur trader who came to Hudson Bay in the nineteenth century.

There was also a photo of Ray and another man. They were in their twenties and standing in the flat, grassy prairie of southern Manitoba. Far in the background was a natural gas processing plant. It was a large plant from before the invention of the Shanghai process.

"That's me and Danny thirty years ago," said Ray as he gave the beer to Paul. "We grew up here but went south to work for Manitoba Hydro."

"When did you come back?" Paul asked.

"Danny got homesick and returned after five years and got married," said Ray. "I got married too but stayed in the south. I visited Churchill frequently, though. After my wife died, I retired and came back five years ago."

Paul looked at other photos of Ray and Danny and their families over the years. "You guys kept in touch for decades, didn't you?"

"We sure did." Ray picked up a model rocket. "Danny visited Baikonur Cosmodrome and gave me this toy from there. He was fascinated by spaceships because he worked at Iceberg Rocket Base when he came back."

"Ah, Iceberg. I've heard of that company," Paul said. Before Stanley Aerospace, there were several failed attempts to create a commercial spaceport on the ruins of the old research rocket launch site. Iceberg Rocket Base was one of them.

"Look at this," Ray said, pointing at a shoebox full of postcards and envelopes.

He pulled out a postcard showing an old space shuttle. "Danny sent this to me from Kennedy Space Center, Florida. I collect stamps, so he sent me a traditional postcard, not an e-card."

"I didn't know he was so interested in space travel," Paul remarked.

"Oh, he was," said Ray. "He was thrilled by the idea of launching spaceships from here. That's why he came out of retirement to work at the methane plant. He even got me to work there too."

"Which brings me to the reason I'm visiting," said Paul. "You're our most experienced plant worker. You know the Shanghai process. You helped us start up the plant. I know you were planning to retire again after we found a successor, but we can't find and train one before the time we have to launch."

Ray shook his head. "Like I told Jonathan, it was fun at first, but after Danny died, I wondered if it was worth it. Was it really worth his death?"

"Danny wanted spaceships to launch from Churchill," Paul said. "Can you do it for him, at least for my flight?"

"No, not anymore," said Ray, smiling weakly. "Thirty years ago, I would've fought back, I would've defied those protesters, but now I'm too old for it. It's become hand-to-hand combat."

Unsure of what to say, Paul glanced at the computer on Paul's desk. The monitor showed the electronic version of *The Journal of Aerophilately*. An image of a Curtiss JN-4 "Jenny" biplane danced on its cover.

"What's aerophilately?" Paul asked.

"It's the study of airmail, a specialized area of stamp collecting or philately," Ray replied. "I've been collecting stamps since childhood."

"Oh." Paul pointed at the shoebox. "May I look at your envelopes?"

"Sure. Sit down at the table. By the way, an envelope that has gone through the mail is a called a cover. The decorative illustration on the cover is called a cachet."

Paul looked at the covers. Most commemorated new air mail routes, but some had cachets and stamps showing spaceships and astronauts. The space covers bore stamps and postmarks from space centers in the United States, Russia, China, Brazil, and French Guiana.

"Wow, this one actually flew aboard a Shenzhou Gold," Paul said, noticing the special postmark in Chinese: "Aboard Shenzhou Gold Mission 38". The cachet showed the *tàikōnaut* crew standing in front of a Chinese flag.

"Shenzhou Gold Mission 38 carried one thousand covers. Most of them went to Chinese collectors, but I got one," said Ray, beaming with pride. "I've got the largest collection of space-flown covers in Manitoba."

"Ray, I've got an idea," said Paul. "Here's your incentive to create liquid methane for me . . ."

Paul went to Kate's office. "How much of my discretionary expense account is left?" he asked.

"Let me check," she said, accessing the accounting records on her computer. "About five thousand dollars."

"Check the municipal website. How many people live in Churchill?"

"About one thousand plus another two hundred who came to work at the spaceport. These totals don't include the forty protesters in the tent city."

"Forget about them," Paul said. "Can you do me a favor? Can you draw a picture of the Inuit goddess Sedna?"

"Sure, I'll do it. Just like the sculpture?"

"Yes. Draw a picture of Sedna and get a printer to print it on the left side of one thousand and three hundred envelopes. Then buy a stamp for each envelope and have your secretaries put stamps on the envelopes."

He pulled out his pocket computer and typed a message on it. "I'm sending you some words that I want printed on the envelopes."

Kate looked puzzled. "What are you planning? Sending a letter to everyone in town?"

"I'm going to create some positive *qi*, something to counteract the bad *feng shui*," Paul said.

Ray Cassidy returned to work the next day, and production of liquid methane restarted. So too did preparations for the flight.

Jonathan convinced the police to arrest Hackbart and the protesters for illegally squatting on private property, the land in front of the methane plant. Danny Eastman's death and the post office riot had finally exhausted the patience of the police. With the protesters gone, the countdown to launch began two weeks later.

The *Polar Bear* had space for three people: one pilot and two passengers. Paul shook his head when he saw the fiberglass lions strapped into the passenger seats.

He looked anxiously at his watch. Where were Kate

and her secretaries? He hoped they would finish their job on time.

At five hours before blastoff, Kate and two secretaries rode the supply tower's elevator up to the platform leading to the *Polar Bear*. Kate ran to Paul and hugged him. Behind her, the secretaries pushed a cart carrying a large sack.

"You're not going to believe the stamp the postmaster sold us," Kate said.

One of the secretaries, a Métis woman, giggled.

Kate smiled wryly, opened the sack, and pulled out a cover. It had a cachet showing Sedna and a postage stamp showing Louis Riel.

"Oh, no, I wanted the Canadian flag stamp!" Paul said. "Louis Riel means nothing to the Minister of National Heritage of China."

They heard the elevator rise again. Ray Cassidy arrived on the platform and went to Paul.

"You'll be flying through the aurora borealis, won't you?" Ray asked.

"Yes, I will, but not for long," Paul said.

"Good. Can you take this postcard with you? The Cree say the spirits of the dead are in the aurora borealis. I think he would want to know about your flight."

Paul looked at the postcard. It showed an aerial view of Churchill Spaceport. On the message side, it was addressed to Danny Eastman. Its Louis Riel stamp was cancelled with the special *Polar Bear* postmark, the same as the one on the covers.

Its handwritten message read:

Danny, your dream has come true. A manned spaceship lifted off from Churchill and went into orbit today. See you later. Ray.

"I can't stop in space and deliver it," Paul said.

"No, that's not what I want. Take it up with the rest

of the mail," said Ray. "Just being in the aurora will be close enough for him to read the postcard."

"I'll take it up there," Paul said as he put the postcard into the sack.

A ground crew technician came and said, "Mr. Chu, the final preparations are starting. Could you please ask your visitors to leave?"

"I better get back to the methane plant. *Bon voyage*," Ray said. "I'll see you when you come back."

Kate gave Paul a deep, lingering kiss. "I'll give you your Canadian astronaut wings when you land," she promised.

The visitors rode the elevator down the supply tower but left the sack of mail behind. The technician stared at it and asked, "What's that doing here? It's not on the payload list."

"It is now," said Paul. He pushed the sack to the Polar Bear's hatch.

"This isn't authorized," the technician complained.

"I'm the mission commander. I authorize it," Paul said. He pointed at the one of the lions. "Take that lion out and put the sack in the seat."

Gigantic flames, bright blue with burning methane, erupted from the Long March rocket as it blasted off into the night. The aurora borealis danced in the sky. The rocket rose steadily against the backdrop of green, red, and white light.

The rocket flew toward the northeast. After speeding through the aurora borealis, the Long March's first stage separated, falling into Hudson Bay. Later, the second stage fell away. The *Polar Bear* went into orbit.

"Mission Control to *Polar Bear*," said a flight controller from Churchill Spaceport. "Telemetry shows all systems are nominal. Can you confirm?"

"Mission Control, I confirm that," Paul replied.

He saw the aurora borealis along the curve of the Earth. Although he was not a religious man, he wondered if Danny Eastman's spirit was smiling on him, pushing away the hexes of the *feng shui* and guiding the spaceship.

"Here's to you, Danny Eastman," Paul said.

After Paul completed one full orbit, the flight controller said, "Mission Control to *Polar Bear*. Stand by for a transmission from the observation deck."

Kate's image appeared on the video monitor. "Hey, Paul, congratulations on your first orbit! We're all cheering for you down here. Can you hear them?"

Cheers and applause broke out from the people behind her. Paul heard Inuit throat singing and the banging of Cree drums.

"I can hear them loud and clear," Paul said. "It sounds like the whole town is there."

"Most of them," said Kate. "What do you see up there?"

"I'm passing over North America now," Paul reported as he looked out the window. "I can see Hudson Bay. Can you see me waving at you?"

The *Polar Bear* flew over Canada. Paul saw almost the whole country, from the Yukon-Alaska border in the west to Cape Spear in the east, from Cape Columbia in the north to Middle Island in the south. From space, the country appeared as large masses of green, brown, blue, and white: the forests, the tundra, the waters, and the ice.

"You should see the view from here," Paul said. "Everything looks so calm and beautiful."

Below on the ground, the various tribes of Canada squabbled with each other, as they always have. But from space, Paul saw one peaceful dominion.

*   *   *

After two orbits of the Earth, Paul ignited the rockets that slowed *Polar Bear* into reentry. The space plane glided back to a runway at Churchill Spaceport. Within moments of climbing out of the spaceship, he was surrounded by a horde of ground crew and reporters.

Paul wrote "No. 1" on one of the covers and gave it to Ray Cassidy. "Ray, you get the first cover."

"Thank you!" Ray said as he shook Paul's hand.

Paul also gave the postcard back to Ray.

"I'll give this to Barbara," Ray vowed.

Kate kissed Paul and pinned an astronaut wings badge to his flight suit. "You did it, you created positive *qi*," she cooed.

The celebration continued inside the spaceport's main building, where the Chinese ground crew improvised a dragon dance with a dragon from Winnipeg's Chinatown. As the beast swirled through the room, Jonathan toasted Paul with a glass of punch.

"By the way," Jonathan said, "I have to ask you about the payload."

The spaceport manager pointed at a solitary fiberglass lion sitting on a table. "Lions always come in pairs. You never see just one lion in front of a gate. How can I send just one lion back to Ming? How can Ming give just one lion to the Minister of National Heritage?"

Paul pulled an envelope out of his pocket. "Send these covers back to Hong Kong. We've made one for Ming, the Minister, and each member of the Politburo."

Jonathan looked at the picture of Sedna and the stamp of Louis Riel. He sighed and said, "How does this envelope symbolize Chinese science and culture?"

"Look at its back."

Jonathan turned over the cover and read the words printed in English, French, Chinese, Cree, and Inuktitut:

This cover is made of one of the four great inventions

of China: paper, which caused great cultural change all over the world.

The next day, the townspeople went to pick up free covers flown aboard Canada's first commercial orbital spaceflight. For the first time in years, the town hall resonated with the sounds of celebration.

Cree musicians sang a round dance song and banged on drums. Barbara Eastman, Danny's widow, explained to Paul, "They're singing about birds flying. August is the Month of the Flying Moon. It's when young birds fly from the nest."

She looked at the postcard that Ray had written. "Danny would have been happy to see you fly."

"I think he did," Paul said.

Mayor Alaralok held up her cover. "It's so nice of you to give a souvenir to everyone in town."

"We appreciate how much the people of Churchill have done for the spaceport," Paul said as Kate entwined her arm with his.

"That's a beautiful drawing of Sedna," Alaralok remarked.

"Thank you," said Kate. "Drawing it was a pleasure."

"The relationship between natives and non-natives has not always been happy. Outsiders have stolen our land, our culture, and even our children," said Alaralok.

"But you are different. You have given us the stars."

She pointed at the picture of Sedna. "But best of all, you gave us our dignity back."

A month later, Paul and Kate left for Montreal, where Paul became a pilot for a small airline, and Kate resumed working at an art museum. Ray Cassidy retired again after training people to replace himself. Jonathan returned to Hong Kong after handing the spaceport to a manager from Alouette Aviation. Most of the Chinese crew went back to China, but a few stayed and became Canadian citizens.

When Paul and Kate visited Churchill five years later, the town had two thousand people and numerous businesses. Satellites and space tourists flew into orbit from the spaceport. And the methane plant provided fuel not only for the spaceport but also for several communities in northern Manitoba.

But some things hadn't changed. The aurora borealis still appeared in late August evenings. Launch Pad 1 still had a supply tower with X's and a pyramid and bad *feng shui*. And Sedna, the goddess of marine animals, still adorned the lobby of the post office.

However, now the image of Sedna was a framed spaceflight cover carried on *Polar Bear*. On its frame was a small brass plaque engraved with the Chinese character *qi*.

Lips of Ash

Emery Huang

IT was a mud and stick hut tucked deep in the forest. A week of asking around for a true blood shaman had led Zhou Liang there. Inside, the hut was dark but for a fire crackling in the middle and a cone of light coming from the smoke hole in the ceiling.

"They always come to me when they need to traffic in the *evil* spirits," the shaman said. She was a wrinkled old crone who looked more like an overripe kiwi than anything a man could love. "Can't come to me for prayers or blessings, no. They give the Buddhist and Taoist monks the easy coin. They only come to me when they want to play in the dark bits."

Zhou Liang smiled sheepishly. "It's not like that."

"No?" Her eyes popped open, yellowed and froglike. "And what great things are you planning to do with a fox demon? Just a randy young man looking for a frolic with the spirits?"

She looked Zhou Liang over for a minute and shook her head. "No, you're too old for that. A fox girl would wear you out within the week. Best you go spend your time at the brothel." She made a shooing motion with her hands.

Zhou Liang stifled a laugh. "Oh, I agree, old mother. I've already said goodbye to those days. It's not for me, though."

Her eyes narrowed in suspicion. "Looking to sabotage someone then. Ruin a marriage? Destroy a family? You know, shamans are healers. We *restore* the balance."

Zhou Liang sighed in exasperation. "Let me explain the situation." Then he told her his story.

He was a cosmetics artist in the employ of Mistress Fei. Each morning, he was called in to apply her makeup, touch it up throughout the day, and remove it at night. Usually, this was a woman's job, but Zhou Liang was an exceptional talent and Mistress Fei was a stubborn woman.

A week ago, he came in for his morning duties and found Mistress Fei looking despondent. She sat on a bed of pillows at the back of the room, wrapped in a stiff damask robe with her hands resting in her lap. Next to her stood a lacquer table with tea and cakes. She did not offer him any.

He made the proper obeisance, then sat on a stool by her side. Her hair was already done up in the elaborate arrangement in vogue at the time. Her skin was smooth, pale, and lightly scented with litchi fruit. His cosmetic services had always been more an artistic accentuation of her features than a masking of flaws.

He got out his skin creams, his brushes, his mineral powders and rouges. She may have been in a bad mood, but he would do his work and be gone. Let her vent her anger on someone else.

"Zhou Liang, we have a problem." Mistress Fei's expression was clouded with doubt and her lips pursed with worry.

He paused in his work, the thin powder brush hanging loose from his hand. "What is the matter, Mistress Fei?" He hoped he had not done something to incur her displeasure. She was his primary patron and could leave him and his family without work and out begging in the streets.

"The duke. He tires of me."

Zhou Liang's heart almost stopped. It would be a serious turn in fortunes if Mistress Fei lost her master's favor. It was also surprising. She was still young, twenty-one to be exact, and was in the full flower of her beauty. She had high, full breasts, a plump round face, and fine soft skin.

"Impossible. You're the most beautiful of his mistresses." Zhou Liang resumed applying makeup to her face. There was comfort in his work and he felt as if his nerves were being smoothed along with the powder on her cheeks.

"His chamberlain brought a new girl from the east. They say she's from a merchant family, that she's bright and young but smart as a civil exam graduate. She reads poetry and dances and plays chess like a man." Mistress Fei's face grew angrier as she listed what the girl could do.

Zhou Liang paused, a lump forming in his throat. "But you've studied those subjects for years."

"I'm hopeless when it comes to scholarly pursuits. You know that."

His response was silence.

"I know my limitations, but I cannot lose the duke's favor. You must help me." She looked into Zhou Liang's face with a young vulnerability that showed how scared she was. "Find a way to win him back, and I will never forget your service to me."

"So, you're going to steal a fox demon's wit?" the shaman asked. Her eyes lit with amusement. "A clever idea. Your own?"

Zhou Liang nodded. "Is there any way to give my mistress the demon's wit without being possessed?"

The shaman rolled a small copper hoop around in her hand, a mishmash of rooster feathers and beads dangling from it. "Perhaps. You'd need a medium to hold the fox demon's essence. Make it something you can put on the girl like a fur bracelet or a necklace of the fox's teeth. But be careful she doesn't wear it too long. She can lose herself that way."

"So the fox demon has to be slain?" Zhou Liang asked. "I can't make a bargain with it?"

"No bargain. Are you mad? You want to bargain with a fox demon?" The shaman gave him a look of great irritation. "Maybe it's you that needs the fox's wit."

"Sorry, old mother."

"Find one when the moon is full. Hopefully, you can find a weaker one, young, unable to take the shape of a human yet. The demon will have enough intelligence for your needs but won't have the force of will to push out the girl's soul."

"Thank you." Zhou Liang reached into his pouch to find the two silver ingots he'd brought as payment. It was an exorbitant sum, but the shaman wouldn't even speak of demons if he hadn't promised that much.

"Not so fast. Remember, you never know what traits she'll gain. Maybe it'll be the fox's wit, maybe its lust, or maybe its wicked spirit. None of them are the same. Stay vigilant. The fox demon's powers seduce both men *and* women."

He thanked her again and handed over the two ingots, their heavy weight rolling off his palm and into her waiting hands.

"Take this with you." She gave him three leather pouches. "The first pouch holds herbs a fox demon can't resist. It's like catnip. Chop the herbs up, mix them with fresh soybeans, and make a tofu out of it. The second pouch has five flavor fruit. Boil them in a small amount of water and drizzle it over the tofu. They will put the fox to sleep. The last pouch holds a rock of cinnabar. When the fox is asleep, shove it as far down its throat as you can. It will disrupt the life essences."

"The cinnabar will kill the fox?" Zhou Liang asked.
"Yes."
Zhou Liang gave her a grim look and nodded.

Half a month later, the moon was a large, round white orb. It was time. Zhou Liang had confided in his wife all that had occurred, but tonight, he shared with her his doubts.

She gave him an incredulous look. "What do you mean 'you're not sure if you'll go through with it?' "

"Think of all the things that could go wrong," he said.

"Think of what could go wrong if you *don't*. You want to lose your job? Our daughter needs her dowry soon. We need a way to feed ourselves. Give the woman what she wants and be done with it."

Zhou Liang sat in his bedchamber, worried and confused. On one hand, he knew how to satisfy his mistress's demands. On the other, he fretted over what effects the amulet could have on her.

"Enough. It's time to be a man. Your family needs you. Give me the pouches. I'll go make the tofu."

He lay on the hard wooden bed, listening to her tinker in the kitchen. Earlier in the day she had soaked, crushed, and boiled the soybeans. Now he could hear her splashing handfuls of seawater onto the curds.

A while later, she came into the bedroom with a bamboo bucket. The bottom half of the bucket was shiny with silken tofu. Speckles of green dotted the surface, which Zhou Liang took to be the herbs from the first pouch.

"I already poured the five flavor fruit over it. Now go and bring fortune back to our doorstep." She put the bucket on the floor and reached over to give him a rough kiss on the lips.

*   *   *

The forest was bright with the moon full in the sky, and Zhou Liang had a good idea of where he was going. Forest spirits were likeliest to emerge where water met wood, and along the west side there was a large pond amidst a grove of trees.

When he got to the pond, he saw a large flat stone. He laid his bucket on it and pulled the top half away, leaving the tofu on a circular wooden tray. Then he went to find a comfortable hiding spot between some tall ferns.

A few hours later, a fox approached. In the meantime, Zhou Liang had armed himself with a walking stick to ward off other wild animals that tried to eat the tofu.

The fox came padding along the forest floor, its fur red as apples. Zhou Liang watched it lift its snowy white muzzle to the sky, following the fragrant scent of the tofu.

Then a thought came upon him in a burst of alarm. *What if the fox wasn't a fox demon, but merely a regular fox?* He hadn't thought to ask the shaman how to identify one. His mind raced as he tried to figure out how to make sure the fox was in fact a demon.

But as he was tensing his muscles for action, a small blue fire flickered along the fox's muzzle. As the fox ate, the fire grew thicker, almost like a wild fog bubbling around its jaws. It slowly licked at the tofu, each lap of the tongue sending blobs of fire spraying along the stone's surface.

It ate this way for several minutes, consuming about a third of the tofu. Then it sat on its haunches, wrapped its tail around its legs, and promptly fell asleep.

Zhou Liang couldn't believe how easily the plan had worked. He waited a full ten minutes before pushing his way out of the ferns and tiptoeing over to the fox's comatose body. It looked small and vulnerable, barely the size of a small dog with limbs delicate and furry.

He dumped the rest of the tofu onto the ground and

kicked dirt over it so no other animals would find it. Then he scooped the fox up in his arms. Its small body was so light, it was like holding a pouch of feathers. Even the creature's bones felt loose beneath its silky fur.

Zhou Liang had never seen a fox up close, but now he understood why beautiful women were called foxes. There was something alluring about the vivid redness of its fur, the sensual grace of its tail, and the daintiness of its whiskers.

He rushed home beneath the moonlight, half dreading the butcher's work that lay ahead and half in wonderment that he had actually caught a demon with such ease.

He stood in the kitchen with his wife. The fox's body lay between their feet. Its ribs rose and fell in a gentle motion.

"Do you have the cinnabar?" his wife asked.

"Yes. It's still in the pouch." Zhou Liang showed her, fingering the hard lump of rock with one hand.

His wife looked dubiously at the large bulge. "The shaman said to stick it down its throat?"

Zhou Liang sighed and fished the cinnabar out of the pouch. It was a rough texture and reddish-purple, like a pomegranate seed. "Do you think we could use a pair of chopsticks to push it down? I'll get queasy if I feel its teeth."

"I'll get them," his wife said. She came back a moment later with a pair of large cooking chopsticks and put them in his free hand. "Come. Let's get it done."

Zhou Liang squatted down next to the fox, using the chopsticks to pry its jaws open. Its teeth were small sharp nubs of white, and its tongue lolled out, pink and long.

As Zhou Liang pushed the cinnabar down its throat, he tried not to imagine how it'd feel to have a rock pushed against the tender flesh of his own mouth. The thought made him hurry, and he pressed hard with the point of his chopsticks. The cinnabar's rough edges broke skin and a thin trickle of blood pooled out of the fox's mouth.

"Hurry," his wife cried. "It might wake up if you're cramming it in like that."

"It's going to wake up if you're screaming in its ear, too," Zhou Liang whispered back.

From beneath his hands, the fox's body began to twitch madly. Husband and wife jumped back in surprise and Zhou Liang threw down his chopsticks in his haste to retreat.

The fox jerked around, rising to its feet and moving erratically.

"Kill it," his wife shouted.

Zhou Liang grabbed his walking stick and gave the fox a hard whack on the head. But in his panicked state, he struck too hard a blow, sending it rolling across the kitchen floor and into the fire pit.

As the pair watched in horror, the fox twisted and writhed atop the hot coals. Its fur burst into flames and it shrieked in great agony, sounding uncannily similar to a young woman.

The shrieking awoke their daughter from bed. She came bleary-eyed into the kitchen.

"What's going on?" she asked, looking confused and frightened.

"It's nothing. Your mother was trying to butcher one of the chickens and it accidentally ran into the fire."

"Wouldn't she break its neck outside?" their daughter asked.

"No. Go back to bed." Zhou Liang's wife hustled their daughter out and shut the kitchen door before the girl could get a good look inside.

The fox's shrieks had died down by then. Zhou Liang

grabbed a pair of wooden cooking spoons and tried to pull the body out of the fire to no avail. It had burnt unnaturally fast. An animal would have taken several hours to reduce to ash but the fire had consumed the fox demon as if it were paper.

"What do we do now?" Zhou Liang's wife wrung her hands.

Zhou Liang stood in front of the fire pit, staring mutely at the mess of ashes that was his future. There would be no amulet for Mistress Fei. There would be no dowry for his daughter. There would be nothing but ruin for his house.

"I don't know."

The two spent the rest of the night huddled around the fire pit trying to come up with a plan.

In the morning, Zhou Liang stood bravely in front of Mistress Fei's chamber. He had the guard announce his arrival like every other day and added the caveat of having the solution to his mistress's worries.

As soon as the guard made his announcement, there was a flurry of activity as all of Mistress Fei's maids were ordered out of the room. Zhou Liang walked in, smiling wide and trying to show confidence.

"You've found a way to help me?" Mistress Fei turned the jade bracelet on her left wrist back and forth in nervousness.

"I believe I have," Zhou Liang said. "I need your full trust in the matter, though. This endeavor holds great danger."

Mistress Fei frowned. "I will not be a party to assassination. I'm trying to get the duke's attention, *not* the county magistrate's."

"No, no. It's nothing like that. Here, let me show you."

Zhou Liang scooted closer, plopping himself on a stool next to her and putting his cosmetics box down on her bed. He opened one of the small wooden trays and took out a round jar.

"Look at this." He opened the jar and showed her its contents. It was a fine black powder with a pearly sheen.

Mistress Fei closed her eyes and took a deep breath. "Zhou Liang. Makeup is *not* going to work this time. Were you listening at all when I explained the problem?"

"I did. I even went to a shaman to get you help."

Mistress Fei's face wrinkled in disgust.

"The powder's special. It's made from crushed pearls mixed with the ashes of a fox demon. If I apply it to your lips, you will be able to talk with the fox demon's wit." Zhou Liang spoke slowly so she could digest it all.

"What do you mean 'the ashes of a fox demon'? Where did you find a fox demon? Did the shaman sell you this?"

"No." Zhou Liang stood up in annoyance. "I mean, no, mistress." He got his feelings under control and sat back down. "It truly is the ashes of a fox demon. Please, just trust me in this. All will be well."

Mistress Fei gave him a hard look. "Expect the worst if this goes wrong."

"Everything will be all right," Zhou Liang said. He turned his concentration to applying her makeup.

The next morning, Zhou Liang was seized from his house by the duke's guards. He felt his face burning with shame as he was dragged through the streets past the other villagers. Some of them laughed at him in amusement while others just looked surprised.

He wasn't a hated man, but he wasn't popular either. Some resented him for his easy life. He had been handsome in his youth, and some villagers surmised the duke's ladies had paid him for services rendered aside from cosmetics.

Zhou Liang tried to concentrate on what was important.

What had gone wrong? Had a different facet of the fox demon manifested itself? Maybe it was the wicked side of the fox's tongue that had come out. Maybe she had gone mad with possession.

He had no way of knowing. He thought using it as lipstick would salvage the ashes, but apparently they failed. The shaman had only mentioned using the fox's body to make amulets, nothing about its ashes.

Maybe he should have abandoned Mistress Fei for another lady. It's not as though it would have been impossible to find more work. Zhou Liang began to examine why he hadn't left her. Was it really the money?

He'd always had a love for the female face, for its grace and delicacy. There was a promise hiding there in the shadows of the cheekbones, a rich vista waiting beyond the eyes that beckoned him onwards, asking him to discover what new wonders could be found with brush and powder.

And Mistress Fei was his muse. He didn't care if she had no talent for chess or calligraphy. Not with a face like that. Hers was a canvas on which he could paint his dreams. It wasn't even the prettiness *per se*; it was more the adaptability of it, the dramatic angles. Suffice to say, Zhou Liang found it hard to pull away, and now he was paying for that mistake.

The guards dragged him into the duke's dungeon and threw him in a dirty cell. He begged them to explain what had happened, but they didn't say a word. He began to wonder if he would catch some dreadful sickness from lying in such squalor before his thoughts inevitably turned to his poor wife and daughter. What would they do without him? He couldn't remember if there was enough money left for his wife to go back to her parents' village.

These dark thoughts were playing in Zhou Liang's mind when he heard a rustle of rich fabrics. He sprang up from his crouch and pressed his face against the bars.

Mistress Fei stood outside. She had a furious expression on her face.

"What has happened?" Zhou Liang asked.

"What happened? I was made a laughingstock is what happened," Mistress Fei said. "The lipstick you gave me was *black*." Her voice rose in anger. "That damned girl from the east even had the gall to make a joke of me. She said, 'I do believe Mistress Fei has confused her eyebrows with her lips.'"

Zhou Liang was mortified. He'd had a fleeting moment of doubt when he had mixed the lipstick, but there was nothing he could do. He had tried to make a red pigment blend with the ashes, but they came out a dreadful muddied brown. He thought maybe with the pearly sheen it would at least be presentable, almost like a black lacquer.

"You're lucky I didn't throw your wife and daughter in here with you. I will at least spare you that," Mistress Fei said. "You served me well these past years, but not anymore."

"Did you feel any change at least? Any quickening of wit?" Zhou Liang asked.

"Oh, enough about the fox demon already. You're such a silly twit." Mistress Fei began walking away.

"Please. Mistress Fei," Zhou Liang shouted down the hall. "How much longer will I be in here?"

"Until the duke likes me," she shouted back, turning the corner and out of sight.

It was three miserable days in the dungeon. Three days of itchy skin, starvation rations, and unbearable darkness. Even worse was the constant stench of urine and excrement. So it was like a gift sent from above when the guards pulled him out of his cell and took him down to the river to get cleaned.

He scrubbed at his body happily in the cold, fresh water, using a rough cloth and a lump of soap. They gave him a clean hemp robe and a pair of cheap slippers, and told him to be prepared for a visit from Mistress Fei.

She came alone and sent the guards away. It began to dawn in his mind that something good had happened. Mistress Fei grabbed him by his hands and held them with great tenderness.

"Thank you so much, Zhou Liang," she said. "I'm so sorry I doubted you."

"Not at all." He shook his head. "But what has changed?"

"Everything," she said. "That same night I talked to you in the, uh, in the night, the duke came and spoke with me. He asked me what was wrong and why I was trying to get attention by wearing black lipstick. He was very understanding. He told me that I was still his first mistress and not to worry about the new girl."

"And then?" Zhou Liang asked.

"And then, somehow, without knowing how, I quoted a line from one of his favorite poems, and it perfectly fit the situation," she said in excitement. "It's exactly the sort of thing he likes."

"You didn't know the poem beforehand?"

"Not at all. I can't stand poems. The lipstick *worked*."

"What's happened since then?"

"The duke's been coming night after night. He enjoys talking with me now. I talk about topics that interest him. I have an opinion on politics. It's all very new and strange."

"How often are you wearing the lipstick?"

"Oh, every night. I don't wear it in the daytime because I don't want to make a scene with the court, but the duke said he finds it quite fetching in private."

"How much of it is left?"

"Quite a bit. I don't think it takes much to work. A dab here, a smear there, and we're set to talk the night away. Well, some of the night." Mistress Fei winked.

"Good. Once you've won the duke's confidence, it would be best if you did not use it anymore. I worry the more you use, the greater the chances of possession."

"Possession?"

Zhou Liang nodded. "Yes. You're borrowing powers from a fox demon."

"But I thought it was dead."

"It's a spirit. I don't think life or death applies to them quite the same way."

Mistress Fei shrugged. "No matter. I'm beginning to understand this talking business on my own anyway. It's not so hard. Mostly just drop the right phrases here and there and bring up something related when he mentions a new topic."

That last thought brought Zhou Liang up short. The old Mistress Fei would never have said that.

"Do you think I could see the lipstick again? I'd like to try to see if I can make a red pigment with the mix."

"You could do that for me?" Her voice was tinged with hunger.

"I can try."

"Do so," she said.

Zhou Liang managed to bring back a quarter of the jar. Mistress Fei insisted on keeping a good portion for her own use but thought it'd be worth giving up some if it allowed her to wear the lipstick in the daytime.

He promptly turned around and gave her an ordinary red lipstick, claiming it was mixed with the fox ashes. She was overjoyed and thanked him a great deal.

Over the next few months it became common knowledge that the duke had become much infatuated with

Mistress Fei. So much so that the other ladies in the court began to wear black lipstick and mimic her mannerisms. His cosmetics business boomed as court ladies sent dozens of orders for his pearly black lipstick. Of course, none of them had fox ashes in them.

Mistress Fei had not forgotten her debt either. After securing the duke's affections, she sent a large chest filled with silver ingots. A note delivered by the guards said that it was for his daughter's dowry and for the comfort of Zhou Liang's old age.

It was a prosperous time for the Zhou family. His wife busied herself with the new money. She married off their daughter to a tea merchant's handsome son and hired builders to construct a large residence for their retirement.

There was only one shadow that darkened Zhou's happy heart. It was many months after his daughter had married and he had been invested in his sumptuous new home. Mistress Fei had called him to her chambers to bid farewell.

She sat once more at the back of the room. But unlike the first time, she did not wear the stiff damask robes of a court lady. Instead, she wore vivid red silks that flowed and draped her body.

Her look had changed as well. No longer was she the plump and rosy girl of before. She was leaner now, more graceful, and her breasts were small and pointed. Her eyebrows rose like bird wings, and her cheeks stood out like contours carved into jade. Her eyes were different too. No longer wide-eyed and innocent, they smoldered with a wild intensity.

Nor did she have tea and cakes on her table. Instead, she had a large bowl of silken tofu swimming in syrup. He watched as she ate one spoonful after another.

"I'm going to the capital, Zhou Liang," she said between bites.

"How long will you be gone?"

"I expect quite a while. We're going to visit the emperor. The duke's nephew wants advice on matters of war, and, of course, the duke will not go without me."

"This is excellent news."

"Isn't it?" She smiled even wider. "It will be such fun." Her eyes flashed green in the light.

The look sent a hot jolt of desire through his body. She was so much more than a girl with a few daubs of fox wit now. Her very presence swam with sexual energy. His brow was damp, and he resisted the urge to wipe it.

"Will you be needing my services on your trip then, Mistress?"

"No, I suppose I won't. The imperial court's more formal. I wouldn't want to cause a scandal bringing a man along for makeup. Besides, I don't think I have much use for the stuff anymore." She spoke with carefree leisure, the words sort of skipping along her tongue.

Zhou Liang bowed his head in silence. In a way, he was relieved. Throughout the ordeal, he had waited for something to go wrong, for the fox demon to possess his mistress, for the duke to catch on to their plot, for Mistress Fei to turn on him. Any number of things could have happened.

But there was a part of him that grew dim with sorrow as well. His muse was leaving, and there was nothing ahead of him but the humdrum path of a merchant. His cosmetics business left him flush with money, but it didn't nourish his soul. Only the daily painting of faces would bring him that joy, and now he was bidding farewell to the most precious one of all.

Mistress Fei had grown exquisite in a wholly different way. Something fierce and torrid glowed in her face, and Zhou Liang wanted nothing more than to spend an eternity of mornings with her. In his mind's eye, he was already tracing a new eyebrow design for her, maybe using silver foil to gild her forehead, or adding light purple accents to her cheeks.

"You may go now." She waved him off with a hand.

Zhou Liang wanted to ask for one more session, but he knew it would be too risky. There were boundaries of propriety to be recognized.

"Thank you for your kindness, Mistress." Zhou Liang kowtowed thrice and retreated from her chamber.

Many years later, Zhou Liang had grown soft with age. His business had been combined with his son-in-law's and transformed into a trading company. It sold tea, cosmetics, textiles, jewelry, anything that was used by the affluent classes. They had also moved, setting up a large estate outside a vast port city to the south. The family was prosperous and well respected. A few years ago, he even witnessed the birth of his grandson, who had kept his wife busy ever since.

But Zhou Liang had also fallen into decadence. He had taken several concubines, spent long hours smoking opium, and frittered away large sums of money on gambling. He was wasting away in indolence.

One night, while trying to cure himself of boredom, he rummaged through his old cosmetics box and found the jar of fox ashes. He held it in his hands with a sigh. The porcelain jar still held its lustrous blue glaze despite being caked with dust.

He unscrewed the lid to look inside and found the lipstick had dried and cracked. He reached in and pinched the makeup, rubbing it between his fingers. The grains were crumbly. Any other time, Zhou Liang would have tossed it out in disgust. This lipstick was special, though. The sight of it brought him back to that day long ago when he stood in Mistress Fei's chamber.

As the old man stood there in his storage room, a glimmer of an idea came upon him, and he latched onto it with great fervor. For the next month he was obsessed. He had the servants scour his old workshop clean, demanded that nobody disturb him, and sequestered himself inside. His opium pipe sat in the parlor, cold and unlit, and his gambling companions found new haunts to frequent.

He spent his every waking hour trying to salvage what he could of the old lipstick, using all the tricks he knew and sparing no expense on new ingredients. Finally, at the end of the month, he emerged tired and triumphant.

He stood outside his workshop with his hands raised high, holding a new jar of pearly black lipstick, a feeling of accomplishment swelling in his chest. But all around him was silence and dust. What use was lipstick without a woman to put it on?

And so Zhou Liang went on a hunt for the perfect mistress. He searched the teahouses and brothels; he looked in the slave markets and asked his merchant friends for help; he even took a wagon to neighboring villages to see if the pickings were better somewhere else.

In the end, it was his son-in-law who quietly brought a girl to him, explaining that it was losing the family face to have the patriarch run about like some hot-blooded youth sniffing around for girls.

Her letter of introduction said her name was Jiu Xiang and that she hailed from the wild provinces to the west. She was very pretty, and her body glowed with a healthy vigor quite unlike the women of the city, but Zhou Liang clucked his tongue when he saw how tan her skin was. He would have to keep her indoors for a while to make her pale.

She wasn't a shy girl. The first morning he came to her, she disrobed in a perfunctory manner, then turned to face him with an expectant look. It took a few minutes of embarrassed mumbling on Zhou Liang's part to explain that he only wanted to do her makeup.

Her expression changed, as if his request was some sort of deviance, but she sat on the stool and allowed him to do his work. He smeared the lipstick on her with his fingers. He'd grown to enjoy the feel of it during his time in the workshop.

Over the next few weeks, he applied lipstick each day, giving her clear instructions not to remove it until night. He also kept her hidden away from the rest of the family, moving his effects to an isolated wing of the estate.

She began to experience the same changes Zhou Liang had seen in Mistress Fei. Her face narrowed, her cheekbones lifted, and her eyebrows thinned. She took on more sensual mannerisms, wore the red silks, and would only eat soybeans.

The daily contact with her began to arouse a great desire in Zhou Liang's body, and one night he invited her to bed. She'd nodded demurely but smiled at him in a knowing way.

That night, he lay in his soft silk bed, listening to the crickets as they sang outside. Jiu Xiang announced her arrival with a light knock on his door before slipping inside, a small red lantern bobbing as she held it behind her back.

"Come closer, girl. I'd like to see your face."

She stepped closer, her face and figure still hidden in the shadows of the room as her dainty slippers peeked out into the moonlight.

"You shouldn't have come looking for me, old man," Jiu Xiang said. Her voice slid over him like the fragrance of peach trees in warm summer air. "I was going to consider your debt paid when you gave me Mistress Fei's body, but having you so close is too great a temptation to resist."

Jiu Xiang lifted the lantern to her face. Her eyes

flashed green in the light, and she gave a great snarl, showing sharp bladelike teeth.

Zhou Liang screamed in terror, backing up against the wall as her mouth bubbled over with globs of blue fire. She sprang onto the bed after him, setting the silk sheets ablaze as she sank her jaws into his neck and tore his throat out.

The Man on the Moon

Crystal Gail Shangkuan Koo

THE Man on the Moon carried a small suitcase with him to Earth and checked in at the hotel.

While he was away at a press conference the next morning, the cleaning lady who came to make his bed and replace the empty plastic bottles in the shower indulged her curiosity on the suitcase that lay on the luggage rack with its lid open. The bundles of red silk cords in it disappeared from sight when she touched them, which was a little too odd for her, so she pulled out the Book underneath them instead.

Two columns divided each page, filled with names that were matched neatly by row in the Man on the Moon's tiny cursive. The cleaning lady found her parents' names next to each other. Her grandparents weren't matched, but then her grandfather had been a philanderer. When she discovered that the name next to hers wasn't her husband, she cried at the foot of the bed, wiping her tears on the sheets.

After she had put the sheets back into order, she found her husband's name and a blank space in the column next to his. Excitedly, she tried to fill it with her name using a pen from the desk drawer. The pen wouldn't write on the Book but worked perfectly when she scribbled impatiently on the slip of cardboard reminding guests to reuse the towels. Finally, she hurled the pen away and vainly tried to tear out the pages.

They found her huddled against the foot of the bed again, crying over the Book, and had a housekeeping boy watch her as they informed the floor manager. The boy sat next to the middle-aged cleaning lady, awkwardly crossing and uncrossing his arms. There was never anything comforting to say about being disappointed by destiny.

The hotel's address was printed below a picture of the Man on the Moon's ageless face in all the newspapers the next day. If a young man were to pick up the newspaper, he would discover that the Man on the Moon was looking for contestants to enter a beauty pageant he would be holding at the hotel's grand ballroom. Once the winner was decided, the Man on the Moon would write his name next to hers on the Book of Matches and tie one of his red cords between his and her ankles, as he had done for thousands of years to all the couples that he had predestined. When the Man on the Moon leaves Earth to resume his matchmaking duties, he would compensate her with eternal youth while she waits for the end of the world, when he will return to bring her away and marry her.

After reading this, the young man would put the newspaper down to finish his cereal and prepare for his shift at the appliance store. It is possible that he would cut the article out and shove it into the back pocket of his jeans to show to his friends later at the pub. It is also possible that he would keep it as a talisman, hoping that he and the girl who always fishes the lime out of her drink with a spoon and slips it into his are matched in the Moon's Book. Anything is possible for young people. Even if she has told him that she will be leaving the country at the end of the year when her studies finish, he would still hope that he had not misunderstood the choice of her microwave oven to break down on his shift when they first met a year ago. He might wait for a revelation or decide to act. Anything is possible for young people.

Sad songs and poetry have been written about the Man on the Moon, but he had stopped reading them a long time ago. When the journalist asked why, he said that they distracted him from his duties. Like the prayers that lovers offered him from mountaintops or temples during the midautumn festival, they were remarkable in their variation but ultimately none of his responsibility.

The general manager of the hotel began to run out of rooms for prospective contestants who wanted to preserve their youth for one reason or another and had made reservations too late. Tickets for the contest audience sold out for exorbitant prices, and news networks set up tents around the building.

When asked by philosophers if he was responsible for wrong circumstances that plague lovers, the Man on the Moon replied that there were no such things as wrong circumstances.

When asked by psychologists on how to fix a broken heart, he insisted that it can only be prevented by learning to wait instead of gratifying every momentary impulse that besets the heart.

When asked by human rights advocates on what grounds he made each matchmaking decision, he answered that he only followed the forces that trace across the world in intricate, ordained patterns which they would not comprehend.

When asked by religious groups about the end of the world, he answered that only his bride would be able to survive the collapse of all the patterns of the universe. In the hubbub that this produced, the general manager of the hotel, who hovered solicitously wherever the Man on the Moon went, announced that they had only one question left.

When asked when the world would end, the Man on the Moon said that even he has to wait for its occurrence. This answer brought a bigger slew of organizations that flooded the hotel's restaurants and coffee shops, much to the general manager's delight.

From the balcony of his suite, the Man on the Moon watched the vague figure of a young woman on the street below lean over to kiss the young man standing next to her under the lamp.

The Man on the Moon lit a stick from a cigarette pack that the general manager had given him to help him relax.

The young man picked her up in his arms, their laughter rising up as briefly as the smoke from his cigarette. It was too far to see if they had cords around their ankles that led to one another, but the Man on the Moon noticed that they held each other in a tight, too-fierce embrace, which meant that they were aware something was wrong. Perhaps it was too little time or too much space in between. Perhaps there was another person. Anything was possible. Precarious lovers were all alike in their desperation, and the Man on the Moon assumed that there was something written in the Book of Matches that would eventually cause a breaking of hearts and more sad songs and poetry.

The couple on the street walked away arm in arm, and the street lamp seemed to dim in their absence. The Man on the Moon took a puff, coughed violently, and decided he didn't like the taste of it.

For each contestant who preened and wriggled before him, the Man on the Moon would look at her feet and consult the Book of Matches to check whether he had already predestined her to someone else. Then he would study her face to see if there was something that deserved to survive for eternity. No one knew what prompted him to tell her to stand on the back of the stage or to step down.

This angered many of those who had bought tickets to the contest to gather information on their own destinies. Some of the audience heckled him. Others tried to grab his Book. Most of them dissected the lack of excitement on the Man on the Moon's face, which was shown in closed-circuit television screens in the hotel building.

Groups of people stood outside the hotel every day. Those waving bullhorns shouted that the Man on the Moon should save everyone when the world ends. Those waving bulky cardboard props of his Book shouted that he should not have the freedom to choose his lover if nobody else has it. A small group was cheering on the most significant beauty pageant in history, but because they weren't waving anything, they were largely ignored.

Many of the contestants offered to aid him in making up his mind. They behaved so spiritedly in his bed that when he refused to promise them victory, they could not help but turn against him with insults about his performance.

Some of them said nothing at all, choosing only to slap his face. Surprised at their reactions, he held the door open for them and repeated that a week was really not too long a time to wait for results.

Just pick one. Toss a coin, if you want. Toss a thousand coins. You do it so easily for us, don't you? Why can't you do it for yourself?

Annoyed with his impatience, the Man on the Moon did not answer the general manager. The suite where he stayed was papered with photographs of women. They smirked, they simpered, they leered, depending on the light. They watched him tally their attributes against each other and spend many hours trying to tell their glaring smiles apart. At the end of the day, he always felt that if he chose one, he would be choosing all of them.

The Man on the Moon learned to smoke and kept the curtains open to air the room. His Book of Matches lay forgotten on top of the bureau. From the street that his balcony overlooked, he was often seen knotting his red cords together in irritation until they looked like a tangle of hair that clung to the shower drain.

In an effort to clear his mind, he put on the croak and hobble of an old man and walked unnoticed through the news vans and the groups of waving people.

He went to the park first, where lovers sat together exploring fingers and lips and the prospect of staying in that moment for eternity. In that sea of red silk that only he could see, cords twisted around to look as if they linked with each other, but the Man on the Moon knew that most of the couples were either bound to no one or to someone else. Although he could not blame them for being blind, their happy ignorance upset him all the same. Frequently he had to stop himself from telling the truth by choking back his words and coughing in a manner that made his disguise even more believable.

He hastily set off for somewhere with fewer provocations, and soon passed by a block of old brick apartments.

She was seated on the apartment stoop, waiting for someone. She drummed her fingers absently against her knees, watching a bird that had alighted on top of a grated air shaft on the pavement, and looked at him politely as he intruded into her line of sight.

It was when her eyes veered away to return to the bird that the Man on the Moon, in a moment of astonishment, suddenly found himself wishing that she were waiting for him.

She sat on the edge of time, between past and future, and it was not called the present because the present was a word that humans used only to deceive themselves into thinking that they can learn from the past to prepare themselves for the future. There was no point in panicking about the end of the world when it was inevitable. Humans compelled themselves to go through exercises in choice, thrashing like epileptics, grasping at the wrong threads and knotting them this way and that. Who would not be irritated to find his handiwork treated in such a manner?

But she sat so coolly on her seat in the arena of the city. She wanted nothing; she only waited to know what it was that she would want. The stoop steps could crumble at her feet, the Moon could come crashing down from the sky, and she would only bend down to pluck a piece of debris off her sandals. She would listen to the sound of the wind blowing through his gigantic web of silk as the world plunges upside-down, twisting within itself, as she waits for him.

He realized he was terrified of speaking to her, so he let the old man do so while he listened anxiously at the clumsiness of his words. He asked her what time the library closed. He asked if he may sit with her. He asked, in a studied way that ensured he appeared wistful rather than overly curious, for her name.

She answered everything and added that she was waiting for a male friend, the light tone that tinted her voice implying that she was trying to keep him from embarrassing himself. A look of horror crossed the old man's face, but when he looked at her ankles, it immediately vanished. Then the old man smiled brilliantly at her, as though all the light of the world was in him to do as he pleased.

She responded with a quick smile of her own that showed her awareness of an incoming lull in the conversation. As she waited in silence, the Man on the Moon felt an urge to burst out of his disguise and store each impression of her deep in the hollows of his elbows and knees, where no one would find it.

He sat placidly with her instead, imagining how he would tie a red cord around her ankle, and left only when he realized that he could wait no longer.

The news that the Book of Matches had been stolen appeared in all the papers the next day.

The Man on the Moon hunched on the sofa, head in his hands, mindless of the flashing cameras around him. He smoked and emptied his ashtray frequently. Sometimes he wept. He would not answer questions about the end of the world. He would not offer speculations of what would happen to new predestined couples without the Book. Only when asked about the contest results did he say that he had already chosen the winner, but without the Book he could not write his name on the empty space next to hers. When the reporters pointed at the photographs on his wall, he would not tell them which one she was.

Advertisements for the missing Book were sent out.

Many came to his suite, and their demands for a reward were just as diverse as the Books they claimed to be his. Some wanted to survive the end of the world. Some asked to be transformed into a demigod. Some wanted the same power in matchmaking. They were easy demands to turn down in their impossibility. As the days wore on, the Man on the Moon refused to even look at the Books they brought. None of them had given him the right reason to steal it.

*   *   *

He dreamed for the first time. He was in a hotel, and a soft, warm hand was touching his, but he was blind and could not see who she was. He could hear the silent wail of the world ending, but he had to search with his hands to remove the veil from her head.

Desperately he prayed that it was her. His fingers groped for her face, but he was already bowing to the disintegrating heavens and turning around to bow to her. *Wait, wait,* he screamed, and he reached out and pulled at her clothes so violently that they tore. They felt like paper, and he ripped off the pages a fistful at a time until his hands burned.

He awoke in the darkness, and for a moment, he thought he was still blind.

A man aware of the danger of being separated from his lover could choose to wait or choose to act. If he chooses to wait, he would force himself not to think about what would happen after the year is over. He would use all his paid leaves from work to take her to the coast because that is all he can do to distract himself. Afterward, he will keep her microwave oven and the beach kitsch she had bought from the man whose board shorts had too many pockets and help her pack her books before taking her to the airport. They will talk again about her career goals and family obligations in vague terms, and he will watch her leave. He would spend the following years waiting for a revelation, which he hopes will come in a neatly wrapped package and which he knows will arrive as a sack of uncertainties that would slowly crush him.

If he chooses to act, he would sit his lover down and talk about possibilities. He would talk of how the Man on the Moon's balcony overlooks the street where they usually walked and how its guest liked to keep his curtains drawn during the day. He would talk of how a friend of his who works as a linen keeper in the hotel knows that the Book of Matches lies on the bureau, its ash-littered pages flipped only by an inquisitive breeze.

Then the young man would tell her to wait for him at his apartment. If all goes well, he would return with the Book, flushed youthfully with more triumph than apprehension, and they would leaf through the pages on a small desk stacked with photographs of her and her limeless drinks. They will look for their names and discover that both of them are destined for no one.

Then the two choices would spread before them again, but by this time it would be too late to change paths.

The documentary about the end of the world began with an assortment of possible ways in which the world could be destroyed. This was followed by footage of the beauty pageant where the Man on the Moon was caught pursing his lips fastidiously as a contestant mounted the stage. Instead of showing how he turned around to shush the man who was whistling at the contestant, they cut to a review that contrasted the Man on the Moon with more heroic messianic figures that the world had seen so far.

Surrounded by cigarette butts, the Man on the Moon sat on the sofa in front of the television and waited for dawn to break.

The last person to come to the suite was dressed in a gray collared T-shirt with the name of an appliance store printed on his left chest. He brought only a curious calm and an offer to exchange the Book of Matches for one request regarding a girl whom he loved.

The Man on the Moon hid his elation. A shrewd negotiator, he asked the young man to bring him to the Book first.

*   *   *

The Man on the Moon opened his suitcase and packed his belongings, which consisted of only a tangled ball of red cords. He quickly removed the photographs from his walls and threw them into the wastebasket. Beside him, the general manager clamored for the name of the future bride. He told him to wait.

The taxi halted, and the Man on the Moon looked up from untangling his cords to see a block of brick apartments outside the window. The young man unbuckled himself and opened the door, saying that the girl was keeping watch over the Book.

This is how the world will end.

In the chaos, the Man on the Moon will return to where a hotel used to stand. There he will watch the universe unravel the web of red silk he had crosshatched from one side of the Earth to the other.

He will be holding the Book of Matches, where sad songs and poetry would have been scrawled on each of its pages.

He will be writing one at that moment, about a young woman who sits on the steps with her eyes focused on the horizon.

As he writes, he will see her face before him, smiling as the object of her waiting arrives. He will return the smile, as though it is him she is looking at. But then her eyes will move away to follow the other man behind him, and he will have to turn around and see nothing but the debris.

Alone, the Man on the Moon will finish his poem while the world is crushed under its own weight.

Across the Sea

Emily Mah

CHOPSTICKS made from bone or ivory, a piece of jade carved into the face of a dragon, and a piece of a lacquered bowl. The objects were laid out on a weathered plastic tray set on an unsteady card table at one end of the dig site. Kate Hu stared at them, her stomach churning.

"We'd put these at about six hundred years old," one of the archaeologists said. "So, beginning of the fifteenth century."

"Right," Kate replied. "So you called—"

The sentence was cut short by the arrival of a shiny black Hummer that pulled up to the dig site and stopped short enough to spray everyone with gravel.

"—Michael Scott," Kate finished.

"Well, yeah," said the archaeologist, a pencil-thin grad student with thick spectacles perched on the bridge of his nose. Kenderson was his name, Doug Kenderson. "He's been talking about writing another book."

The Hummer door swung open, and out stepped a man in his early forties with silvered hair and a perfectly tailored sport jacket over jeans. Kate wished she could turn away, but her traitorous eyes stared at him openly.

He caught sight of her at once and blinked. "Kate?" At least he remembered her name.

"Mr. Scott," she replied.

"*Dr.* Scott," Kenderson whispered. Then, louder, "You know Kate Hu, then?"

"We have met." Dr. Scott chuckled as he sauntered over. "What brings you out here?" he asked her.

"I'm the Deputy Manager of Cultural Affairs."

"Really? For the Tlingowa?"

No, she thought in her mind, *I joined some other tribe and just decided to show up at this dig on Tlingowa land out of nosiness.* She turned her gaze towards the beach, half a mile away. The sun was setting out over the ocean, painting the sky with pale peach light and turning the clouds molten gold. The weather had been beautiful all week—not something that could always be counted on along the Oregon coast.

"How's your aunt?" Dr. Scott asked.

Kate didn't respond to that. She just turned and started hiking toward her beat up old jeep.

Michael Scott had shown up at her father's apartment fifteen years ago, when Kate was nine. It had been a rainy day in Eugene, and her father had answered the door to reveal a chubby, pimple-faced grad student with a nervous air about him.

"I'm a linguistic anthropologist," Mr. Scott had explained, "and I'd like to do my field work with the Tlingowa."

Kate had stood behind her father's legs, peering out.

"You've got to be kidding," said her father. "The tribe's got three hundred members, most of whom live in the city, and two fluent speakers."

"Rumor has it there are three fluent speakers," said Mr. Scott. "I'm looking for Bess Jenkins?"

Kate gripped her father's belt loop. Great Aunt Bess was sitting in the kitchen, rambling to herself as was her wont. Kate felt her father hesitate before he stepped back. She scampered out of his way.

"She's here," said her father. "I'll introduce you."

Even though Kate was only nine, she understood that her father expected this grad student to take one look at Bess and then politely take his leave. Bess rambled and ranted and was never more than half aware of where she was or whom she was with. When her father led Mr. Scott to the breakfast nook, Bess was sitting at the table muttering something about people on television trying to steal her glasses.

Her skin was fair, her eyes light gray. Like most of the Tlingowa, she had very little native blood. The tribe had been assimilated long ago.

"Bess?" snapped Kate's father. "Someone here to see you."

Usually Bess didn't even acknowledge that she'd been spoken to, but this time she turned, blinked, and looked up at Mr. Scott. "Hello," she said.

"Hello, I'm—"

"A giant canoe, one driven by the wind pushing against its great cloth wings, was dashed upon the rocks near the mouth of the river," Bess said. "Long ago, long before any whites came to our land. These men were from across our sea, the only sea my people knew."

She was speaking half in English, half in Tlingowa. Mr. Scott sat down in the chair across from her, rapt.

Kate slipped into another chair and listened. She couldn't tell if Mr. Scott understood what her aunt said.

"Five men survived and swam to shore, clinging to pieces of their canoe. Their skin was paler than ours, their hair jet black. Their eyes were tilted and dark brown, and they sang to each other rather than spoke.

"Our people helped them ashore, pressed the water from their bellies, and lit fires to warm them. They welcomed them as friends, putting beaded shell necklaces around their necks and frying them a feast of fishes. Three of the men were thin, one was very fat, and the fifth was round with a very round face, like the moon."

It was rare for Bess to string so many coherent sentences together. Kate listened eagerly and didn't notice when Mr. Scott got out his tape recorder.

"Something wrong, Kate?" Randall McGinty asked. He was the Manager of Cultural Affairs for the Tlingowa, a job that he did in the evenings and weekends. The rest of the time he was an attorney at a small real estate practice. Kate worked as the receptionist. The fact that they were both registered Tlingowa was almost laughable, as neither of them looked native, nor did they participate in any cultural events. None of the Tlingowa did. The last of their fluent speakers had died years ago.

"Kate?" Randy prompted.

Kate blinked. "Um, Michael Scott—"

"I hear you got to see him. I have his book. He said he'd sign it for me." Randy looked downright giddy. He even bounced on the balls of his feet.

"Oh," said Kate. "That's nice. I was just wondering if we wanted him here on the dig. I mean, as Manager of Cultural—"

"Can you imagine the publicity this'll net?" Randy said. "I bet we'll get hundreds of archaeologists here next summer. Here—" he dug into his briefcase and came up with a hardcover book "—will you sign this too? You're Bess's closest surviving relative."

Kate stared down at the glossy dustcover for a moment, then shut her eyes. Michael Scott had recorded Aunt Bess's entire story and written a paper on "The Emerging Tlingowa-English Creole" using her tale to illustrate when and how a fluent Tlingowa speaker used English. It was a dry enough topic, but with the oddness of Bess's story, it became one of the most popular papers of its time.

It was so popular in the world of anthropology that Dr. Scott had fleshed it out into a book. It was supposed to be a textbook on how linguistic anthropologists cataloged and quantified language shift. Again, he used Bess's story in its entirety, and the book shot up the *New York Times* bestseller list, making the Tlingowa one of the most well known Athabaskan tribes in the country . . . and exposing Bess to universal ridicule.

To make matters worse, Kate's father, who had been the Manager of Cultural Affairs at the time, had blurbed the book, calling it "hilarious" and "absorbing."

"I'm not signing this," Kate told Randy. She pushed the book back toward him.

"What? You don't like it?" he said.

"No," she replied. "I don't."

"I'm not sure if there's another book here or not," Dr. Scott was saying as Kate arrived at the dig site that evening. "There's the beginning of one. I mean, these Chinese artifacts are most likely the product of trade along the coast. There's a lot of evidence that there was a small Chinese community in northern California in the 1400s, people who got left behind when one of the junks dropped them off and never returned."

"Right," said Kenderson, the same archaeologist who'd done all the talking the day before. "So you write about how these artifacts could support Old Bess's story, but then give the more scientific explanation."

"Sure, that's the idea," said Dr. Scott. "But I've got to do some more looking into all this." He turned to Kate as she approached the table. "Evening," he said to her.

She just stared back in reply.

Dr. Scott's smile faltered, but only for a split second. "I need one of you to help look for documentation of a wrecked junk along the coast near here. A wreck so bad that only five people would survive."

"There is one," said Kenderson. "I already looked it up. See, if you let me use your laptop there, I can show you on Google Earth. It's here, where the river runs into the sea, or thereabouts."

Kate clenched and unclenched her teeth. "Look," she said, "you're here with permission from the Tlingowa people. You can't just—"

"Randy already gave us permission to let Dr. Scott take over the dig," said Kenderson. "If he wants to."

"We'll see, we'll see," said Dr. Scott. "Huh, there was a junk wrecked just a mile out from the beach. Interesting." He squinted at the computer screen.

"The pale men wanted to go home, that was clear. They sang to each other in forlorn tones and stared off across the sea. Although our people fed them and gave them space in our huts to live, the men preferred to sleep under the stars.

"While four of them just wept and despaired, the moon-faced man started to take long walks. He came back every evening with rocks that he would grind into powder, and he'd mix the powders together.

"One night, he added ash from the fire pit to his rock powder, then held a flaming brand to his mixture, and it flared up. The rocks themselves burned."

"He says it's too early to know if there'll be a second book," Randy was saying into his phone when Kate arrived at work the next day.

Kate wished she had her own office. She would have shut the door and locked it. As it was, she had to sit out in the open, at the receptionist's desk, while Randy blabbed away with his office door open.

"Here she is!" Randy said. "Kate Hu. Her great-aunt was the one who told the story, and her father was Chinese-American. She's got a double interest in all this, what with the archaeologists finding actual Chinese artifacts. I'll ask if she wants to speak to—whoops, she's gone."

Kate had gotten up and made for the bathroom. Once there, she shut herself into a stall and sat on the toilet lid, knees pulled up to her chest, forehead resting on her folded arms. It was all too much. While the cold porcelain seeped the warmth from her body, she struggled to suppress the memories that were bubbling up in her mind.

Bess had always ranted insanity for as long as Kate had known her. That story she related to Mr. Scott was the only coherent story she'd ever told, and ridiculous as it was, Kate treasured it. She wished she knew its origins, whether it had been a Tlingowa legend or just the product of Bess's addled brain.

That story and the broken Tlingowa that Kate could speak were the only relics of her native heritage she possessed. Her mother had died in a car accident when Kate was four. Her father had used his position as Manager of Cultural Affairs to accompany Dr. Scott on a signing and lecture tour, and then when the limelight faded, he remarried and moved to Des Moines. Kate lived with him for a few years, then moved back to Oregon at age eighteen. It was, after all, her ancestral home.

Even though Kate was only one eighth Tlingowa and seven eighths a mix of Chinese and Danish, Bess had nurtured her cultural ties to this tiny tribe of three hundred souls who lived and worked in southwest Oregon and owned a minuscule stretch of the coast. Their language had died out in her lifetime, and now archaeologists with no ties to their people were on their land to dig up their history and tell their story. It wasn't right.

"Kate?" Randy called out. He knocked on the women's bathroom door. "Hey, Kate? Mike found what looks like an ancient saltpeter mine. Can you believe it?"

"The moon-faced man hollowed out a stick and packed it full of powder. He carved the outside of the stick just so

and bound it with a length of twine. One evening, he lit the twine, and our people watched as the hollow stick shot up into the air leaving a trail of sparks."

Kate's father placed a peanut butter sandwich in front of her and turned to Mr. Scott. "You hungry?" he asked.

Mr. Scott looked up from his hastily scratched notes and shook his head.

Bess continued on, heedless. *"The moon-faced man knew only a little Tlingowa, but he pointed at the flying stick and said, 'We go home like this.'"*

Although her first impulse had been to ignore the evening news and just turn in early, Kate found herself sitting in front of her television as the news anchors interviewed Dr. Scott. Her apartment was a tiny studio, so the television illuminated the entire room in flashes of blue and white light.

"There's definitely material for another book here," Dr. Scott was saying. "This one will be a primer on archeology. What I'll do is use Old Bess's story and contrast it with the archaeological evidence."

"Well," said the anchor, "it sounds like the evidence supports her story."

At that, Dr. Scott laughed outright.

Kate shrank back from the screen, picked up a throw pillow, and pressed it to her gut.

"The Chinese artifacts are most likely the result of trade. The saltpeter was no doubt used for fertilizer and as a food preservative. The sulfur mine we found nearby was probably the source of ingredients used in medicine. See, what's interesting is that we're learning that the Tlingowa were probably agrarian and had a very advanced understanding of chemistry in the fourteen hundreds, and no one even guessed that before. But of course we'll use Bess's story as a narrative to tie all of our investigations together."

"Even though you don't believe it's true?" the anchor asked.

Again Dr. Scott laughed. "No," he said, "I don't."

Kate buried her face in the woolly fringe of her throw pillow, then threw the pillow at the television and got out her phone.

Randy answered on the third ring.

"Can't you send him away?" Kate asked.

"Dr. Scott?"

"Yes. He's turning this whole thing into a circus."

"Did you watch the news? He's helping us learn all sorts of fascinating things about Tlingowa history."

"And he's ridiculing Bess."

"Kate, her story was—"

"Untrue? So what? How many other tribes' legends are true? You don't see people out making fun of Anasazi tales or—"

"Oh, come now. You never watched Wile E. Coyote cartoons? That's Coyote the Trickster turned comical. Besides, this isn't a legend we're talking about. It's one of Bess's wild tales. The last time I saw her she told me her first husband was a toaster oven and that she could tell colors apart by the way they scratched her ankles. She could come off looking a lot worse. And did you watch Dr. Scott's interview, even? There's evidence that the Tlingowa had advanced medical technology and agriculture. They were a very interesting people."

"Don't you mean we?" said Kate.

"We. Right. Of course."

Kate hung up and stared dumbly at the television for a long moment. She glanced at her watch, got to her feet, and headed for the door, donning her windbreaker on the way. Ten minutes later she was pulling her car into the small strip of parking lot next to the pottery co-op. Located in a large metal warehouse on the edge of town, it was where she always went when stress overwhelmed her. The door squeaked when she pushed it open, and fluorescent lights blinked to life when she hit the switch, illuminating a wide open space with tables set out in the middle and drying racks along the far wall. In one far corner were the kilns. The place smelled like moisture and clay and drying glaze.

Kate made her way to the racks and started sorting pieces for the kiln. That was her job, to get everything fired before the next class, and although she hadn't meant to start the next batch until the weekend, the pieces were ready now and she had time.

She separated the polymer clay pieces from the natural clay pieces and set the latter down on a kiln rack, careful not to clink them together. She'd joined the co-op and started taking pottery classes in her teens, on the misguided notion that this would put her in touch with her heritage. There was plenty of natural clay on Tlingowa land. She could see several pieces that were made from it with their telltale black streaks of coal. However, her father had set her straight. There were no pottery artifacts in any of the Tlingowa sites. Her ancestors were most likely basket weavers.

And so pottery now seemed to her like one of her many wrong turns taken in her lifelong search for home and people. Her decision to drop out of college because her anthropology teacher had based a unit on Michael Scott's book was another. At the time she'd felt righteous. Now she just felt petty and stuck in a dead end job that didn't hold her interest.

"The next day the moon-faced man and one of the skinny men drew pictures of tall, straight trees in the dirt and asked where they could find them. Our people explained that the winter was coming and we could spare no one to fell trees, but the moon-faced man drew other strange pictures on the ground. Crooked lines and symbols and a

picture that might have been of the flying stick he'd made.
He sang insistently, furiously.

"Our shaman saw this and begged our elders to help
the strange men, lest they bring a curse down upon us.
The next day, four of the strange men left with six of our
best hunters. The fifth, the fat man, showed the women
how to boil beetles until a paste came from their shells.

"When the men returned with two long, straight tree
trunks, the strange men ordered them hewn out like ca-
noes and cut into long strips that they painted with layer
after layer of the paste from the bugs. These long pieces of
wood were then left to dry, glistening in the sun."

"We know that there are tall trees fifty miles from here.
But six hundred years ago, the land no doubt looked
different. I'm not sure how that pertains to our investigation, though." This quote was in the next morning's
paper, which Kate read online from her desk at work.

"There's no evidence of lacquer work, no. Other than
the bowl we've already unearthed. Right now we've got
three dig sites. One at the community where the Chinese
artifacts were found, one at the saltpeter mine, and one
at the sulfur mine. The University of Oregon's been kind
enough to provide additional funding for all this."

Kate glanced at Randy's open office door and saw
that his desk was unoccupied. He'd probably gone to the
break room for coffee or had to go out to meet a client.
She was so distracted that she didn't remember if he'd
passed by her desk or not.

She picked up the phone and looked up the University of Oregon's website on her computer. It took her
three calls to get to the chair of the grant committee that
had funded Kenderson's dig.

"I'm concerned that this is all becoming a circus," she
explained. "The dig was supposed to be a small one, focused on that one community. Now you've got a person,

who isn't an archaeologist, setting up more digs at other sites without any scientific reason."

"I see," said the tired-sounding woman on the other end of the line. "You say you're the Manager of Cultural Affairs?"

"Deputy Manager."

"So you speak for the tribe on this matter?"

"Well, no."

"Because I have a fax from the Manager saying that Dr. Scott can have access to any of the tribal lands that he wants."

"Oh," said Kate.

"Did you not get the departmental memo?"

Kate didn't want to admit that the "department" was nothing more than her and Randy, and that they rarely even used the tribal letterhead, let alone wrote memos. There was little point when they worked a mere twelve feet apart. "So there's nothing you can do?"

"I'm not sure what you're asking. Is this letter valid or isn't it?"

"It . . . yeah, it is. Sorry to bother you." Kate hung up and looked around, grateful that Randy still hadn't returned and that none of the other attorneys had their doors open.

"The five pale-skinned men directed our strongest hunters to bind the long wooden planks together to make a great tube. The moon-faced man demanded that its outside be carved and shaped just so and that the inside be divided into chambers. Some were packed with powder. At the top of the tube a little hut was fashioned with a peaked roof.

"All the while, the moon-faced man drew more strange symbols in the dirt and sang in triumphant tones to his fellows. They did not seem to be as happy as the moon-faced man, but they obeyed his instructions."

*   *   *

After work, Kate drove out to the dig site once more. The sun was low in the sky and, much to her dismay, she saw a long line of cars parked around the site. There seemed to be three times the number of archaeologists alone since she'd last visited.

Dr. Scott wasn't there, so she took her jeep across the sand flats toward where the archaeologists said the saltpeter mine was located. The vehicle's suspension creaked and groaned in protest as she sped along, raising a cloud of dust in her wake.

Another large cluster of cars was parked around this second dig site, and Dr. Scott stood on a low rise, bellowing instructions. At the sight of Kate pulling up, he paused, mid-bellow, then said, "Carry on." He dropped his arms and turned to face Kate as she trudged across the loose dirt to him.

The site was littered with screens, shovels, and twine strung between pegs. Kate stepped over and around these various obstacles until she stood on the rise, facing Dr. Scott. He was a full head taller than she was.

"Kate," he said. "I'm so sorry I haven't had a chance to visit."

"Visit?" she said.

"Yes. To see how you are. It's been a long time, hasn't it? You're all grown up. How's Bess?"

Kate folded her arms across her chest. "She died last year."

"I'm sorry to hear it."

"We had to put her in a home."

"That's rough."

Kate looked out over the dig, at the swarm of archaeologists screening dirt and laying artifacts on plastic trays. "Why are you doing this?" she asked.

"I take it that you don't . . . agree with my methods."

"I'm tired of having my family made fun of."

"I never meant to be disrespectful."

"Sure you didn't."

"Kate, please. I gave your father a cut of the royalties, and I'll do the same for you if that'll make it better."

"I'm not interested in money," said Kate. "I just want you to leave. *Now*. This was supposed to be a little dig, looking at one little community."

"I'm sorry," said Dr. Scott. "I can see that you're upset, but I promise you, your tribe will benefit from this exposure. People will know more about you and have a greater respect for your lands and history."

"How can you talk about respect given what you did to Bess?" Kate shouted.

The archaeologists all stopped digging and looked up at her. Kate felt her face go hot.

Dr. Scott let out an uneasy chuckle. "Now, Kate—"

Kate turned her back on him and stormed off. She ignored the uncomfortable silence in her wake and got back into her jeep. As she pulled away, she stole one last glance over her shoulder. Dr. Scott had returned to directing the dig.

Tears stinging her eyes, Kate turned her jeep away from the road and toward the coast.

"The strange men built their craft on the flats near the sea, out of reach of the highest tides, by the rock with the dark stripes from which we watch the whales migrate north."

There was one high, flat rock along the coast, at the very edge of the Tlingowa land, where Kate's father had taken her whale watching. It was the highest point for several miles and had several exposed coal veins. Now the formation loomed in front of her.

Her jeep lost traction on the loose sand, so she put it into park and got out. First she walked, then jogged, then ran.

*   *   *

"On the first day after the new moon, the men sang their farewells and gave us tokens. Green stone carvings and fine sticks to eat with. Then they scaled the wooden craft and disappeared into their little hut at the top."

A stitch was forming in her side, so Kate slowed to a walk and stumbled on toward the beach. She tripped over a pile of rocks and went down, skinning her knees smartly.

"One of our men lit the end of the length of rope they had bound the craft with, and the flames consumed it slowly, deliberately, leaving a trail of ash on the ground."

Kate looked back at the pile of rock. It was odd how it was stacked like a little, low wall.

"The fire leaped into the hollowed tube, and flames spewed out, causing the sand and rocks to fly as the craft lifted off the ground."

Kate's gaze followed the length of the rock pile, then jumped to a low hillock, then to another larger pile of rock. She blinked, then turned full circle. She stood inside a large depression.

"It lifted off with the sound of thunder, and fire a thousand times brighter than the little flying stick."

Kate scuffed the dirt under her feet with her sandals, then got down and dug with her hands. The moist sand moved aside easily, pale yellow giving away to dark soot, a great, thick layer of it.

"As our people watched, the strange men flew off, toward the horizon, leaving a trail of smoke that shone gold in the sunset."

"Wait," Mr. Scott had said. "You mean to say that men from across the Pacific, from China, came here, and built a gunpowder rocket?"

Bess's eyes focused on him for a fleeting moment, then she was back to her muttering, chanting the jingle from a laundry detergent commercial. As quickly as it had come, her moment of coherence had fled.

Kate stood up and looked around again. Ten paces from her was a shallow trench. She stepped over to it and started digging. About eight inches down she found rocks laid out to form a channel, charred black as pitch. She followed the length of the channel with her gaze, then dug another hole at the far end of it. Again she hit soot.

Her fingers brushed something smooth and cool. She dug around it and found herself staring at a clay fragment. She tugged it loose and held it up. Its surface glowed rose, a reflection of the sun setting on the horizon. She took it in both hands and twisted, feeling it press deep into the pads of her fingers. She tapped against the rocks she'd exposed and heard the familiar clack. This was too hard to be dried clay. It was fired clay.

Kate pressed the fragment to her chest and let the tears flow down her cheeks.

Mortal Clay, Stone Heart

Eugie Foster

"*AI-YAH*, Shu-mei!"

I started, nearly dropping the unfinished earthenware bowl. Baba has said—sometimes exasperated, sometimes amused—that the element that governs my spirit is not metal or fire, wood or water, but clay. And I suppose it's true. As far back as I can remember, I've had an affinity for finding the hidden grace inside pliant earth, the hard strength and flowing forms that the industry of my hands and the fire of the kiln can set free. But this affinity frequently makes me unmindful of such things as the passage of time and Baba's homecoming.

"Clay on your face, and is that slurry on your sleeve?" My father continued to scold me as I fumbled the bowl aside. "Do you think you could manage not to disgrace me with a grimy-faced welcome for the visitor I'm expecting tomorrow? The daughter of the Emperor's Overseer of Terracotta Sentinels should be refined and decorous."

"*Hmpf.* Do the terracotta soldiers concern themselves with the impression they make upon me?"

"Shu-mei, you're no longer a child. Have you considered how other girls your age are already married, even mothers?"

I pretended to scrutinize the bowl, hoping that Baba

wouldn't notice the heat suffusing my cheeks. I couldn't tell him my heart already belonged to another. Although I didn't delude myself that the man I admired regarded me with the slightest measure of consideration I held for him, it was too embarrassing and absurd to admit my one-sided love to anyone.

"What do I need a husband for?" I mumbled. "Kong Fuzi says that contentment can be found 'with coarse rice to eat, water to drink, and—'"

"Be silent!"

I couldn't have been more astonished if Baba had spouted hooves and bleated like a goat. "The mouth is the gateway to misfortune" was how other fathers instructed their daughters. But Baba had dismissed my nurse when I was four, after she had scolded me for demanding to be taught the abacus. He'd taught me himself how to do sums and read, and the arts of philosophy and debate.

Baba relented. "Forgive me. You couldn't have known. The Emperor has prohibited any discourse regarding the Hundred Schools of Thought."

"What?" Relief that my father was not, after all, transforming into a goat vied with shock.

"The only principles one may extol are those prescribed by the School of Law."

"That's ridiculous. How can any man prohibit another from thoughtful contemplation?"

"Qin Shi Huangdi is not a man. He is the Emperor. And he has decreed that all the histories and analects in opposition to the School of Law be consigned to fire."

The treasury of bamboo slip scrolls in my studio hung before my mind's eye. "But how can the empire move forward if it cannot study the past?"

Baba fixed me with a hard stare. "Shu-mei, I am in the habit of indulging your stubbornness, but you must understand the position I am in as one of the Emperor's officials. There can be no hint of sedition from this house."

I'd never seen my father look so grim. "I understand."

In the morning, Old Baishi, Baba's retainer, loaded our library into the firebox of the little dragon kiln built into the natural hillside at the garden's edge. Bleak and disconsolate, I turned to clay for commiseration, and it obliged me with a yellow Qilin. Adorned with the antlers of a deer, the hooves of an ox, and the tail of a lion, Qilin are the celestial emblem designating the element of earth, the natural foil to water—absorbing it. And water was the element and symbol of Qin Shi Huangdi.

As seditious acts went, it was admittedly a feeble one. But it helped, venting my outrage in this manner until late into the night.

I woke the next day to the afternoon sun chiding my eyes, with barely enough time to make myself presentable for Baba's guest. I donned a malachite coat and an ebony skirt that swirled like the sea, all the while wishing for a comfortable *shenyi* and the company of clay. As I finished securing the jade-green sash, I heard the *hi-hiin* whinny of a horse.

I hurried out, rehearsing appropriate phrases of welcome. But at the entrance, all words deserted me. It was not Baba with some stuffy official but the crown prince of the empire, Prince Fusu, handing the reins of his mount to Baishi.

Although I stood mute and stock-still, he noticed me and bowed. "No one could mistake you for anything but a refined and well-born lady today, Shu-mei."

I was goggling like a fish, but I couldn't look away. Memories of our previous meeting transfixed me, juxtaposing with this moment: Prince Fusu before me now and Prince Fusu from that other afternoon, drenched and seeking refuge from a sudden downpour.

* * *

He'd thought me a servant—my hair in rags, my *shenyi* splattered by clay. His first words to me, by way of introduction, were, "You, girl, could you fetch your mistress and bring me a towel? I'm near to drowning on your doorstep."

I bowed to conceal my embarrassment and irritation. "I'm Shu-mei. My father, the Imperial Overseer of Terracotta Sentinels, does not keep household servants. I'm afraid there's only myself—that is, unless you'd prefer our gardener, old Baishi, to attend you?"

"That won't be necessary," he replied, curt and dismissive. He stepped past me, and I shut the door to the rain, wondering whether I'd invited the more turbulent storm inside.

I fetched one of Baba's housecoats to replace his sopping garments and put a pot of water on to heat, aware of his eyes following me.

"You're not at all as I imagined," he said at last. "I thought the girl who fashioned that exquisite terracotta rabbit in your father's studio and who puts his apprentices to shame with her unflagging diligence would be as stout and formidable as he. But instead I find a willowy girl with rosy cheeks."

My cheeks, however rosy they'd been, blazed.

An eyebrow quirked. "Modest too? Unpretentious, modest, and undoubtedly steadfast. If you're a fraction as diligent as your father claims, you epitomize Kong Fuzi's ideal of virtue."

"You're a follower of Kong Fuzi's teachings?" I all but lunged at the opening, anything to shift the conversation from my rosy cheeks, the merits of my character, or even the terracotta rabbit. I'd fashioned that piece after my mother died—she'd been born in the year of the rabbit—and it was not a subject I cared to discuss with this man.

"Any school that proclaims real knowledge to be in grasping the extent of one's ignorance can be assured of my devotion." Prince Fusu winked, startling a smile from me. His return smile transformed him, making him younger, warmer. Our eyes met, and something within me shifted, realigned. Shaken and off balance, I understood later it had been nothing more or less than the foundation of my world giving way to be replaced by a new one: Prince Fusu.

"Shu-mei?" The prince's voice shook away my paralysis.

I bowed, mortified I'd kept him waiting like a peddler at the door. "Please be welcome. My father isn't home yet, but I expect him soon."

"Until he arrives, could I impose upon you for a tour of your kiln? The rain precluded my curiosity last time."

"Of course." I joined him on the stone walkway, striving to appear composed despite the agitated tremors that shook through me. But at the garden gate, I frowned. "Oh, wait, what if Baba's stuffy official finally arrives?" I clapped both hands over my mouth, appalled. How had I let myself say that aloud?

The prince chuckled. "I wondered if I'd misremembered the girl who glared at me so fiercely when I mistook her for a servant. But at last, here she is. As to the matter of the stuffy official, I suspect I am he."

I smiled shyly back, relieved. "Your Highness could never be stuffy."

"And why not? I've had the finest teachers to instruct me on all the varied forms and methods of stuffiness. I assure you, I'm a master at it."

I bit back a giggle and opened the gate.

"I've been unforgivably remiss in not thanking you for your gift before now," Fusu said, "but I hoped to be able to convey my appreciation in person."

I lowered my eyes. I'd fashioned the marbled tiger from two different clays to create a pattern that was both impetuous and considered—like the man strolling beside me.

"I showed my father your tiger," he continued, "and he wishes you to sculpt a matched team of terracotta horses for his afterlife city." The prince drew a sandstone token stamped with the imperial sigil from a pouch and offered it to me. "How convenient of my father to provide an official reason to call upon you."

I only partly heard him, my attention riveted on the imperial token. "The Emperor wants *me* to sculpt his horses?"

"He desires that his spirit world be as lively as this earthly one."

I glanced up at the tautness in the prince's voice, reminded of the whispered speculations that had arisen when Qin Shi Huangdi had first conceived his afterlife city, revealing his disquieting obsession with the trappings of immortality. Fusu would never undermine the Emperor, but his tone told me how troubled he was by his father's recent directives. The prince believed as I did in Kong Fuzi's teachings, as Baba had taught me: *Ignorance is the night of the mind.* How much more had it sickened him, the mandated destruction of wisdom?

I accepted the token. "My efforts will no doubt be inadequate, but I will do my best."

"I await with great anticipation your forthcoming masterpieces, *sifu.*"

No one had addressed me as a master artisan before. Did modesty require me to protest such honor or would that cause the prince to lose face? Before I could make up my mind, he swiveled, head raised.

"What's that?"

I strained, listening.

Rumbling, a subtle crescendo in the distance. An approaching thunderstorm perhaps?

"Men marching," Fusu said. "A brigade's worth, but not soldiers."

"Not soldiers?"

"The tread of an army is a tide that swells in a measured, beating gait." Fusu's eyes no longer saw me, focused upon some inner reflection. "This is undisciplined and irregular."

"A parade then?" I suggested.

"Shall we go see?" He pivoted and strode to where Baishi had tethered his horse, leaving me to scramble after. He flipped the reins free and mounted while I struggled not to trip over my skirt. He leaned to me, hand outstretched.

Should I have hesitated, refined and decorous like a court lady? I didn't. I gripped his hand, and he swung me up behind him.

My riding acquaintance was limited to infrequent occasions atop draft horses and, once, an indulgent cow. I teetered, feeling as graceful and secure as a sack of rice on a bamboo fence.

"Don't be afraid. Hold on to me if you're unsteady."

"I'm not afraid." I hoped I sounded bolder than I felt. "But I admit to a certain unsteadiness."

"Fei-hua is as courteous as she is swift. Neither of us will let you fall."

I remained dubious, but contrary to my expectations, when Fei-hua sprang forward, I didn't topple off, a feat I credited to luck, as it certainly could not have been skill. I did, however, clutch at Fusu like a drowning woman, kicking Fei-hua with my heels in the process. Fortunately, her disposition was as gracious as the prince had said, and she didn't take offense.

I eased my grip, and, as though he'd been waiting for this, Fusu leaned forward, bringing us low across Fei-hua's back. She, in turn, transformed from an earthbound creature to one of wind, anchored to this world only by the prince's will. To call both Fei-hua and the drays I'd sat before "horses" was like calling a blue-glazed platter the sky. And what I'd taken as a gallop had actually been for her an easy canter.

I laughed in fierce exhilaration, intoxicated by the heady combination of Fei-hua's speed, the heat of Fusu against me, and the thrill of basking in both. The prince turned his head, beaming like a boy.

All too soon, we slowed. I brushed streamers of hair from my eyes and saw why. A procession of hundreds of men marched on the imperial highway; scholars all, their vocation was apparent from their somber robes.

Prince Fusu slipped from Fei-hua's back and handed me the reins. "Wait here."

I didn't know if he'd addressed me or Fei-hua, but fortunately the mare considered it one and the same. I had no notion what to do with the straps of leather he'd given me, and doubted I could've dissuaded her if she'd had other designs.

Where had the prince gone? I scanned the highway until I spotted him engaged in discussion, not with a scholar but with a soldier. Before I had time to speculate about their conversation, Fusu came pelting back.

"I regret that our visit must be curtailed," he said, hurling himself into the saddle. He waited only for me to grasp his waist before spurring Fei-hua into a breath-stealing run.

"What's going on?" I had to yell to be heard above the strident wind.

"The Emperor has ordered the execution of those scholars for adhering to Kong Fuzi's teachings."

I almost tumbled off in horror. The only thing that saved me was Fei-hua, who slowed, allowing me to regain my balance.

"Shu-mei, I must return to the palace to plead with my father to stay this massacre. Forgive me for subjecting you to such distressing circumstances, but can you bear it a little longer? We're almost back to your home."

Shamed that consideration for me had caused the prince to delay, I released his waist. Accommodating me, Fei-hua eased to a stop.

"I know this region," I said, gathering my skirt. "I'll walk from here." It was too much to wish for a graceful dismount, but I hoped I could maintain a modicum of dignity.

"I can't allow you unescorted—"

"Nonsense. This is almost my back door. If I shouted, Baishi would come charging up with his handcart." I gave up on dignity and floundered off, landing on my rump in a swell of silk.

"Shu-mei! Are you hurt?"

I picked myself up, scowling. "I'm fine. Why are you still here? Hurry and save them."

The prince regarded me for a still moment. "You are most remarkable, Shu-mei." He wheeled Fei-hua, and they were gone in a storm of hooves.

When they were out of sight, I brushed myself off and began the hike home. Distance flown atop Fei-hua translated to an exhausting plod, made worse by the hateful skirt tangling my legs. But physical discomfort was nothing to the turmoil in my head. Those scholars. Surely Prince Fusu would be able to dissuade the Emperor from slaughtering them.

When at last I straggled through our gate, Baba came charging out, the stark lines of worry on his face flooding me with guilt. Prince Fusu's visit, the glorious ride, and the Emperor's condemnation of the scholars spilled from me in a disjointed babble.

*   *   *

By evening, everyone had heard of the four-hundred scholars executed, buried alive, and Prince Fusu's exile to the northern frontier for daring to champion them.

Baba caught me when I crumpled and rocked me as I sobbed. He carried me to my room, tucking me in my coverlet as though I were a child.

When I had cried all the tears I had, I lay awake, eyes open and mind abuzz. I didn't court sleep. When my mother died, sleep had brought nightmares, dark images that laid my grief bare on nerves already keening. Solace for me resided in wakeful activity. As soon as I heard Baba's soft snores, I rose and slipped to my studio to pray for healing and strength, the cool resistance of clay my benediction at the altar of my worktable. Immersed in my litany, immersed in clay, my head cleared.

I recognized this desolate empty place that had opened in me. It was the same as when Mother had died. More insights came, one after another like beads on a string. This crushing grief was not because of the scholars' deaths—a great loss and tragedy to warrant tears, yes. But what had sent me to my knees was Prince Fusu's banishment.

How shallow my character that I grieved more for a single man's exile than for hundreds of deaths. Moreover, I had no claim on the prince, had never had any claim on him. Realistically, he was no farther from me in the depths of Suizhou than he'd been in the palace.

I contemplated the shape beneath my hands. Although I'd given my fingers no directive, they'd fashioned an equine's long, fine nose, big, intelligent eyes, and delicately outlined nostrils. I knew this particular equine.

"Hello, Fei-hua."

I fetched the Emperor's token, tucked into my sleeve and forgotten in the afternoon's turmoil. Tracing the roughness of the imperial stamp against the slippery sandstone, I recalled a snippet of Kong Fuzi's teachings: *One should sorrow but not sink under sorrow's oppression*, and also, *If one takes no thought about what is distant, one will find sorrow near at hand.*

Qin Shi Huangdi was an old man. One day, Prince Fusu would guide the empire back upon the path of enlightenment. And after his inauguration, I would present him with a terracotta horse in Fei-hua's image, so lifelike one might expect it to toss its head and stomp the ground. I would offer as well another of Kong Fuzi's proverbs: *He who exercises government by means of his virtue may be compared to the north polar star, which keeps its place and all the stars turn toward it.*

Days unfurled to months, the flowers of the calendar—orchid, osmanthus, chrysanthemum—losing their petals as I cast and recast Fei-hua in clay. Evoking nuances of gracious strength and refined swiftness tasked me to my limits, but anything less than perfection was unacceptable. I'd remolded Fei-hua's head yet again when the news came of the Emperor's death.

I donned the proper mourning attire, but inside, I rejoiced. The work on Qin Shi Huangdi's afterlife city grew fevered, and Baba was called upon to attend the funerary ceremonies, a weeks-long affair.

As I checked his satchel to ensure I'd packed everything, a courier hurtled to our gate bearing another imperial writ. Baishi, shuffling with as much speed as his creaking joints could produce, delivered it to my father, and he and I hovered at Baba's elbow, brimming with curiosity.

The document was spare, but its meaning was clear to anyone versed in matters of court intrigue. The Imperial Secretariat had conspired with the youngest prince to discredit Fusu in a bid for the throne. In a coup of innuendo and forged documents, they'd presented Fusu with a letter from his father proclaiming him seditious and disloyal.

There was only one recourse for a son so dishonored. The prince had swallowed poison.

Fusu was dead.

My eyes burned, but I couldn't cry. How ridiculous I was to bawl like a child when the prince had been banished yet be utterly dry-eyed at his death.

Baba wanted to postpone his departure, but I wouldn't let him. History was littered with the corpses of hapless officials caught in the turbulence of violent succession. His constancy and worth as a servant of the empire must remain above suspicion.

Alone, I drifted to my studio, my mind estranged from my body by a juncture of white numbness. When my fist slammed into Fei-hua's clay features, I felt only surprise, as though another dictated my actions, another will that pounded the clay until all signs of careful labor had been erased.

Still under the control of this unknown craftsman, my hands mounded the clay anew, fashioning an elegant brow, expressive lips, and aristocratic nose. Recognition ran through me like a burning wire: Fusu's brow, lips, and nose—an unquestionable likeness. I caught my breath and raised my palm to wipe the features away. But a tiny incongruity made me hesitate. Was that crease about the eyes something I'd done? I shook my head. Foolishness. Of course it was. I raised my hand again. This time, I couldn't mistake it. In the space of a blink, the lips had thinned, suggesting a frown.

I touched the down-turned mouth. The contact sent a tingling intimacy through my fingers of a nature I'd never known before. I snatched my hand back and squinted shut my eyes.

"Prince Fusu," I whispered, "don't you think I'm too insignificant to haunt?"

I peeked open an eye.

One eyebrow arched higher than the other. It was the same expression Fusu had worn when he'd teased me and proclaimed me modest. An ache blossomed in my chest, the first taste of wrenching grief.

"No." I jerked around, giving my back to the clay head. "Don't. If it's vengeance you want, I'll serve you. But don't be kind or gentle. Be terrible or fearsome or nothing at all. Otherwise, I'll march out and tell Baishi to throw you into some pit or bash you flat, and I'll never touch clay again."

I waited for the hurt to fade, for the merciful numbness to seep back before I dared turn around. On my worktable, the clay face had emptied of expression and personality, just as I had demanded.

Without my father's comings and goings to punctuate my days, I could work unchecked save only by my stamina. Under the scrutiny of vacant, clay eyes, I crafted a body to match the head, kneading and molding until I collapsed from weariness upon the straw mat in my studio.

Grueling pace notwithstanding, this work was the easiest I'd ever done. Limbs and torso manifested effortlessly, as though I didn't sculpt the clay so much as remind it. In a matter of days, quicker than I thought possible, all lay finished and drying.

I rose from my workbench to summon Baishi, and the accumulated complaints, fatigues, and distresses of my body, disregarded this while, came alive. Bent over, hands on my knees, I waited for the sickening dizziness to ebb before wobbling outside and trekking to the little dragon.

Baishi had already removed the large bricks from the kiln's entrance and stacked them nearby. I crawled inside, edging past the firebox to the stacking floor. Crouching beneath the low ceiling, I measured the space, using my forearm as gauge. I'd never fired so many large pieces at once, and if I loaded them too closely, they could fuse disastrously.

I eased out of the dragon's maw and was unsurprised to find Baishi waiting for me with a soft cloth. Wiping the soot from my face, I wondered, for the thousandth time, how he seemed to know when I needed him at the kiln.

It required two days and two nights of ceaseless blast fire to mature the clay to terracotta. Baishi and I camped outside, alternating shifts to feed wood nonstop into the furnace. He tried to bully me into letting him take two shifts for my one, but I'd have none of that. So instead, he foisted huge quantities of lumpy rice and salt fish upon me until gratitude and annoyance became the same. Exasperated, I shooed him away, preferring to oversee the final hours alone. At last, weary to the core, I cast the last stick of wood in and stumbled home, too spent to change out of my smoke-drenched *shenyi* before surrendering to sleep.

Discomfort goaded me awake—nettles and grass plastered by oily soot to tender flesh. I blinked, the darkness outside my eyelids the same as within, and fumbled for a lamp. Its wan glow caught my reflection in the bronze mirror. I yelled before I could stop myself. Hair matted by clay and ashes, face and *shenyi* layered in grime, I looked like a *yaoguai* demon from the underworld. If Baba saw me like this, he'd scold me deaf. Or summon a priest to exorcise me.

I heated bathwater and soaked and scrubbed until as much skin felt scoured off as dirt. *Yaoguai* purged, I was left wide awake. So I put on a fresh *shenyi* and tramped across the garden, bearing a single lantern to augment the moonlight. The little dragon would take as much time to cool as it had to fire, but inevitably, I would spend the next days retracing my steps between kiln and house as a feeble sop to impatience.

I groped the air above the bricked up mouth. Its breath should have been balmy as summer, but there was no change to the night's chill.

Could I have slept for two full days?

I heaved bricks aside and squeezed in as soon as I'd cleared enough space to fit. On the stacking floor, I set the lantern down and groaned.

I'd set the pieces too close. They'd fused into slag. I crept over to survey the magnitude of my failure. Would it even be possible to remove the botched mess without shattering it first?

My outstretched hand contacted warmth—not cooling terracotta, but living warmth, a body of flesh. I sprang back as the man in the kiln stirred. A crash, like a hammer upon rock, and I wondered what had fallen before darkness tossed me down.

Waves lapped beneath me, the peaceful tide. They rocked me, lifting and falling, and as a counterpoint, a drowsy rhythm drummed in my ears: *tong-tong, tong-tong.*

Realization jolted me alert. Not tide and drum, but breath and heartbeat. I shot up. Pain lanced through my skull, and I winced, hand to temple.

"Softly. You hit your head and knocked yourself insensible. I carried you to your studio."

I knew that voice, would have known it waking or asleep, even though I'd heard it only twice before. My hand fell away, the pain forgotten.

"Fusu?" I whispered.

Somber eyes met mine, not quite the color I remembered. Touched with heat, like red-baked earth. Or terracotta. But still his eyes, still Fusu.

"They said you swallowed poison."

"Ah. Yes, I did. Imagine my surprise when I woke from that and then discovered myself lacking an essential accouterment—by which I mean my body."

I followed the tilt of his head until I grasped what I'd been too dazed to notice before. The prince was naked save for a thin blanket.

I flushed and looked away. The blanket rustled, a liquid spill, as the prince closed the space between us. Strong fingers caught my chin, compelling me back.

"You restored me, gave me this mortal sheath of perception and sensation, breath and light."

His words brushed my lips, like kisses I thought, until his mouth chased his words, and I saw I'd been mistaken. Fusu tasted of wood smoke, fire, and, faintly, the salt-bitter tang of fresh water drawn from our well. He unfastened the sash of my *shenyi* and, bemused, I marveled at the adeptness of fingers I had sculpted. He parted my *shenyi*, and I marveled at the firm smoothness of skin born in the scorching blaze of a kiln. He parted my body, and all thoughts became lost in a swell of movement and heat and joy.

I swam from a languid doze to find Fusu gazing out the window in one of Baba's housecoats—the same one I'd lent him on a rainy afternoon so long ago. That he was clothed made me shy, and I tugged on my rumpled *shenyi* before padding over to join him.

Outside, night still ruled, but its authority had waned. The sky held its breath, waiting to herald in the new ruler advancing in a golden chariot upon the horizon.

"I must go soon," Fusu said.

"Yes. To avenge your death."

He cocked his head. "Do you truly think me the kind of man to hold death as reason enough to discard the virtues I cherished in life?"

I frowned.

"And can you conceive of nothing other than vengeance, no other purpose powerful enough to entice my spirit from the void?"

"What?"

He sighed. "Shu-mei, do you recall what Kong Fuzi said about vengeance?"

I shivered. "'Before you embark on a journey of revenge, dig two graves.'"

He cupped my face in his hands. "Indeed. So why would any true disciple of Kong Fuzi desire that path?"

My heart leaped, frantic wings against the cage of my chest. "But . . . you're leaving."

Fusu's eyes darkened. "*Sifu*, not even your wondrous craft can make the heavens forget that dead is dead."

I broke away. "You didn't come back for me. Please, say you didn't."

"Why?"

"Because—" I balled my hands into fists, trembling. "Did I do something to invite your hatred?" I stammered.

"Not hatred, you fool, lo—"

"Don't!" I hugged myself, fighting for composure. "I-I told myself I was a fool. I was nothing to you, and I would forget you eventually. But when you died, those comforting lies were ripped away, leaving me flayed and reeling. The only way I could endure it, the only way I could survive, was to let my heart be stone. But I can't be stone if you love me."

"Would that be so terrible?"

"How could it not be terrible? Thrusting someone starving and parched to a banquet and allowing one taste, one sip before snatching it all away? It's the same, offering me words of love before forsaking me to grief." I rubbed my eyes, and my fingers came back wet. My tears had spilled unnoticed, postponed but not averted. "It's too late, it seems. Stone does not weep. Better that you hated me, that you were an evil spirit. This night will haunt me my whole life, the sweetness I'll never taste again and the knowledge of what we might have been. Even if you say you hate me now, I will know you lied, and that you lied from kindness. From love."

Fusu held me with his eyes, sorrowful and stricken. "What do you want me to do? Already dawn comes to chase my wayward shade back."

"Take me with you. Anything would be better than foundering in all the tomorrows before me, bereft and alone."

He inhaled, a ragged shudder. "If you are fixed on this course, give me one last gift. Give me your heart."

Like the other time, when he'd offered me his hand to some unknown adventure, I didn't hesitate. I took the pottery knife from my worktable and, effortlessly, as though I'd practiced it a hundred times, slit open my chest. The knife unseamed me with the same couth regard that it parted clay, producing neither pain nor blood. I lifted out my heart, although the state of it embarrassed me— misshapen, drab, and riven by faults—an altogether unsuitable gift. Yet it was also appropriate that Fusu have it, inevitable. It had always belonged to him anyway.

He accepted my heart as though it were a delicate flower or rare jewel. Reverently, he smoothed away the flaws and cracks with a few deft strokes, easily finding the harmony and balance that had eluded me. That, too, was only inevitable.

"Why is this so familiar?" I asked.

"We are bound." He breathed on my heart, suffusing it with color—warm ginger, bright vermillion, tawny red—until it was no longer mortal clay, but hard terracotta. "These acts of remaking—my body, your heart— bind us and will bind us again, choices made and yet to be made rippling out like fated echoes. Our paths are destined to converge."

I wrapped my arms around his neck. "Then let's continue to our next assignation together, with clasped hands."

"And joined hearts." Fusu drew me close and set the newly fired terracotta back into my chest.

Baishi knocked softly at the studio door, concern vying with uncertainty. Usually he knew when the young mistress visited the little dragon, just as he knew when a tree in the garden needed pruning or the flowers watering. But this morning he'd found the kiln partially opened—enough for a slender girl to slip in—without any inkling of when she'd been there.

She'd unpacked it too, all by herself. Always so impatient, that one. It must have taken her several trips to lug the terracotta pieces back to the house, when he and his cart could've done it in one. Well, she was considerate, sometimes to a fault.

He knocked again. The girl had a habit of overworking herself. What if she'd fainted or had a fever, too weak to summon help?

The door swung ajar.

"Shu-mei?" he called. "Are you asleep?"

When she didn't answer, he nudged the door wide enough to poke his head around.

Baishi furrowed his brow. "Huh. Not here?" About to withdraw, he paused, his attention caught by the pair of terracotta figures at the window. He crept into the studio, curiosity winning out.

The couple stood entwined, highlighted in a nimbus of sunlight. They were so close they might have been sculpted as a single piece, although he knew that wasn't possible. Leaning for a better look, Baishi marveled at the exquisite detailing, admiring the girl's evident skill and masterful technique.

The maiden's face, upturned to her lover, was ethereal and lovely, radiant with joy. The man embraced her in an attitude of tender adoration, though there was a sadness about him, so lifelike, so poignant that tears pricked Baishi's eyes.

He clucked his tongue at an old man's foolish sentimentality and turned to go. On his way out, he spied the pottery knife lying on the floor. Absently, he picked it up and set it on the worktable.

The young mistress could be so heedless sometimes. She might as well be clay.

Dancers with Red Shoes

Melissa Yuan-Innes

$\mathbf{A}$S an apprentice in the Wizard's Hospital, Leah Chang was used to a certain amount of noise at night. "The night is a fertile time," the wizard, Noah, had explained early on. "Many spells, from voodoo to demon summoning to the simple wart cure, are most powerful at certain hours of darkness."

Leah yawned. No need for demons tonight. Her friend Andrew, a corps member of the Royal Academy of Magical Ballet, had danced beautifully but then kept Leah up past midnight, doing shots and agonizing over his parents disowning him. They couldn't handle him being a ballet dancer, let alone a magical ballet dancer. Leah had poured iced coffee and sympathy down his throat for hours on a muggy July Montréal night. Now she needed sleep and silence. She placed orange foam earplugs in her ears, which worked as well as her imperfect silence spell, and closed her eyes.

Thump! Th-th-thump, thump, THUMP!

Leah tried some yogic breathing. *In. Out.*

Thumththumththumpthump . . .

That was the worst part. It had some sort of rhythm to it. So instead of blocking out random noise, her treacherous mind started analyzing it. She muttered a spell for a breath of wind. Wind was the most responsive element, though also the most fickle. This time, it answered with a small breeze. It smoothed the edge off the heat while creating a bit of white noise. Leah dozed off.

Ththum THUMP!

She jumped out of bed, ran up the curved stairs to Noah's sanctuary, and banged on the door.

The door opened a crack. She couldn't see his face, but his voice floated out. "Yes, Leah?"

"Noah, I'm sure you're working on something important, but for the past few weeks, I've hardly slept! Could you *please* put a silence spell on it?"

He paused. "Or a sleep spell on you?"

"Ha ha. I don't need to wake up in a glass coffin with seven dwarves."

The door opened a bit more. A shaft of light fell on his wrinkled parchment paper face and still-brilliant blue eyes. "Come in quickly, then."

Leah slipped inside, inhaling the usual tang of smoke and something darker, like licorice and rosemary and blood. It took a second for her eyes to adjust to the light. Then her mouth fell open.

At the far end of the room, in front of the extinguished fireplace, between a faded pair of purple velvet armchairs, a pair of amputated feet danced.

The feet did a step-twirl, step-twirl, step-LEAP, pas-de-bourré toward her in red ballet slippers. Leah recoiled. The ankle bones were smooth and white in cross section, surrounded by dun-colored muscle and papery skin. In contrast, the *en pointe* shoes were a brilliant, spotless scarlet. Their ribbons wound around the dead ankles and the empty air above them as if there were still legs to cling to.

The feet smacked down flat on the ground and paused for a second. It was like a drummer's cymbal, marking the grotesqueness. Then the feet spun away again.

"My God," Leah said softly.

Noah nodded. "She's getting more and more impatient, too. I'm not sure what to do with her."

Leah watched the feet spin, one on the ground, one in the air. "What are they doing here?"

He smiled and shrugged. "You remember Hans Christian Andersen's story about the girl with red shoes?"

Leah's forehead pleated. "You mean that girl who kept dancing and dancing in magical red shoes until a woodcutter chopped her feet off?" Her eyes bulged. "These are *the* shoes? The feet?"

The shoes jumped *en pointe*, then flexed their toes, as if curtsying.

"That's disgusting," she whispered.

"Yes, I myself dislike how Hans turned a young girl's misfortune into a parable about vanity. You should re-read it, Leah. The girl tricks her foster mother into buying red shoes, which are eventually spelled by a 'soldier' into endless dancing, until the unfortunate ending you describe. Of course, Hans then focuses on the girl's returning to the breast of the church thereafter. He never bothers to follow the feet."

Leah shook her head. "Why do we have to have the feet?" They danced more slowly now, the left foot still while the right arched up in the air.

"My friend Cartaphilus bequeathed them to me for safekeeping."

Leah breathed shallowly through her nose. There were some things up with which she could not put. "So what have you been doing with them?"

"Well, I thought she would enjoy staying in a wizard's chambers, but she seems to be growing impatient. Though I applaud as often as I can, she seems to imagine a more appreciative audience lies beyond my door." He shook his head. "She can see the mundanity of traffic lights and pizza parlors from the window, but she jumped up to tap-dance on the glass pane."

Leah's brow pleated. "Can they see?"

He shrugged. "She dances around obstacles, so she must have some sort of sensory system."

Great. Seeing-eye feet. After centuries of dancing, they deserved a rest. Vaguely, Leah noticed that Noah called them "she," as if the girl were still alive, but Leah couldn't stop thinking of them as an abomination disguised as feet. She'd seen a lot in med school before she quit, and even more as a wizard's apprentice, but this one gave her the ooglies. "Can you do a disanimation spell?"

The red shoes leaped on Leah's feet. Hard. She yelped. They sprang away before she could snatch them.

Noah said, "I must say, I agree, Leah. Those shoes clearly want to keep on dancing. And Cartaphilus certainly wouldn't thank me for burying her."

"The girl's feet have rights, too!"

"Leah, my dear. After all this time, her feet and the shoes have come to an agreement. It's called dancing."

Leah's toes throbbed. She leaned against Noah's workbench to rub them, glaring at the red shoes. "Well, why don't you send them to a dance company?"

He smiled at her. "The human mind is so logical."

In other words, he agreed.

The red shoes capered around in delight. Leah caught herself smiling before she smothered it. The sooner the shoes were outta here, the better off they'd all be.

In the morning, Leah read up on various dance forms while the shoes beat on the wooden floor, practically flamenco-style. But the only magical dance corps were ballet, jazz, and modern.

Leah went for the obvious. She woke Andrew up from his hangover. He connected her with the spokeswoman for the Royal Academy of Magical Ballet. The cool British voice expressed interest in acquiring "such a unique prop." Leah felt a twinge at that as she coaxed the red shoes into a cat carrier.

*   *   *

Leah thought her role would be to stop, drop, and run, but the business manager asked Leah to stay as the shoes' "guardian." More likely he wanted an apprentice wizard on hand in case the slippers started beating a tattoo into his face. Since Leah's toes still ached from the shoes' stomping the night before, she felt some sympathy for that point of view, although she thought the prima ballerina was even more of a pain than the footgear. "Who will look at me if there's a pair of disembodied feet prancing around?" the diva demanded before storming out.

As if in response, the red shoes began what looked like the *pas-de-deux* from *Swan Lake*. Andrew Mac-Millan rose to join them.

"For God's sake, Andrew!" The choreographer tore him away. "We're watching her form. She doesn't need a partner now, and when she does, it will be Peter!"

Leah avoided his eyes. On-the-job humiliation was par. Humble pie shoved up your nose in front of an ex-girlfriend wizardling was unbearable.

Only the shoes seemed impervious to the tension. They twirled, they arced in the air, they sustained leaps and splits beyond human anatomy. They were amazing, and yet Leah, the cultural troglodyte, found her mind wandering after fifteen minutes. For her, part of the tension in dance was the effort of the dancers themselves: the cords bulging in their necks, their breath panting, the grimace forced into a perma-smile. These shoes, no longer limited by muscle and bone, seemed more acrobatic and less magic.

Still, the company gave the red shoes and mummified feet a standing ovation. It looked as though they had a new prima donna.

Good riddance. Leah scooped up the cat carrier and waved to the business manager. "Well, break a leg," she murmured to Andrew before she realized how weird that sounded when the new star had not only broken but severed legs.

"Wait," he said, turning his hazel eyes on her in a way that she yearned to refuse but knew she wouldn't. "Could you come see my grandmother after? She's been asking for you."

Leah sucked her teeth. She had to master her air spell, trouble-shoot a love potion, and walk her three-headed dog. But she'd always loved Penny MacMillan, sometimes more than her grandson, so she was sunk.

At the end of the rehearsal, the business manager finally decided to lock up the space while the red shoes kept dancing. And dancing. And dancing.

Andrew's shirt stuck to him in the sticky summer air. At least the hospital entrance was shaded by maple trees, but he held his breath past all the smokers and ran up all eight flights of stairs. The air conditioning had failed again. He wiped the sweat off his forehead with the sleeve of his yellow gown before he donned a pair of latex. At last, he rushed in the room.

"Grammie!"

She was lying in bed, in her blue hospital gown. He ignored her scrawniness and the bedsores, trying to see the ballerina he remembered, before her back injury, the cigarettes, the diabetes, and all the rest.

She turned her blind eyes toward him. "Andy, my love," she said.

"Grammie." He held her hands. Even through the gloves, her bones were so fragile. She reached up to stroke his forehead, but he ducked. MRSA bacteria. They weren't supposed to touch skin-to-skin. "How was your day?"

"The same, the same."

He forced a smile. "Want to go for a walk? We could use your prostheses . . ."

"They don't fit any more."

"Maybe we could buy you new ones." He could taste the lie. So could she.

"That would be throwing good money after bad, Andy. I don't need them. The nurses get me up in a chair every day and the physiotherapist does her best. Now you, my sweetheart. What's new with you and your magical dance troupe?"

"Nothing," said Andrew, while Leah said, "Huh? What about—"

He nudged her, but too late. Penny turned toward Leah. Her pupils were milky, yet strangely compelling. "Tell me."

"Nothing," said Andrew, louder, but Leah was already talking.

At last, Penny spoke. "I need those shoes."

Andrew shook his head. She felt the movement and squeezed his hand. Under the sheet, Leah saw the stumps of her legs stir.

He grinned. "Red shoes. The ones from the fairy tale." She was the only other dancer in the family, but more than that, they had the same spirit. She understood why he dumped an opening in the Royal Winnipeg Ballet for a lower one in a magic company.

For the first time in weeks, he saw a light in her sightless eyes.

"Do you love me, Andy?"

"You know I do."

He entered the hospital slowly the next day, inhaling his surroundings. The steamy smell of reconstituted mashed potatoes and feces. The hallway crowded with linen baskets, wheelchairs, dressers with gowns and gloves, and

an occasional commode. People crammed into rooms.
A man with white wisps of hair, tied to his bed, calling,
"Help me. Help me." An intravenous machine beeped.
A nurse called, "I'm coming, Mrs. Smith!" Through the
window, the St. Joseph's Oratory's magnificent copper
dome oversaw all of Montréal. Andrew paused in front
of the window, trying to ignore the scrabbling in his
backpack.

At last, he silently entered Room 8311. He shut the
door.

His grandmother said nothing. Her fists clutched her
thin blue bed sheet, her face alight with hope.

Andrew turned away from her as he popped open
the cat carrier. The red shoes sprang free and landed
gracefully, almost silently, on the tile floor. They flexed
and pointed again. Limbering up.

At last, he spoke. "You can't even see them,
Grammie."

Her hand reached for his. He made no move toward
her. Her hand faltered in the air. "I love you, Andy," she
said. "Thank you."

Damn. She always knew how to work it. He grabbed
her hand, ignoring its tremor. He repeated, louder, "You
can't even see them."

The shoes ignored them both, launching into a scene
from *The Nutcracker*.

She licked her lips. "But I can hear them. Thank you,
my love."

He choked back tears the only way he knew how. He
danced with the shoes in that tiny box of a room. He
was the toy soldier, the shoes were Clara. He didn't have
to lift her, but his hands rose automatically. The shoes
sprang ever higher, ever greater, in sweeping strokes, as
if they could clear the illness and sadness and regret from
the air. Andrew found himself smiling. Dancing better
than ever. Trying to out-do those goddamn shoes.

Grammie clapped. She laughed, gurgled, and began to cough. Her face turned red. She bent at her waist, covering her mouth.

"Grammie? Should I call a nurse?"

She waved him off. She mastered the cough and sucked in her breath until it was almost normal. "Andy. Please leave me the shoes tonight."

He shook his head but said, "I love you, Grammie."

"Dammit!" It was the first time she had sworn at him.

"I can't. It was too much just to bring them today." He said under his breath, "I know how much you miss dancing."

She snorted. "I miss *walking*."

He gaped at her, realized how futile it was to make faces at a blind woman, and shut his mouth.

"I used to make my own decisions. Now I have to ring a bell if I want to loose my own bowels. More often, the nurse doesn't come in time, and I sit in a filthy diaper, sometimes for hours. I have an ulcer on my buttocks that will not heal because of this."

"Grammie—" He wanted to cover his ears.

"Your mother brings me geraniums. I hate geraniums."

"Grandma!" He almost laughed until she turned her face to his.

She enunciated every word. "I want to live again, Andrew McMillan, or I don't want to live at all."

"Okay. You're upset. I shouldn't have brought these. I'll take them away—"

"No!" she yelled and started coughing again.

"I'm getting your nurse this time." He pressed the bell again and again. No answer, as usual. He ran to the hallway. "Nurse! Nurse!"

Grammie shook her head, still coughing. That boy. He was still so very young.

Thump! Thump! The red shoes landed on the bed.

She swung toward the pressure, pushing aside the blankets. She felt dead flesh and bone rub against her stumps. Then the red ribbons whipped around them, lashing her flesh to the dead girl's ankles.

"Thank you," she managed through a final cough.

Though the shoes trembled with the effort, they kept nearly still as she clambered out of bed and, even more treacherously, balanced her stumps on the cool, smooth, but not unpleasant ankle flesh.

Then the shoes began dancing. First a slow step to each side. She grinned as her shrunken muscles jerked into action. Soon, the red shoes began faster steps, even a spin.

"Grammie!" Andy shrieked. He dove at her feet, hands reaching for ribbons, but she jumped over his fingers and landed on the bed, kicking Highland dance steps.

The Filipina nurse came running and screamed. "Mrs. Sebastien! Mrs. Sebastien! She's—call a doctor! Stat! No, a code! She's—I don't know what—look at her! Is it a seizure?"

Her chest was caving in. She had no breath left. She mouthed "I love you," and her eyes rolled up. Andy sprang at the bed, but her body soared into the air, the head and torso hanging at a bizarre angle as the shoes spun her legs, again and again, in a relentless pirouette.

Leah dashed up the stairs. "Did you hear about Andrew's grandmother?"

Noah nodded. "And the role of the red shoes."

"But—she was dying, right? That's what Andrew said. I mean, he was pretty upset, but it sounded like suicide to me."

"No matter what the circumstances, we forbid magic objects to commit murder or abet suicide. Law number 252."

"They'll deanimate the shoes?" Leah's stomach roiled with guilt. It was all her fault.

"Yes. In the past, a wizard would have been summoned to the hospital and performed his duty then and there. Now we have to conjure the shoes away and stage a trial first." He gave her a crooked smile. "Progress."

They sentenced the shoes to burn.

A large crowd jostled around the bonfire. A few had signs: BURN, BABY, BURN warring with JUSTICE FOR ANIMATE BEINGS. Leah crossed her arms, the breeze blowing her hair. Noah said nothing. Neither did Andrew. He hadn't spoken much since his minimum two-week suspension from the dance company. Despite the heat, he was wearing a long-sleeved black shirt and black cords.

A limousine nudged its way up the hill. A flunky rushed to open the door. The black-hooded executioner stepped out holding the red shoes firmly around each foot.

A free strand of ribbon lashed at his eyes. He jerked his head back. An assistant had to snatch the ribbons out of the air while another man tied their ends in knots. The executioner stood impassive until they finished. Then he marched to the fire, careful not to hasten his pace. He tossed the shoes at the flames. "May you rest at last."

As he opened his hands, the red shoes launched themselves off his palms. The flames reached for the shoes, but Leah muttered a spell, and the winds blew the flames and the smoke toward the audience. When their eyes refocused, the red shoes were gone.

Leah was suspended from her apprenticeship.

"For a month," said Noah. "To ponder what you have done. I will notify you if I will continue your apprenticeship."

The "real" world bit. Her parents in Toronto were pleased but startled to see her. What had she been doing since she dropped out of medical school? Nothing she could explain.

She gossiped with friends. Shopped. Hit the movies. Went clubbing. All things she'd missed, but the lack of magic ate at her. She couldn't drink too much, or she'd catch herself saying things like "That bouncer's pretty big, but I once saw a giant . . ."

The little things cut at her. She missed patting her three-headed dog and controlling the breezes instead of flicking an air conditioning switch.

Five weeks later, she woke up at 5:00 AM to stare at the ceiling. Her life was empty. Her parents were impatient. Had she called med school yet? No? Well, what did she plan to do with her life?

She drank a glass of water and logged on to her computer. "Anonymous461386" had emailed her a picture. She clicked on it. What the hell. A virus might help put off med school.

It was a crappy jpeg. She squinted at swirls of black figures surrounding a fire. At the left side, far from the flames, she caught a glimpse of red.

In fact, she'd swear there were two red blobs. Dancing with the gypsies?

Leah's heart stopped and started again. Then she clicked on her next email. From Noah. Subject: Coming back. As her server loaded up his message, she cranked up her Nelly Furtado CD and whooped as she danced.

Intelligent Truth

Shelly Li

"LET me raise a white deer on my green slope, And ride to the great mountain when I have the need; How can I bow and scrape to men of high rank and men of high office, Who never will suffer from being shown an honest-hearted face."

Katie Huang glanced up from the paper she held in her hand, focused in on the robot sitting across the table from her. According to the robot's paperwork, his name was Searle, produced in 2076, making him part of the Cobalt Generation.

"Searle," Katie said. "These four lines are the last lines of a poem by Li Bai, a Chinese poet of the Tang Dynasty. Will you give me your interpretation of them?"

Searle blinked, his human-looking eyes staring back at her. No words came out of the robot's mouth.

Katie leaned back in her chair and waited as Searle processed the words, probably keying each line into his inner dictionary, comparing notes with various Internet sites, trying to find an answer to her question.

But, in the end, Searle had to give his own interpretation. After all, that was what Katie had asked of him, and a robot could not disobey a human order.

So Katie waited, meanwhile letting her thoughts separate. She thought of Charles, waiting at home with dinner. She thought of what he was cooking up today. He always had silly little surprises for her, whether it be a love letter hidden under the dinner plate or various presents taped to the bottom of the dining table.

A smile crossed her face. Out of all the presents in the world, though, the only one she wanted was the one that Charles had yet to give her.

"My interpretation of the four lines that you read to me," Searle's words bled into her thoughts, "is that this person lives on the outside of civilization. He spends his days with nature, because he does not like to interact with others." Searle paused. "He thinks that everyone looks down on him because he was not blessed with an honest face."

Katie nodded and looked down at Searle's robotic grading rubric. She scrawled at the bottom: *Does not understand how to compare verses to historical allusions and cannot firmly grasp extended metaphors. Human status denied.*

"Thank you, Searle," Katie said as she looked up. After another day of analyzing the psyche of all kinds of advanced robots, she still hadn't been able to categorize one, just one, as a legal human being.

After another day, she was still a failure.

"You are dismissed."

Katie watched Searle walk to the door. He even had the swagger of a human, that little hunch sitting on his shoulders.

In fact, if Searle were out walking the streets, Katie didn't think that even she, one of the many doctors who conducted the robotic psychological examinations here at BioCorp, could tell the difference between him and a human.

But if he can't understand the inner meanings of a poem, Katie thought, *then he will never be anything more than a robot.*

A machine.

*　　*　　*

It took Katie less than ten seconds of sitting down at the dinner table to realize that something was off about Charles today.

Her fingers started to tingle.

Could this be the night? she wondered as she watched her boyfriend set the table.

Over the year and a half that they had been together, Katie had gotten to know Charles pretty well. Well, more than pretty well. She knew Charles like she knew the back of her hand.

And right now, Charles looked nervous. Charles never looked nervous, or frenzied, unless he had something important to say.

Charles sat down at the table and noticed Katie staring at him. His lips formed a shaky smile. "Katie," he said, reaching over the table to grab her hand.

Katie had to grind her teeth together to keep from smiling. *This must be the moment*, she thought, readying herself. She could hear her heart thundering, pounding against the walls of her chest.

He's going to propose.

"I have something I want to show you," Charles said, his eyes glued to the table, refusing to look at her.

"Oh. And what's that?"

Charles slid out of his seat, pulling Katie up with him as he led her to the bedroom.

Katie's hold on Charles' hand tightened as he opened the door. "After you," he said, staring deep into her eyes.

And so Katie, barely able to breathe, entered the room.

She took a look around, not seeing anything out of the ordinary. There was the king-size bed, carefully made that morning by their robot, Queenie. Queenie had also cleaned the wood floor and wiped down the floor-to-ceiling window that exposed Chicago's glittering Lake Michigan.

"Charles," she said, turning around. "What—"

All of a sudden the closet door burst open, and a woman jumped out between her and her boyfriend.

Katie stopped.

Her mouth dropped open.

This can't be happening, she thought, fighting the urge to scream as she stood in place, staring.

After a few seconds, she found her voice. "Mom. What are you doing here?" Her gaze shifted to Charles.

There was a helpless expression covering his face.

"Aren't you surprised, honey?" her mother said, opening her arms and pulling Katie into an embrace. Her mother was a couple sizes skinnier than her, and hugging her was like hugging a stick.

"Very surprised," Katie said. "But what are you doing here?"

Her mother's eyebrows furrowed to form a frown, and she made that *tssk* noise with her tongue, making Katie's insides cringe, her stomach twist. That *tssk* was all too familiar, too haunting.

"Why must you talk like that?" her mother said. Her English, after all these years, still carried an accent, a reminder of a separate life back in China. "Can't a mother come visit her child when she misses her?"

Her mother turned to face Charles, giving Katie an opportunity to pierce a glare into him.

"Now, Charles," her mother said. "Before we all eat dinner, will you help me carry my things from the car? It's parked downstairs."

"Yeah, no problem, Nina," Charles said and followed Katie's mother out of the room.

Katie let out a sigh as she watched her mother and her boyfriend disappear out the door of the apartment.

I can't believe I was actually expecting a proposal to-

night! Now, standing alone in the silence of her home, she wanted to slap herself.

The reason Charles had been so antsy was because he had hidden her mother to surprise her.

Dear God, Katie thought as she strode out of the bedroom.

This wasn't a surprise present. This was damnation.

Her mother's last piece of luggage arrived with yet another surprise, one that Katie was not sure how to feel about.

"Do you like him?" Nina said, motioning for the robot to put down the luggage. "I got him cheap, on sale at an outlet mall in Indiana."

Katie took one look at the robot before tearing her eyes away and telling her mother, "Mom, there's a reason you got this thing cheap. It's an Aqua Generation robot. A *first*-generation machine that was made in the 2050s."

"Hey, this 'robot' has a name, honey buns," the robot interjected.

Katie's head snapped back to the robot, who then said, "The name's Carter."

"Carter." Katie smiled and said to her mother, "The thing is even dysfunctional. A robot doesn't interrupt communication between two humans. It's one of the rules in his programming."

"Bite me," Carter said.

"Now, cool down, Carter." Nina cast a disapproving look at Katie. "He's more human than any of the 'advanced' robots that are sold nowadays, and I'm keeping him."

Katie threw her hands up in the air and looked to her boyfriend, who, again, offered no support. He was helpless against the five-foot-two bully standing in the room with them.

"Whatever," she finally said, walking out of the room. She could win an argument against anybody, but when it came to her mother, it felt as if all the words in the world retreated from her.

What do I know, right? I only have a PhD in robotic diagnostics.

"I cannot believe you," Katie said, as Charles climbed in on the other side of the bed.

Charles lay down with a sigh and turned to face her. "What was I supposed to do, Katie? It was your mother's idea to surprise you. You want me to refuse her?"

"Yes!" Katie exclaimed. "You could have told her that I was really busy and that she should come stay with us some other time."

"She's just staying for the weekend. It won't be too bad."

But Katie's mind was no longer on her mother. Her thoughts had now jumped to the robot in the other room.

Carter.

"Is it just me, or was that a malfunctional robot that my mother brought into our apartment?" she asked Charles. As an operations manager at the same company, Charles worked with the BioCorp scientists on the mechanical functions of the different generations of robots.

Charles rubbed his eyes and set his glasses down on the nightstand. "Look, Carter is an Aqua Generation robot. He's a prototype, modeled after the *average* human being. He's going to be a little on the sassy side, and not too pleasant either. And even work ethic-wise, he's not going to be as efficient as, say, Queenie."

At the mention of her name, the robot standing at the corner of the room blinked to life. "What can I help you with, Charles?" she asked, the color returning to her flesh.

"Nothing, Queenie," Charles said, waving the robot away, and so Queenie retreated to the corner of the room and shut down again.

"Every generation of robots is different, Katie," he said. "And the older they are, the more unsophisticated, the more inhuman they are."

But that answer failed to satisfy. Even with her eyes closed in the darkness, Katie couldn't stop thinking about Carter.

In the silence, she could hear the echoing noise of the second hand in her head, ticking to a new minute, then a new hour.

Finally, when she could no longer take the curiosity welling up inside her, she slid out of bed and, careful not to disturb the sleeping Charles, tiptoed out the door.

Darkness pressed on the hallway from all sides, oozing into her senses as she made her way to the study at the end, her footsteps silent.

With her mother breathing in the same house as Katie's again, she could feel herself transported back to her teenage years, slipping silently out of the house late on Friday nights, while her friends waited in a car down the street.

Her mother always said that nothing good happened after midnight.

Then again, nothing fun happened before.

Katie rubbed the sleep out of her eyes and set her hand on the doorknob, slowly opened the door and stepped into her study. It was her and Charles' joint study, but since Charles almost never ventured into the room unless he needed to surf the Internet or answer emails, it was Katie's diagrams that were plastered over the walls, Katie's papers that were scattered across the floor.

She hadn't logged off work, so the database search engine popped up right away.

Aqua Generation. She hit the search button. In her five years of working at BioCorp, she had never tested a first-generation robot, possibly because the Cyan Generation had just popped onto the market at the time, making robots like Carter outdated machinery.

There were only eight reported psychological examinations for Aqua Generation robots, and of the eight, only three had examiner comments. The rest were "Yes" and "No" checkboxes for robotic performance. Almost all examiners checked "No" for "Willingness to Perform Tasks." Half checked "Yes" for "Ability to Think at Normal Human Speed," and only one checked "Yes" for "Pleasant Demeanor."

The category "Ability to Understand Poetry" was nonexistent.

Katie ran a hand through her hair as she scanned the rest of the data on the screen. *Eight psychological examinations were reported,* she thought. The second-generation robots, the Cyan Generation, logged a total of three thousand and sixty-six examinations.

How can this be? Katie leaned back in her chair, thinking. She remembered the first day she had arrived at the robotics testing office. Outside, there had to have been thousands of deactivated Aqua Generation robots hanging off the trucks.

"So where did their examination reports go?" she wondered out loud. *Could an administrator possibly have erased them?*

If so, it didn't make sense.

"Hey," a voice suddenly said, a few feet away.

Katie jumped an inch off her seat and turned toward the shadow leaning against the framework of the door, where the light in the study couldn't reveal him.

"Who is it?" she said, standing up quickly.

The person stepped into the study, and relief washed over her.

"Oh," Katie said and dropped back into her seat. "Carter. What are you doing, walking around at this hour?"

Carter shrugged. "Nina is sleeping, but with all the racket you're making in here ..."

Katie frowned as she looked at Carter, at his humanistic face. He couldn't walk as smoothly as his successors, who moved with flawless step and meticulous swings. Even when Carter talked, his lips couldn't form perfect *Os*.

She shifted her stare from Carter to her computer, where the list of examinations for Aqua Generation robots was still pulled up.

An idea hit her.

"Please, sit down," she said, gesturing to the chair across her desk.

Carter sat. He didn't look happy or even pleasant.

"Have you ever read a poem, Carter?"

"No," Carter said. "You see, at slave school, we learned how to cook meals, vacuum, repair leaks ... those kinds of things."

Katie couldn't help but smile. "Is that bitterness I detect?" In the back of her mind, her curiosity was piqued. *Robots have never been programmed with an understanding of things like bitterness or sarcasm.* Katie had written a paper on the subject in grad school—and if her professor had met Carter, she would have failed the class.

"Actually, hold on," Carter said. "When I was examined, way back in the 2050s, the man in the room read me a poem."

"Really?" Katie sat up in her seat. *Then why were there no records of the poem interpretations?* "Which poem did the man read you?"

Carter shrugged. "Something by Walt Whitman."

"Ahh."

Carter then proceeded to say, "I don't remember the

title of the poem. But man, it couldn't have been any more communistic."

She hadn't expected an answer like that. "What did you just say?" Katie said.

"Transcendentalism is just a mask for communism," Carter said. "Being one with nature, transcending the physical and empirical . . . Whitman is just a better-groomed Karl Marx."

The joke would have been funny if it had come from the mouth of a human. But in Carter's case . . .

A shiver traveled down Katie's spine. Could she really have a human-robot on her hands? A robot with his own thoughts, his own opinions?

"Well, I'm going to read to you a poem by my favorite poet of all time," Katie said, grabbing the Chinese version of *The Selected Poems of Li Bai* out of her drawer.

A robot, though it was the most complex piece of machinery in the twenty-first century, could not possibly comprehend the deep meanings in human poems. Because to understand poetry, one must identify with the emotions expressed on the page.

And robots did not have emotions.

But, looking at Carter, Katie began to doubt.

She flipped to a page, translated the first few lines of the poem to English in her head, and began. "Blue mountains to the north of the walls, A white river winding about them; It is here that we must separate, And go out through a thousand miles of dead grass."

She stopped and looked at the robot, meanwhile grabbing a pen and a notepad. "These are the four opening lines from Li Bai's famous poem, 'Farewell to a Friend.' Will you give me your interpretation of them?"

At this question, every robot that Katie had ever examined would pause and start up their internal search engines, combing the Internet and the dictionary for the most accurate answer.

Carter, on the other hand, immediately said, "Easy. In the first two lines, Li Bai is using the image of mountains surrounded by a river to illustrate the relationship of two friends, as inseparable as Mother Nature's children. It's the basic form of love."

He just explained to me what love is, Katie thought, her pen shaking as she set the tip down on paper. *How in the world does he understand love?*

"As for the last two lines," Carter continued, "there comes a day that the mountain and the river, the two friends, must separate and go their own ways. Li Bai is saying that, after spending so much time alongside your best friend, traveling the road with no voice to talk to but your own is going to seem scary and dead."

Katie dropped the pen. It clattered to a stop on the floor.

Carter frowned and said, "Hey, butterfingers. Your pen is on the ground."

After a pause, Katie scooped up the pen and stood. "Please wait here, Carter," she said. "I have to go make a phone call."

"Hmm. Will it be a quick thirty-second conversation, or will you be confessing your sins to a priest?"

Katie didn't answer the question; instead, she tossed her Li Bai book at him. "This might keep you occupied," she said and left for the second spare bedroom a couple doors down.

After three rings, her manager picked up.

"Hey, Dennis, I've got something hot on my hands," Katie said.

"Well, it better be if you're calling me this late and on a personal line."

Katie took a deep breath and said, "I just did a psychological examination on a robot. He passed the poetry comprehension test."

There was silence on the other end.

"Dennis?" Katie said. "Did you hear what I just said?"

"Let me connect you to Jeremy Lawrence. He's the director of robotics distribution at the company. Hold on."

The wait was short.

"Hi. Is this Katie Huang?" a voice came on.

Katie cleared her throat. "Yes, this is she." She had never spoken to anyone this high up on the management chain, and the upper levels didn't speak to her, either—unless something major had happened.

"Well, Katie, it's nice to make your acquaintance. My name is—"

"Dennis told me who you are."

"Ahh. Good. Let's see—first, I want to thank you for making this a priority and contacting us straight away. If this robot indeed qualifies for human status, you will find a generous bonus on your desk soon."

"Umm. Thank you, sir."

"Of course," Lawrence said. "Now, tell me: This robot that you just examined, which generation is he?"

"Aqua," Katie answered. "He belongs to my mother. He started exhibiting unusual behavior upon arriving at my home. I only examined him when I searched for prior psychological examinations of Aqua Generation robots and found that there was almost nothing in the database. Why is that?"

"Oh. You saw that, huh?"

Katie was about to say something, but then thought it would be best to keep quiet. He had obviously heard her.

After a few seconds, Lawrence said, "Well, it was just a matter of some spring cleaning." He chuckled. "The Aqua Generation robots are so outdated that I didn't think anyone would go hunting for their examinations."

"Yes, but you didn't even leave it up there for referencing in the future?" Katie pressed. Lawrence's answer didn't make any sense. Database storage was so extensive and cheap. Nobody cleaned anything off systems anymore.

"Yes, I suppose we could have," Lawrence said. "But anyway, is it okay if we stop by in the morning and take the robot back to BioCorp, have our scientists run some tests?"

Katie frowned. "I don't know if that's possible," she said. "You see, the robot isn't mine. He's my mother's."

"BioCorp has the right to take away any robot at any time for reasons that will be disclosed to the robot's owner after the robot has been readmitted to the labs for a period of twenty-four hours," Lawrence answered. "It's in the safety clause in the buyer's contract."

"Oh."

"So we'll be by in the morning."

But before Lawrence could hang up, Katie asked, "Sir? Umm . . . what will happen with Carter the robot if he tests positive for human status?"

The silence that followed sent chills down her back.

Oh, God, Katie thought. And in that instant, everything hit her. The erased information on the database, the urgency in Lawrence's voice . . .

They're trying to erase the existence of all Aqua Generation robots.

Finally, Lawrence said, "Don't worry about it," and hung up.

Oh, God. Katie leaned against the wall of the room, shaking. *What have I done?*

The sound of a scraping chair from the study reminded her that Carter was still waiting for her.

"How was your call?" Carter asked as Katie stepped into the study.

Katie took a deep breath. She owed him the truth.

"I was just on the phone with the director of robotics distribution. He's sending some people to come get you tomorrow."

"I know," Carter said. "I heard everything."

Katie nodded. She half-expected that he would listen in. "I think that—"

"They're going to kill me?" Carter said. A smile played at the corners of his lips.

"They're going to deactivate you, yes." Katie kept her eyes trained on the ground as she spoke, afraid to meet his gaze. "But, Carter, I didn't know until after I had told him. I mean, when I saw that most of the Aqua Generation information in our database was missing, I was confused, maybe even suspicious, but I was just doing my job. Nothing clicked for me until—"

"I know," Carter said again.

Katie frowned and returned to her seat. "How do you know?"

"Let's just say that, after forty years of serving under humans, watching their expressions and listening to their tones of voice, I've become skilled at seeing the emotions under the skin."

Katie couldn't believe it. Despite the wires and systems under his synthetic skin, Carter could feel. He couldn't be anything but human.

Carter cocked his head to one side and said, "You looked rattled when you came back, whereas before you left, you were full of excitement, like you had just bought a pair of shoes for fifty percent off."

Katie chuckled, the noise echoing off the walls of the study. "That would be my mother, not me," she said. "She's always going after the bargains."

"That she is."

Katie nodded. "Well, Carter . . ." She paused as she stared into Carter's eyes. Were they the windows to an internal computer? Did he even have a soul?

She decided to give him the benefit of the doubt and said, "You should leave. I'll just tell them that you heard me talking on the phone and decided to escape."

Carter frowned. "Escape? Save myself?"

"That's right. They'll be here in the morning. That gives you at least four hours to disappear."

A few seconds passed before Carter shook his head and said, "No. I can't."

Katie didn't understand. "What do you mean, you can't? Of course you can, Carter. It's a human instinct—it's called self-preservation. They're going to demolish you."

"I can't leave," Carter said. "Don't bother asking me why. Every part of me is pushing me to run." He looked down at his lap. "But something inside of me tells me that I *can't*."

"Oh, my God." Katie took a few steps, jolted by the shock he had delivered to her. "Oh, my God." The surprises wouldn't stop coming.

"What?"

"You're so humanistic, in every way," she said. "But you don't possess the basic instinct of self-preservation."

Carter chuckled nervously and leaned back in his seat. He sounded scared, and with good reason. "Sucks for me."

An awkward moment of silence passed.

"Well, I'm going to go to—" Katie smiled, not knowing what to say. "I have to wake up my mom and tell her—" She stopped. She didn't know what she was going to tell her mother, though the truth itself would be cumbersome enough to grasp.

"I'm going to be gone by morning," Carter said as Katie stood up from her seat.

Katie paused.

"Do you think we could chat?" Carter looked up at her with his pleading human eyes. "I know that I haven't been the nicest little house slave, but—indulge me? Grant a robot's dying wish."

Katie fought back a smile and thought about his request. She had just been responsible for sending an innocent being to his death. The least she could do was sacrifice a few hours of her time.

"What do you want to chat about?"

Carter shrugged. "Human things. Human life."

"That's a pretty broad topic."

"Then let's narrow it down." He gestured at the study door, though his eyes never left Katie's. "Why are you so wary to see your mother?"

Katie forced out a laugh and said, "I'm not *wary*. I'm just—" She stopped herself. Why bother keeping up this pretense? She was talking to something that would be silenced by tomorrow morning. "Yeah, my mother and I, we don't get along."

"And why's that?"

Katie sighed. "Different values, I guess. She emigrated from China when I was still in the womb, so that I could be a citizen of this country. And she's always dangled that 'sacrifice' in front of me, pushing me to be the best. No, to be better than the best."

Carter smiled and said, "I've never had a mother, but I think that all mothers want the best for their daughters. Their worst fear is seeing their daughters follow the same path that they did."

"Yeah." Carter was right on the money with that statement. "But I don't know. Her priorities in life are different from mine. You see, my dad left us when I was three—"

"I know. Nina told me."

"Right. Well, my mother's always told me that love is overrated. When finding a husband, security is the most important." Katie shook her head and looked out the window behind Carter.

Raindrops pitter-pattered against the glass, cutting through the silence of the night.

"Mom always said that every type of love in this world is just a reflection of self-love," she continued. "If you love yourself, you won't need the love of others."

"Then what about your boy toy, sleeping in the other room over there?" Carter asked. "Are you in love with him?"

Katie opened her mouth to say "Yes," because when someone asks you a question like that, the answer is so obvious that it's almost a reflex.

But this time Katie paused. Stopped.

Seconds ticked by.

And then she asked, "What's your definition of love?"

Carter chuckled and shook his head. "If you have ever been in love, you wouldn't need someone else to define it for you."

The words stabbed into Katie's chest, planting pain like fire. "How would you know that?" she shot back. "Don't tell me that you've been in love before."

Carter snorted. "No, I've never been in love, nor have I ever *been* loved. People don't love pieces of machinery. They kick you around and abuse you, knowing that if you break down and cease to perform, they can take you down to the shop and replace you."

Katie said nothing and looked down at her hands, folded across her lap.

"Anyway, enough about me," Carter said. "Tell me more about you."

Katie blinked away the tears clouding her eyes and said, "What do you want to know?"

Carter shrugged. "Tell me why you wanted to go in robotic diagnostics. The guy who examined me thirty years ago treated psychological examinations like a job, something that would pay the bills and feed his family.

But you . . ." He moved his seat closer. "But you have a passion for robotics. You were so determined, even desperate, to seek out humanistic traits in me. Why?"

Katie smiled through the bitterness mushrooming in her heart. "I grew up as an outsider," she said. "It's not that the other kids didn't accept me. I always had a lot of friends. But my mother, she never let me get too close with anybody. There were no such things as sleepovers, birthday parties, and after-school activities. So, when I was little, I had no such thing as a best friend to tell all my secrets to. As I grew older and more rebellious, this changed, but—" She swallowed the lump in her throat and continued. "I've never forgotten what it was like to be on the outside looking in, desperately wanting to break the glass between me and the people I wanted to be."

Carter nodded. "And so, by analyzing the psychological awareness of robots—"

"I wanted to break the glass between robots and human society," Katie said. "I thought, if I could find a robot that was so humanistic that he was no different from a real human—"

She had to laugh at herself, realizing that voicing her thoughts out loud sounded even more stupid than it seemed inside her head.

"I don't know. Maybe then I would feel like I achieved something, like I've helped someone else break the barrier."

The more she talked, the more things she revealed about herself, thoughts and ideas that she had been planning to take to the grave. As she spoke, Katie felt something inside her escape, little by little. As if the boulder that sat on her chest were eroding away.

As though, finally, everything was beginning to make sense.

*   *   *

The men came to the door before the sun even crept up.

"What is going on?" Nina demanded as she stepped out of her room, still dressed in her pajamas.

Katie, Charles, and Carter were already standing at the front door.

"Katie, why are you all making all this racket at—" Nina stopped when her eyes fell upon the five other men in the room.

"You must be Ms. Huang's mother," one of the men said. He handed Nina a business card. His name was Ian Roberts. "We are with BioCorp's robotic collection division, here to pick up a certain robot. Carter, I believe?"

Before Nina had a chance to reply, Carter stepped forward and said, "That would be me."

Standing there, Katie felt her stomach twisting, turning.

"Now, hold on," Nina said, grabbing Carter by the arm as he walked toward the men. "Carter, where are you going?"

"We're taking him to the testing lab at BioCorp," Roberts said. "You see, Carter here has passed our robotic psychological examination and is now pending human status."

Nina looked confused. "I never submitted Carter for any examinations."

Roberts' pleasant smile faded. "Umm . . ." He looked from Nina to Katie.

"I gave Carter the psychological examination," Katie said. Her mother's eyes jumped to her. "I read a poem to him last night, just to see whether or not he could interpret it as a human could, and he passed."

"You gave him one of your nonsensical psychological examinations?" Nina exclaimed with a glare. "Why in the world—"

"Nina, it's okay," Carter interrupted. "I'm just going with these men down to the lab to get tested. I'll be back soon."

None of the men said anything, and Katie stood with her eyes glued to the ground, her heart racing with an unsteady beat of guilt and fear as Nina rounded on her again. "Katie, how could you?"

"Ma'am." Roberts stepped in between them, a sheet of paper in his hand. "This is the buyer's contract you signed in Indiana when you bought Carter, a little over three months ago. If you read the safety clause below, you'll see that BioCorp is perfectly within its rights to take possession of any robot, at any time, without giving a reason until BioCorp has kept the robot for more than twenty-four hours."

Nina's eyes scanned the paragraph. She said nothing afterwards.

"All right," Carter said, smiling. "I guess it's time for us to go."

Roberts nodded and motioned for the men behind him to file out.

As Carter placed his first foot out the door, he suddenly stopped and turned around.

"I almost forgot," he said, looking down at Li Bai's book of poems, still clutched at his side. He handed the book back to Katie. "Thank you."

Katie looked down at the book. "You can read this?" She had a hard time keeping her voice steady. "When did you finish?"

"While I was waiting for you to finish your phone call," Carter said. "It took a little longer, using the Internet to translate the Chinese, but I did finish. By the way, this Li Bai guy is a total cheese ball of emotions. I can see why you like him. You're both so much alike."

Katie tittered, pushing down the feelings that were convulsing inside her. It hurt. It was supposed to hurt.

"Oh, don't be so sad," Carter said. "You look as though someone just burned your favorite doll."

And with those words, he nodded to Roberts, standing a few paces in front of him. "I'm ready."

Katie called out, "Wait."

Carter stopped.

"Wait." She took a deep breath, examining Carter from head to toe. She wanted to remember him. She needed to.

We had it right the first time, she thought as she stared into Carter's eyes. *On the first try, we created a breed of robots that could feel, that could think.*

And the company, terrified of its own creation, was trying to erase all evidence of Aqua Generation robots having ever walked the Earth.

"This is murder," Katie blurted out. "You can't do this. Carter may not have a beating heart. He may not have blood streaming through his body like you and me. But his brain, the free-thinking system that BioCorp installed in him, tells him that he is human. He is *human.*"

She stepped forward and grabbed Carter by the arm. "And for this reason alone, I cannot let you haul him away and recycle his parts like a defective machine."

Silence blanketed the room for a moment, and then Roberts, standing beside Carter, spoke. "Ms. Huang, I'm not sure where you're getting these ideas. We are only taking the robot down to the lab for an extensive checkup, as you probably expected we would. You were the one who called in."

Katie had nothing to say. She clenched her teeth as tightly as she could, but the tears that she fought against eventually crept down her face.

"Hey, look, don't worry about me," Carter interjected.

All eyes in the room found their way to him.

The robot grabbed hold of both Katie's hands, looked

deep into her eyes and said, "Remember, don't live your life caring about the criticisms of others and changing yourself in order to realize dreams that weren't even your own. You'll lose sight of who you really are."

Feeling weak all over, Katie said, "What if it's already too late?"

Carter shook his head. "It's never too late," he said. "Because I see who you really are. I see you, trapped inside who you've become, waiting to burst out." He gave her hand a squeeze before letting go, stepping back. "So don't be afraid to laugh when something's funny. Don't be afraid to cry when you're hurt. But most important of all, don't be afraid to speak up if you're unhappy. Life's too short to be unhappy."

Though every part of her ached, Katie thought that the last impression she would give Carter should be covered with a smile.

Carter smiled back. "Everything will be all right."

The words froze Katie's heart.

Everything will be all right, she repeated. Her father had told her the same thing, on the night that he packed his bags and left.

She watched in silence as Carter and the men walked out the door, disappearing from sight. This time she made no attempt to stop them.

Bargains

Gabriela Lee

"SO how's the writing going?" Jeff asks me when we meet up for dinner. He's wearing that cute paisley button-down that we got from Levi's last week, and it fits him perfectly. I dig into my *nasi lemak* and assault the fried chicken.

"It's going," I answer between bites.

"So what's it about?" He laces his fingers together and rests his chin on top of them. A lock of hair falls straight across his eyes. He looks like a cross between one of the Four Flower guys and the Korean singer Rain. If he were straight, I'd totally go for him.

I thoughtfully chew on a spoonful of coconut rice. "You know what, I'm still thinking about it."

"You know what?" Jeff points his chopsticks at me. Bits of *hokkien mee* still cling to the bamboo surface. "We have less than a week here. You need to turn in that story when we get back. Amelia, you need to start cracking."

I nod and finish the rest of my food. It didn't taste as good anymore. "I know, I know. How's your progress?"

Jeff shrugs. "I'm done. Just giving myself a couple of days to breathe before editing."

I push my plate away and glare at him. "Come on then. I want to get back and have a few pages done before turning in for the night."

169

We walk out of the *kopitiam* and into the cool night. It's hovering between summer and the monsoon here, and the air seems heavy with the promise of a storm. We wander the bazaars of Temple Street in Chinatown, passing hawkers selling cheap knockoffs of Prada and Louis Vuitton, plastic toy cars, and display case perfumes by the dozen. Bright orange lanterns crisscross overhead, and there's the rising scent of cooking satay in the air. Jeff takes out his digital camera and starts snapping photos.

I wander off to a stall selling bright Thai silks, wondering if I should buy a bolt or two for my mother, when a flickering light catches my eye. I stop haggling with the stall owner and turn toward the light. It's there, dancing, right at the corner of my eye, like my own personal St. Elmo's fire. I walk toward the light, and realize that it's behind a barred door, with small windows cut out at the top. Intricate carvings slither in and out of the woodwork, seemingly alive. I can see scrolling clouds, dragons with curling whiskers, lotus flowers blossoming against the wood. I lift the heavy brass doorknocker and rap against the door.

"Come in," I hear a voice say.

The smell of camphor hits me as soon as I enter, and incense smoke surrounds me like invisible fingers ushering me inside. I feel as if I am walking onto a movie set, a fantasy Chinatown land, replete with stereotypical lacquer boxes against a scarlet-painted wall, handwoven straw baskets full of dried things that have no name, and carefully carved jade ornaments hanging on the wall. A fat golden Buddha sits on the counter, its carved face shining with good fortune. Wall scrolls depict delicately painted bald men, as white as a sheet, clad in ornately decorated robes of state as they ascend toward the top edge of the scroll, where presumably Heaven lies. There are myriad signs in Chinese calligraphy, none of which

I could read. They cover the entire top half of one wall, gilt-edged and framed, watching me as I make my way through the aisles.

"Hello," says the same voice. I turn around, and there is a little old lady standing behind me. She is wearing a yellow blazer and matching slacks, and her white hair is neatly tucked into a bun at the back of her head. She has the kind of face that you want to kiss, the one you want to start confessing all your secrets too, hoping that she will give you a kind word, a quiet benediction. "Welcome to my shop."

"It's very lovely." I am suddenly aware of my size, all five foot four inches of me, sweaty with the humidity from outside and smelling distinctly of charred meat. My cotton tank and shorts don't belong in this world. I have the sudden urge to take a bath in rose petals and sandalwood, and brush my hair a hundred strokes. "I'm sorry, but I didn't catch your name—"

"You may call me Auntie Wang," she says, moving past me and making her way behind the counter. She takes out a small set of weights, perfectly carved in miniature. A dragon curls up the middle pillar of the scales, its sapphire eyes glinting in the ruddy light. "Now then, my dear—Amelia, was it? What was it you wanted to buy?"

"I, ah—didn't want to buy anything. I just wanted to take a look." I don't recall giving her my name, but she looks at me, and her face crinkles into a soft smile, and I want to tell her *everything*. Then the door jangles again, and Jeff enters, slipping his lithe frame past the door, camera held out in front of him.

"Oh, there you are," he says amiably. He waves at Auntie Wang. "Hello!"

She nods and smiles, then turns back to me. Her face glows softly, like the full moon. "Now, where were we? Oh, yes, you wanted to purchase something."

Jeff joins me at the counter. "Buying souvenirs already? You can go shopping later. I want to go try some of that rose drink they have down at the corner."

I wave him away. "What can I buy here, Auntie Wang?" I hope my voice has a respectful tone in it. I'm so used to yelling at editors, and being yelled at in return, that the notion of respect hasn't quite sunk in.

She touches the tip of her nose with a wizened finger. "Ah, well, this shop, see, is full of cures for all kinds of ailments, of sicknesses here—"

She leans over and touches my forehead—"and here." Her fingernail brushes lightly over my heart.

"I can brew you a special tea that will make time stop, make it go forward and backwards. Or maybe an ointment to soothe a broken heart, hmm? Powder to make your mother stop asking you so many inappropriate questions. I can give you a jade charm for happiness, or money, or intelligence." She gives me another smile. "The only thing I cannot do is tell the future. That is best left to soothsayers, not medicine women."

Jeff lets out a laugh. "Seriously? Oh, God, come on Amelia. This woman is clearly off her rocker. We'd better get going." He moves away from the counter and toward the door.

I wave him on. "I'll meet you outside."

His face suddenly darkens. "Oh, God. Don't tell me you believe in this crap."

"For goodness sake, Jeff, just go."

I hear the door close behind Jeff, and once more we are alone in the shop. I turn back to Auntie Wang. "Are you pulling my leg?"

"All I say are true."

I take a deep breath. It wouldn't hurt, right? And besides, Singapore has great healthcare, the best in the region. If I get a stomach ache, at least I'm not in some backwater village in Laos, retching behind a banana tree.

"All right. I'd like to buy some inspiration for a story. I've been trying to write this damn thing for ages now, and whenever I see a blank page, I just—" I look back at all the hours wasted and wonder what the hell I was doing. "Well, you know what I mean."

She gives me a shrewd look, her lacquer-dark eyes narrowing. Then she turns her back on me and starts grabbing small glass jars arranged in shelves behind her. They look dead and old, and they smell of decay and age. Their labels, written in cramped calligraphy, are taped in the front, the ink already bleeding against the paper. I hear her muttering to herself as she mixes the compounds, grinding everything into a powder with her mortar and pestle. After a few moments, she turns to me and presents me with a small bag of powdered material that looked suspiciously like potting soil, tied neatly at the top with a piece of red thread.

"Steep this in boiling water for exactly three-quarters of an hour, then drink under the light of the full moon. You will find yourself in a frenzy, a . . . hmmm . . . a need to write." She wraps the bag in brown paper, stamped with what was probably the name of the store. "The effect lasts for twenty-four hours, so you must use it wisely."

"Thank you," I say, pulling my wallet out of my bag. "How much does it cost?"

"No." She gestures emphatically. "You pay me in a different way." Placing the paper-wrapped parcel on the weighing scales, she gives me a searching look. "Now then, inspiration is expensive to brew. So it is one of our most valuable items for sale. What do you think is the price for this?"

I stare at her blankly. *This must be a joke.*

She sees the look on my face and nods sagely. "I see.

You do not know the price. Go on then, and take this as a gift. I shall name my own price, and you will have to accept it." Suddenly, she doesn't look like my favorite grandmother anymore; she looks hard and mean, a woman of steel. I take my parcel and rush out the door, colliding with Jeff as I stumble out. He looks at me, half-pitying, half-mocking, and leads me away from the medicine shop.

I plug the electric pot into the socket and unwrap the paper packet. Upon closer inspection, it smells faintly of dried flowers. I shrug and place it in the hotel-provided coffee cup on top of the minibar and wait for the water to boil. I watch a couple of episodes of *How I Met Your Mother* on my laptop while waiting for 45 minutes.

We've been here for over three weeks now, researching and writing for a travel magazine. I didn't want the assignment at first—what with the break-up and the move and all. But Jeff was quite adamant that I get away from all "the negative energy," as he termed it, and our editor was probably more than happy to see me with more than one expression on my face (morose). But while the bracing Singapore heat was more than enough to burn Omar out of my mind, the writing was going nowhere.

The room begins to smell of air conditioning and lavender. I can't believe I was so critical of the scent earlier. I totter over to where the tea bag is steeping and discover that the water has turned golden, as if Midas himself had touched it. I take my cup, blow across the surface a couple of times, and walk over to the balcony window. Moonlight streams across the balcony and I slide open the glass and walk barefoot across the tiled floor. Everything seems tranquil and at peace. I take a sip of the tea, then another, and before I realize it, the entire cup is empty.

As the last drop touches my lips, I suddenly hear voices in my head. I clamp my hands over my ears, frightened, staggering back inside the hotel room. Over the babble, I could hear a sentence, a single sentence I could latch on like an anchor amidst the turbulent sea of sounds. I grab on to the sentence in my mind, a buoy to the harbor that was going to be my story, the ship that would take me to the promised land.

I sit in front of my laptop, pull up a blank page, and begin to write.

If someone had asked me when I was young what I wanted to be when I grew up, I would have answered "a marine biologist" or "a ship captain." But when I was twelve, my mother brought me to a book signing at a local bookstore, where her favorite author had come to visit. We stood in line, clutching hardbound copies of his latest novel, and listened as he came up to the microphone and read a chapter.

I remember sitting down on the carpeted floor as he spoke, allowing his voice to wrap around me like a warm blanket. Everything seemed to make sense when he spoke. He built everything into my mind—the way buildings rose and fell, the way the sun sparkled across an open sea, the way people fell in love. This was probably how serpents felt once their handlers started playing a commanding tune. I couldn't help but follow him, follow every word that came out of his mouth. And it was there and then that I decided, damn, I wanted to be a writer.

But even at school, I knew that there were others better than me. I could carry a pretty turn of phrase, an inspired page or two of writing. But it always felt as though someone deserved it more. I was no product of a broken family, and abuse was restricted to mean sales ladies and absentee boyfriends. My first experience with sex left me bored, wondering where the romanticism was in the act. I felt raw, unready, like a beanstalk that never had the chance to grow. The only time I felt the world made sense was when I was tucked into a corner of the sofa, my favorite shawl around my shoulders, sinking deep into another new book. But no matter how hard I tried, I could never do what that long-ago author did in the bookshop. I could never spin magic.

Until now.

"You look like shit," Jeff comments as soon as I walk into the Jasmine Lounge and slid into the seat in front of him. Against two walls, the buffet breakfast is spread out like a king's feast. "Watched too much TV again?"

"No," I say, trying to tamp down the defensive tone in my voice. I peer at him over the rim of my sunglasses. "I was writing."

He chokes back a laugh and pushes a cup of coffee in my direction. "Oh, really? Can I see it?"

I take a long drink out of the cup, ignoring the scalding heat as it burns down my throat. "No, because I sent it off to Alice already. She gets to be the first to read it." I shake my head to clear out the cobwebs. It seems only an hour ago that my face was reintroduced to the pillow.

"Wait a minute, wait a minute. You sent an unedited draft over to Alice?" He shakes his head. "You've got some balls, Melia. She's gonna have your hide for that."

Suddenly, my phone rings. I answer it before Lady Ga-Ga's voice amplifies over the heads of the hotel guests.

It's Alice, my editor. She says a few glowing things about my story, then casually mentions that they'll be submitting it to an awards committee for vetting. She thinks I have a good shot of winning.

I find that my mouth is dry, and my brain has suddenly run out of steam. I thank her and turn to Jeff. My look says it all.

"They're submitting it to the awards committee," he says quietly. "Am I right?"

I drain the coffee cup and nod, peering into the cup with one eye. "Dude, did you put sugar in this thing?"

"Yeah, two tablespoons. Stop changing the subject." He leans across the table and stares at me as though I'm some sort of science experiment he's trying to figure out. "You drank that thing the crazy lady gave you at the shop, didn't you? And you thought that would help you write better?"

"It *did* help me write!" I clutch my head in hands. There's the sound of distant drums pounding out an erratic rhythm in my head. I run my tongue across my lips, tasting—nothing. I bite my lips, sucking every last bit of coffee from the fleshy crevices. I can feel the liquid in my mouth, but there is no bitterness, no sweet tang of the dark liquid that I had so recently drunk.

I look up, frightened. I stumble over to the plates and pile my own with food. Rolls of bread, warm from the oven. Pats of butter. Pancakes, doused with maple syrup and topped with strawberries. Whirls of chocolate logs, Frosties in cold milk, cubes of bright red watermelons and honeydew and papaya.

Jeff gapes at my plate, slack-jawed, as I shovel food into my mouth. My tongue runs along each and every morsel of food, but there's nothing to taste. Nothing salty, or sweet, or even the faintest bitter aftertaste.

"What the hell are you doing?"

"That woman," I scream as I inhale food, "has done something to me and now I can't taste anything!"

Jeff grabs me by the arm and half pulls, half drags me away from the table. The other guests look at us as if we're crazy. Servers and waiters are poised to help Jeff, if needed. "Okay, that's it. We're out of here."

*   *   *

I stare at my face in the mirror. My eyes seem rimmed in shadows. They are shiny, bloodshot. There's a bright spot of color on my cheeks, as though I am out of breath, hyperventilating. *Everything will be all right.* None of it is logical, or rational, but deep down inside, I know—I know the price I paid for this.

The phone rings once more and I flip it open. It's Alice again, all the way from the home office. Everyone loves my story. I am on my way, a rising star in the literary world. I could do anything and everything. I thank her for the kind words. She asks me if I have anything else for her, something to cement my status as her new favorite. I stare at my fingers. I would give anything to be able to taste even a morsel of freshly baked bread again.

"She wants you to stay here?" Jeff asks incredulously.

We are sitting at a seafood restaurant along the Singapore River, and his hands are stained with chili sauce. The steaming *mantou* gleams in the yellow light, the crabs are still warm, tomato-red, streaked with egg white. I pick at my food, pushing the morsels around with my fork. I know I should eat something, but ever since this morning, my appetite seems to have decided to take a permanent vacation.

"Alice says that I should go around the region, let myself be inspired by the exotic locations and all that." I push a lock of hair away from my eyes and wave the hovering waitress away. "So I guess I'm staying here. She wants you to go back, though. Pronto. Says that she wants to see your work ASAP."

"Are you sure this isn't just more of that hocus pocus that old lady cooked up?"

"I wish it were. No, wait, scratch that. I don't even want to see her again."

And then there's that flickering light at the corner of my vision again. My heart starts pounding, cramming its way into my throat. I clench and unclench my fists, trying to tamp down the rising—panic? elation? excitement?—and wonder, irrationally, if I was really this ambitious, this crazy to even *believe* in this kind of shit.

"Hey, where are you going? Hey—Amelia, wait up! Hey!"

I feel as though I'm walking on air, floating from the pavement. Lights sparkle on the trees, reflecting against the water lie iridescent fishes, liquid fireflies. I pass by Indian maitre 'd's and Thai waitresses in tight cheongsams, British and Australian and American men all congregating around a giant TV in some pub, their beefy arms slung across a girl's hip or shoulder. I pass by knots of friends, couples holding hands, a family of four. I can hear Jeff running after me, but I reach the door of the shop first, tucked between an neon-lit club and a swanky uptown café. He reaches out to grab my shoulder, but I shrug him off, still buoyant, and close the door behind me.

Inside, the room is dark. Auntie Wang perches behind the counter, strangely luminescent. I approach her warily. There is a part of me wanting to ask for more, to always give more and more and more. I want to be, as that cartoon theme song goes, the very best. This is only the beginning. I see myself standing in front of a crowd of hundreds, thousands, waving copies of my books in the air. A whirlwind of daytime talk shows, book signings, framed awards, and honorary degrees. Children in Africa reading translations of my stories. I am offered a position at the United Nations. I can do anything—*anything* I can think of. I giggle, imagining what I would say to the Nobel Prize for Literature. This is a chance at making magic. This is a shot at living forever.

Auntie Wang looks at me slyly. "I see you've made up your mind."

"Name your price."

Auntie Wang looks at my thoughtfully. "Your sense of taste was sold at quite a high price. I can only imagine how the others will sell. However, I must caution you: Once a bargain is made, you can never go back."

I take a deep breath. "Look, whatever you did with your mumbo jumbo, it helped me write. And now I need more. In fact, I need everything you can give me to make sure that I'm the best."

"That is a steep request, and for that, you must pay a price that I do not think you can afford. Not even I would bargain my soul for such a paltry thing." She taps her finger against her chin. "However, I can make sure that you will never want for anything in this regard. But are you willing to pay?"

I drum my fingers against the glass surface of the counter. A part of me is trying to pull away, pretending this is a bad dream. I can go back home, go back to a normal job where Jeff constantly knows better, where he is the prize staff member and Alice is glaring at me over her morning coffee, wondering what she has done to be saddled with the likes of me. A place where I can enjoy a bagel with cream cheese, a bag of sour cream potato chips, where I can still taste butter melting on my lips, the salty tang of another's kiss. Where I am normal, where I am not special.

And then another thought takes over: a great black creature, serpentine, hissing angrily. How dare I even think for a moment that I would want to go back? How can I not take this chance at something more than what has been given to me? My mind is surrounded in a scarlet haze, rising like a fire, feeding on the dreams I've had since I was twelve.

I can be special, I tell myself.

The other voice is now feeble and weak, a dissonant tone. I push it away, lock it behind an iron door. The creature flashes a sharp-toothed grin and coils around the space inside my mind, pleased, replete.

Auntie Wang looks at me as though she is satisfied. "Very well. I will make this for you. But after this, you will never see me again."

I nod and smile. "Thank you."

I hobble onto the stage, carefully navigating the steps. My nurse, Maris, holds my hand, but I cannot feel her grip. Five steps to the podium, and shakingly, I turn and hear tumultuous applause. I wish I could see them, but this is the price you pay for greatness.

Once the speech is done and the theatrics of another university commencement are over, I tell my nurse to drive me back to the hotel. We are in Zurich today, and in two days, my agent tells me, we are off to Madrid, then home for a week. I am tired, and my feet are probably swollen once more. Old age is a burden more than anything else, and if I knew what I had bargained for over forty years ago, I would have included perennial youth as well. However, given popular culture, I probably would have been accused of being a vampire—or worse.

I hear the car stop and wait for the door to open. Maris clucks at me in sympathy; I must take my medicines, take a nap, get ready for the evening. There's a publishers' dinner at eight, and they're awarding me some other plaque for my achievements—in other words, for lining their pockets with money. I shuffle in the direction she leads me, feeling the weariness with each heavy step. Even though I cannot tell soft from rough anymore and do not care whether or not I am wearing perfume from Germany or France, I know, in my bones, that I am tired.

This is not what I wanted. This is not what I dreamed of. There is no magic in this.

"Madam, we need to take off your shoes." I encounter an obstruction and realize that it is the hotel bed. Maris lifts my feet, and I find myself horizontal, sinking against a rise of pillows and sheets. I wave Maris away and close my eyes. I am in a gray fog, surrounded by shadows of things I used to know. All the stories in my mind have faded, receded back to unmappable shores.

They tell me I have made my mark on literature. Critics say that I was Helen Keller returned from the dead, that I am the most important writer of my generation. I do not tell them that marks can be erased, that another will take my place, that I am already dead.

I grasp the sheets underneath my fingers, wondering if they are made of Egyptian cotton or combed wool. I am incapable of luxuriating in sensation anymore; everything is dead and dull, cauterized by a wish made forty years ago. Everything returns to that place: the scarlet walls, the smell of camphor and incense smoke, jade stones polished until they stare at you, wide-eyed and waiting. I remember the taste of the golden tea, as though it came from some fabulous tale, and the frightening need to be something more than myself. I wish I could go back. I wish I could tell myself, my younger half, something about the world, about the choices she made, the choices she is making. But don't we all wish for something like that?

There is a flickering light at the corner of my eye. I wonder, irrationally, if Maris has left a candle lit somewhere in the room. I have never seen light since I wrote my third book—that was the one that won the PEN Faulkner award. I can smell camphor in the room, and sandalwood burning. Slowly, I get up from the bed and walk carefully to the source of light. Somehow, the world is getting brighter, moving into focus, like a camera lens being adjusted by careful fingers. I wonder if this is hell, if I am being punished for my bargain with the devil.

There is a wooden door in front of me, carved in familiar markings. Here is the dragon, the lotus flowers, the clouds of heaven. I run my fingers across their raised relief, marveling at the smooth, polished texture of the wood. I lift the heavy brass knocker and announce myself. The door opens and I step inside.

Auntie Wang sits at the edge of the counter, sipping a cup of tea. Her ornate golden scales are in front of her. I navigate through the bales of dried items and stacks of lacquered boxes and stand in front of her. Her jade necklace shimmers around her neck.

"Hello, Amelia," she says to me, smiling. "Did you enjoy yourself?"

"'Enjoy' is probably not the right word." I look at her regretfully. "Why are you here again? I thought I would never see you again."

"Well, we have one last bargain to make. I remember what you asked for earlier: a chance to tell yourself about the decisions you made, was it?"

"I thought you said you can't go into the future."

Auntie Wang puts her cup down. "This is not about the future, but the past. But are you ready to pay the price?"

I look at her and see the road stretched out behind me. The loss of family and friends. The loss of feeling, of scent, of sight. I would turn back the hands of time, gladly, for a chance to tell myself that happiness is not on this road, that it is elsewhere, somewhere, but not here. "What is your price?"

She leans over and whispers into my ear.

A chill runs down my spine. But yes—I will do this. For myself.

I can feel her outside. She has found the door. "Come in," I say.

She is small and slight, her hair held back by a piece of

cloth. She is every inch the tourist: young and carefree, ready to take on the world. But I can see the sadness in her eyes, the need to be somewhere else, someone else, other than herself.

"Hello," I greet her. "Welcome to my shop."

Threes

E.L. Chen

"**Y**OUR mother is the ocean," Dad said when I first asked him about her.

Is. Not *was.*

Later, when I told Em-n-Jen, they said I was lying. Our mother wasn't the ocean because she was dead-dead-dead in a box deep beneath the earth, and even though the coffin had been closed during the funeral, they knew she was in there because everyone had said so. I was only four, but I knew then that Em-n-Jen would always take someone else's word over Dad's.

A month ago there had been children playing on this street. There had always been kids playing road hockey along this stretch in the summer. Em-n-Jen and I used to play ourselves. Em had actually been a pretty good goalie until she discovered boys. Now all the children were indoors, playing video games or surfing the internet or watching TV. They didn't care about what was happening as long as their parents weren't yelling at them to get off the couch and play outside.

I braked slightly when I saw white figures in the distance, shimmering under the heat. A clean-up crew wearing surgical masks and latex gloves picked star-lings off the pavement. The city said that the birds that

185

didn't survive the fall were being brought to University of Toronto for tests. But so far nothing conclusive had come back.

I almost expected the workers to shout "Car!" and scatter as I rolled by, but they lined the curb and waited indifferently for me to pass. It was just another street in another Toronto neighborhood and another flock of birds that had given up on flying.

Most houses in the Beach neighborhood were too old to have garages, only makeshift driveways at the owner's discretion. The antiquated family station wagon sat out front, so I found a spot on the street. When I turned off the ignition, even inside the car I could hear a dull drone from the backyard. I climbed out. The summer air slapped me in the face like a wool blanket, thick and hot and suffocating.

I drew an umbrella out of the trunk and opened it over my head. The gate to the backyard was unlatched, so I walked through without ringing the front doorbell. Something small bounced against the side of my umbrella and fell to the ground with a soft *thunk*. I didn't look. There was nothing I could do anyway.

Dad was maneuvering a piece of plywood through a table saw. I stood back, not wanting to surprise him. The backyard was even narrower now that he had turned it into a workshop. The patio furniture had been moved to one side, the chairs stacked, and the table strewn with power tools. A carpet of sawdust covered the patio stones.

After a few minutes he turned off the saw and peered at the wood from behind dusty goggles. "Hi, Sara," he said without looking up. "Come inside."

He slid open the screen door to the kitchen. I ducked inside and closed the umbrella. He followed. "What's wrong now?" he asked.

"The neighbors are complaining," I said. "You're

using power tools twelve hours a day when everyone's supposed to keep the A/C off to save energy."

Dad pushed the goggles up his face. A sheen of dirt and dust dulled his ruddy cheeks. "Who's complaining? Mrs. Weller? The Kims?"

"I don't know. Em-n-Jen just said that the neighbors were complaining about you."

"Then why didn't Emily and Jennifer tell me themselves?"

My eyes flickered to one of the photos on the fridge. The colors had faded under the sun, but my father was still resplendent in his family's tartan, and my mother willow-slender in a red cheongsam patterned with gold curlicues that resembled waves. *She barely spoke English when we met,* he'd told me once, *but we understood each other perfectly.*

When one looked closely at the pattern, one could make out dragons peeking out from beneath the waves. I knew this because Dad had given me the dress last year on my twentieth birthday. "Don't tell your sisters," he'd said, not because they would be jealous but because they would think it strange that he'd hung onto our mother's wedding dress after all these years.

The dress smelled like sand and surf. They were married on the beach where they'd met, the beach that would one day swallow up my mother and spit her out on its shore.

"He has fewer memories of you with *her,*" Em had said once, and only once, as it was the kind of statement that resonates for a lifetime. We had both been very drunk and very bitter at the time, she because I was Dad's favorite, and I because she and Jen believed that I was.

Dad shook his head and slipped back outside. I was always surprised that he was on speaking terms with any of us. *My little changelings*, he used to call us when we were kids. It certainly must have seemed that way to him. How could a ginger-haired giant of a man have spawned three pale and almond-eyed little girls?

As a child I'd always thought of Em-n-Jen and myself as being princesses, as in the stories I read. Fairy-tale princesses always came in threes. They never had mothers, and the youngest was always the king's favorite.

"What are you building?" I shouted from the doorway as he fired up the table saw again.

"A boat," he said.

"What do you need a boat for?" I shouted. To my knowledge, he'd never even been on the ferry to Centre Island.

"To take me to your mother," he said.

"He's crazy," Jen said.

"He's always been crazy," Em said, "but it's gotten worse since you moved out."

As if it were my fault. Next they would divide up Dad's property, and I'd be married off to the King of France, as if we were a dysfunctional family of Shakespearean proportions.

"He thinks Mom was a Chinese dragon," Em said.

"He thinks Mom was a shape shifting water-spirit," Jen said.

"Because that's how they met, and that's how she died."

"By water. Oh my God!"

Jen jerked back in her seat as a seagull tore through the awning and smacked onto the table. The bird's wings spread and flapped, their tips grazing Em's shoulder. She shrieked.

The seagull staggered to its feet, snatched a heel of garlic bread, and hopped to the ground. "Get lost!" Jen snapped, kicking at it. The bird flapped its wings again but did not fly away.

A gaggle of apologetic waiters rushed us inside. "I told you the patio wasn't a good idea," Jen said to me.

"I thought there weren't any birds left in the sky," I shouted over the whirr of a ceiling fan. The A/C ban was in full effect for businesses as well as residences.

"Christ. This bird thing is nuts," Em said.

"I bet it's because of climate change," Jen said.

Em nodded. "Yeah. You have to wonder, what's next? The oceans rise? The dead walk?"

"You're right," I said. "Everything always happens in threes."

"That's silly," Jen said.

"Is it?" I said. "Look at us."

Kalman wasn't home when I turned the key in the lock. There was little respite from the heat in the apartment, although it did smell better, humid and clean like the inside of a laundromat. I flicked on the electric fan by the window; the old high-rise wasn't air conditioned, so the energy ban made little difference.

I took my phone out of my purse. No texts, no messages. I felt a slight pang, and then guilt. Of course Kalman was working late again. The lab where he was a grad student was running twenty-four hours now, cataloging dead birds.

I stripped down to my underthings and tossed my sweaty clothes on top of my open suitcase. I still hadn't finished unpacking from the move, mainly because there was nowhere to put my things in Kalman's tiny apartment. I turned on the TV. I could barely hear it over the fan, but I didn't care. I only wanted to make the apartment feel less lonely.

As I rummaged through my suitcase for a clean shirt, my hands touched cool silk. I don't know why I had packed my mother's dress—perhaps to bring me luck with Kalman or to keep it out of Em-n-Jen's clutches. I

drew it out. As my arms swept through the path of the
fan, the scent of sun-warmed salt water wafted toward
me. I liked to think it was what my mother had smelled
like. I pictured my father curling up every night behind
her in bed, putting his lips to her glossy black hair and
imagining they were on a beach, lying under the sun.

I'd shown the dress to Kalman the night after I had
moved in. He'd snorted as if he had wanted to laugh but
was holding it in. "That's going to make you look like a
Thai hooker." I hadn't brought it out since.

Although it had been folded haphazardly, there were
no wrinkles, only ripples in the fabric as I shook it out.
The silk was the rich poppy-red that traditional Chinese
brides wear. A pattern of waves was embroidered across
the silk in gold thread, and when I looked out of the corner of my eye I could see a claw here, a whisker there, a
patch of scales.

I had never tried it on before. I had expected it to
be too tight; I had inherited some of Dad's height despite having my mother's small bones. But the high neck
slipped easily over my head and the long, slim skirt cas-
caded over my hips like a waterfall.

I looked in the bathroom mirror. I didn't know what I
had hoped to see, but I didn't see my mother. I only saw
myself wearing her dress. She was still a mystery. Was
she a dragon, as Dad imagined? To me, she might as well
have been a mythical creature, patched together from
his and Em-n-Jen's memories.

Kalman had been somewhat right, though. The dress
did make me look more Asian. It was odd to see this
variation of myself, one who was my mother's daughter
instead of having been born a changeling to a tall, sad,
ginger-haired man.

The silk's light touch was comforting against my skin.
I stretched out on the bed and dreamed of birds falling
into a black, turbulent sea.

*   *   *

I woke to my phone buzzing beside me on the bed. The apartment was dark and had cooled down. The TV was showing an infomercial. Kalman still wasn't home.

The call was from Em's cell. "Hello?" I said.

"You have to come over."

I pulled the phone from my ear and blinked at the display. It was 4:30 in the morning. "What's wrong? Is Dad okay?" I tried to scramble to a sitting position, and then realized I was sheathed in red silk.

"He's fine. Except this time he's really lost it. Jen and I can't get through to him."

I rubbed my eyes. "Can't you put him on the phone?"

"He won't come inside, and you know how he feels about cell phones."

"Is that Sara?" I heard Jen say in the background. There was a fumbling sound as Em handed her the phone.

"Get over here right now," Jen snapped.

I sighed. "Give me ten minutes."

Em-n-Jen didn't even say goodbye. The connection ended, and I glanced again at my phone's display. There were still no messages from Kalman. I called him and got his voicemail. I didn't know what to say, so I hung up. His cell would show that I had called anyhow.

I took off my mother's dress and folded it back into the suitcase.

Em opened the door as soon as I hopped up the front steps. The station wagon was parked in the street. In its place on the driveway sat what looked like a triangular frame with wheels.

"Thank God you're here," Em said.

"Are the neighbors complaining again?" I asked.

"No, but I'm sure they're going to call the cops any

minute," she said, and as if on cue, a power tool roared to life in the backyard. "He's been at it all night."

"I had a date," Jen said, emerging from the family room. She nearly spat out the words. "I'd been trying to get Jeremy from IT to ask me out for weeks. You should have seen his face when he dropped me off. Dad was putting out the trash. He looked—well, he looked like Dad. You better talk to him, Sara."

Jeremy had probably been appalled that Jen was still living with her father. But I said nothing, and hurried through the kitchen into the backyard.

"Oh good," Dad said when he saw me. "You can help."

There was something large and wedge-shaped propped up on the sawhorses. It looked like a child's idea of what a boat should be, like a bathtub with a side that came together in a point. "I need you to help me take this out front and put it on the trailer. Then we're going to go down to the beach."

I glanced back at the kitchen doorway. Em-n-Jen looked as if they were trying to bore holes in the boat with their eyes.

"I want to see if it floats," he said.

"Dad," I said, "Em-n-Jen are mad about the noise." And about being known as the women with the crazy father.

"Why?" He stopped. He'd asked it before. *Why don't they tell me themselves?*

I shrugged and said, "I'm the youngest. It's my job to tell you the truth." Like in fairy tales, when the youngest princess tells her father she loves him more than salt. "What do you want me to do?" I looked back again at Em-n-Jen. Em's lips were tight; Jen's arms, crossed. They closed the door.

The boat wasn't as heavy as it looked, but it was bulky, and it took us a while to maneuver it along the side of the house to the driveway. Pushing it down the street on the

trailer was easier; our street sloped slightly downhill toward Queen Street, and at that hour there was little resi-
dential traffic. As we crossed Queen, the people sitting in
the few cars on the road didn't give us a second glance;
we were heading toward Beaches Park, and never mind
that people rarely ventured into the water.

I remembered the park being dense and shady, but
the heat wave had browned the grass and shriveled the
leaves on the magnificent old trees that normally shel-
tered the path to the beach. At this hour it was eerily
quiet without birdsong to greet the dawn. The wheels
of the trailer, although well-oiled, grated my ears as it
trundled along the pavement. After a few minutes, the
sight of blue-green water broke out from behind the
tree trunks. I squinted from the brightness.

I smelled the fish first.

Then I heard them: an arrhythmic slapping, like a flag
whipping in the wind. The paved path ended in a bank
of sand, and I saw that the water's edge was a flicker of
olive and gold and silver. A ribbon of fish gasped and
flopped their way up over sand and pebbles. A handful of seagulls stepped over them, pecking and snapping
and flapping their wings to keep their balance as they
feasted.

"Dad, I think we should go back." I wanted to leave
the boat, run back to the house, and turn on the TV to
see if this were happening elsewhere in the city. Like the
falling birds, I suspected it was.

"It's okay, Sara. Everything is going to be okay." He
smiled, but he looked at the beach and not at me. "You
know, this is where your mother and I were married."

"Dad, you were married in B.C." On the salty, frothy
edge of the Pacific, not the calm, cold waters of Lake
Ontario.

He shrugged. "All beaches are the same. A place between land and water. That's where we were married."

I wasn't the youngest fairy-tale princess after all. I was the Fool, guiding King Lear through his delusions as he wandered madly over the moors. "Sure, Dad. Whatever."

"We'll stop here," he said. "We won't be able to get the trailer over the boardwalk. Take this end and we'll get the boat down to the water."

"Shouldn't we try to help the fish? Or call someone? I've got my cell—"

He said, "Don't worry about the fish. It means she knows we're coming."

"Who knows we're coming?" I asked, although as soon as I said it, I knew who he'd meant.

That night Kalman stumbled back to the apartment, exhausted after having spent forty-eight hours in the lab. "You smell like fish," was the first thing he said before heading straight to the shower. Afterward he crawled under the sheets without bothering to put clean clothes on. He was too tired to do anything but kiss me on the cheek.

I lay in his arms and watched the news. Fish had washed up everywhere in the city: sweeping over the shores of the Toronto Islands, leaping onto the docks at Harbourfront, bordering every inch of land around Lake Ontario. The only upside was that there had been no more reports of falling birds.

Every channel paraded out its experts. "He doesn't know shit," Kalman said, gesturing at the U of T professor who was currently on screen, reassuring the public that the drinking water was still fine. "He never comes by the lab. My supervisor is the one doing all the research, and even she can't figure out what's going on. Nothing is wrong with those birds. It's as if they all decided to give up on flying at once. It's probably the same with the fish."

"First the birds, then the fish," I said. "And then there'll be something else. It's going to happen in threes, I know it."

Kalman raised his eyebrows. "I didn't know you were superstitious."

"It's not superstition," I protested. "Threes repeat themselves through history and myth. It's ingrained in us. You know, like Roman triumvirates, religious trinities, Three Wise Men, Three Fates, Three Graces—"

Kalman laughed. "Things happen in threes because humans have bad memories and short attention spans. *Who's been sleeping in my bed?*" he said in a mocking, high-pitched voice. "It's a storytelling device from the oral tradition. The second event reinforces the first. And then the third comes along and changes things. The third event is the punchline."

"But—" I said, pulling away from him. "Birds falling from the sky. Fish coming out of the water. Next up should be land. It's like an earth trinity."

He snorted. "Next up could be locusts and the death of first-born children, for all we know. Come on, Sara. You have to stop seeing patterns in everything. You might as well point out that the Earth is the third planet from the sun and that pi makes the world go round. Have you been reading Joseph Campbell again?"

"No," I lied.

He crawled out of bed and padded to the bathroom. I was struck by how distant he was, even though he was only one bachelor apartment-length away, urinating with the door open, his backside bare. We were intimate without being intimate.

"Kal," I said.

"Yeah."

"What's my greatest regret?"

He flushed the toilet but didn't leave the bathroom. He turned to look at me, standing naked in the doorway. "I don't know. That you didn't try to get into that Women in Shakespeare course last year?"

"No, that's not it," I said, more to myself than to him.

"Well?" he said.

"Well what?"

"What's your greatest regret?"

"I—oh, never mind," I said, saddened. I didn't know either. I had expected him to know me better than I knew myself, but he didn't.

"Dad," I said. "Kal and I broke up. I need to move back here for a little while."

He nodded and said nothing. Not that he was trying to repress the *I told you it wouldn't work out* that Em-n-Jen would tell me later, but because he really had nothing to say.

"There's leftover pizza in the fridge if you're hungry," he finally said, opening the sliding door to the backyard.

I lugged my suitcase up the stairs and entered my old room. Jen was turning it into a home gym, but I rolled up the yoga mat and tucked it behind the treadmill she'd set up.

I closed the door, sank on the bed, and cried for ten minutes.

When it was over, I dried my eyes on the pillowcase. I unzipped my suitcase and found a fresh T-shirt to change into. I was sticky from the day of packing. I had wanted to leave before Kalman got home. I hadn't called because I hadn't wanted to bother him at the lab. He was busy with something that was bigger than the two of us.

Downstairs, Em was sitting at the kitchen table, flipping through a fashion magazine. Half a bottle of red wine and an empty glass stood by her elbow.

"So you're back," she said. "The Galbraith sisters ride again."

"Things weren't working out with Kal," I said.

"Join the club." She got up and grabbed another glass from the cabinet. I held out my hand in protest, but she poured wine for us both anyway.

"I'm going to look for a new place soon." I opened the fridge. It was empty. Either Dad had been wrong about the food, or Em-n-Jen had polished it off. "I'd like to be back downtown when classes start."

"That's what Jen's been saying for the past eight months. Face it, Sara. You're not going anywhere until you find another boyfriend, and when you do, you'll screw it up like you did with Kevin."

"Kalman," I said.

"Whatever." She waved her hand at me. She was still wearing the diamond Mark had given her even though she'd signed the divorce papers last month.

"And I didn't—" I started. But I *had* screwed it up. I'd stupidly believed that he knew me. "Isn't there anything to eat in this house?"

"No." Em handed me the second glass of wine. This time I took it. It was warm and sour. I drank it anyway.

"It's all Mom and Dad's fault," she continued.

"For what?"

"My divorce," she said. "Your breakup. Jen's parade of bad dates. I swear she came back home because she'd dated everyone in Calgary and still couldn't find a boyfriend."

"Don't say that," I said, although I knew she was right. There'd been more opportunity at Jen's company out west, and yet she'd transferred back to the Toronto office.

"I guess knowing what Mom and Dad had," I said, "it's hard to find anything that compares."

"What are you talking about?"

"Mom and Dad had this great romance, you know? It's set our expectations too high."

Em stared at me, and then she laughed. She sounded like Kalman had last night. "Oh, come on. You don't believe—"

"They really understood each other, even though English wasn't her first—"

"Mom being from China meant Dad could think whatever he wanted about her. Get it through your head, Sara. Mom wasn't the saint you think she was. You never knew—"

"But they really loved each other, and then she—"

"They found her off the coast of B.C.," Em shouted. "British freaking Columbia. What the hell was she doing all the way out there?"

"I thought she was visiting family when she died," I said in a small voice.

"Mom had no family in Canada," she said. "She *left* us. She ran off with someone, and Dad loved her too much to believe that she could leave. He thought she was special, but she was just stupid and crazy. Like him."

I slapped her. I think I shocked myself more than her. She didn't even flinch. She just looked at me with scorn. "Oh, grow up," she said. "Mom was cheating on him for as long as I can remember. She would slip out at night when she thought we were asleep. I'd see her running down the stairs like she was an eighteen-year old meeting her prom date. Jen saw her too, once."

She rubbed her cheek absentmindedly, as if she'd forgotten already that I'd hit her. "One night I waited up for her to come home, and she told me that where she'd been was a secret, our secret that we could never tell Dad because it would make him sad."

Her mouth tightened as if a drawstring had been pulled through it, and I couldn't help thinking, *No wonder Mark walked out on her, if he'd had to live with that mouth.* "By the time I figured it out, she was dead and Dad was too crazy to listen to anyone.

"God," she said, suddenly sagging. "Dad was such a fool. He was totally blind. I mean, Mom would come back stinking like sand and saltwater. Even in winter. Her boyfriend must've had a boat and would meet her down at the beach."

"Em," I said, slowly, "Lake Ontario is a freshwater lake. Why would Mom smell like salt?"

Dad had moved the workbench and sawhorses off to one side. The boat perched on the trailer in the middle of the backyard, illuminated by a halogen work light. Dad sat inside the boat, his shoulders slumped.

I climbed up into the bow. As Dad had only built one seat, I sat on the floor facing him, knees pulled up to my chest. I felt as though we were sharing a large bathtub.

"I don't know why she doesn't come," he said. All the lines of his face drooped downward. He hadn't shaved in days.

"Dad," I said, "Em says that Mom was having an affair."

"And why would Em think that?"

"Mom would leave the house at night."

Dad smiled sadly. "Of course she did. She was going down to the beach. Your mother thought I didn't know, but I knew. That's why we moved here. She needed to be near water."

I thought of Em's words. *Dad was too crazy to listen to anyone.* But why had my mother smelled of salt? I shook my head. All I had were a child's memories and a widower's sorrow to go on. Neither was reliable.

He said, "She warned me that one day she would have to go back to her true form, that her family wouldn't allow her to live like this for long."

"Did you ever meet her family?" I asked.

"Once," he said. "When they came to the funeral. She said they lived far away in the most rural parts of China, but they came to the funeral without anyone inviting them. They were fine-boned, like her, and smelled like ocean salt and sandy wind. They burned incense and paper money and placed a small jade carving of a fish in her mouth. They brought a paper effigy of a boat, and instead of paper cars they brought paper dolphins and seagulls. They broke her comb in half and put one piece in her hand and gave the other to me."

It was the most I had ever heard Dad say at once. I didn't know whether to be touched or troubled. I'd never known he was capable of such eloquence.

I thought of Kalman and wondered if we were all strangers to each other no matter how hard we tried— and that was why my mother had been so special, so otherworldly. No matter what was true about her, she had made Dad feel less alone.

That night I dreamed I was a child again, playing down at the beach with Em-n-Jen. I ran out into the water, and when I looked up, my sisters were gone and I was alone.

"Mother," I cried out.

Frothy waves rolled up around my legs, each one larger than the last. All the colors of the ocean shimmered under the sun: blue and green and white, silver and copper and gold. The tide churned, and I saw shapes in the water: the little mermaid, resurrected from her sea form existence, the deadly kelpie tossing back its mane, a sinuous dragon clutching a pearl under its bearded chin.

The waves rose and enfolded me, and suddenly I was crying against the mother I had never known. She knelt in the water, her arms around me. Seaweed twined in her black hair.

"I don't want to be alone anymore," I sobbed.

"Hush," she said. Her voice was a whispered roar, as

if it were coming out of a seashell. "All you had to do was ask."

The ground shifted beneath my feet, and for a second I felt only terror. She stroked my hair. "It was bound to happen anyway. We were due to take back our children. This way, it is done with love instead of indifference. We will be one again, I promise."

She touched her clammy lips to my forehead. Something tumbled from her mouth. I caught it in my hand. It was a jade fish. I placed it under my tongue and tasted salt.

I woke to the sound of thunder.

"Finally," I heard Jen say from the bathroom. "Maybe now we'll get some relief from the heat."

I stumbled out of bed and downstairs to the kitchen. Dad was staring out at the backyard. Rainwater was spattering through the screen onto his socked feet. I closed the glass sliding door.

He turned to me. "What did you do?" His eyes were bright, feverish. "*What did you do?*"

"I called her back," I said.

He stared at me for a second and then pulled me into his arms. He hadn't hugged me since I was four, on the day of my mother's funeral. *Be good*, he'd said. Something hard and plastic had pressed into my shoulder. I realized now that it had been his half of my mother's comb that her family had given him. The tradition was that the pieces, as well as my parents, were to be reunited in the afterlife when he died.

"Thank you," he whispered, and I knew that he still had that half-comb and had been waiting, waiting so long for this.

A reporter and cameraman showed up on our doorstep the next morning. I'd already seen the images on the web:

a cell phone snap of a boat, floating out onto the rising levels of Lake Ontario under the thunderstorm. The boat was as awkward-looking as a child, dwarfed by the man sitting in it. But it didn't matter whether it was a proper vessel or not. It just had to float. For a little while.

I recognized the woman from the local news station. "Sara Galbraith?" she said. She struggled to keep a huge golf umbrella aloft, but her face was still wet with rain.

"Yes?"

"May I ask you a few questions? It's about your father, Andrew Galbraith."

"Sure."

The woman nodded at her companion, who turned on the camera and pointed it at me. "Miss Galbraith, what did your father hope to accomplish by this dangerous stunt?"

"I don't know," I lied. I looked past the woman at the street. The Kims and Mrs. Weller were standing on their respective front porches, peering toward us.

"Do you have any hope for his survival?"

"No." I knew he wasn't coming back.

"And how do you feel about this tragic event?"

I turned my attention back to the reporter at this last question. The cameraman shifted, ready to catch my response.

"I'm glad," I said, looking straight at the camera. "I'm glad he found what he was looking for. I'm glad I could be the one to give it to him. The water has taken him back. The water is taking us all back. The water, my mother. Everyone's mother."

The man turned the camera off. From upstairs, Jen yelled, "Who's at the door?"

"Just some people who want to talk to us about Dad," I yelled back.

"What's he done now?" she said, descending the stairs. I met her halfway and whispered, "Dad took his boat

onto the lake." Jen looked at the reporter waiting on ten-
terhooks for her reaction and made the connection that
something Very Bad and Newsworthy had happened.
Relief flashed briefly across her face like lightning, and
then tears welled in her eyes.

On the six o'clock news, you would have never known
that Andrew Galbraith had three daughters because
they only showed two. Em-n-Jen, like Regan and Gon-
eril, selling their father for the sake of good television.
"Ever since our mother died, he's been a little off."
Sniffle. "We didn't think he was any harm to himself."
Sob. The tragedy was that they'd had to live with him all
these years, not that he had drowned.

They repeated the footage again at 11. By that time
Em-n-Jen were hoarse from discussing arrangements
with Dad's relatives over the phone.

"You could help, you know," Em said, dropping a
phone book on the sofa beside me as I watched TV.
"Look for florists."

"There's no point," I said.

"It's time for you to grow up, Sara," Jen said. "Mom
and Dad are dead. You're nobody's little girl anymore."

*I don't want to be a grown-up if it means being like
you two. Who are the ones who keep running back to
Dad's house when their relationships don't work out?* I
remembered Kalman, and would have bitten my tongue
if I'd spoken aloud.

Anyway, they would understand when the time came,
when our mother took us back into her body.

Em rustled me awake the next morning. "The street's
flooding," she said. "The army's arriving soon to evacu-
ate the neighborhood. Pack what you can. I'm going to
wake up Jen."

I climbed out of bed and went to the closet. *The third*

comes along and changes things, Kalman had said. I took my mother's cheongsam off its hanger and put it on.

"Sara," Em snapped as I descended the stairs. "Sara! Where are you going?"

I opened the front door. Angry black clouds blotted out the sky. Rain slammed into the ground like gunshots. My hair whipped around my face. A thunderclap shattered over the house, and I thought I saw a golden, serpentine shape twined in the clouds. But it might only have been lightning. Behind me, I heard Em shriek and Jen swear at the sudden noise.

The storm drains had overflowed. A sheet of rainwater crept up the pavement, carrying dead leaves and fish and sparrows. The lines between land, sky, and water were blurring in streaks of falling rain.

I sat on the front steps in my mother's dress, waiting for the punchline.

The Son of Heaven

Eric Choi

*T*SIEN *Hsue-shen was born in 1911, in the last weeks of Chinese imperial history, and at twenty-three he traveled to the U.S. to study aeronautical engineering at the Massachusetts Institute of Technology. Preferring theory to the practice that MIT then emphasized, he soon moved to Caltech and began to follow a path that would lead to his becoming one of the most eminent rocket scientists in the U.S.*

—Aviation Week & Space Technology
2007 Person of the Year

Pasadena, California
September 7, 1950

They came for him in the late afternoon.

The two agents from the Immigration and Naturalization Service strode up the walk to the small one-storey redwood clapboard and brick house at the end of East Buena Loma Court. Arriving at the front door, one of the agents knocked.

Jiang Ying opened the door, her baby daughter Yung-jen in her arms.

"Is this the Tsien residence?"

"Yes."

The agents flashed identification. One produced a piece of paper.

"We have a warrant for the arrest of Mr. H.S. Tsien."

Jiang Ying silently stepped aside. The baby began to cry.

The INS agents entered the house and surveyed the small, sparsely furnished living room. In the corner, at the foot of a bookshelf, two-year-old Yucon cowered, his eyes wide.

"Mr. Tsien!"

Tsien Hsue-shen appeared, his expression resigned. His hands were clasped over his stomach, as if nursing a wound.

"Please come with us."

Shanghai, China
August 1935

As the steamship *President Jackson* pulled away from dock, Tsien watched the crowd at the pier recede into the distance. Tsien Chia-chih, his father, and Chang Langdran, his mother, were still waving. The name they had given him, Hsue-shen, meant "study to be wise," reflecting all the hopes they had for him.

The *Jackson* turned for open water, picking up speed. Tsien took a deep breath and thought about the irony of his good fortune: His post-graduate education in America was made possible by a conflict between China and the United States.

Under the terms of the 1901 peace treaty following the Boxer Rebellion, the victorious foreign powers imposed reparations against China. But the American share of the indemnity turned out to be twice the amount of actual U.S. claims. President Theodore Roosevelt decided to return the surplus by establishing the Boxer Rebellion Indemnity Scholarship, allowing the best and brightest Chinese students to study in the United States.

Tsien looked out to sea, to the new ocean before him.

California Institute of Technology
March 1937

"... and the older woman says, 'There's a terrible curse attached to this diamond.' So the young woman asks, 'What curse?'" Paul Epstein paused dramatically. "The older woman lowers her voice and says, 'Mister Plotnick.'"

Theodore von Kármán shared a laugh with his colleague from the Physics Department. The two professors were in von Kármán's office, taking a break from grading undergraduate exams.

"And when will *you* be cursing some unfortunate woman, Theodore?" Epstein asked.

The old aerodynamicist grinned mischievously. "I never found the need to."

There was a knock at the door.

Von Kármán looked up. "Oh, come in, Hsue-shen."

Tsien walked into the office, dressed in a suit and tie as he always was on campus. He was a short man, with a smooth round face that looked younger than his twenty-six years. He parted his thin black hair awkwardly on one side.

"Professor Epstein," Tsien said, standing straight. But when addressing his doctoral supervisor, he bowed slightly. "Von Kármán *lǎoshī*." He handed over a stack of papers. "Here is the numerical analysis of the transfer functions you asked for."

"Thank you, Hsue-shen. I have something for you as well." Von Kármán rummaged through the journals and papers scattered across his desk. "You mentioned that you want to learn about rockets." He pulled out a journal, folded it open to a page, and handed it to his student.

Tsien read the names of the authors. "Frank Malina and William Duncan Rennie."

"Bill is in Canada, visiting his parents," said von Kármán. "But Frank is around. You should meet him."

"Thank you, von Kármán *lǎoshī*." Tsien turned and left the office.

Epstein looked at von Kármán. "What did he call you?"

"It means 'old teacher,' " von Kármán explained.

Epstein understood. "He respects you greatly."

"The feeling is mutual."

"Tsien was in my relativistic quantum course," Epstein continued. "He is brilliant."

"Yes, he is good," von Kármán said. "The other Chinese students have a nickname for him: 'The Son of Heaven.' "

"Tell me," Epstein said with a twinkle in his eye, "Do you think he has Jewish blood?"

Arroyo Seco, California
October 1937

They were called the Suicide Squad.

Lead by Frank Malina, with the sponsorship of von Kármán, they were a mad monk outfit of Caltech graduate students and local enthusiasts that conducted rocket experiments. After an unfortunate incident in the Gates Chemistry Building, the group was exiled from campus and forced to continue their work at Arroyo Seco, a dry river bed canyon a few miles from Caltech.

Malina, Tsien, and Rennie, along with a chemist named John Parsons and a mechanic named Edward Forman, had worked until 3:00 AM to prepare a rocket motor for their latest test. After catching a few hours of sleep, they drove at dawn to Arroyo Seco and mounted the motor onto its test stand. They connected the fuel and oxidizer lines, then piled sandbags around the apparatus before retreating to their viewing site.

Malina handed Tsien the trigger. "Will you do the honors?"

Tsien pressed the button. The rocket motor ignited, bright flame leaping from the nickel-steel nozzle into the early morning air.

The five young men cheered.

Rennie checked his stopwatch. "Forty-four seconds and counting. That's a record, guys!"

Parsons pointed. "What's that other flame there?"

"I believe the fuel line has broken," Tsien said calmly. "It is on fire."

Malina's eyes widened. "Uh, guys . . . *Run!*"

The Suicide Squad fled across the canyon, moments before the rocket engine exploded behind them.

Pasadena, California
December 1938

Tsien was in a foul mood.

Last night, he had gone to see *The Adventures of Robin Hood*, taking a break from the stress of finishing his PhD thesis. A patron at the theater had demanded the usher eject Tsien from his seat. He did not want to sit next to an Asian.

Someone knocked gently on the corner of his desk. Tsien looked up. It was Frank Malina, his tall, lean frame towering over the desk. His angular face, topped by a short crop of curly dark hair, sported a razor-fine moustache.

"Are you all right?" Malina asked.

"Yes."

Malina looked skeptical, but continued. "Hey, do you know Sid Weinbaum?"

"No."

"Sid's one of the research assistants in the Chemistry

Department. He's throwing a party at his place tomorrow tonight. Do you want to go?"

The following evening, Tsien and Malina found themselves strolling up the walk to Sidney Weinbaum's small
gray bungalow on Steuben Street. Inside the house,
some twenty or thirty Caltech students were sprawled
out on the furniture and chairs of the living room. Tsien
and Malina had come neatly dressed in vests, ties, and
polished shoes—a dignified contrast to the sloppily at-
tired Bohemian crowd around them.

Normally a loner at social events, Tsien found it surprisingly easy to talk with this group. He found sym-
pathetic ears for his outrage at the recent Japanese
atrocities in Nanjing. They discussed other international
crises, including the Great Depression and the rise of
fascism in Europe. Someone suggested Tsien should
read the works of John Strachey.

Later, after refreshments were served, Tsien found
himself talking to an attractive young blonde, telling her
about his idea for a transcontinental rocketliner that
could travel from New York to Los Angeles in an hour.
Even trips to the Moon, Tsien told her, might be possible in the near future.

The young woman listened for a while, then smiled
politely and excused herself. Perhaps she thought the
strange little Chinaman had been drinking too much.

Caltech
November 1943

Blackboards went around all three sides of the lecture hall. Tsien had already filled two of them with his
small, precise handwriting and was well into the third,
the chalk making gentle squeaks as he wrote.

"Professor Tsien, I don't understand the third equation on the second board."

Tsien continued to write without responding.

Moments later, another voice called out. "Sir, are you going to answer his question?"

"That was a statement of fact, not a question."

Finally, with the third blackboard filled, Tsien completed the last equation with a flourish and put down the chalk.

A timid hand was raised. "Sir, this method you have here, using the calculus of variations—is it foolproof?"

Tsien gave the student a cold stare. "Only fools need foolproof methods."

"Sir, we've had no quizzes, no midterms, no problem sets. Can you at least tell us something about the exam?"

"If you understand everything, you will be fine." His patience exhausted, Tsien turned and strode briskly out of the lecture hall.

A few days later, Tsien was called into von Kármán's office.

"Hsue-shen, a number of students have come to me expressing . . . concerns about your class." Von Kármán had lost weight and appeared to be in poor health. "You might consider changing your approach."

"Von Kármán *lǎoshī*, we are not teaching kindergarten. This is graduate school!"

"From my experience," von Kármán continued, "a good lecture is when one-third of them understand what you are talking about, a third has a pretty good idea, and the rest have no clue."

Tsien shook his head. "I am interested only in lecturing to people who understand everything."

"I know you prefer to do research," von Kármán said, "but as a professor you must recognize that teaching is also an important part of your responsibilities."

Tsien nodded. "I will do better, von Kármán *lǎoshī*."

Mojave Desert, California
December 10, 1944

The Private A rocket sat poised at the base of its inclined launch tower, an angular gray metallic truss that stuck out starkly against the beige desert floor. On the horizon, the sharp peaks of the Granite Mountains could be seen.

Tsien focused his binoculars on the Private A. The rocket was small, barely eight feet in length, with four stubby tail fins for stabilization. Its main engine was augmented with four solid propellant boosters, which together would deliver over twenty thousand pounds of thrust in less than one-fifth of a second at the moment of lift-off.

As Tsien lowered his binoculars, he marveled at how far they had come since the crazy days of the Suicide Squad. Their experiments had eventually attracted the attention of the U.S. Army Ordnance Corps, which began funding Caltech to advance the development of long-range rockets. With von Kármán's endorsement, Tsien obtained a security clearance to work on the military projects. A new institution, the Jet Propulsion Laboratory, was established to carry out the research.

"Any news on Theodore?" Frank Malina asked. Von Kármán had recently undergone surgery for intestinal cancer.

Tsien shook his head. "The operation went poorly. He is not well."

The eyes of the Caltech engineers and Army personnel were focused on the distant rocket.

"Here we go," whispered Malina.

There was a flash of flame, a cloud of smoke and sand billowed out, and the Private A raced up the rails of the launch tower. It cleared the structure and streaked into the heavens, a small black cruciform soaring against a crystal blue sky.

The onlookers cheered and patting each other on the back. It was the first successful launch of a large solid-fuelled rocket in the United States.

Shanghai, China
July 1947

Jiang Ying sang like an angel.

Her powerful soprano voice soared from the stage to the highest rafters of the Lanxin Theatre. Dressed in an elegant silk *qipao*, her lustrous black hair gleamed like lacquer under the lights, accentuating her delicate cheekbones and unblemished skin. She was the most beautiful woman Tsien had ever seen.

This was his first visit back to China since he had set sail on the *Jackson* twelve years ago. His mother had passed away in his absence, but his father was still alive, and Tsien had spent several weeks with him in Hangzhou.

He was now in Shanghai, and earlier in the day had delivered a keynote speech at his alma mater, Jiaotong University. It was at the dinner following his speech that Tsien was offered the presidency of Jiaotong. The recital at the Lanxin was the final gift from his hosts.

The audience was on its feet before Jiang Ying's final note had faded.

Tsien bribed his way backstage and somehow managed to find his way to her dressing room. She actually came out to see him, thinking to indulge another autograph seeker. But Tsien had other ideas.

"Will you go out with me?" It was all he could think to say. He was, after all, just an engineer.

Jiang Ying was annoyed. It was by far the worst pick-up line she had ever heard. But she said yes.

Tsien Hsue-shen and Jiang Ying were married less than two months later.

Caltech
June 6, 1950

It was raining the day the FBI came to Tsien's office.

"Can I help you?" Tsien asked.

"I'm agent Hanssen, FBI. This is agent Roberts." They flashed identification and sat without being invited.

"What do you want?"

"Let me get right to the point," Hanssen said. "Are you now, or have you ever been, a member of the Communist Party?"

In shock, Tsien was unable to answer for several moments. Finally, he said, "Absolutely not."

Roberts produced a picture. "Do you know this man?"

"Yes. That is Sidney Weinbaum."

"What is your relationship with Mr. Weinbaum?" Hanssen asked.

"He was a research assistant in the Chemistry Department. I used to go to his parties when I was a PhD student, but I have not seen him recently. How is he?"

Roberts leaned forward. "Mr. Tsien, are you aware that these so-called 'parties' were in fact meetings of Professional Unit 122 of the Pasadena Communist Party?"

"No!" Tsien exclaimed.

Hanssen produced a piece of paper. "This is a copy of a membership list dated February 1, 1938. Your name is on this list, associated with the alias 'John Decker'."

Tsien's face was ashen. "This is impossible!" he stammered. "I am not a Communist! I have never been a Communist! I have no idea how I got onto such a list. I have never heard the name John Decker."

The FBI men waited for Tsien to calm down. Then, Hanssen said, "Tell me about Weinbaum. Would you say he's a loyal American?"

Tsien struggled to answer. "I am an engineer, and

as an engineer, the only yardstick I have to measure anything is data. Since data cannot be applied to such intangibles as a person's character or political beliefs, I cannot speculate on the loyalty of Mr. Weinbaum."

Hanssen and Roberts looked at each other, then closed their notebooks and stood.

"That will be all for now," Hanssen said. "Thank you for your cooperation."

Later that day, Tsien received a hand-delivered letter from the headquarters of the Sixth Army at the Presidio in San Francisco, informing him that the U.S. Government had revoked his security clearance.

June 12, 1950

"What are you going to do?"

Von Kármán had never seen his former student so upset. Tsien was white as a sheet, his hands trembled, and his eyes appeared moist. He was struggling to maintain his composure and looked about to burst into tears.

In truth, von Kármán was not in much better shape himself. He had never fully recovered from his cancer surgery in 1944 and was forced to turn down a position to lead the Scientific Advisory Group at the Pentagon. Though his mind was ever sharp, his body had become thin and weak.

"I want to return to China," Tsien said.

"You must not do that!" von Kármán exclaimed.

"Why not?"

"Because you will immediately bring further suspicion upon yourself. It will make you look guilty."

"I am guilty of nothing," Tsien said, "but I cannot work without a security clearance."

"You cannot work on the military rocket programs without a security clearance," von Kármán pointed out. "Your theoretical studies and your teaching are not affected."

"In China—"

"What is there for you in China?" von Kármán interrupted. "Do you still have a chance at the presidency of Jiaotong University?"

"The offer was withdrawn. The 'new administration' was suspicious of my wife's links to the Kuomintang." Jiang Ying was the daughter of one of Chiang Kai-shek's military advisors. Tsien snickered at the irony.

"When you were in China, you toured some of their universities," von Kármán continued. "What did you think of their research facilities?"

"It is obvious, von Kármán *lǎoshī*. There is nothing in China that matches what is in America."

"Then if you return to China, your days of groundbreaking scientific research are over," von Kármán warned. "China needs people to rebuild the country, not sit around thinking about space travel."

Von Kármán's tone softened. "Think about what you are doing, Hsue-shen. Do not make hasty decisions. This crazy business will pass. I have been in America over twenty years, and I have seen how quickly things can change."

Tsien looked at his mentor with gratitude. "I am thankful that you are still at Caltech to counsel me. I do not know what I would have done without your wisdom . . . perhaps something I might have regretted later." He bowed. "Thank you, von Kármán *lǎoshī*."

"You have called me that for twelve years, Hsue-shen, but I would be grateful if you could start calling me something else: *Lǎo péngyou*."

Tsien smiled. His old friend's pronunciation was excellent.

Los Angeles, California
Fall 1950

Following his arrest on September 7th, Tsien was incarcerated for two weeks at a federal facility on Terminal

Island. Under the Subversive Control Act of 1950, Tsien was charged with failing to divulge his membership in the Communist Party when he reentered the United States after his 1947 visit to China. He was eventually released on bail but was forbidden to travel outside Los Angeles County.

Tsien's first deportation hearing took place on November 15th, in a government building at 117 West Ninth Street in downtown Los Angeles. With his attorney Grant Cooper at his side, Tsien waited for the proceedings to begin. Presided over by INS examining officer Albert Del Guercio, INS hearing officer Roy Waddell, and State Department observer Nick Di Carlo, the hearing began with an investigation of Tsien's background and recent activities.

"What were you doing in China in 1947?" Del Guercio asked.

"Visiting my father and getting married," Tsien deadpanned.

Later, two retired police officers named Hynes and Kimple took the stand.

"We have a membership list for the Los Angeles area Communist cells." Hynes handed a sheet to Del Guercio. "You can see that Mr. Tsien's name is on the list, next to the alias 'John Decker.'"

"How was this list obtained?" Di Carlo asked.

"I'll ask the questions here," Del Guercio snarled. "Mr. Kimple, how did you get this list?"

"I was undercover," Kimple replied. "I had infiltrated the Communist Party as an assistant to their membership director. Every time a list or membership card came by my desk, I'd write down the names."

Grant Cooper leaned forward. "So this list is not an original. It's a copy in your handwriting."

"Yes," Kimple replied.

"And Mr. Tsien's name," Cooper continued. "Did you

copy it from an actual membership card or from another list?"

Kimple paused. "I don't remember. Probably another list, maybe."

Cooper pressed. "Assuming another list, was it an actual membership list or a recruitment list?"

"What difference does that make?" Del Guercio asked.

"My client is a *rocket scientist!*" Cooper exclaimed. "It makes perfect sense for the Reds to try recruiting him, but that doesn't mean he ever joined them."

Del Guercio waved his hand impatiently. "Let's move on." He took a piece of paper from Waddell. "Mr. Tsien, you state in your deposition that you had no idea the gatherings at the Weinbaum residence were meetings of the Communist Party."

"That is correct," Tsien said.

"This is hard to believe, since you said yourself that you attended these events on a regular basis." Del Guercio put down the paper. "Is it *possible* that these *could* have been Communist meetings?"

"It is possible, but I had no way of knowing that," Tsien insisted. "They were always arguing about politics and world affairs. Sometimes they would ask for my opinions because I am Chinese. There were heated political discussions, but I thought this was part of the university experience in America."

"Mr. Tsien," Del Guercio asked, "in the event of a conflict between the United States and Communist China, would you fight for the United States?"

Cooper threw up his hands.

"What kind of a question is that?" Di Carlo interrupted.

Del Guercio glared. "Mr. Di Carlo, this is an INS hearing. You are here as a courtesy to the State Department, which insisted on your presence because of Mr.

Tsien's unique background. So, kindly stick to observing and be silent about it!"

"Don't answer the question," Cooper said.

"Mr. Tsien, you will answer the question," Waddell ordered.

Tsien did not respond for a long time, until Del Guercio looked about to prompt him, and then he spoke. "My essential allegiance is to the Chinese people. If a war were to start between the United States and China, and if the war aim of the United States was for the greater good of the Chinese people—and I think it would be—then, of course, I would fight on the side of the United States."

Pasadena, California
April 30, 1951

The dark Ford Tudor had been parked outside the Tsien household since the late morning. Tsien would periodically take a peek through the venetian blinds. The car's windows were tinted, making it difficult to see if anyone was inside.

"No light, *bàba*?" Yucon asked.

Tsien picked up the toddler and carried him to an armchair. He sat and reached for a scientific journal but didn't even have time to open it before the telephone rang. Fearful of waking the baby, Yung-jen, Tsien immediately got up and answered the phone with Yucon still in his arm.

"Hello?"

There was no response.

"Who is this?"

The caller hung up.

Tsien replaced the handset, summoning his will to keep from slamming it down in anger. He went to the window and peered outside. The dark sedan was gone.

Jiang Ying emerged from the nursery.

"Is Yung-jen still sleeping?" Tsien asked.

"Yes," she replied. "Who was that?"

Tsien handed Yucon to his wife. "I am going to see Professor von Kármán."

"Is he on campus today? You should call to check."

"There is something wrong with our telephone," Tsien said.

Tsien drove to Caltech and found von Kármán in his old office on the second floor of the Guggenheim Building.

"I do not know how much more I can stand," Tsien said. "I have not been able to do meaningful work for almost a year. I cannot answer questions from the JPL engineers about my own papers. I cannot go to conferences. I am not allowed to even go to the beach in Orange County!" Tsien gripped his hands. "And I am certain I am being watched."

"I don't doubt it," von Kármán said grimly. "Things have gotten crazier with the fighting in Korea. I read in the *LA Times* that the FBI has even been spying on the Chinese Hand Laundry Association."

Tsien signed. "I fear my days in America are numbered."

"We're not finished yet. Grant Cooper is still pursuing appeals, and Lee DuBridge has been campaigning tirelessly for us," said von Kármán, referring to the president of Caltech. "Lee had written numerous letters on your behalf. He is even planning a trip to Washington."

"I do not want to go back to China," Tsien said, "but I may have no choice."

"There are *always* choices." Von Kármán thought for a moment, then reached into a drawer and pulled out a letter. "This is from Frank Malina. He only recently took that job with UNESCO, but he's already thinking about leaving the United States and going to Paris to pursue his art."

"I am not an artist."

"No, of course not." Von Kármán tossed the letter on his desk. "Do you know who else was here last week? Bill Rennie. We met for dinner, and he told me about some interesting projects going on in Canada."

"What kind of projects?" Tsien asked.

"Oh, he mentioned something about a fighter plane and a new missile, and he said their National Research Council is upgrading their high-speed wind tunnels in anticipation of future projects." Von Kármán rubbed his chin. "Yes, it was all very interesting."

Shortly after returning home, a mailman arrived with a registered letter for Tsien. It was on INS letterhead, dated April 26, 1951. The letter stated that the INS had reached its decision and determined that Tsien was "an alien who was a member of the Communist Party of the United States and is therefore subject to deportation."

Los Angeles, California
November 1952

Grant Cooper's legal tactics and Lee DuBridge's eloquent letters, and even a small campus protest (rumored to have been "encouraged" by von Kármán) were all for naught. In early November, Tsien's last appeal was denied.

"This is very bad," Cooper said grimly. "It means you can now be picked up at any time and taken into custody."

Tsien and von Kármán sat silently in Cooper's office, letting the attorney's words sink in.

"I'm sorry," Cooper said.

Tsien shrugged. "Our bags are already packed. We are ready to go to China at any time."

Von Kármán pounded his fist on Cooper's desk. "America or China. No, I do not accept it! This is *not* a binary condition." He thought for a moment, then reached for the telephone.

"No." Cooper pointed to the door. "Use the pay phone across the street. I'm sure this one's bugged."

Von Kármán returned a few minutes later. "I've invited Bill Rennie to join us for lunch."

Tsien, Cooper, and von Kármán met Rennie at a restaurant on East First Street. A large red vertical neon sign with the words "Far East Chop Suey" ran up the building's beige facade.

"This Chinese stuff is good," Cooper said, chewing a mouthful of chicken and bean sprouts.

Tsien grimaced. "It is not Chinese."

Von Kármán put down his fork. "Bill, you just got back from Canada?"

Rennie took a sip of water and nodded. "Yeah, spent some time with my parents, then went to a seminar at the University of Toronto Institute of Aerophysics."

"And what have our northern friends been up to?" von Kármán asked.

Rennie wiped his mouth. "Quite a few things, actually. They've started flight testing a subsonic fighter plane called the CF-100, and there are proposals floating around for a supersonic interceptor." He pulled out a notebook. "I met this really sharp kid at UTIA, one of the PhD students." He flipped to a page. "Gerald Bull, that's his name. He's doing aerodynamic modeling for a missile project called Velvet Glove."

Tsien's eyes widened. "A rocket?"

"An air-to-air missile for their fighters," Rennie said. "But there's talk of a sounding rocket program for space research."

Von Kármán turned to Tsien. "Are these projects of interest to you?"

Rennie held up his hands. "Before we get too far, I should point out most of this stuff is being done by industry, which might not be the best fit for Hsue-shen. But I have some contacts at the High-Speed Aerodynamics Laboratory in Ottawa. It's a great facility, and they need fluid dynamics people to support the Velvet Glove program."

"Canada . . ." said Tsien, his tone uncertain.

"It is a possibility, and I think you should give it serious consideration," von Kármán said. "The research facilities in Canada must be much better than in China, and I believe it would be advantageous for you to stay in a Western country. You don't want to close any doors."

Tsien recalled his master's studies at MIT and the harsh Boston winters. "Is it cold in Canada?"

"Oh, yeah," Rennie said.

Cooper shook his head. "The government will never go for this."

"But we haven't asked," von Kármán pointed out. "In any event, my *lǎo péngyou* must first make a choice."

Two weeks later, Tsien made his decision.

December 15, 1952

Neither the INS nor the FBI returned Grant Cooper's calls. But one person did respond: Nick Di Carlo from the State Department, who flew out to Los Angeles to meet Tsien and Cooper in the attorney's office.

"Your proposal is interesting," Di Carlo said. "I'm going to bring it to my superiors in Washington."

Cooper looked surprised.

"The INS still wants to send me back to China," Tsien said.

"Yeah well, I like to think that we in State have a more . . . strategic view of things than some of the other three-letter Washington bureaucracies." Di Carlo leaned back in his chair. "I'm sure we could get the Department of Defense on side too." He pointed at Tsien. "I had a chat with Navy Secretary Dan Kimball about you a few days ago. Do you know what he said?"

Tsien shook his head.

"Kimball said he'd rather shoot you than let you go back to China."

"I assume he was joking," Cooper muttered without humor.

Di Carlo continued. "I can't promise anything, but I'll do my best to advocate for this."

"Thanks," Cooper said.

Tsien asked, "Why are you advocating our proposal?"

Di Carlo looked Tsien in the eye. "We Italians have a saying, Mr. Tsien. I'm sure you've heard it, the one about keeping your friends close?"

Tsien understood. "I believe Sun Tzu said it first."

Di Carlo rose from his seat. "Merry Christmas, gentlemen. Let's see what the future brings."

Malton, Ontario, Canada
October 4, 1957

The afternoon of the Avro Arrow's rollout was cool and sunny. A steady stream of cars, buses, and limousines had been arriving at the A.V. Roe Canada aircraft company parking lot since noon, disgorging scores of people.

Tsien could feel the excitement as the crowd swelled into the thousands. On stage were a number of dignitaries, including Air Marshal Hugh Campbell, Minister of National Defense George Pearkes, some Royal Canadian Air Force vice-marshals, several Members of Parliament, and the senior management of the A.V. Roe Company, lead by president Crawford Gordon.

Scanning the crowd, Tsien spotted his friend Jim Chamberlain, the aerodynamicist and chief of technical design for the Arrow. It was Chamberlain who had invited Tsien to the rollout. Their eyes met, and Chamberlain waved.

Tsien returned his attention to the stage as Defense Minister Pearkes took the podium.

"Fifty years ago, the great Canadian pioneer John McCurdy, who is with us on the platform today, flew the Silver Dart, the first aircraft in Canada, and in fact the first heavier-than-air plane to fly in the British Commonwealth. History recognizes that event as the beginning of Canada's air age.

"Today, we mark another milestone—the production of the first Canadian supersonic airplane. I am sure the historians of tomorrow will regard this event as being equally significant in the annals of Canadian aviation."

As soon as Pearkes finished his speech, he pulled a gold cord that symbolically opened immense blue-and-gold curtains stretched across the mouth of the hangar. On cue, a fly-past of CF-100 fighters swept overhead as a band struck up a fanfare, and with deliberate majesty the CF-105 Arrow was slowly towed out. The crowd broke into applause as the gleaming white delta-winged aircraft was revealed in the late afternoon sunshine.

This was the first time Tsien had seen an actual Arrow, having worked only on theoretical analyses and wind tunnel models at the High-Speed Aerodynamics Laboratory. Tsien's expert eye spotted the aerodynamic improvements to the nose and engine nozzles he had worked on with Chamberlain, drawing on his experience with rockets, to increase the Arrow's speed.

Later that afternoon, as Tsien wandered through the crowd, he felt a tap on his shoulder.

"Excuse me, sir." It was a young airman. "Are you Dr. H.S. Tsien?"

"Yes."

"Please come with me."

The airman led Tsien to the parking lot, out to a waiting black limousine with tinted windows. Tsien entered the car and, to his surprise, saw Air Marshal Campbell and Defense Minister Pearkes inside.

"Are you Dr. Tsien?" Campbell asked.

"Yes."

"Dr. Tsien," Minister Pearkes said, "the Russians have successfully launched an artificial satellite."

"A satellite!" Tsien exclaimed.

"It's called Sputnik," Campbell said. "TASS reports it was launched from Kazakhstan at 20:28 Moscow time."

"A satellite," Tsien repeated. "This is . . . incredible!"

"Yes, and now we need to totally rethink our strategies for the defense of North America," Campbell said. "Sputnik changes everything."

"Dr. Tsien, we have a job for you." Defense Minister Pearkes leaned forward. "The Government of Canada needs to learn everything you know about rockets."

Jeanne Sauvé, Minister of State for Science and Technology, yesterday announced the appointment of Tsien Hsue-shen, 64, as the first president of the newly created Canada National Space Administration (CNSA).

"I am honored to be entrusted with the responsibility of leading the Canadian space program, and I will focus my efforts on ensuring that Canada remains at the frontier of science," said Tsien in a written statement.

The CNSA was created by an Act of Parliament that came into force on July 1, 1975. Established to develop the robotic arm that will be Canada's contribution to the NASA Space Shuttle program, the CNSA will also take over current space projects such as the Communications Technology Satellite and the Black Brant sounding rockets.

Born in Hangzhou, China, Tsien received a doctorate from the California Institute of Technology and played a key role in the early U.S. rocket programs before emigrating to Canada with his family in 1953. As a senior researcher at the National Research Council in the 1950s, Tsien worked on both the Velvet Glove missile and the Avro Arrow.

After becoming a Canadian citizen in 1957, he founded the Scientific Advisory Group at the Department of National Defense. Unlike many of his contemporaries, Tsien remained in Canada following the cancellation of the Arrow in 1959. Prior to his appointment to the CNSA presidency, Tsien was chair of the Department of Mechanical and Aerospace Engineering at Carleton University.

Tsien is married to Jiang Ying, the award-winning Chinese-Canadian soprano whose acclaimed final performance in the opera Eugene Onegin *opened the National Arts Center in 1969. They have two adult children and recently celebrated the birth of their first grandchild.*

The appointment of Tsien is controversial. On CTV Question Period, *Progressive Conservative industry critic George Hees questioned Tsien's suitability to head the CNSA. "The allegations of Communist affiliations that lead to his departure from the U.S. have never been unambiguously resolved," Hees said, citing also a 1970 CBC interview in which Tsien said the deaths attributed to Mao's disastrous Great Leap Forward were "probably exaggerated."*

Sauvé defended Tsien's appointment, dismissing Opposition concerns as "baseless and irrelevant."

—The Globe and Mail
July 16, 1975

Shadow City

Susan Ee

A body thumped against the barge. The waxy face still had a look of ecstasy. One open eye had a fresh bruise, maybe only a day old by the look of the red and black. The face dipped under water as it slid along the boat. The silver water flowed over the face, softening the bruises, flashing fool's gold over the eyes.

Zian bowed to the body as it flowed by, giving it the respect it deserved. Among all the things that floated in the river, a dream addict was the most precious. Without their dried and ground flesh, the dust that gave the gate-keepers so much power in Shadow City would be impotent with hardly more power than a passing daydream.

The barge scraped the bank of the river beside the dock. The dock sat in a gap in a rickety wall of houses built on stilts. A string of red lanterns strung along the houses gave a festive feel to the city that belied the sorrow hidden within. City dwellers, whom the gatekeepers called Shadowers, reached out their tattered arms through the bars of the gate surrounding the dock. Didn't they understand the futility of pressing against the reinforced metal? Didn't they know it was fortified with the power of suggestion by the daily prayers of the monks?

Zian took a deep breath and bid himself peace. The

humid heat, the stench of sewage, the buzzing of insects, stirred his emotions and churned them into something ragged and raw, like the nightmares of a guilty man. He vowed to investigate the incident as quickly as possible and return to the peace of the Gate House.

The mob of reaching hands and maddened voices made him want to shrink back and not leave the safety of the barge. But he held his posture, exaggerated it even—straightening his shoulders, puffing out his chest as he tied the barge to the dock. Just out of reach of the grasping arms, Zian dipped into his pouch, pulled out a handful of dust, and sprayed it above the crowd's heads. The Shadowers—animal eyes and broken hair, skeletal faces and distended bellies—scrambled like rats to catch a grain of dust and place it on their tongues.

While the Shadowers were occupied, Zian quickly unlocked the gate, slipped out, and slammed it shut behind him. Unmolested, he walked past the city dwellers fighting over the grainy bits of precious drug. It wasn't so long ago that he had scrambled for dust along with the other tattered wretches, longing for the rush of pleasure as soon as the grains touched his tongue, craving the high that blighted the nightmare of Shadow City for what seemed like months.

A man smacked a grubby woman and snatched her finger toward his own tongue to lick the traces of dust. But before the man could drag the resisting hand to his face, the woman lurched at him in a blur of broken teeth and snatched her hand back, leaving the man to howl over his bitten arm.

The woman's fingers froze in midair on their way to her tongue when she saw Zian. Through the wispy hair streaking her face, through the dirt-encrusted rags, he almost didn't recognize Mei. Her eyes had lost their mischief. Her posture had lost its firmness. But it was definitely her, staring at him with shock. He had an insane urge to talk to her, to buy her a bowl of warm noodles and see how she was doing, to hold her hand and beg for forgiveness.

Zian turned and quickly walked away, pretending not to recognize her. What could he expect from a conversation with her? Mei with her button nose and long lashes. Mei with her tinkling laugh and gentle voice. That's how he wanted to remember her. Not as an addict in a stooping body who'd do anything for a grain of pure dust. His childhood friend had grown into a Shadower who had nothing but her broken dreams.

The old guilt threatened to drown him. But for the whim that made his master accept him instead of Mei, he would be the one scrambling in the dirt and she would be the one doling out the dust. Hadn't he and Mei been inseparable until then?

Zian left the Shadowers to their fevered hallucinations of a sunlit world full of meat pastries and fresh fruit, a full night's sleep on a soft mat, and even an occasional laugh with someone who loved them.

For every fortune, there is an equal and opposite fortune. For every good thing happening to a Sunshiner, an equally bad thing happened to a Shadower. Zian had heard it said that long before anyone could remember, the two cities—they used to be called something other than Sun City and Shadow City—were once equally balanced. But then war broke out between the cities that lasted seven generations. The Shadowers eventually lost, and a new balance was set. To allow the Sunshiners to live their fortunate lives in Sun City, the Shadowers had to live their unfortunate lives in Shadow City.

Zian walked with one hand on his gatekeeper's key to show any who might challenge him. His other hand rested on his dust pouch in case he needed to scatter a crowd. He was careful not to touch the dust unless he had to, careful not to caress it with his hungry fingers.

In the city's skyline, one of the buildings flickered and shifted, at the mercy of dream tides. It was the tallest building in the city, shaped like a cone of hats with the four corners of each brim tapering up like a lady lifting her skirt to avoid the filth of the streets. The binding chants that held together the stone and cement, tinged with the blood of those sacrificed during the inauguration prayers, weren't working. Zian had never seen it like this. The daily prayers of the monks had always anchored the buildings. Had always anchored the inhabitants.

A crowd gathered across the street from the flickering building. The last of the building's occupants ran out with their precious belongings tied in a blanket. Everyone stood watching, wondering whether it was an opportunity or a disaster.

Zian recognized the flickering for what it was: an unauthorized gateway. His master had suspected something wasn't right, but if he had suspected an actual gateway, even if it was weak and flickering, he would have sent someone more senior.

Throat dry, Zian broke out of the crowd and approached the building. He felt the crowd's eyes following him. Perhaps he should go back and tell his master this task was beyond him? No. That would only prove he was unworthy; that he didn't belong with the gatekeepers. Zian forced his feet to enter the building.

Inside was an empty vestibule with stairs spiraling up to the living quarters and stairs spiraling down to the basement. He headed down. Beyond the first couple of steps, the feeble light withered and died. It was so dark that Zian had trouble finding his worm pouch as he groped his feet down the stairs. He poured out the mass of worms onto his palm, trying to ignore the shifting sliminess. He tried to forget the story he'd heard of the apprentice who kept the worms in his hand too long without feeding them. That boy ended up with the tiny worms wiggling their way through his skin, living inside him and multiplying until they burst out of every orifice. The boys loved to tell this story late at night, of how the unfortunate apprentice had been eaten hollow from the inside out.

Zian quickly sprinkled dust on the worms. Then, just to be sure they were satisfied, he sprinkled another pinch over them. They immediately began to glow. Their squirming intensified, the pile of worms going into a copulating frenzy. The worm glow grew to illuminate the basement enough for him to see the columns lining the cavernous space.

He had expected the building's anchors to be columns of stone or some other practically shaped object tethering the building, but these anchors were anything but practical. They were shaped like people, contorted to wrap their stretched arms around the stalactites of the basement ceiling like ivy clinging to a post. The anchors stretched and strained, impossibly strong. Their legs reached and twisted around stalagmites in the foundation. The sculptures were so realistic, so full of pain. Excruciating expressions were carved with the finest detail into their stone faces. Lines of anguish shaped their tapering eyes and elongated cheeks. Their mouths were open in eternal screams.

Near the corner, the grid pattern of the anchors was broken by a missing support. Zian walked past the sculptures to the empty spot. The statues around that spot seemed even more contorted than the rest. In the empty blotch, the stalagmites on the floor were ripped and amputated, covered in a thick, dark ooze. The stalactite on the ceiling still had a sculpted hand grabbing it, with part of the forearm wrapped around it. The forearm ended in a ragged edge, more like flesh than stone. Dark goo oozed out of the torn arm and dripped onto the darkness below.

He backed away from the gap. His shoulder brushed against something. He jumped away, thinking someone was behind him, but it was only a statue.

A low moan sounded above him. It sounded as if it were coming from the gaping mouth of the statue he had bumped into. An echo bounced off a nearby anchor. Then another. Then another, until the basement filled with moans from every direction.

Zian ran, trying to ignore the nightmare image of a stretched hand reaching for him. The moans chased him through the basement and up the stairs.

He stopped running only when he burst through the doors out into the flickering light. In his palm lay the remains of a few crushed glowworms. He must have dropped the rest in the basement when he ran. He frantically checked the dust pouch. It was still tethered to his belt. Enormous relief flooded through him. He could take the punishment of losing glowworms in a deserted basement, but if he had lost his dust, he'd have to go back into the building and search for it, groping in the dark along the feet of the moaning statues.

Zian walked toward the crowd, composing himself. A gatekeeper had an image to keep, and looking scared and confused was not part of it. But no one was looking at him. They were all looking up at the flickering tower. An old couple looked out the window from the second floor, too old to walk down the stairs to escape the unstable building. They clung together, apparently trying to give each other enough courage to jump out of the window. They flickered . . . here for a moment . . . gone . . . then back again. Then, in a flicker that was no different than the others, the old man disappeared and did not come back. The old woman wailed over her empty arms.

The words, "Sun City," spread through the rabble.

Breaking out from the safety of the huddled masses,

a thin woman ran toward the building. Her bare feet slapped the concrete, her colorless shirt flapped to show the bones of her ribs. This time, Zian recognized Mei immediately.

Two men, well fed and wearing new clothes, grabbed her before she made it into the building.

"You think a chance to go to Sun City would be free for a dirt smear like you?" asked a woman. She was positively *chubby*, with rosy lips and puffy wrists. She wore a yellow dress, wrapped fashionably tightly around her body to show off the ridges of flesh bulging along her back and sides. It was said that the only fat people in Shadow City were politicians and gangsters.

"This area," announced the chubby woman to the crowd, "is now under our protection." A man in an accountant's robe stepped behind the woman. He held a pen poised over a ledger. An accountant signified an official gang presence, one in which all events and transactions would be recorded.

Mei looked back and forth between the gangsters with wide eyes, her long lashes making her look impossibly innocent. "What do you want?" she asked.

"What do you have for me?" asked the fat woman.

"I have nothing left," said Mei, as though only now realizing it.

"Then what are you wasting my time for? Get out of here."

The beefy men shoved her away.

"Please! Please," said Mei, her expression dark and needy.

"Ah," said the gangster woman, her chubby cheeks dimpling in a grin. "You got something. You know what they say, 'a desperate girl is a rich girl.'"

"I can't," said Mei. "It's the only dream I have left. Please."

"So what's the problem?" asked the fat woman. "You

don't trust us to help you reach your goal if you give us your dream?" She put on a hurt expression.

Mei was too smart to become prey to her hopes. Everyone knew it was a bad bargain to sell your last dream to the gangs. They would let her pass but wouldn't bother to remind her that she had been willing to do anything to get into that tower. Having sold her last dream, she no longer remembered why she wanted to go there.

"No, no," said Mei, taking a step back. "Of course I trust you. It's just . . . I don't know if I want it bad enough to give up my dream. That's all."

"Well, we're not unreasonable. We would accept several smaller dreams."

"I don't have any. I already sold them all." She hung her head. "Or I've lost them." Mei used to dream about being a gatekeeper. She'd regaled little Zian with fantasies of majestic halls and pretty dresses, of endless tables laden with food, and parties attended by regal people. Zian now knew that her dreams had been far more grand than reality. At the time, though, her dream had been enormous and all encompassing. They had treasured it, and it had nurtured them through their darkest times. Somehow, she must have lost it through the years, along with her firm gaze and glossy hair.

The gangster woman twitched her head toward the street. Her boys threw Mei away.

Mei stood there, staring up at the flickering tower, a tear streaking down her face. A few brave people stepped up to the gangsters and commenced negotiations. The crowd jostled Mei until she turned and shuffled away.

Zian grabbed her as she passed. She was as light as a bird with hollow bones. She looked up at him with a child's eyes, filled with anger and disappointment.

"How are you, Mei?" As soon as the words left him, he regretted it. How was she? Did he really need to ask? He'd become soft over the years, steeping his life in meaningless niceties spoken only by Sunshiners and politicians' daughters. Mei stared at him as though he'd just spoken in another language.

"Have you seen anyone leave with a statue?" asked Zian.

Mei's eyes rolled white, her head lolled, greasy strands of hair sliding over her face. Fainting from hunger was something Zian remembered well.

"Wake up," said Zian, shaking her and feeling her bones rattle. Terrible things could happen to an unconscious woman on the street. She slumped, her bones melting, and sat on the stained ground like a pile of discarded rags.

Zian dug into his robe pocket for his lunch. He pulled out a sandwich, a delicacy of the Sunshiners. He unwrapped it from the waxed paper, realizing that the exotic paper alone would be worth a meal to her if she traded it. He waved the sandwich in front of her. She opened her eyes and looked at it, indifferent. He opened the bread pieces for her, showing her the meat in between. Still, she gazed through it with no interest, as if she had forgotten what real food looked like.

He reached into his pouch with his other hand, pulled out a pinch of dust, and showed her the sparkling crystals. Her attention was immediate, her eyes sharp and focused as she reached for it. Zian snatched his hand away. "First, you eat this." He handed her the sandwich.

She accepted the food without hesitation, her eyes still on his pinch of dust. She bit into the sandwich and chewed. He remembered his first taste of Sunshiner food. Who could forget that first burst of flavor, the incredible taste of the bundle of nutrition that the Sunshiners called food. He had crammed the sandwich into his mouth, convinced someone would take it away from him. Had he expected the same of Mei? Had he been hoping for a glimpse of the old Mei with an echo of her old dream shining in her eyes?

She chewed mechanically, showing no more enthusiasm than she would when eating refuse. She did, however, lick off every scrap and crumb. But she would have done that as well with a rotting piece of fruit found in a gangster's trash.

"Someone stole an anchor out of that building," said Zian. "A statue without a hand. Do you know anything about it?"

She nodded, all her concentration on Zian's dust pouch. He had brushed the dust back into the pouch so his hungry fingers wouldn't be too tempted. A single taste of dust was enough to expel an apprentice. And expelled apprentices were thrown back to the streets of Shadow City.

"Can I have some dust now?"

Zian hesitated. "Do you know where the statue is?"

She nodded. "I can take you there. I just need a tiny bit of dust to get me going."

"Take me to the statue first, then you get the dust."

She licked her lips and nodded. When they were kids, she had been the one who made the decisions. She had been the one who kept them fed, secured their shelter for the night, walked the fine balance of negotiating with adults and feral children. All he did was follow her until the day the masters saw them and picked one of them for an apprentice. Deep inside, they both knew it should have been her.

She got up, full of new energy, reminiscent of the old Mei. She slipped through dark alleys between butcher shops and whore houses, through the open market of unidentifiable meats and yellowed vegetables, through the money district where the politicians and gang bosses looked down from their windows, framed by billowing curtains, forgetting what it was like to walk the streets.

After a while, Zian realized that Mei was still more clever than he'd thought. She was following a trail of dark ooze, smeared and rubbed into the edge of the grimy streets. He suspected she didn't know where the statue was; her bravado was enough. He followed her through Shadow City with complete confidence, just like in the old days. They nearly lost the trail when it crossed the streets, where the feet of a thousand people pulling carts ground the trail into nonexistence. But she managed to pick up the trail again every time.

At the riverbank, Mei stopped. She pointed to a couple leaning against the gates around Zian's barge. They stood looking down at the water, leaning as far as the bars would allow. The woman, who was hardly more than a girl, wore the crimson robe of an apprentice monk, her shaved head still pale and unseasoned. The man—tall and lanky, barely out of childhood—was gray from head to foot. The gray man cradled his arm, which ended in a wet stump covered in a mass of bandages. The woman's hand reached up and stroked the gray man's cheek, and he leaned his head toward her. Their tenderness was a sight Zian hadn't seen in Shadow City since he was a child.

Without thinking, Zian touched Mei's thin shoulder, feeling her warmth through her rags.

"Can I have my dust now?" asked Mei, her voice empty.

Didn't she at least want to talk to him a little? Wasn't she curious to hear about the last few years of his life? Didn't she want to hear about the marvels of life outside Shadow City?

She watched him with tired eyes. No curiosity, no hope.

Reluctantly, Zian dribbled dust onto her cupped palms. He held himself back from giving her a generous portion and just gave her enough for a few hours of ecstasy. Given more, she could be lost forever. As soon as she got the dust, she turned without a word and ran.

She didn't look back.

A hot wind blew from the river, bringing with it the sweet smell of lost dreams, with a hint of rotting flesh.

He watched her disappear into a dark alley. He had a crazy urge to follow her, to let her lead him through the sewers and secret hiding spots of the old days. But, of course, he couldn't.

Zian took a deep breath, and turned to the strange couple. When they saw him coming, the monk apprentice stepped protectively in front of the man, putting out her hands in a warding gesture. Zian stopped.

"Just let us go," said the girl. Her hands trembled, and stains of exhaustion circled her eyes. She must have used all her powers to release the anchor, and even then, she couldn't release all of him.

"Go where?" asked Zian. There was nowhere the gatekeepers wouldn't find them.

"We're going to be Sunshiners," said the man in a voice filled with pain and hope. "We're going to float down river and make it to Sun City."

Zian glanced at the girl. She wouldn't meet his eyes. He guessed that she knew it was suicide. "Everybody drowns in that river," said Zian to the girl. "You know that."

"No, some people make it," said the man who was a boy, gripping the gate with his one hand. "We can make it if we have the barge. She can cast a spell to let us ride it, and we'll be all right." He looked at the girl, who gave him a small smile. To Zian, it looked as though that smile cost her last bit of effort. Although she was obviously talented, it would still take more than the skills of an apprentice to navigate the currents of Lost Dreams beyond the regular route between the Gate House and the city.

He thought about showing him a fistful of dust. It

would lure him as easily as it lured the addicts. But the girl wouldn't be tempted, for she knew the secret of the dust and had sworn off it along with the rest of her brethren when she joined the monkhood. It was her he had to convince to put the anchor back in the basement.

"If you're lucky, they'll throw you back onto the streets," Zian said to her. "If you're not lucky, you could end up as part of a building. Or maybe they'd throw you in the river if you haven't already drowned. I'm guessing that a drowned monk would be especially valuable."

She stepped closer to her man, their shoulders touching. Her childlike eyes were beautiful, almost as beautiful as Mei's. She reminded him of the old Mei, who used to be as protective and loyal to him as this woman was to her gray man. If Mei had become the gatekeeper and Zian had been the one on the streets, would she have found a way to help him regardless of the risks?

"We have no choice," said the girl. "Sorry about having to take your barge."

A twinge of fear ran through Zian. The master could be cruel to those who failed him. "You haven't heard about what's happening to the building you deanchored, have you?" he asked.

"I hope it came crashing down," said the gray man in a cold voice. He was cradling his stump again.

"It's flickering. Wavering between here and *there*."

"Where?" asked the girl.

"Where do you think? The gangs are already charging for entry." That gave it legitimacy. The couple's eyes widened with hope. "All you have to do is come back. I can get you past the gangsters."

"Why would you help us?" asked the girl.

"Let's just say you two remind me of some kids I used to know. My master will eventually forgive me if I fail to find the missing anchor. The city's a big place to search, and I'm just one person."

They looked at each other, unsure.

Zian looked directly at the monk. "It's your best option." He left her some dignity in front of her friend by not saying out loud what they both knew: It was her only option if she wanted to live. The River of Lost Dreams was not kind to those who were desperate.

She nodded. Zian waited for the sense of triumph. They believed him. He was about to stabilize the city, to restore order and maintain the balance. His master would be impressed.

But the only thing he felt was a heaviness in his chest.

They walked back toward the center of the city. Zian let the man shuffle out of earshot before whispering to the girl, "Why did you throw away everything for him?"

She kept walking without looking at him.

"He wouldn't do the same for you," he said with certainty.

"Of course he would."

"You took care of each other on the streets, didn't you?" he asked. "Before you were chosen to be a monk and he to be an anchor? You gave him everything." He let himself steep in his thoughts. "And yet, if by some miracle, a master came to him and told him they would save *you* but not him, do you know what he would do?"

She feigned disinterest but clenched her jaw.

"He would tell the master that he'll fetch you. He'd run to get you, you being the one person he loved. But along the way, his footfalls would get heavier. His stride slower. And before he reached you, he would turn around. He'd curse himself ten thousand times but he would still turn around." The words ripped through Zian's throat, leaving it raw and ragged.

"He'd go back to the master and tell him you refused his offer," said Zian. "That you begged the master to take him instead. Your loyal friend would get on his knees and beg the master to save him instead of you." His nails dug into his palms until the pain was all he felt. Until the pain almost blotted out the memories. "And without ever telling you of your salvation. Without even saying goodbye. He would leave you to rot on the streets. That is what he would do."

She glared at him. "He's not like that. Only the worst filth would do that." She walked ahead to join her friend.

Zian watched her walk away from him. "You're right," he whispered to himself. "Only the worst filth would do that."

When they returned to the city center, the tower was severely flickering. The tower's tip was already gone with a dark shadow bleeding down from the missing chunk like a spreading bruise. A crowd pushed against the gangsters, who had multiplied tenfold. They were taking payment as fast as they could grab, their pockets stuffed and overflowing with shimmering wisps of precious dreams, some of which floated away in the wind, drifting into the sky. The ones who had sold their last hope to get past the gangsters wandered away as often as they wandered toward the building, no longer remembering they wanted to escape Shadow City.

Zian pushed his way through the crowd, making sure the monk and gray man followed. The gangsters left them alone when they saw he was a gatekeeper and she a monk.

Inside, the building rumbled and creaked like an old man breaking in the river. "This way," he told the couple as he led them to the basement. He had only moments to put the anchor back into place. The gray man hesitated, fear and distrust coming over his face.

"Do you want to go to Sun City or not?" Zian asked.

The man looked to the girl who nodded. The man who used to be an anchor hesitantly led the way back to his prison. The girl shot Zian a suspicious look.

The building flickered, making Zian's heart skip a beat, making him lose his breath, and confusing his thoughts until they finally neared the basement.

A low moan rose as if the basement itself was in pain. It was only then that Zian remembered that he had no glowworms and would have to scamper around in the dark. But a glow rose up from the basement through the stairwell. The light shifted the way it does with glowworms, only it would take thousands of them to make this much light.

Zian ran down the stairs. A burst of light flashed below him. A statue groaned as glowworms burst from his eyes, mouth, and nose. The statue glowed with a thousand worms, like rays of sunshine bursting out of him. Through his skin, the telltale illumination of glowworms slid along his face, arms, and feet.

The anchors were still alive. If the anchors had been enchanted stone like the rest of the building, the worms would have harmlessly crawled around looking for a host, then died when they didn't find any. The anchors couldn't move, couldn't even cringe away. How aware were they as the worms crawled leisurely up their legs and chewed their way into their stomachs?

For every fortune, there is an equal and opposite fortune. Fifty anchors were dying in the most horrible way. And he had caused it. He had to keep it from cascading. He had to restore the balance.

If he didn't equalize it, something freakishly happy would happen in Sun City. Maybe fifty people would come back to their families from the dead. Or maybe a bunch of old ladies would suddenly find themselves young again. He didn't know the details, but it would be miraculous enough for the rest of the Sunshiners to want it to happen to them too. They would pressure the masters into causing more disasters in Shadow City of equal or greater proportion to what just happened. And soon, this level of horror would be the norm.

"Stay here," he said to the couple. "You can leave the basement but stay in the building."

They looked at him in confusion and distrust.

"You're going to be Sunshiners," said Zian. And this time, he meant it. He ran out of the building. He had to be careful that the final outcome would be balanced. If the end result was positive for Shadow City, Sunshiners would complain, and the masters would hunt the Shadow refugees and bring them back. The balance had to be just right.

Outside, the accountant was furiously scribbling in his ledger while keeping a keen eye on the transactions. "How many have gone into the building?" asked Zian.

"Forty-two. And these two have almost paid their price," said the accountant, pointing his quill at two addicts who leaned their heads toward the gangsters to let them scoop another dream out of their heads.

Zian had seen two disappear, plus there were forty-three in the building including the old lady who lost her husband. So forty-five people were on their way to Sun City. "I'm taking them," Zian said. "And this one." He pointed to the nearest person. Forty-eight.

Those around him stirred and began reaching out to him, yelling, "Me! Pick me!" Zian scanned the crowd, trying to find Mei, but the people near him grabbed and pulled on his robe, yelling for his attention. He backed off behind the gangsters where the crowd wouldn't dare pass.

"Mei!" He yelled into the crowd but his voice was drowned out. "Mei!" Time was running out. The dying anchors couldn't hold the building for much longer. He motioned for the chosen people to step forward, which they did with trepidation, despite their desperation.

"Let these people into the tower." He handed the accountant his bag of dust. He wouldn't need it where he was going. A half bag of dust could make the accountant a gang boss if the others didn't kill him first. "No one else comes into the building."

The accountant took the bag as if in a dream. But he had to tug at the bag before Zian could make himself let go.

"Mei!" He yelled one last time but wasn't sure if his voice carried beyond the edge of the crowd. There were two more spots—one for him and one for her. Fifty anchors eaten alive. Fifty Shadowers freed in an impossible bid for freedom. Zian hoped it evened out. In Sun City, he wouldn't need to worry about punishments, and she wouldn't need to fear the streets. Where was she?

"Mei!" His voice drowned in the crowd. She was nowhere to be seen.

He finally pointed to a grimy child with hair so tangled it seemed like a single mass. He nodded, letting her know she had been chosen. She ran toward the tower with hungry eyes.

The chosen ones rushed into the building. A roar of despair rose behind them from the crowd as they entered the flickering doorway. Zian turned to follow them.

Then he saw her.

Mei was arguing with the gang woman, pleading, with her hand extended. Her palm sparkled in the flickering light. Clever Mei. Through unfathomable willpower, she had saved her dust. Held it in her bare palms, fought the siren's call of her addiction. All so she could trade it with the gangsters for a once-in-a-lifetime passage to Sun City.

The gang woman shook her head, her neck jiggling, and pointed at Zian. The flickering was so fast now that it looked to Zian that Mei turned her head to look at him in a series of still images. What had taken her so long to get here? Had she taken a grain of dust and lost time? More likely, she had to defend her precious dust against others who might have sniffed its tantalizing scent.

It should have been her. Mei was always the smart one, the deserving one. But there was only room for one more if he was to keep the balance.

In his mind, Zian waved for her to come. He imagined her ecstatic face as she ran past the crowd toward him. They would run together, holding hands just like in the old days. When they reached the flickering door, she'd say, "I forgive you." And he'd let her go inside while he stood outside. He'd let go of her hand just before the building flickered out for the last time.

Afterward, only a gaping crater would sit in its place, charred and twisted with broken roots. An open wound in the city's foundation. The buzzing would fade along with the flickering light, leaving him eternally alone on the streets of Shadow City.

Zian came back to the moment and met Mei's gaze across the dirt gap. She stood half hidden in the crowd, behind the fat woman blocking her way. An endless sea of suffering surrounded her—jagged elbows and scuffed knees, starved faces full of desperation, people waving their skeletal arms to catch Zian's attention. Mei's eyes shined an intense hope he hadn't seen since she was a child. Her body tensed, fully loaded to run toward him as soon as he gave the word.

"I'm sorry," he said. He didn't know if she heard him.

"I just can't . . ." He turned away, but not before catching a glimpse of her hope crumpling.

His chest felt weighted, his fingers icy. He cursed himself ten thousand times for being the worst kind of filth as he walked toward the tower with his head hung low.

But somewhere before he reached the door, his footfalls got heavier, his stride slower.

His hand blindly waved Mei to come forward.

He never saw her face as she ran past him and into the building. But just before the tower flickered out, just before the chosen ones disappeared, Zian managed to lift his head to see Mei look back to meet his eyes.

The Water Weapon

Brenda W. Clough

THE arching glass roof of the Crystal Palace was wonderfully high. But it was not high enough for the Chinese dragon, which had to be housed outside the Great Exposition of 1851. Throngs of English and foreign visitors crowded close to gape, even daring to extend a hand to feel the steam-hot wood. Its sinuous neck, cunningly jointed and riveted, flexed with a creak of bamboo against bamboo. When steam shot from the red-painted nostrils, the mob groaned with amazement.

"Oh, my stars!" Mrs. Grace Stulting held her bonnet onto her head and leaned back to look as the carved head swayed above.

"Purely mechanical." Mr. Bucket wagged his head tolerantly. "You can see the metal gears, moving the neck. *And* the stokers for the steam."

"Still, it's a marvel," Grace sighed.

Mr. Bucket drew her gloved hand through his arm. His tweed coat was too warm for the London summer and shiny at the elbows. He looked like the elderly uncle taking a country cousin to see the Prince Albert's Great Exposition of 1851. "Let's pay attention to the job here," he said quietly. "That monster's just a show—a fancy steam engine. Scotland Yard's got a tip about some bigger magic here. So now we're going to edge in closer,

Mrs. S, and you keep your ears sharp. Those Chinese, they won't be expecting a young white lady to understand their lingo. They might let fall something we need to hear."

In her happy excitement, Grace hardly listened. She has been recruited into this jaunt merely because the preferred candidate, her husband, was busy addressing the Anglo-American Mission to the Orient Society. But Hermanus would have dismissed the Great Exposition as frivolous time-wasting, unlikely to further the spread of the Gospel. Now, on a legitimate patriotic mission with no less than the famous Inspector Bucket paying the entrance fee, Grace intended to enjoy herself.

"Oh, look! Souvenirs!" Exotically dressed Chinese attendants were coming forward with wide baskets. Eager hands reached for the gifts.

"For free? Huh." Bucket snagged one for his companion. "A paper toy. What's that in aid of, I wonder— they could easily charge halfpence."

"It's cute! Look, the little stick makes it stand up!" A bamboo skewer served as a handle, to support a red and black paper copy of the steam-powered giant dragon.

"Come along then, let's get closer." They edged forward through the crowd. Bucket had brought a pair of gilt opera glasses, through which he pretended to examine the gears and wooden joints of the construction towering above him. "Now, Mrs. S., ears sharp. What's that johnny saying? He's no coolie. From his robe, he's a magician, right?"

"Yes, that's what the tassels on his cap mean. Three gold ones mean he's a wizard at the Imperial Court." Grace gazed fixedly at the Chinese stokers shoveling coal into the furnace that heated the boiler. "He says English people are very quiet. So true! In Nanjing the cacophony would be immense."

"Don't waste energy on commentary, Mrs. S.," Bucket reproved her. "Quick—what's his pal saying?"

Ruffled, Grace said, "He's agreeing, that's all. Says Englishmen are like zombies."

The glasses slipped from Bucket's upraised hand, rescued from disaster only by their silk cord around his wrist. "You're sure of that?"

"My Mandarin is excellent, Inspector."

"Now don't take my manner wrong, Mrs. S.," Bucket said. "You're doing the British Empire a vital service here . . . Is that the princess?"

"Lady Mei," Grace corrected him. "She's not really a princess. She's the granddaughter of the last emperor and a concubine." Along with everyone else they gaped at the splendid silk-clad figure in the gold sedan chair. Carried in full panoply through the Exposition, the exotic lady drew even more crowds to view the dragon. Half the ragtag and bobtail of London seemed to be following her, all the poorer people who had bought the cheap end-of-season tickets into the Exposition. The servants filtered through the press, distributing paper dragons hand over fist.

The foreman in charge of the stokers shouted in Chinese, "Back, all of you! He's going to go!"

Suddenly the Chinese were in retreat, scurrying past them. Grace grabbed Inspector Bucket's tweed arm. "Inspector, let us step back. I think there are problems with the boiler."

"The way they were stoking it, the pressure must be terrible. Look nonchalant, now. Talk to me about your husband's mission work."

"Our plan is to start a school in Nanjing—" Grace felt the tug on her skirt instantly. A lady always has to be aware of her surroundings—in addition to pickpockets and purse-snatchers, there were always unsavory men who tried to get too close to women in public. And then even a street-length skirt was always getting caught in things or picking up dirt. Pulling surreptitiously with one hand had no effect. She shot a quick glance back. "Oh, sweet Jesus!"

An enormous brass-tipped claw had speared down, pinning the flounce of her skirt to the earth. Hot humid steam puffed around her, and a huge hissing voice huffed in Chinese, "Little foreign-devil lady. You understand me. Do you not?"

Grace gaped up at the tremendous bamboo head, big as her own body, swaying above her. The red eyes, which she had taken for panes of tinted mica, were lit not with flame but with life. White steam shot from the carved nostrils. "You're alive!" she blurted in Mandarin.

"Behold me, the new Prometheus," the dragon hissed, very low. "It's a poor magic that can only reanimate dead flesh, eh?"

"By Jove, the clockwork's amazing clever." Bucket, trapped in monolingual ignorance, let go of her arm and stepped back to stare upward.

With another huge hiss of steam the dragon lumbered forward. Suddenly, Grace was divided from the Inspector and the rest of the crowd by the coil of an enormous hot bamboo tail. It occurred to her that if the dragon encircled her completely, she would boil like a Christmas pudding. "Inspector!" she called in English, before he was shoved out of hearing. "It talks!"

Bucket cast another glance up at the dragon, which winked a glowing red orb at him. As he vanished from her view, Grace saw Bucket's eyes bug out with astonishment.

The bearers set the sedan chair down, and the lady within took effortless charge. "You say she speaks properly, Lung? In this barbarous land—amazing! Who are you, woman? What do you seek here? Let her go, Lung."

Slowly the enormous claw pulled up and away, and the hot humid bamboo coil widened its compass. Drawing a grateful breath of cooler air, Grace no longer felt like a dumpling in a bamboo steamer. "Thank you." She twitched her skirt free. A good Christian woman told the truth—Bucket surely knew she could not lie. "My parents are Presbyterian missionaries, and I have lived fifteen years in Nanjing. There were rumors of Chinese magic at the Exposition, and I see they are fully true!"

"They do not believe, these English," the Chinese wizard said to his mistress. "Their own New Prometheus was hushed up, and there are no magicians among their common folk. Either the peasantry here are lazy, or fools. It's taking them too long. We should have concentrated our efforts in India."

Surely this beast was what Scotland Yard had sent Grace to find. "You need not think that Britain is going to stand by while magically animated monsters invade!"

Lady Mei giggled, and Grace saw that under the brocade and headdress she was very young, perhaps sixteen years old. From the height her chair lent her Lady Mei reached over and patted the hot bamboo neck with a tiny pale hand. "Lung here? He's nothing but a worm-boy, my favorite bug."

"More," the dragon muttered very softly, huffing steam between each syllable. "More. Feed me, slaves!" The sweating stokers leaped to the work again.

Grace kept in mind Bucket's earlier musings. "Then what is it for?"

"Why, for this." Imperious but girlish, Lady Mei flicked her fan around. "To attract many English people." She snapped her fingers. "More paper dragons! I want every one of the foreigners to have one. And let some tea be brought, and my maid, to mend our guest's garment."

Servants hurried out with more overflowing baskets.

A wooden stool was set for Grace, and traditional handleless porcelain tea cups were offered. A young maid with needle and thread knelt shyly by her seat to cobble together the hole in her flounce. It all seemed quite hospitable and innocuous; no English host could do better. Constitutionally inclined to believe the best of everybody, Grace took a careful sip of the hot tea.

"I know what to do," Lady Mei declared. "They have eyes but they don't see. Tell this one the story—the one about the water."

The wizard stared at his mistress, pondering, and then nodded. To Grace he said, "Were you in Nanjing during the last war?"

"The Opium War? No, I was at school here in Britain."

The wizard smiled at her with an unpleasant glint of teeth. "Perhaps you will be there for the next one. Or the one after that. The end of the nineteenth century in China will be full of incident."

"Don't frighten her, magus," Lady Mei said. "Scaring British people makes them angry. These big scary magics, like Lung here, do not win wars."

"Better to be like water, seeping through the earth, penetrating everywhere but impossible to grasp." The wizard glared at Grace as if it were her fault. "Some small simple magic. Perhaps like the one in the children's story—your *ah-mah* will have told it to you. The one about the spell that turns bullets aside."

"I have heard that fairy tale," Grace said uneasily. "If it were true it would be destructive for all empires, everywhere." Soldiers and armies kept the world in order; without the suasion of guns, how would governments stay in power, or kings on their thrones?

"I don't care." Lady Mei shrugged a green silk shoulder. "Another Opium War will destroy us. In a hundred years there will be no more Chinese Empire. It would be only fair if there were no British Empire either. Look, here the fat one comes back again." To the stokers she added, "Give over!"

"Mrs. S.!" Bucket came pushing through the throng, a short plump figure with a couple of tall bobbies in his wake. "Mrs. S., you're safe now!"

In justice Grace felt she had to say, "Inspector, nothing bad has happened to me."

"Tea," the Chinese wizard said in tinny English, bowing to Bucket. "The maid, to mend accidental damage."

"Unauthorized magic use within a Royal Park," Bucket retorted. "A dangerous magical animal on the rampage."

"Would it were so," the wizard said with another bow. "Our dragon is difficult to maintain."

And indeed, with the stokers at rest, the bamboo dragon sagged. Joint by steamy wooden joint it drooped down to earth, groaning and creaking. Coolies with iron rods supported its descent to prevent breakage. The vapor from the wooden nostrils thinned and died out.

The Exposition mob all around shouted in disappointment. "*Get 'im fixed!*" "*Pretty poor show, chinks!*" Their clamor was angry. Grace remembered uncomfortably that the entire point of the Exposition was to entertain and distract a restive populace.

"More paper dragons," Lady Mei ordered in Chinese.

"False alarm," one bobby said, inspecting the brass gears. "Sadly taken in!" And the other accepted a paper dragon as he murmured in reply, "Well, old Bucket is getting on in years."

Grace jumped to her feet, to distract Bucket from that last hurtful remark. "I am so glad you came back, Inspector. I long to tour the rest of the Pavilion! Great lady, thank you for your kindness and hospitality."

Their eyes were now nearly on a level. Lady Mei eyed

her thoughtfully, while the little maid took her teacup. "The British are enemies," she said, "but I do not believe missionaries are enemies."

"You went to a mission school," Grace deduced. A minor Imperial scion could do that, and Lady Mei had quoted Jeremiah. In return she admitted, "Well, I do not feel that the last war was a Christian one."

"Indeed!" The two women stared, silently acknowledging that in some other time and place they might have been friends. "If ever you have a daughter," Lady Mei said at last, "name her Pearl. It will be a name of warding, in the storm to come."

Hermanus had already declared that their first daughter was to be named Caroline, after his mother. But there might be a second daughter, or failing that a granddaughter. "Pearl would be a beautiful name," Grace said. "Farewell!"

The bobbies went ahead, but Inspector Bucket tucked her arm through his. "You became mighty cozy, Mrs. S. What in thunder did they blab to you?"

"I'm not sure," Grace confessed. "I think we were talking about children's stories." She repeated as best she could the gist of everything. "They can't be trying to warn us. Why warn someone you plan to fight another war with?"

"And if it's a warning, then why tell you? Why not deliver the threat through official diplomatic channels?" With his other hand Bucket rubbed his chin. "Something cunning's going on—those Chinese are always at it. The stories I could tell you! I'm sorry we can't stay and see more of the Exhibition. I have to go over to the Yard and report. I'll see you safe to the Presbyterian Mission on the way." Under his guidance they made their way speedily to the cab stand at the edge of the park.

As one of the bobbies opened the door of a hansom for her Grace said, "Inspector, I told her that Britain was wrong to fight the war in China. I hope that wasn't treasonous."

A Chinese servant thrust yet another paper dragon at him, and Bucket stuffed it absently into his tweed pocket. "Right or wrong, the Opium War is over and done with, water under the bridge. Come along then, up you go."

Obediently she climbed up into the hansom. A bobby and Bucket followed, sitting across from her. He slammed the door shut and tapped on the roof. Immediately the vehicle lurched into motion.

"Pardon me, ma'am." The bobby's voice was loud but humble. "Is this yours?"

"Oh dear, I must have trodden on it." She took the paper dragon from him and smoothed it flat. Perhaps it could be refolded into shape? Then she peered more closely at the crudely printed red and black pattern. That was not a design of scales—it was English letters, oddly drawn as if with a brush, but easily readable. "An Infallible Spell," she read aloud slowly, "To Make Him That Work It Invulnerable to Weapons."

"Good lord!" Bucket's round commonplace countenance suddenly seemed suety, slick with more than the summer heat. He took out his own dragon and flattened it. The spell was closely printed on the underside in black.

"The Exhibition opened in May—"

"And now it's August," Grace said.

They stared all three at each other in dawning horror. Thousands upon thousands of these paper dragons must have been distributed, water trickling unstoppably throughout England. No wonder there were rumors of magic at Regent's Park!

"The wizard said we were slow," Grace remembered. "They poured out the secret, and nobody noticed."

"For a little while." On his plump fingers Bucket

tallied up the enemies of the Empire. "Ireland, Wales, India, Burma. And do you know how many anarchists and revolutionaries the Crown has already arrested? Every one of 'em will know about this soon, if they don't already."

"And what about that Marx chappie?" the bobbie said. "The Yard is keeping an eye on him. Russian bloke, but lives right here in Chelsea—spends his time writing about how the common Englishman should rise up and throw over the government."

"If the common man learns how to make bullets bounce, the Empire is in the soup," Bucket said flatly. "And that's what they've been doing, those Chinese— giving the secret to the common man, here and in India and Lord knows where else."

"The Yard," the bobby said feverishly. "We've got to get to Scotland Yard." He put his head out, to shout at the driver.

"I can help," Grace said to Bucket. She was not sure if she was doing an un-Christian thing, but she was certain it had to be done. The only hope for civilization now was if all nations had this terrifying knowledge at once, together. Then one and all could face rebellion and chaos. "I will translate it back into Mandarin. We can empower the Chinese peasantry. They hate their masters as much as—"

As much as the British poor hate their rulers, she would have said, but one could not say such things aloud.

"Yes." Bucket nodded slowly. "Let's all go down into the abyss together."

The Right to Eat Decent Food

Urania Fung

W HILE my fellow American teachers and I taught
English at a private boarding school in China, we
were fascinated by what we saw as exotic superstitions.
On the streets of Changping and Beijing, pictures of warriors posted on doors guarded against intruders. During
the Year of the Ring, girls would wear rings on their fingers to ward off bad luck. Restaurants often had altars
offering food to gods in return for good business. A TV
program showed farmers smoking out foxes because of
the belief that some foxes were shape-shifting demons.
Despite their officially secular government, the Chinese
still had a healthy regard for both gods and demons.

Naturally, we had complaints, too, and our biggest one
concerned the cafeteria food at our school: dry, tasteless
buns; stir-fried meats and vegetables flavored with an
obnoxious-tasting radish; greasy metal trays; rats nesting
in a corner; hair in the noodles. At first, we easily avoided
the cafeteria by eating out. Less than two US dollars
could get us Peking duck. One US dollar could buy us an
order of ten little steamed buns that exploded with soup
when we bit into them. A few cents could get us a wide
assortment of snacks. But in April 2003, these cheap and
delicious luxuries were snatched from us because of the
Severe Acute Respiratory Syndrome (SARS) epidemic.

Though public schools had closed, the administrators at our private institution chose to quarantine teachers, students, and workers in hopes of keeping the campus SARS-free and able to continue with lessons. With the foreign teachers seated around a conference table, the principal, whose body shape resembled that of an upright walrus, informed us that the SARS outbreak should be over soon and that there was no SARS on campus: "Anyone with so much as a cough has been sent home until either they are well or they have a doctor's note saying their illness isn't SARS. Please rest assured that the cafeteria is a clean and safe place to eat."

My eyes slid toward my tall, blond roommate, Mike, who had a cough, yet was obviously still on campus. The next day, I was walking to the cafeteria with him when dread slowed our steps to a stop.

Mike wrung his hands. "They don't get it! Even if I don't come down with SARS, I'll die of something else unless those rats are out of the cafeteria and the hair is out of the food. What do you say, Steven?"

Back in the United States, I had been known for being so straitlaced I didn't even jaywalk, but I couldn't handle the cafeteria either. "We need decent food."

We feigned interest in the students playing on the grassy field in the middle of the campus, all the while searching for a place where we could hop the fence. We scouted around the teacher apartments, student dorms, workers' dorms, the administration building, financial office, primary school building, middle school building, and clinic. No good. Security guards in black uniforms and red berets paced in front of every possible escape route. We passed the basketball courts and found that tall boards in mismatching shades of gray had been placed against the otherwise climbable wire fence. The administration must have already suspected people would try sneaking out.

As we dragged ourselves back to our fifth-story

teacher apartment, I sensed something following us. A bush rustled. Probably a squirrel.

Stomachs rumbling, we settled down in our two-bedroom apartment to discuss alternatives. Perhaps Mike could call up his girlfriend and have her throw food over the fence to us while we tossed her the money.

A loud knocking jolted us.

I answered the door to find a slender, teenage Chinese girl in a black student uniform, the name of the school in yellow block letters across her chest. She had a long, elegant nose, and her eyes were as bright and clear as an infant's.

I caught myself staring and turned to Mike. "Not my student."

Mike looked blank. "Not mine either."

The girl smiled. "My name is Rabbit. May I come in?"

Neither Mike nor I laughed. I already had students who had chosen Beaver, Tigger, and Harry Potter for their English names. Mike nodded, so she stepped in, and I closed the door behind her.

She wouldn't sit, and her Chinese accent thickened when she spoke again. "Teachers, I heard you want, ah, decent food."

I don't know why I squirmed as though I had been caught with porn magazines. "It's no big deal."

"But, of course, you have, ah, the right to eat decent food," Rabbit said, her voice full of sympathy.

Mike's eyes widened. "You mean, you can do something about this?"

Rabbit's smile broadened. "Trust me?"

Our growling stomachs decided for us. We gave her some money with the understanding that she would keep the change for her services.

She brought back burgers and fries. Curious to know how she managed it, we made plans to watch her. One of us would wait in the apartment for the food while the other would stand outside somewhere along the path we thought she took. We could always see her enter and leave the apartment complex, but somehow, we would lose her after she turned at the financial office building.

A few nights later Mike and I decided to watch a DVD we had bought off the street before the quarantine. In the middle of the movie, Mike suddenly stood and walked around in front of the screen.

"Hey, what's up?" I said.

He kept pacing. I asked again. No answer. What should I do? After a while, he sat back down and stared at the screen with ridiculous intensity. Toward the end of the show, he shuddered, then relaxed, then frowned.

"What's going on?"

"What do you last remember?" I asked.

He only remembered the first half. I filled him in. Instead of wondering what might have come over him, he raised an eyebrow at me before going to bed. I don't like it when people change personalities after a few drinks, and I like it far less when they change for no reason.

For the first time since arriving in China, I slept with my bedroom door locked.

I was anal about keeping my room tidy, but two days later, I awoke to see my closet open, my desk overturned, and clothes, hangers, and books all over the floor. The door was still locked. The window was fine. Could I have trashed my room? I thought carefully. We had been quarantined for a week. Had cabin fever ever done this to anyone? Could Mike and I have caught the newest in scary diseases? Maybe I should have tied myself down at night.

Four days passed normally before the next episode. This time, I was watching CNN when I heard clangs and thuds from the kitchen. I leaned forward to peer in. Mike was swinging a butcher knife at the refrigerator.

I crept out of the apartment and found a security

guard. My Chinese was too poor for me to explain, so I gestured for him to follow me upstairs. When I opened the door, the apartment was quiet except for the TV. The guard looked around.

Mike sat on the couch with a soft drink. "Something wrong?"

Annoyed, the guard walked out.

I checked the fridge. It was scarred enough to belong in a horror flick.

Immediately, I sought out a local English teacher named Judy. She was Mongolian and had a round, flat face. While I taught ninth graders listening and pronunciation, she taught them grammar and vocabulary. With a cup of tea in my hands, I sat down across from her at her plastic table and looked out the window at a dirt yard fenced in by a brick wall. Beyond the wall, brown patches of dead trees in a sloping forest looked clearer than ever as my mind grasped at the world as though for dear life.

I didn't want to appear as scared as I felt, so we first talked about the quarantine. The principal had said it would last two weeks. Now he was saying it would not be over until the May holiday. We debated whether or not we should believe even that. Then I told Judy how strangely Mike had been acting and asked her if she had any idea what Mike and I had been doing differently.

"You two do not eat with us in the cafeteria," Judy said as correctly as an instructor on a language tape. She even looked the part in her silk blouse and black slacks.

I smiled because I thought it was cute. "Can't stand it."

"What do you do?"

"Can't say."

"You sometimes have a burger smell."

I felt my face flush. "So?"

Judy gazed at the forest, which was often obscured by white, smoky ribbons of pollution. We sat in meditative silence before I noticed workers shoveling near the brick wall.

"Is something wrong with the wall?"

Judy watched the workers add bricks beneath it. "No, they are keeping out foxes."

"I didn't know we had foxes." I hadn't even seen birds and thought pollution had killed them. "What do they do?"

Judy made a face as she concentrated. "They play."

I couldn't tell if she had meant to sound so ominous, but I could tell the answer was too complicated for her to fully explain in English. "What games?"

Judy looked as though I'd asked her to name every Chinese dish in the country. Then it occurred to me that someone else might have been suffering the same sorts of problems I was and had filed a complaint, attributing the problems to fox demons. Ridiculous superstitions.

"Can filling in the holes really keep them out?"

Judy shrugged. Of course not.

But, with Mike the way he was, I was willing to try anything. "Can they be killed?"

Again, that look of concentration on Judy's face. "Foxes? Yes. Fox demons? Very difficult."

"I've heard of garlic keeping vampires away. Can it work on fox demons?"

Judy shook her head. "The only people they leave alone are enlightened."

Great.

I returned to my apartment and packed, prepared to stay at some other teacher's apartment for the rest of my contract, which ended in August. Mike was still watching the news. I placed myself near the front door and faced him while gripping the straps of my duffle bag.

"Have you seen the fridge?"

Mike set his cup down on our coffee table. "Yeah, I've been meaning to ask you what's up with that."

"You went berserk at it with a butcher knife."

Eyes narrowed, Mike leaned back and stretched an arm along the back of the couch. "Yeah, right."

"Do you never wonder if, like, maybe you're doing strange things?"

"You're the one losing your mind, throwing stuff around. How many times do I have to tell you? I'm tired of cleaning up after you. Must be this freaking cabin fever."

The warmth from my body drained into the tile floor. The days that had seemed to pass normally must not have. I took a deep breath, hardly able to believe what I was about to say. "Rabbit's food might have something to do with this. Let's try the cafeteria food instead."

Predictably, Mike laughed. "You are so out of your mind, dude."

I had hoped to leave before Rabbit delivered dinner, but then came a familiar pattern of loud knocks.

"Well?" Mike said. "Get it."

"I don't trust her anymore."

"Oh, for Pete's sake!" Mike pushed himself off the couch, shoved me aside, and opened the door. He pulled his wallet out of his back pocket and paid Rabbit, who handed him a bag. Then she handed me a bag.

Before, I couldn't have resisted the smell of burgers and fries, but now it made me sick. I backed away. "No thanks. No more for me."

Rabbit wrinkled her brow. "Why?"

I stared at her, wondering how I had come to suspect she was a shape-shifting fox demon. Was it like human rights, something that existed if enough people in the country believed in it? When I returned to America, would I still think she might be a demon?

Rabbit's bewilderment mutated into a sly smile. She held the bag behind her back while her other hand slid down my arm, the one with the duffel bag. "I know what you really want. Why not take it?"

A treacherous desire trembled through me. I bolted down two flights of stairs and pounded on a fellow foreign teacher's door before risking a look back up. No sign of Rabbit.

I settled in with the other teacher before braving the cafeteria's greasy trays and hairy food. Like the rest of the campus, the cafeteria was half empty, which was no surprise since many students had left the boarding school. As I told the cafeteria workers what to add to my tray (there was no line to wait in anymore), I thought about how even young, healthy, local students could get diarrhea from this stuff. But diarrhea was the least of my problems now. I ate with some other teachers, who told me the best news ever. Since the demand for teachers had diminished, I could sign an early termination agreement with the school.

This I did. I should have dropped by my old apartment to say farewell to Mike, but I kept imagining him greeting me with the butcher knife. After I flew back home, my parents enforced the American government's recommended quarantine of ten days for travelers from SARS-infected areas, which I accepted as a fitting touch to the end of my Chinese adventures. This last confinement was a breeze, thanks to my mother's cooking.

I emailed Mike many times, but he never replied. The last news I heard of him came a year later when I met with a fellow former teacher at a dim sum restaurant. We were toasting to all the good times back in China when she mentioned that Mike had disappeared about a week after I left, officially dismissed for "wild behavior." She couldn't elaborate because that was all the principal would say to the remaining foreign teachers.

Away from Rabbit, Mike should have recovered. To this day, I still don't know what happened to him. But whatever the case, I've kept him in my prayers.

Papa and Mama

Wen Y. Phua

PAPA was swimming listlessly in his glass tank, so Ning wrapped her hands around him, and though he writhed and flapped his reddish-gold tail, she managed to get him into a bowl of fresh water. He looked sicker than yesterday. She hoped the spoonful of salt she'd stirred into the water would invigorate him.

As she hoisted his heavy tank to the bathroom to scrub, she started singing what used to be Papa's favorite tune. Sometimes, she wondered if he could hear her. After all, he was immersed in water, unlike Mama, who was perched in her carved wooden cage and could sing far prettier songs. But despite Ning's doubts, she sang for Papa as he had sung to her when she was little.

Two years ago, not long after Papa and Mama had died in the train wreck and left Ning an orphan, Uncle had come home one morning with a fish in a red bucket and told her this was Papa.

She didn't believe him at first. She was thirteen already, not a gullible little girl. But as she yelled at Uncle for lying to her, the fish popped its silvery gold head out the water, and as its gleaming black eyes met hers, a flash of tingling warmth shot through her, and she just knew . . .

Uncle didn't scold her, as he sometimes did for being disrespectful, but sat patiently with her to explain.

Each morning since the seventh and last day of her parents' funeral, Uncle had risen before dawn and ridden his bicycle west along the dusty village streets till he reached the old bamboo grove Mama had enjoyed strolling through with Papa. There, Uncle would get off his bicycle and push two sticks of smoking incense into the ground. After telling Papa and Mama he was there, he'd hike down the beaten trail to the lily-covered pond where Papa had spent most Sundays fishing. For an hour, Uncle would trudge around, peering into the clear water, after which he'd head for work.

For ninety mornings, Uncle had left the bamboo grove empty-handed. But on the ninety-first morning, he glimpsed a dazzling shimmer amid the reeds growing along the pond's shallow edges. When he strode over, he spotted a luminous fish. It was shorter than the span of his hand and had a silvery head, a vivid yellow body blazing with orange streaks, and a reddish-gold tail.

Uncle knew there was no other fish like it in the pond. When he dipped his hands in to scoop it up, it didn't swim away or struggle, removing any doubts in his mind that this was his brother reincarnated.

Now the fish was Ning's to care for, which was her duty as his daughter.

Three days later, on the hundredth day following her parents' death, Uncle found Mama flapping through the grove. Mama was a golden yellow bird with a silvery white crown, orange wing tips, and a red streaked tail that glistened under the sun. It was from these colors that Uncle knew her, and when he called her name, she came. Mama matched Papa in so many ways. They both were fond of the same colors, and now in their reincarnated forms, their body hues matched.

Uncle had bemoaned the fact that Mama couldn't share Papa's tank. But Ning secretly rejoiced when he said they could start eating meat again, for there was no longer any danger of them unwittingly eating her parents.

Two years had since passed. Papa had grown to almost twice his initial length. But now, he was ill. The more Ning thought of it, the more convinced she was of her failing. Uncle had always said it was his duty to give his brother and sister-in-law a home and keep them safe, but it was the daughter's duty to see to their health and happiness. Ning wondered where she might have gone wrong.

Mama squawked when Ning transferred Papa back into the big tank. "Just a moment, Mama," Ning said.

Mama continued squawking, making Ning's skin prickle, but Ning finished tossing food into Papa's tank before stepping to Mama's cage in the corner.

"I'm here, Mama. Shh . . ." Ning cooed to Mama, but Mama still screeched raucously.

Ning felt at a loss. Mama had never been hard to take care of. All Ning had to do daily was clean the cage and give her ample fresh water, seeds, and nuts. She'd done this already after coming home from school. Why then was Mama so riled up? Ning poked a finger through the bars, intending to stroke Mama, but Mama pecked at Ning's hand, almost nipping her.

"Mama, please, what's wrong?" Ning asked. She tried singing a lullaby, but Mama didn't quiet down.

Soon, Ning had to leave Papa and Mama alone in their room, for it was time to meet her friend. With a heavy chest, Ning got on her bicycle and rode to Liwei's house.

When Ning met Liwei, her petite classmate with a head of unusually frizzy hair, Ning smiled and laughed as usual. However, as they were halfway through their homework, Liwei dropped her pen.

"You're not happy," Liwei said. "What's the matter?"

Ning faked a laugh. "Who says I'm not happy?" Tightening her grip on her pen, she looked down and continued with her essay.

"I'm your best friend," Liwei said, but didn't pursue the issue.

Ning forced herself to keep writing. Liwei's understanding warmed Ning's heart. *Sorry*, she wanted to say. But what could she tell Liwei? That Papa was a fish and Mama a bird? Her stomach felt knotted. She spent another hour scribbling, and then realizing she could barely concentrate, she told Liwei her head was hurting and went home. She hoped Liwei wouldn't be too upset.

"Uncle, what do you think is wrong with Papa and Mama?" Ning asked when she sat down to dinner. "Papa has no energy, Mama is agitated."

"Maybe they're unhappy or worried about something," Uncle said as Aunt piled white rice into a blue porcelain bowl and handed it to him. "How have you been doing in school? Do you have any problems? Animals can sense things, especially charmed ones like your Papa and Mama."

Ning frowned. "Papa and Mama look pretty ordinary to me."

"What do you mean, ordinary? Have you seen another bird or fish looking like them?" Uncle dipped a pot sticker into a bowl of black vinegar and sucked loudly as he bit into it.

"I mean they haven't done anything special," Ning said. It wasn't as if they'd seen all the birds and fishes in the world, so how could they conclude Papa and Mama looked unique?

"You haven't answered my question." Uncle put his chopsticks down. With his thin angular face, thick brows and stout build, he looked awfully stern as he stared at her. "How have you been doing in school?"

"The problem isn't me," Ning said, hiding her exasperation. "I got ninety-five points in the last test. I haven't done anything bad."

Aunt gave Ning her bowl of rice. "Yes, Ning, you've taken good care of your parents." Aunt's small lips stretched out into a long smile as she rubbed her bulging belly. "I hope my child will be as filial as you." Her glasses slipped down her flat nose, and she pushed them up with a knuckle, leaving a grain of rice stuck to her nose.

Uncle didn't notice the white blemish on Aunt's face and just picked up his chopsticks. "Ning will make a good big sister to our child."

Ning stifled a chuckle and grinned at Aunt, who was always so caring that she made her feel at home from the first time she stepped into their house two years ago. "Uncle, why do you say Papa and Mama are charmed?" Ning popped some cold bean sprouts into her mouth, chomped fast, and swallowed so she'd be ready to respond promptly to whatever Uncle said.

"They were reincarnated just within a hundred days of their passing." Uncle's voice emerged muffled through his mouthful of rice and pork. He finished chewing and swallowed. "When I found your Papa, his body was glowing. Usually, when people are reincarnated, they lose all their memories, but your Mama—she knew her name. After I called her, she even settled on my hand."

"What does it mean?" Ning asked. "Are they magical? Do they have special powers?" Could her parents bless them with good health and prosperity? Could they help her win a scholarship to a good university when she was older?

Uncle flicked his bushy brows up and down. "How would I know? I don't know everything. But though they are charmed, they were not blessed." He put down his chopsticks again and shook a finger at her. "Don't you get attached to any single place, I'm warning you, or you'll end up like your Papa and Mama. I want to be reincarnated as a man. And your poor Papa and Mama—one in the water, one in the air." He shook his head as he retrieved his chopsticks.

For the next few days, Papa continued in his lethargy, while Mama continued squawking whenever Ning entered their room. Ning noticed Mama squawked more frenetically whenever Ning attended to Papa.

"I know," Ning said one Friday afternoon after returning home from school. "Mama, you're worried about Papa. And you're angry with me for failing to take good care of him."

Mama's screeches escalated in pitch.

"Shh ... Mama." Ning felt like clamping her hands over her ears, but approached Mama's cage instead. "Mama, I promise I'll make Papa well again." Mama was so agitated Ning didn't dare open the cage, so she just tossed seeds onto the cage floor.

Mama flapped her wings and squawked furiously.

"I'm sorry, Mama," Ning said as she slowly backed out the room and closed the door. The squawking dropped to a muffle, then ceased altogether.

What was wrong with Papa? Ning pondered this as she paced around the backyard. Her white shoes soon became brown with mud, for the ground was still soggy from this morning's rain. The sky was beginning to clear, however. Sunlight pierced through broken clouds, reflecting off beads of water on the tree leaves and potted plants. While Ning made another circle around the backyard, a yellow glare caught her attention. It was a yellow flower with a pool of shimmering water gathered in its center, and as she blinked and looked away, its brightness left an imprint in her vision. She remembered Uncle saying how Papa had been glowing when he'd first found him in the pond. Ning wondered why she'd never seen Papa glow. Had it only been temporary, or could it have something to do with the pond?

At this new thought, Ning grabbed her bicycle and a plastic bucket and rode off for the bamboo grove. She took almost forty-five minutes to get there because she made a wrong turn on one of the little dirt roads and ended up getting halfway lost and having to make a big detour. The ground in the bamboo grove was uneven and squelchy, so she leaned her bicycle against some bamboo and walked.

Through a brushwork of mist and a faint drizzle of rain, the pond looked like a painting, surrounded by dark green reeds and supple willow trees whose slender branches and leaves drooped into the water, which was strewn with lily pads. An aura of serenity coupled with a fresh green fragrance made Ning smile. Now she understood why her father had loved fishing here.

Not wasting any time, Ning dunked the bucket into the limpid pond. Soon, Papa would get better. She filled the bucket almost to the brim and struggled off, sloshing water. Her arms ached, but she refused to rest. She heaved the bucket up into the wire basket at the rear of her bicycle, spilling more water.

The bucket was only three quarters full when Ning got home. Ignoring her aching back and limbs, she transferred Papa into a bowl and washed his tank to the background sound of Mama's screeching. The pond water filled only half the tank, but it was just enough.

To Ning's disappointment, Papa didn't glow or dart about with newfound energy. He only lay at the bottom, almost motionless except for the in and out movement of his gills and that ever so slight wavering of his fins.

Ning ran to Aunt, who was watching television in the living room.

"Aunt," Ning said, clenching and unclenching her

fists, "I tried my best. I brought Papa his pond water, but he's still sick."

Aunt patted Ning's damp hand. "You can't expect him to get well immediately. Anyway, how can pond water be the same as the pond?" She clutched Ning's hands in hers. "Don't worry. Your Papa was a good man in his previous life. Now he's a good fish. He'll be fine."

Yes, Ning realized. How could the pond water compare to the pond itself? Maybe Papa missed his pond.

Papa wasn't doing any better the next morning. Since she was off school on Saturdays, she put him in a bucket and carried him off on her bicycle. Luckily, Uncle was at work.

"Papa," she said, staring at him in the bucket. He looked up at her with his round black eyes. "I'm going to put you in your pond for a while." She caught his slick body and plopped him into a shallow recess of the pond where the reeds were growing.

Seconds after Papa landed in the water, he blazed like a lantern in silver and gold, red and orange. Squealing, Ning clapped her hands.

"Papa!"

As she was jumping and laughing, Papa shot off in a brilliant streak.

"Papa?" She stopped jumping. "Papa!"

Ning dropped to the ground. "Papa, please come back. Papa . . ." She covered her face with her hands. "Uncle will kill me."

For hours, she sat by the pond beneath the burning sun. Sweat rolled down her neck and back. Her stomach rumbled. But after she spent two to three hours clutching her belly, her hunger pangs disappeared. Still no sign of Papa.

"I'm sorry," she murmured repeatedly.

She drew her knees to her chest and hugged herself. Uncle would never forgive her. She recalled Aunt was due in a month or two. Very likely, they would both be busy with their baby and forget about her. The thought was small comfort, however.

She waited till the sun dipped below the horizon of bamboo before trudging away morosely.

"How could you be so stupid?" Uncle banged his hand against the door as he stared at Papa's empty tank. "Anything can happen to your Papa now that he's out in the wild." Aunt patted his shoulder, but he shrugged her hand off.

Ning cringed. "Sorry," she said, clasping and twitching her hands behind her back. "I just wanted Papa to get better."

The furrows in Uncle's forehead deepened. "And now he may get eaten by an eagle. Or just turn up dead one day because he's all alone and defenseless. Stupid, stupid!"

"Ning was so worried over her Papa," Aunt said.

Uncle banged the door again. "Worry should not make you switch off your head."

"I'm sorry." Ning wished she could sink into a dark hole. "I'll go to the pond every day till I get him back."

As Ning promised, she watched the pond daily. During the weekdays, she headed there straight after school, ignoring her friends, and on the weekends she spent her daylight hours sitting by the water. Sometimes, she spotted flashes of light flitting far within the pond. But though she called, Papa never came. When she got home at dusk, she had to suffer Uncle's glares and curt remarks. Over the days, Aunt gradually softened him. His brother was where he was happiest, she told him, to which he could not help but nod.

Ning cringed whenever Uncle yelled at her and called her stupid. She was sure once their baby was born they would remember she was just someone else's child, or worse, their bad niece who had failed to take care of her own father. Aunt was, as always, sweet to her, but once she had her own baby she would have no time for anyone else.

Each night, Ning lay staring in the darkness for over an hour before dozing off. Ning imagined that if Mama were her human self she would lie with her in bed and hold her tight until she fell asleep. Everyone was upset with her, including her friends, who thought she had abandoned them. Liwei had called Ning three times over the first few evenings, but Ning always felt too troubled to talk. Thereafter, Liwei stopped calling.

What hurt Ning most was seeing Papa's empty tank. For the first few days, she kept it filled with water, but mosquitoes began to breed, so she had to empty it.

At least now, strangely, Mama was quiet. She even chirped and sang sometimes.

Exactly two weeks after Papa's disappearance, he came to Ning in a trail of light. She'd been fretting by the pond the whole morning when suddenly she opened her eyes and spotted the approaching light. Papa's head bobbed out the water and their eyes met. Gasping, Ning leaned over and dove her hands in to grab him. To her surprise, he didn't struggle.

Now that Papa was home once more, Uncle was all smiles, while Mama was back to her squawking self. Ning was beginning to wonder if Mama was jealous.

Papa no longer glowed. Though he wasn't sluggish, neither was he as lively as he was back in the pond. Had she been selfish in taking him away? Mama kept squawking whenever Ning was in their room, making Ning feel knotted in the chest.

One day, Ning unlatched Mama's cage door on impulse and flung it wide open. Mama froze, as if stunned.

"Mama, I don't know what's bothering you. I guess

I wouldn't be happy either if I was locked up. Do you want to fly?" Ning's heart pounded in her ears as she spoke, but she steeled herself.

Mama twitched her head, then pecked at the seeds on her cage floor.

To show her sincerity, Ning strode to the window, and with trembling hands, slid it open. The cool night breeze swept in.

"Mama, do you want to fly back to the bamboo?" Perhaps a trip there would make Mama happy. And perhaps, like Papa, she too might return freely.

Mama remained calm and didn't fly out.

"I don't know what to do anymore, Mama," Ning said. Leaving the window open, she plodded to her room and took a warm shower.

When Ning returned to check on Papa and Mama before going to bed, she spotted Mama perched on the edge of Papa's tank. At the sound of Ning's entry, Mama flew back into her cage. Ning lingered in the room for half an hour, but Mama stayed still and silent behind bars that no longer locked her in.

The next morning, Mama was gone.

"Do you hate your parents?" Uncle asked, glaring down at Ning.

Ning shook her head, feeling lightheaded.

"Yes, your Mama was making a lot of noise. But how could you throw her out?" Uncle's eyes burned with anger and disappointment. "What would happen to you if we threw you out?"

Ning's skin prickled. "I'm sorry, Uncle. I didn't know what was wrong with Mama. I didn't know what to do anymore, and I—I—"

"Now your Mama is at the mercy of the outside world!" Uncle raised his right hand, making Ning shrink back for fear he would hit her, but he just let his hand drop.

"I'm sure Ning has her reasons," Aunt said as she stroked Ning's back.

Ning sucked in a deep breath and gathered her courage. "I just wanted to make Mama happy." She went on to describe how Mama had stopped screeching once the cage door was open, and how she had hopped onto Papa's tank and waited till the next morning before leaving.

After Ning was done speaking, Uncle just looked away and stormed out the room.

"I know you only did what you thought was best." Aunt squeezed Ning's shoulder, but Ning didn't feel any better.

Every day, Ning visited the bamboo grove. Sometimes, when she was lucky, she spotted Mama flying or perched amongst the slender bamboo. Occasionally, she heard her sing. Despite the vibrant yellow and orange of Mama's feathers, there were days when Ning missed glimpsing her. She often called to Mama, asking if she was okay. Once, Mama replied with a melodious trill.

Papa grew more lethargic by the day. Ning was so concerned she spent less and less time at the bamboo grove. She realized the situation was dire when he went a whole day without touching the flakes of food she had strewn into his tank. Even Uncle was worried.

"Maybe he needs to go back to his pond," Aunt said as they stared at Papa in his tank.

Uncle pursed his lips and slowly nodded. "I had thought to care for him, but—" He drooped his head, sighing.

Ning bit her lip. "It's my fault. I must have done something wrong. He's supposed to be happier with us family, isn't he?"

Aunt put an arm across Ning's shoulder and hugged her gently, keeping her other hand over her huge belly. "No, you've always done what you thought was best.

I think you've done a great job. Walk me back to my room, then go with Uncle to take your Papa back to his pond."

Ning held Aunt's arm and blinked hard, for her eyes were beginning to smart.

While Aunt rested in bed, Ning left with Uncle for the bamboo grove. This time, Papa rode at the back of Uncle's bicycle in the same red bucket Uncle had put him in two years ago.

The bamboo grove was alive with the chirping of insects. The sound calmed Ning as they got off their bicycles and continued on foot.

"Soon," Uncle told Papa.

Soon, Ning thought, Papa would be happily glowing again. She heard a familiar warbling. As she glanced skyward, she spotted Mama flying from branch to branch with another bird. Like Mama, the bird was golden yellow, but except for its black chest, it had no peculiar color markings.

"Look," Ning said, pointing.

Uncle smiled. "She found a friend."

"Yes." Ning clapped her hands. "Mama, now you have someone to talk to." How Papa and Mama must have suffered all along—so close to each other, yet separated in more ways than one. Though they still couldn't be together, at least they'd have their own companions.

Uncle grinned even wider when he saw Papa lighting up the water around him. "I'm sorry, you were right," he said as the beam of light that was Papa cut across to the other side of the rippling pond.

When they got home, Ning immediately picked up the phone and called Liwei. "Would you like to come over for dinner tonight? We can watch TV later."

"Sure," Liwei said after a moment's silence. "What's the occasion? You've been so busy these days."

Ning grinned. "Now I'm free."

* * *

For the next few days, Ning went out with her friends after school. Aunt and Uncle thought she spent each afternoon at the bamboo grove, but though Ning made it a point to visit, it was only for half to one hour before dusk. That really didn't give Ning sufficient time to look for Papa or Mama, but it was enough for her just to be there. Ning didn't tell Aunt about this. She didn't want Aunt to think she cared any less for Papa and Mama. She knew, in the same way, just because Papa and Mama wanted to live out on their own didn't mean they loved her any less. She remembered how Papa had come back for her sake and sacrificed his freedom, albeit temporarily.

On Saturday morning, Ning decided to spend some quality time with Papa and Mama, assuming of course she could find them. She happily hummed Papa's favorite tune as she rode her bicycle and carried seeds for Mama and fish food for Papa, although she didn't know if they'd still care for such ordinary fare.

When she reached the pond, she spotted flies buzzing about the water's edge. Curious, she skipped over.

Something was floating amongst the reeds.

She screamed.

Papa. His once bright black eyes were now sunken, his skin and scales were no longer incandescent, and his stomach was bloated. She stooped down, hands quivering as she lifted his lifeless body off the water. Her stomach churned.

"Papa," she whispered, tears rolling down her cheeks. What had happened? If she had only spent more time here yesterday and tried to look for him, she could have seen what was wrong. She bit her lower lip until she tasted blood.

Ning sat for over an hour, staring at Papa as she swatted away flies and insects. A rank, fishy odor emanated from his motionless body.

"I'm sorry," she said in a cracked voice she barely recognized. At the back of her mind, she knew Uncle would be furious, but she was too upset to feel afraid.

The least she could do was give Papa a funeral. She carried his bloated body to his favorite spot along the banks where he used to sit and fish during his last life. There, she stooped down and clawed a hole in the ground.

"Papa, wherever you'll go, whatever you'll be, I hope you're always happy." She pushed the dark, damp soil over him.

Ning's face was wet and smudged with dirt. She walked off, feeling numb. She stumbled a few times and tripped over a loose stone, grazing her knees and elbows. As she picked herself up, she heard Mama's twitter. Glancing up in a daze, Ning spied her colorfully feathered Mama squatting in a nest wedged between several slender branches of bamboo.

"Mama," Ning said, and then her face contorted.

Another bird chirped. Through bleary eyes, Ning saw beside Mama the same black-breasted yellow bird Uncle and she had seen the other day. It dawned on her that Mama had found a mate.

Ning ran off, stomach churning. What about Papa, she wanted to shout. Poor Papa. He was dead, while Mama had a new love.

When Ning returned home, the house was dark. She dashed about, bumping against doors and furniture, but she couldn't find Aunt anywhere. At last, tired and bruised, she staggered into the kitchen and washed her face in the sink, which was still stacked with breakfast dishes. With a dripping face, she yanked open the freezer door and grabbed the tub of chocolate ice cream. As she slammed the door shut, she spotted a note Uncle had scrawled and stuck to the refrigerator with a frog magnet. In unusually haphazard writing, Uncle said tersely: *Going to hospital.*

Ning dried her face on her sleeve. What had happened with Aunt? Would Aunt lose the baby just weeks before it was due? This was a day of ill fortune.

Ning sprinted out the house, leaped onto her bicycle, and pedaled frantically. In less than twenty minutes, she was at the hospital.

She found her uncle and aunt on the third floor. Aunt was sharing a room with a few other patients. She was sitting in bed without her glasses and cradling a bundle swathed in red cloth.

Uncle and Aunt smiled at Ning, their brown eyes sparkling. Ning forced a smile back.

"His name is *Mingliang*," Uncle said, wrapping a warm hand around Ning's left arm.

Brightness. Ning's eyes started welling up with tears again. Uncle had named his son for luminescent Papa, not knowing what had befallen him. She resolved not to tell them yet. A birth and a death—the two should not mix. She couldn't ruin their happiness.

"Why are you crying?" Aunt asked, brushing her fingers against Ning's cheek.

"My good niece is so happy, she weeps," Uncle said, throwing an arm around Ning's shoulders.

"Look at him." Aunt moved her sleeping baby closer to Ning. Mingliang had rosy cheeks and a round, chubby face that warmed Ning's chest.

"He's cute," Ning said, despite her churning stomach.

The baby's eyes fluttered open. As his dark brown eyes met hers, she felt a tingle, and a wave of warmth rushed through her.

She knew him. . . .

"How are your Papa and Mama?" Uncle asked.

Ning smiled, still staring into Mingliang's eyes. "Happy."

Běidǒu

Ken Liu

*I*N 1590, the daimyo *Toyotomi Hideyoshi completed the dream of his dead liege lord, Oda Nobunaga, and unified Japan by conquest. As* kampaku *to the figurehead Japanese Emperor Go-Yozei, Toyotomi was ruler of all Japan. Seeking to engrave his name eternally in history, he turned his eyes west to the glory of Joseon Korea and the beauty of Ming China.*

In 1591, Toyotomi demanded Korea's surrender and aid in the conquest of China. King Seonjo refused, as Korea was a close ally of China. Toyotomi raised an army of one hundred and sixty thousand veterans hardened by decades of battle in Oda's and Toyotomi's domestic campaigns and invaded Korea in 1592. It was the largest army ever deployed in Northeast Asia up to that time.

Within a few months, Hanseong and Pyongyang fell, and Toyotomi's army occupied most of Korea. Villages burned while starving refugees streamed across the Yalu River into China. Only the tactical brilliance of Admiral Yi Sun-sin and his destruction of the Japanese fleet on the west side of the Korean Peninsula halted the Japanese advance. King Seonjo fled to the Chinese border and rushed waves of emissaries to Beijing for aid.

*   *   *

In the private audience chamber of the Forbidden City, Tan Yuansi was struck by the youth of the Wanli Emperor. Save for his yellow robe and jewel-encrusted belt, the Emperor could pass for any of the young *xiùcái*, the scholar-gentlemen who had passed the first level of the Imperial Examinations. The Emperor's unlined face was kind, his eyes on the verge of a smile.

"You know," the Emperor said, "You are not supposed to look directly at me, and you haven't properly paid me the respect of Five Bows and Three Kowtows."

Cold sweat broke out along Yuansi's back, and the twenty-year-old infantry commander silently cursed himself. Not paying the Emperor the proper respect was not only discourteous, it indicated a rebellious heart. Immediately, Yuansi lowered his eyes, fell to his knees, and rushed to dip his head to the ground.

But before his forehead touched the ground, a pair of strong hands held him up by the shoulders.

"It's all right," the Emperor said. "I like the simple manners of soldiers, unadorned by the slavish habits of the Court. There was a time when an emperor and his general would sit on the floor as equals, but our simple Confucian ideals have become corrupted in these latter days." He lifted Yuansi until he was standing. Then he pointed at a chair to the side. "Sit, and let's talk about the situation in Korea."

Yuansi bowed and sat. "*Bìxià,* Your Imperial Majesty, I do not believe that Korean reports of the Japanese invasion force being but 'a few thousand greenhorns' are true. When I was a child, the Japanese *wōkòu* pirates who plagued my village in the Zhoushan Archipelago abducted me on a raid, and for many years I lived as one of them, learning their language and ways. We would beach our boats in a village, and swift-footed villagers would run to the local garrison to get help. We learned that those villagers always underreported the number of pirates who attacked them. If there were ten pirate ships, they would say there were only three, and if there were three pirate ships, they would say there was only one."

"Why? Wouldn't the villagers exaggerate the number of pirates in their fright?"

"If the villagers reported the true strength of the pirates, the garrison commander might hesitate to give aid. After all, if there were ten ships full of pirates, a garrison of fifty soldiers would have a difficult fight. The commander might request more reinforcements from the Prefecture or he might send spies to investigate further, but he would certainly not send out his soldiers right away. If the villagers wanted immediate help to salvage whatever they could, their best bet was to lie and minimize the danger."

"So you think that's what King Seonjo is trying to do? To get China to send troops without knowing Toyotomi's true strength?"

"I don't think we can rule it out. Korea is a very powerful country. It is inconceivable that King Seonjo would be driven out of Hanseong and Pyongyang unless Toyotomi has an overwhelming force. And this all might be a trap in a Japanese-Korean alliance to lure our troops into Korea for an ambush."

The Emperor was stunned. "Well, I really haven't thought of that possibility. It will not be possible for us to raise a large army quickly. Toyotomi has been at war for decades and has perfected his logistics, and an invading army can live off the land and rely on the sword as a tax collector. But if we send an army to help Korea, we will be acting as guests in someone else's house. We will have to keep the soldiers disciplined and leave the crops undisturbed and the village women unafraid. Our logistics will be ten times more expensive.

"I can only give you a small army, and so this will be a

hard campaign. But the greatest general I've ever known is General Li Rusong, and he speaks highly of you as a resourceful commander. I understand you came up with the idea of using trained falcons to intercept Mongol messenger pigeons? And you invented the practice of wrapping armor with wet cotton rags to dampen musket fire? Clever! I am sure that General Li and you will do well in Korea."

Yuansi clasped his hands and bowed. The Emperor's humbleness surprised him, and the Emperor's trust warmed his *dāntián*, the pit of his stomach, where the *qì* of breath and life began. It reminded him of a hot water-skin that his mother used to put next to his stomach at bedtime on cold winter nights when he was little.

"Before you go, let's talk about something more pleasant," the Emperor said. "Do you know much about painting?" He pointed to a small horizontal scroll on the side wall, the paper faded to yellow with age.

The left side of the scroll was dominated by a jagged cliff hung with gnarled trees. In the bottom right-hand corner, a small fishing boat was drawn in great detail, with the warp and weft of the rattan-covered shelter on the boat carefully limned. A contemplative fisherman sat over an oar in the back of the boat, his fishing pole forgotten behind him. In the upper right hand corner was a poem.

Yuansi, who was barely literate, could not read the cursive script. He had never learned painting or calligraphy and had little use for pictures unless they were pictures of pretty girls—especially the kind that soldiers collected.

"I have never had the opportunity to study the arts," he conceded. "In my wasted life I first lived as a pirate, and then, after General Li rescued me, as a soldier." General Li Rusong had taken a liking to the youngster after capturing him from the pirates and treated him as a son.

"No matter," the Emperor said. "The Bandit Liu Zhi was once teacher to Confucius, and native talent graced with insight sometimes far excels years of careful instruction. Let me try to explain to you how to look at a good painting.

"This painting was made two hundred and fifty years ago by Master Wu Zhen, who called himself the Plum Monk. We'll never have another painter as great.

"The highest of all the arts is calligraphy, which is the art of harnessing the writer's energy, his *qì*, and unleashing it in the service of freezing thought and capturing feeling. Practicing calligraphy is like doing *tai chi*, and there must be no wasted motion. Before even putting down the first stroke on paper, the writer must already know where the last stroke will go."

Yuansi nodded. He had seen General Li practice calligraphy, and it did look a little like a dance or some kind of martial art. He could appreciate that.

"Painting, properly understood, is but a form of calligraphy. Do not focus on nonsense such as the sketch's mimicry of life, the composition of figures, or the shading and perspective. Rather, look at a painting as a calligraphy scroll, and see how the painter's *qì* took shape on paper. Envision his movements and breaths, his broad brushstrokes and fine bone work.

"You may examine a true masterpiece as long as you like, but you will not find a single failed stroke in it. In a painting, the painter lays out his spirit with no lies and no embellishments, much as a wild goose taking off leaves behind ever widening ripples in the lake.

"And so we can sit here together today, admiring the spirit of Master Wu."

Yuansi was amazed. He stared at the painting, trying to see everything the Emperor showed him. "I will treasure your lesson, *Bìxià*. Hearing you speak for an hour is like going to school for ten years."

"Oh, don't flatter me. Here, take this copy of the scroll made by the royal painter so that you can have something beautiful to look at when you have a moment off the battlefield. Do not neglect the civilized side of life even in war. Otherwise there is no point to fighting."

General Li Rusong's horse, Red Tiger, snorted in the cold air of Jianzhou in late fall and gazed suspiciously across the Yalu River into the dense forests of Korea.

By the river shore, Li welcomed Yuansi and his small squad of scouts, returning from three weeks of reconnaissance inside Korea. They were disguised as Korean refugees in dirty rags and cotton headcloths.

"Come, have some warm rice wine to revive your spirits," Li said.

Yuansi thanked him and drained his cup in a single gulp. "As I suspected, the Korean envoys were lying about the size of the Japanese army. Some Japanese soldiers claim that over three hundred and twenty thousand troops landed in Waegwan back in April, but that may be just puffery. If I had to put a number on it, I'd say the fighting strength of Japan in Korea right now is above one hundred and fifty thousand, maybe two hundred thousand.

"The Japanese garrisons are extremely effective, due to a combination of cruelty and manipulation. They would behead entire families and enslave whole clans if even one member resisted, and simultaneously they would buy off the local gentry. Despicable collaborators." Yuansi spat on the ground.

"Using locals to control locals," Li Rusong said, shaking his head. "Toyotomi knows what he's doing."

"Almost all surviving Korean forces have either surrendered or gone into the woods and mountains as guerrillas. Toyotomi would have crossed over the Yalu into China months ago if the heroic Admiral Yi Sun-sin hadn't destroyed all the Japanese supply ships and transports off Jeolla Province. I saw Admiral Yi four days ago, and he gives you his regards." Yuansi handed Li a message from Admiral Yi, written in Korean. Li's parents were Korean, and it was the language of his childhood.

Li said nothing, mulling over the news. Yuansi was a careful young man. If he thought Toyotomi had one hundred and fifty thousand troops in Korea, then that was as good as proven. Admiral Yi's estimates of Japanese strength also confirmed Yuansi's report. Li had under his command about twenty-four thousand cavalry, ten thousand infantry, and three thousand matchlockmen. He was outnumbered four to one and likely worse.

"The good news is that we still have the element of surprise," Yuansi interrupted Li's thoughts.

"Oh?"

"None of the Japanese commanders I spied on suspected that China would send troops into Korea. Most thought China too scared to come and meet them after what happened to General Zu Chengxun."

All the men were silent for a moment, remembering the three-thousand-man cavalry vanguard commanded by the impetuous Zu. A few months ago, Zu ignored Yuansi's advice for caution and led his men into an ambush in Pyongyang, where most of his men died at the hands of the samurai.

Yuansi gritted his teeth. "I saw a mound Toyotomi's troops had built out of the noses and ears cut from dead Korean and Chinese soldiers. Some Japanese commanders joked that the Wanli Emperor is so young that Toyotomi could be his father and that the Ming princesses would make excellent concubines for the *daimyo*."

Li Rusong roared and swore in Korean. Red Tiger whinnied and reared up.

Yuansi continued, "No one knows that our army is here. The Japanese believe that they will have the whole winter to rest, secure their supply lines in Korea, and begin the invasion of China in the spring. We have to make them pay."

Li shook his head. "But the surprise will be lost as soon as we march into Korea. It takes more than a week to go from here to Pyongyang. I don't know how we are going to keep almost forty thousand marching men hidden. It's a setup for an ambush."

Yuansi paced alone in the silvery light of the almost-full Moon. His body was exhausted, but his mind could not sleep.

There was no torchlight. Moonlight reflected from the sheepskin tents where all the soldiers were asleep. Yuansi knew that patrols circled the perimeter of the camp to keep them safe. If you were in the woods only a few hundred feet away and didn't know where to look, you could hardly tell that thousands of men were camped right here.

It's easy to hide a sleeping camp, Yuansi thought. But how do you hide a marching army? In order to go from the Yalu River to Pyongyang, the army would have to go through the narrow plains between the tall mountains of the Rangnim Range in the east and the coast of Korea Bay on the west, easily visible to Japanese lookouts from miles away.

Perhaps the solution was to hide in the dark? If the troops could march at night by Moon and starlight and stay hidden in camps in the foothills during the day, they would be able to get all the way to Pyongyang without detection. But how could an army navigate in the dark? They would have to avoid the broad roads and villages and go through the uninhabited woods. They would have no way of knowing where they were or how far they had to go. It would be far too easy to get lost or stumble into a Japanese garrison.

Yuansi sighed and looked up at the night sky. He found the North Star and, at a slight distance from it, traced out the imaginary lines connecting the seven stars of *Běidǒu*, the Northern Dipper. He remembered lying on the deck of a *kenminsen*, the large trading/fighting ships used by the *wōkòu*, and watching the Northern Dipper spin all night around the fixed North Star, like seven men marching in formation, guided by a distant pole.

One of his favorite things to do, on those long-ago nights, was to make and fly Kongming lanterns. He would make the frame out of a lattice of light bamboo, shaped so that the lantern tapered down to a small opening at the bottom, like the hat worn more than a millennium ago by General Kongming, the greatest strategist who ever lived. He would then glue a layer of thin rice paper onto the lattice, making sure it was airtight, and then suspend a small candle in the center of the opening with a bamboo skewer or two. When the candle was lit, the warm air trapped by the Kongming lantern would lift it out of his hands, its warm glow receding from him until it was just another star in the sky, a distant point of light. Other children, on other pirate ships, would sometimes answer with their own Kongming lanterns, and Yuansi had loved to see them—giant fireflies hovering over the dark East China Sea.

Tired, cold, and still without a solution, the frustrated Yuansi headed back to his tent. He lit a candle and brought out the Emperor's scroll. He tried to distract himself by practicing the Emperor's lesson, tracing the brushstrokes on the scroll, imagining the Master's posture and movements, savoring the marks left on the paper by his energy and spirit; not one single stroke out of place.

He noticed something: all the strokes in the trees and the cliffs seemed to point to the boat in the bottom right corner. It was as though the *qì* of the whole painting had a focus—the hunched-over figure of the fisherman. Invisible lines seemed to connect every spot on the painting to a single fixed pole, like the North Star, a center around which all other things measured themselves and knew their place.

Yuansi smiled to himself. He had a plan.

"Let's check our position," Li Rusong gave the order to Yue Lijing, his field clerk.

Li and Yue pulled their horses aside as the column of marching soldiers continued past. The January air penetrated their coats and cotton-covered armor and made them shiver. Red Tiger's breath, ghostly white in the moonlight, curled around them.

Yue quickly set up a field desk and spread out a map of the sector of Northern Korea they were marching through. They had to work quickly, before the cold winter air froze their fingers. While Li prepared the covered lantern that cast a focused cone of light on the map, Yue took out his goniometer and surveying pole, got a reading on the North Star to fix true north, and began to scan the horizon both to the east and the west.

Far in the northwest, over the Yellow Sea and Korea Bay, Yue could discern a small group of six bright yellow flickering lights hovering in the shape of a hexagon.

"I see the Legs of the White Tiger," Yue said. He took a careful reading with the goniometer and gave Li the angle of the cluster of lights from true north.

In the calm waters of Korea Bay, a small armored turtle ship from Admiral Yi's fleet was at anchor. Every night, the ship would sail to that spot and launch those six Kongming lanterns, tied to silk threads so that they would stay anchored in the sky high over the ship.

Yue looked over to the northeast. Far in the distance, over the treetops, he could see another small group of five bright yellow flickering lights hovering in the shape of a small cross.

"I see the Horn of the Azure Dragon," Yue reported. He took another careful reading with the goniometer and gave Li the angle of the lights from true north.

Yue silently prayed that the militiamen over in the mountains were safe. His brother had gone with Tan Yuansi into the mountains a month ago. His mission, like that of the other men Tan took with him, was to get in touch with the various militias hidden in the mountains. Every night, his brother's group would go to a fixed spot and launch that cluster of five Kongming lanterns, also tethered by silk lines. Since their position in the mountains was so remote and inaccessible, made even more so by the December snow, Toyotomi's garrisons could not get men out there to investigate.

The positions of the Legs and the Horn stations were clearly marked on the map before Li. Yue quickly drew out the measured angles from them and triangulated the army's position.

With a few dozen scouts and the help of the Korean resistance, Yuansi had set up a grid of Kongming lantern stations spread tens of miles apart across Northern Korea. Guided by these *Běidǒu* positioning stations, the Ming army marched, undetected, during the nights towards Pyongyang.

"We should turn slightly to the east," Yue said. "In another hour or so we should arrive at a good camp site. We are only about two days march from Pyongyang now. Yuansi and the Korean militias will join us there."

Konishi Yukinaga could not believe his eyes. Before the gates of Pyongyang, the allied forces of Ming China and Joseon Korea ranged in battle-ready splendor.

"What have your spies been doing?" he screamed at his samurai. "How could an army of forty thousand men go from the Yalu River to Pyongyang without any warning?"

But it was too late for speculation. Konishi sent his men scrambling to the defense of Pyongyang.

Li Rusong ordered a general assault on Pyongyang from all sides, sparing only the eastern walls next to the Taedong River. It seemed as if the charging cavalry and infantry would easily overwhelm the Japanese defenders.

But dug in behind reinforced earthworks, the Japanese arquebusiers laid waste to the allied forces with their fusillades. The Japanese guns had much better range, accuracy, and penetration than the Chinese matchlocks. Even Red Tiger was shot from under Li Rusong in the middle of one of the assaults.

"Damn the Portuguese," Li Rusong swore as his wounds were dressed. "All these years we thought we bought the latest matchlock technology, and behind our backs, they were secretly selling more advanced weapons to Toyotomi."

In light of the heavy casualties, Li ordered a change in tactics. Now, the allies would try to overwhelm the Japanese defenses with flame arrows and artillery fire. Soldiers held up well-oiled rattan shields and iron pavises to defend the field artillery and flaming arrow launchers from Japanese arquebus fire. The arquebuses, though more powerful, had shorter range than the arrows, and their bullets glanced harmlessly off of the pavises.

Volley after volley of cannon fire and flaming arrows propelled by gunpowder rockets arced into Pyongyang. Yuansi was impressed by the Korean militia's *hwacha*, a two-wheeled cart that could launch several hundred flaming arrows at once. He made a mental copy of their design.

Soon the houses in Pyongyang were burning, and smoke covered half the sky. But Pyongyang was a big city, and as long as Konishi moved his forces around the walls and stayed under cover, they avoided much of the bombardment.

"We'll run out of ammunition in another day," Li Rusong said to Yuansi. The Ming army was not prepared for an extended siege.

Yuansi hovered in the sky over Pyongyang. He could see miles and miles around him in all directions. No pagoda in the world was as high as he was. It was glorious.

Above him was the biggest Kongming lantern anybody had ever seen, a giant floating cylinder about forty paces across at its widest point. Yuansi had made the frame from thick but light bamboo lashed together with silk ropes and covered it with multiple layers of rice paper.

He sat in a rattan basket attached by woven cords of silk to the hoop at the bottom opening of the giant Kongming lantern. Beside him in the basket were several large leather pouches with iron nozzles. One of them was filled with swamp gas, to provide high-heat flame for takeoff. The others were filled with distilled alcohol, to provide long-burning flames that would keep him airborne.

Now that he was high over Pyongyang, Yuansi could see where all the Japanese troops were hiding. Using a long pole tipped with a red flag, he pointed at these positions, guiding the artillery fire to strike at them. Salvo after salvo of cannon fire and *hwacha* arrows fell where he aimed, and the Japanese troops suffered heavy losses. A few noticed Yuansi's Kongming lantern flying overhead and aimed their arquebuses at him, but he was flying too high for the bullets.

Yuansi put down his red flag and picked up a white flag. He waved it in wide, slow circles. It was time to end the battle.

From the west side of Pyongyang, Japanese soldiers, captured in the fighting, marched from their prison compounds onto the battlefield until they were right behind the pavises of the Chinese soldiers at the limit of Japanese arquebus range.

Before his flight, Yuansi had convinced them that the dream of Japanese conquest of Korea and China was dead. The Great Ming had learned the trick of teleportation—hadn't they seen with their own eyes how the Ming army had appeared out of nowhere, like troops descended from Heaven? But all the prisoners would be allowed to go home to Japan if they would help convince their comrades to give up Pyongyang and retreat.

As Yuansi gave his signal, the Japanese prisoners began to sing an old folk song of Kyushu, from where most of Konishi's men came:

Cherry petals have filled the floor of the valley.
Tears have soaked the faces of the children.
Oh my sorrow, my sorrow is great.
The warriors, they have died as beautifully as falling
*   cherry blossoms.*
My son, oh my son, he is not coming home from
*   battle.*

As the prisoners' mournful song rose in volume, the allied artillery stopped firing. Gradually, the return fire from Pyongyang stopped as well. Only the singing Japanese voices filled the silence.

Yuansi looked down, and he could see that it was no longer only the prisoners who were singing. The Japanese soldiers in the city sang as well. Their voices swelled louder and louder, and through the smoke of the burning city, Yuansi could see that the city was filled with upturned faces full of tears.

Konishi, his heart filled with despair, ordered his samurai to mount their horses and began the retreat from Pyongyang under cover of night.

From the simple but elegant sandalwood throne in the private audience chamber, the Emperor stood up to welcome Yuansi.

"You have fought well to help Korea, and more importantly, defended the homeland. Though we have not yet won the war, you have dealt Toyotomi a heavy blow. You have King Seonjo's gratitude and ours."

Yuansi knelt to kowtow to the Emperor and was once again lifted to be seated by the throne.

"*Bìxià*, I saw Toyotomi's soldiers flogging press-ganged Korean laborers to death and caught his *daimyo* selling captured Chinese soldiers to Portuguese slave traders. I was glad to do my duty."

The Emperor sighed. "Toyotomi thought he was going to bring the blessing of the virtues of the Japanese Emperor to Korea, to China, to India and Siam, and all of Asia, even if it was by the point of a sword. From his view, he believed that he was behaving in the most virtuous way possible, and his superior weapons were the proof of his virtue.

"But let us turn to more immediate matters. General Li wrote to suggest that we establish a network of your *Běidǒu* stations in the Gobi desert in the far west and in the snowy forests of Jianzhou to allow military maneuvers by day and night. He also seeks funds to build more of the man-carrying Kongming lanterns you invented for reconnaissance and to equip the army with our own *hwacha* based on Korean designs and arquebuses modeled on those captured from Japan. I believe these are your ideas?"

"I have given such suggestions to General Li, *Bìxià*. But real credit should go to your virtue and wisdom. It was the painting you gave me and what you taught me about how to look at it that inspired me to think of the *Běidŏu*."

"Ah, Master Wu Zhen would be saddened to hear that his art was used for war. Although I have given your suggestions some thought, I fear the answer must be no."

Yuansi froze. "Why?"

The Emperor, his eyes somber but determined, looked at Yuansi. "Let me tell you a story. Almost two hundred years ago, during the reign of the Yongle Emperor, the great Admiral Zheng went on seven voyages of exploration into the Indian Ocean. He led fleets of treasure ships, each one the size of a floating town, the greatest ships men had ever built, and sailed to India, Arabia, Africa, and Ceylon. He sailed farther than any Chinese had ever gone and saw more than any Chinese had ever seen. He spread the fame of China far and wide, and he went farther and farther with each voyage. Had he kept on sailing, I believe he would have gone around the world and found the lands of Mexico and America, whence we now get our Spanish silver, maize, and sweet potato.

"Yet, after the death of the Yongle Emperor, his successor, the Xuande Emperor, stopped all ocean-going exploration, burned all records of Zheng He's voyages, scuttled the great treasure ships, and forbade any further construction of them. The arts of navigation and ship construction were lost, and today China cannot build a ship even one tenth as large, so that we have been plagued by the *wōkòu* all these years. Do you know why Xuande did that?"

Yuansi shook his head. He was sorry that such knowledge was lost.

"On those voyages, Zheng He and his men discovered many beautiful and fertile lands far beyond the boundaries of the Ming Empire, lands rich with spices, exotic animals, and beautiful women, but little in the way of arms. It would have been easy for China to decide that those lands should also bathe in the virtue of the Ming Emperor and to enjoy the benefits of Confucian civilization, that the squabbling natives should be made to appreciate peace and to learn Daoist values, and that the virtuous thing to do was to send a fleet of treasure ships laden not with goods for trade, but with soldiers with flaming arrows.

"Does that remind you of anyone?

"Xuande believed that path would have corrupted us beyond redemption. He chose to remove all temptation.

"The temptation offered by your inventions are similarly corrupting, Yuansi. There was a time when our ancestors fought hand to hand, with crude bronze swords and wooden spears, and each life was dear. But now at a single command, you can launch a thousand flaming arrows propelled by rockets at a city with little thought. Your inventions would allow us to rain down death upon men with ever greater efficiency, to march troops through darkness to the doors of unsuspecting homes.

"Today, we go fight in Korea to defend ourselves, but who knows where such logic will stop? It is far too easy to make of virtue a cover for all manner of vices. We cannot trust in our capacity to always reason to true virtue; we can only reduce our capacity for evil should we err.

"There has been enough killing, Yuansi. I'm going to order that the prototypes for your inventions be destroyed and the records of them expunged from the histories."

A chill settled in Yuansi's *dāntián*. He felt as if a part of his *qì*, his spirit, had been laid out on and imbued into those machines. His heart convulsed, and he clenched the armrests of his chair.

"*Bìxià*, China must defend itself. The Jurchens are watching in the northeast for any sign of weakness, and in the west, the Mongols remain a threat. We cannot tear down the Great Wall and hope for the kindness of the world."

"If China cannot preserve its virtue, then there is nothing worth defending at all."

The Emperor and the General stared at each other. Tan Yuansi did not lower his eyes.

Toyotomi's invading army did not fully retreat from Korea until his death in 1598. Afterward, the Jurchens, taking advantage of the weakened and ill-equipped Ming army, conquered China between 1618 and 1645. Some twenty-five million Chinese are estimated to have died as a result of the Conquest.

In 2000, China began to launch its own satellite navigation and positioning system. It is named Běidŏu.

Author's note: the painting in this story is Wu Zhen's *Fisherman*.

Afterword

Derwin Mak and Eric Choi

*T*HE *Dragon and the Stars* can trace its beginnings to
2007, when Derwin went to that year's World Science Fiction Convention in Yokohama, Japan. Thanks to
the proximity of the venue, many science fiction writers
from China were able to attend the Yokohama Worldcon, and Derwin was thrilled to meet these peers from
the country of his ancestors.

The SF authors from China were equally eager to
meet a Canadian writer of Chinese ancestry. One of these
authors was Wu Yan, who is also a professor of literature
at Beijing Normal University. Dr. Wu asked Derwin to
write an article about Chinese-Canadian science fiction
writers for the Chinese magazine *Science Fiction World*.
This article, which included profiles of *Dragon* writers
Tony Pi, Melissa Yuan-Innes, and E.L. Chen (as well as
honorable mention of two certain editors), was published
in the May 2008 issue of *Science Fiction World*.

As for the anthology itself, that came about in the same
manner as many other great ideas—over a meal. Shortly
after the article's publication, Derwin met Eric for dinner
at, appropriately enough, an (authentic) Chinese restaurant in Toronto. We got to talking about the poor manner
in which Chinese people and culture are often portrayed
in both speculative and mainstream fiction.

Regrettably, most depictions of Chinese characters and themes occupy a rather narrow range, usually as martial arts fighters or magical Buddhist monks in historical fantasies. It was the Chinese who invented rockets, gunpowder, paper, and the compass, yet we are rarely shown as engineers or scientists—except when Fu Manchu or Ming the Merciless invents a new death ray. When Chinese people do appear, they are usually in minor roles; if they're not villains, the men are sidekicks of the main characters and the women are girlfriends of white heroes.

This is hardly representative of a five-thousand-year-old civilization.

Over the course of those five millennia, and especially within the last century, many Chinese have left the land of their ancestry and settled across the globe, creating a diaspora of remarkable diversity by adapting and merging the rich heritage of China with the new traditions of their adopted homes. As Chinese-Canadians, we are not the same as Chinese-Americans, Chinese-Singaporeans, Chinese-Filipinos, or Hong Kong Chinese. We are all Chinese, yet we are all different.

And so we thought, what better way to show the diverse culture of this great diaspora than through original stories of science fiction and fantasy written by overseas Chinese?

Many thanks are in order. The first must go to Dr. Wu Yan, whose interest in Chinese-Canadian speculative fiction writers kicked off the chain of events that led to this collection. We also wish to express our appreciation to Tess Gerritsen, who so generously took time out of her busy schedule to write the beautiful introduction that opens the book. But our deepest gratitude goes to our *hǎo péngyou* Julie Czerneda, who championed the idea of this anthology from the start and was a constant source of advice and inspiration as it came together.

Měi gè rén, fēicháng gǎnxiè.

ABOUT THE AUTHORS

E.L. Chen was born in Toronto to immigrant parents who, unlike those of most Canadian-born Chinese of her generation, actually met in Canada. Her short stories have appeared in publications such as *Tesseracts Nine*, *Tesseracts Twelve*, *Strange Horizons*, *Lady Churchill's Rosebud Wristlet*, and *On Spec*. "Threes" was inspired by contemptuous ex-boyfriends, Chinese funeral customs and—as always—fairy tale sisters. Everything else she doesn't mind you knowing about can be found at *elchen.blogspot.com*.

Eric Choi was born in Hong Kong but emigrated to Canada with his family at a young age. His fiction has appeared in the anthologies *Footprints*, *Northwest Passages*, *Space Inc.*, *Tales from the Wonder Zone*, *Northern Suns*, *Tesseracts Six*, and *Arrowdreams* as well as the magazines *Asimov's* and *Science Fiction Age*. He was the first recipient of the Isaac Asimov Award for Undergraduate Excellence in Science Fiction and Fantasy Writing (now known as the Dell Award).

An aerospace engineer by training, Eric has a bachelor's degree in engineering science and a master's degree in aerospace engineering, both from the University of Toronto, and an MBA from York University. He worked briefly for a NASA contractor but was forced to return to Canada due to U.S. technology export control regulations. Today, he is manager of business development at the Canadian space company COM DEV. His website is *www.aerospacewriter.ca*.

In our timeline, Tsien Hsue-shen was deported back to China (not Canada!) in 1955, where he is today revered as the father of the modern Chinese space and ballistic missile programs.

Brenda Clough's parents came to the United States from China. She was born in Washington, DC, and still resides in the suburbs of Virginia. Brenda has seven novels published in traditional format and several more in electronic format at Book View Cafe. A finalist for both the Hugo and the Nebula awards, her website is *www.sff.net/people/Brenda*, and she also has an ongoing comic review blog at *blog.bookviewcafe.com*.

Brenda was feeling steampunkish when she wrote "The Water Weapon"; something about steam and bamboo is so Chinese!

Susan Ee is a writer and filmmaker. Her stories have been published in *Beyond Centauri* and *Realms of Fantasy*, and her films have screened at festivals and on television throughout the United States. She studied creative writing at Stanford University, Clarion West, and the University of Iowa. Her blog is *www.feraldream. com*.

Of her story "Shadow City," Susan recalls: "One day, a piece of a scene played itself out on the page. A young man who was a gatekeeper. His job wasn't to keep people out; it was to keep people in. Being a gatekeeper meant so much to him, yet his emotions around it were a swirl of guilt, longing, and fear. I found him intriguing but didn't have a story to go with him. I was drawn back to him several times over the next couple of years until I finally uncovered his story."

Eugie Foster was born and raised in central Illinois, although she now resides in Atlanta with her husband,

Matthew, and her pet skunk, Hobkin. After receiving a master's degree in developmental psychology, she retired from academia to pen flights of fancy. She also edits legislation for the Georgia General Assembly, which she occasionally suspects is another flight of fancy.

Eugie's fiction has received the Phobos Award and has been nominated for the British Fantasy, Bram Stoker, and Pushcart awards. Her publication credits include stories in *Realms of Fantasy, Interzone, Cricket, Apex Magazine, Fantasy Magazine, Orson Scott Card's Intergalactic Medicine Show, Jim Baen's Universe,* and the anthologies *Best New Fantasy, Heroes in Training,* and *Best New Romantic Fantasy 2.* Her collection *Returning My Sister's Face and Other Far Eastern Tales of Whimsy and Malice* is now out from Norilana Books. Visit her online at *EugieFoster.com.*

"Mortal Clay, Stone Heart" was inspired by the exhibit *The First Emperor: China's Terracotta Army,* which she saw when it came to Atlanta's High Museum of Art. Eugie hopes to one day visit the necropolis in Xi'an.

Urania Fung was born in Lawrence, Kansas, and currently resides in Arlington, Texas. She holds an MA in English and an MFA in creative writing. Her work has appeared in the anthology *Ages of Wonder* and the journals *Front Porch Journal* and *Texas Books in Review.* She has been a finalist in the San Gabriel Writers League's Writing Smarter Contest, the Writers' League of Texas Novel Manuscript Competition, and the Texas Association of Creative Writing Teachers Contest. Her website is *uraniafung.blogspot.com.*

While teaching English to ninth graders in Changping, China, from 2002 to 2003, she was quarantined during the SARS outbreak and had to force down the meals described in "The Right to Eat Decent Food." Urania will always remember the "fun" they had trying to get decent food during the quarantine. The Chinese friends she made during her stay told her stories about fox demons, which were the inspiration for the Rabbit character. School administrators did not lift the quarantine until June 2003. The early termination agreements were a blessing!

Tess Gerritsen's father was second-generation Chinese-American, and her mother is an immigrant from Kunming, China. Born in California, Tess studied anthropology at Stanford University and went to medical school at the University of California, San Francisco, where she earned her MD. After several years of working as a doctor, she left medicine to follow her dreams . . . and became a writer.

Now an internationally bestselling novelist, she is the author of over twenty novels including the space/medical thriller *Gravity* and the popular Jane Rizzoli and Maura Isles crime series. Tess is published in thirty-five countries, and twenty million copies of her books have been sold around the world. She lives in Maine, and her website is *www.tessgerritsen.com*.

Emery Huang was born in Fairfax, Virginia, and now lives in Orlando, Florida. He has a degree in creative writing from the University of Central Florida. In 2008, he won the Gold Award for the 25th Writers of the Future competition.

Emery always wanted to write about fox demons because he finds East Asian versions of lycanthropy interesting and vastly different from their Western counterparts. In the West, lycanthropy is perceived as a disease, where the human form is perverted into a monstrosity. In the East, lycanthropes tend to be animal or spirit in their natural state, and it's their human form that's the disguise. The particular details for "Lips of

Ash" were conceived as Emery read a book on Chinese alchemy while sitting in MAC Cosmetics waiting for his girlfriend to finish browsing.

Crystal Gail Shangkuan Koo was born in Manila, Philippines, and graduated with a BA in English literature from the University of the Philippines and an MA in Creative Writing from the University of New South Wales. She is currently an English lecturer at the College of International Education of Hong Kong Baptist University.

Crystal's stories have been published in *The Digest of Philippine Genre Stories, Unsweetened Literary Journal, RUBRIC: Creative Writing Journal of the University of New South Wales, Short Stories at East of the Web, Salu-Salo: An Anthology of Philippine-Australian Writings,* and *Philippine Speculative Fiction IV.* In 2007, her story "Benito Salazar's Last Creation" won the Carlos Palanca Memorial Award for Literature, and in 2009, her play *The Foundling* was performed at the Fringe Theatre in Hong Kong. She maintains a blog at *sword skill.wordpress.com.*

"The Man on the Moon" turns the myth of Yue Lao on its head and explores the places of a mortal man and a deity in a universe of circumstances, choices, and destiny. It is her first story published in North America.

Born in Manila, Philippines, **Gabriela Lee** received her bachelor's degree in creative writing from the University of the Philippines and completed her master's degree in literary studies at the National University of Singapore under an ASEAN scholarship. She has been a fellow for poetry in English at the Dumaguete National Writers Workshop, and her stories have been published in a number of magazines and anthologies including *By Blood We Live, Philippine Speculative Fiction Volume 1,*

A Different Voice: Filipino Fiction from Young Writers, and *Crowns and Oranges: New Philippine Poetry*. Gabriela currently lives in Singapore with her boyfriend, where she develops online content. Gabriela's website is *sundialgirl.multiply.com*.

Her first story published in North America, "Bargains" was inspired by the author's own experience with writer's block. Inspiration, unfortunately, cannot be bought from a Chinese shop—a painful lesson that both Gabriela and her fictional counterpart Amelia have now learned.

Shelly Li is a writer in Omaha, Nebraska. Her work has appeared in several publications including *Nature*, *Cosmos Online*, and Italy's *Robot Magazine*. Her website is *www.shelly-li.com*.

The inspiration for "Intelligent Truth" came from her stepfather, who recalled reading an article about recent advancements in artificial intelligence. A plot began to develop around the idea that robots might one day understand human emotions better than their makers. As Shelly wrote, she also decided to include some of her experiences with the joys and frustrations of life as an American-born Chinese.

Born in Lanzhou, China, **Ken Liu** grew up on both coasts of the United States. He is a graduate of Harvard College and Harvard Law School, and he worked as a software engineer before becoming a lawyer. His fiction has appeared in *Strange Horizons*, *Science Fiction World*, *Writers of the Future*, and David G. Hartwell and Kathryn Cramer's *The Year's Best SF*. Ken lives in the Boston area with his wife Lisa and their two cats. His website is *kenliu.name*.

A popular genre of Chinese science fiction is an analog for steampunk, which Ken has dubbed "silkpunk."

These stories are set in a classical or medieval East Asian setting, and instead of steam, the fictional inventions tend to be powered by wind, water, animals, or uniquely Chinese concepts like *qì*, ox sinew, and *jīguān* (a type of mechanical engineering associated with Mohist philosophers of the Spring and Autumn and Warring States Periods).

Ken was inspired by a discussion with his aunt on the aesthetics of calligraphy and Chinese painting to write "Běidǒu." The Seven Years War (1592-98) provided the silkpunk setting for the debate between the Emperor and Tan Yuansi about our ambivalence toward the interplay among art, technology, war, and reason.

Emily Mah was born in California but grew up in New Mexico. She currently resides in London, England, while her husband attends grad school. Emily is a graduate of Oxford University and UCLA School of Law, and she practiced law for six years. During her attorney years, she attended the Clarion West and Viable Paradise writers' workshops and has since sold to several publications including *Polaris: A Celebration of Polar Science*, *The Black Gate*, and *Shiny*. A member of the Church of Jesus Christ of Latter-Day Saints, she also writes LDS fiction under the name E.M. Tippetts and has published a novel, *Time and Eternity*. Her speculative fiction website is *www.emilymah.com* and her LDS fiction website is *www.emtippetts.com*.

The inspiration for "Across the Sea" came from listening to her friend Char Peery, a linguistic anthropologist and science fiction fan, talk about lost languages and cultural assimilation.

Derwin Mak was born in Peterborough, grew up in Kitchener, and lives in Toronto, all cities in Ontario,

Canada. He is a chartered accountant with master's degrees in accounting and military studies. In 2006, his story "Transubstantiation" won Canada's national science fiction award, the Prix Aurora Award, in the category of Best Short Form Work in English. His novel *The Moon Under Her Feet* was a finalist for a 2008 Prix Aurora Award. He has also written articles about East Asian pop culture and anime for the magazines *Parsec* and *Rice Paper*. His website is *www.derwinmaksf.com*.

"The Polar Bear Carries the Mail" was inspired by Derwin's interests in aerophilately and buildings. Derwin collects space covers, including one that flew aboard a 1983 Space Shuttle mission. He also likes the work of Chinese-American architect I.M. Pei, who designed the Pyramid at the Louvre and the Bank of China Tower in Hong Kong, which is alleged to have bad *feng shui*.

Wen Y. Phua was born in Singapore and graduated from the University of Illinois at Urbana-Champaign with double bachelor of science degrees in food science and food industry. After several years working in the food industry, she turned to her first love, books and writing. Currently a freelance writer and editor, she has written three nonfiction books and numerous articles.

A graduate of the Clarion Science Fiction and Fantasy Writer's Workshop, Wen found her initial inspiration for "Papa and Mama" during her grandfather's funeral. Her family, although not Buddhist, was told to go vegetarian during the funeral proceedings. Shortly afterward, she learned that some Buddhists refrain from consuming meat for a hundred days after the passing of their relative, for fear their deceased kin might be reincarnated as an animal and land on their dining table. Aside from this theme of Buddhist reincarnation, the rest of "Papa and Mama" is, of course, pure imagination.

Tony Pi was born in Taipei, Taiwan, and first encountered an army of Chinese characters on cast metal type, thanks to his grandfather, who operated an in-home printing press. At age eight, he emigrated to Toronto, Canada. His love of words and languages ultimately led him to complete a PhD in linguistics from McGill University. Tony has taught at Queen's University, the University of Waterloo and Simon Fraser University and is currently administering the graduate program at the Cinema Studies Institute, University of Toronto. His website is *www.eyrie.org/~pi/*.

A finalist for the 2009 John W. Campbell Award for Best New Writer, and a Second Place winner in the Writers of the Future Contest (Volume XXIII), Tony also had a novelette on the ballot for the 2008 Prix Aurora Award. His work has appeared in *Ages of Wonder*, *The Improbable Adventures of Sherlock Holmes*, *Orson Scott Card's Intergalactic Medicine Show*, *On Spec*, *Abyss & Apex*, *Beneath Ceaseless Skies*, and *Tales of the Unanticipated*.

For "The Character of the Hound," Tony took his idea that tattoos prime the body for spirit possession and combined it with his fascination with General Yue Fei to divert the history of Song Dynasty China onto a unique and magical course.

Charles Tan is a writer from the Philippines. He graduated from Ateneo de Manila University with a degree in creative writing and currently works as editorial assistant for *The Fookien Times Philippines Yearbook*. His fiction has been published in *Philippine Speculative Fiction Vol. 4* and *The Digest of Philippine Genre Stories*. His blog is *charles-tan.blogspot.com,* and he has a sampler of speculative fiction at *philippinespeculativefiction .com*.

"The Fortunes of Mrs. Yu" is his first story published

in North America. Growing up in a Chinese family, they would eat out in a restaurant and order the same menu (the eight-course lauriat) whenever there was an occasion to celebrate. Fortune cookies, however, are not authentically Chinese and are actually rarities in the Philippines.

William F. Wu is the author of thirteen novels, sixty short stories, and a book of literary criticism. His story "Wong's Lost and Found Emporium" was adapted for an episode of *The Twilight Zone* in 1985. A six-time nominee for the Hugo, Nebula, and World Fantasy Awards, Wu is also the author of the young adult series *Isaac Asimov's Robots in Time*.

Wu was born and raised in the Kansas City area and attended the University of Michigan. He has a bachelor's degree in East Asian studies and a master's degree and PhD in American culture. His doctoral dissertation was published as *The Yellow Peril: Chinese Americans in American Fiction, 1850-1940*. He lives in Palmdale, California, with his wife, Fulian, and their son, Alan. His website is *www.williamfwu.com*.

"Goin' Down to Anglotown" is an alternate world story based on old tales about Chinatowns, from nineteenth century fiction to movies like *Chinatown* starring Jack Nicholson. In these depictions, Chinatown is often a weird, scary place, with beautiful but treacherous Chinese women and threatening Chinese men. "Anglotown" turns these racial stereotypes on their head.

Melissa Yuan-Innes is a full-fledged emergency doctor now, but when she toiled as a family medicine resident she fantasized about a hospital for wizards where magical beings came to be healed. She wrote four stories, one for each season. "Dancers with Red Shoes," the summer story, is her favorite.

Melissa was the winner of several contests, including Writers of the Future and the 2008 InnermoonLit Award for Best First Chapter of a Novel. Her work can be found in *Nature, Weird Tales, Island Dreams: Montréal Writers of the Fantastic*, and other publications. Melissa's website is *www.melissayuaninnes.net*.